MOON SISTER'S HUNT

JAY HOBSON

CONTENTS

For my wife and daughters.
The loves of my life.

Acknowledgements

I would like to thank everyone who helped make this book a reality.
A special shout out to all my beta readers that helped tighten my messy first draft up, I appreciate your help so much.
Cover design by Deranged Doctor Design

WOODS HOLE
SEA
COUSTEAU
OCEAN
SEA OF
SORROW
N
W
E
S
Major trade route
Moon Sisters' Path

A Sisterhood Threatened

The series of events that would change the path of my life forever started on an unremarkable night, much like any other, as my two companions and I set up camp in my jungle. It was *my* jungle because no one else dared to live in it. To be fair, it wasn't supposed to be my home, either. When Jack dropped me off on a beach in the middle of nowhere, at my request, before he sailed back to Earth, I was planning on wandering the land, trying to explore the few corners left that I hadn't already seen.

Instead, I found myself rescuing stray, brutalized women and girls one at a time from the various outlaw tribes that inhabited the savannah just outside the jungle's borders. From that nothing, we had grown into two towns, one in the jungle's heart where I spent most of my time, and one on the edge of the plains, destined to be our outward face to the outside world. In fact, that was where we were headed now, my quarterly visit and inspection of Sanctuary. It was six months overdue. I felt a twinge of guilt about that, but there was my garden to tend to, and Council meetings to lead that sucked up a lot of my time.

I winced at that thought. That sounded like bullshit reasoning, and I couldn't buy it, even if it came from me. The truth is, I was a monster and had been for a very long time. Many of the girls I rescued wanted to become monsters like me, so I obliged several of them. I couldn't protect everyone I saved all the time, so I gave them the tools to protect themselves. But they had to show me they could survive. So I carefully tested them. There were many different kinds of strength, and I only Changed the ones strong enough to bear the burden of what we became. When I was done, they had the outward power to go along with their inner strength, enough to meet any challenges they might face in the future.

I sighed, and lay on my blanket roll, clasping my hands behind my head. That was all well and good, but I could very clearly see the path in front of me, and I didn't like it, not one bit. I was a monster, but I was a monster that wanted to fade into obscurity. I was just afraid that that wasn't my destiny, and the gilded cage that came with the mantle of leadership I saw in my future terrified me to no end. Silently I gazed up at the bejewelled night sky, hoping for it to bring me a measure of serenity. It never did, however. It just reminded me of what was out there.

"I notice you spend a lot of time looking at the stars, Lyr."

I glanced over at Babs. She was a middle-aged looking woman with brown hair shot through with gray, and brown eyes. I was freakishly tall for a woman, taller than all but the biggest men, and strong to boot. Babs was average height, about a full head shorter than me, and solid, seemingly almost as wide as she was tall. Calm and unflappable, she looked like she could take a club to the face and power right through it to get to the person behind it. In her case, looks were definitely not deceiving. Technically, her name was Barbara, but most everyone called her Babs.

Apparently she was keeping an eye on me as well. I continued to gaze up at the diamonds scattered haphazardly across the velvet of the night sky. "Just looking for shooting stars."

Babs raised an eyebrow. "Shooting stars? Or the spaceships you're always going on about?"

"Shooting stars could actually mean spaceships, and that is a concern of mine for sure. There could be a starship in orbit tomorrow. It might take a thousand years. But it is inevitable that we will be visited at some point. Hopefully they're friendly, but given human nature, I wouldn't bet any money on it."

"What's the plan if that happens?"

I shrugged. "Don't have one, really. Stay hunkered down in our little corner of the world? They'll have the ability to destroy any city or number of cities they choose to, but I don't think they'll have enough bodies to occupy the whole of the planet, at least not at first. If we have to, we'll withdraw into the forest, and do our best to make the invaders think the forest is haunted, or so deadly as to not be worth their time. Our only obligation is to each other. We won't be able to meet them in the field in open battle, but I like our chances against any small group that wanders in."

"You do know that not everyone believes your stories about spaceships and visitors from beyond, don't you?" This came from Greta, my other companion, who was staring intently at the fire, not looking at me. Greta looked to be in her early twenties, petite and blonde, with startling blue eyes that reminded me of a pool of melt water from a glacier. They could be just as cold, too. She was a tiny thing, but she was blindingly fast, aggressive, and completely vicious in any kind of fight. Anyone that tried to brawl with her had better be prepared to go all the way. I tensed angrily, wondering if she was challenging me, then forced myself to relax. She had spoken in a very neutral tone, as if she was wary of upsetting me.

Irrational rage was one of the downsides to our condition, and we had to always guard against it.

"Is it something I'm going to have to defend myself against?" I asked carefully, keeping my tone calm and even.

She turned from the fire to look at me. "Not right now. All of the Sisters revere you too much. The ones that don't believe you think it's a funny little quirk of yours. As the Sisterhood grows, maybe some will be more ambitious and use it as an excuse."

I thought about it, then shrugged. "I'll deal with it as it comes, then. In the end, it doesn't matter what anyone believes, it only matters that I know that it's true. I've ridden in a flying ship with Jack, the only one on this world to do so. If it makes problems for me in the future, so be it. I'll deal with it then. Now, let's get some sleep. I'll take the first watch. And Greta, stop staring into the fire. You know it ruins your night vision."

She snorted, not disagreeing, but letting me know that she really didn't care about my admonishment. We had done this so often, it had become a running joke between the two of us, practically a cornerstone of our relationship. She suddenly raised her face, nostrils flaring as she tested the air. I tensed in reaction to her movement, then caught the same scent a moment later. I relaxed again, recognizing the scent.

"Hallo, the camp," a voice called out softly from the darkness.

"Come on in, Lupita. Adalyne. You know you're always welcome," I replied.

A figure separated itself from the darkness as she stepped into the firelight. Lupita was long, lean, and intense, with brown eyes set deep in a face weathered brown by a life outdoors. Her name used to be Carmen, but she changed it to Lupita when she became a Sister, a custom gaining popularity among some. It was supposed to signify them being born anew when they became Sisters. Lupita picked her name because it meant "Little Wolf," a reference to werewolves of legend, even though that isn't what we were, although I supposed the term worked as well as any. (Also a trend growing in popularity.) Whatever. Adalyne joined Lupita a moment later. Shorter and rounder where Lupita was tall and angled, she looked like a mythical cherub to me with her blond hair and apple red round cheeks.

They were a couple of my Long Hunters, Sisters who spent most of their time deep in the jungle, trapping, hunting, and scouting, learning about the particular plants and animals that inhabited this jungle, unique amongst Kaler's environments, unless there was something similar on the Kiisian island. I didn't know, having never been there. The Snake People didn't welcome outsiders. Lupita especially, had been a Long Hunter for so long, there was a feral air about her. Adalyne had recently joined the Sisterhood. I thought she was young to be a Long Hunter, but she felt more comfortable out here than anywhere else, especially when it came to learning about the different plants that lived here and their properties. Lupita's specialty was dealing with the Army Wasps. She had a lucrative little business collecting Army Wasp venom and selling it to Stel, Serenity's local tavern owner, for her Skull Hammer drink. In fact, I noticed the thick bundle of her ghillie suit that she used around the Army Wasp Nests rolled up on her back as she sat down.

"What brings you out here to civilization?" I asked dryly when they had made themselves comfortable.

"There's something somewhere by Sanctuary that's upsetting the balance of the jungle. I thought someone should know about it," Lupita replied.

"Do you have any idea what it could be?" I asked.

Both Lupita and Adalyne shook their heads. "We were close to the area a couple of days ago. Something didn't smell right there, and I trust my instincts," Lupita said.

I nodded. To survive as a Long Hunter took a special skill set. I wasn't about to gainsay those instincts. There were things out here that could kill even a Sister, so those instincts were what kept her alive out here for this long. "So what are you saying? Do you think we should go back to Serenity and organize a force in strength?"

Lupita pursed her lips, thinking about it for a long moment, then finally shook her head. "I wouldn't feel right, rousing everyone over just a *feeling*."

"So what? Do you want us to help you scout?"

She shrugged. "Well, you're not exactly familiar with this jungle, but you're three of the strongest fighters we have, so if we ran into trouble, I'd feel confident that we could fight free of it at least," Lupita replied.

I bristled a little at her remark. I'd been knocking around this jungle before she'd been an itch in her daddy's trousers, but then made myself calm down. I had merely traveled through the jungle. She lived in it. Every day, every night, day in and day out. It was a different depth of experience. "What about the horses? Can they navigate where we need to go?" I said instead.

Adalyne piped in, shaking her head. "The undergrowth gets really bad in that part of the jungle. It's going to be impassable for your horses."

"I'm not going to just leave them here, or take them all the way back to Serenity," I protested. "If I do that, I might as well get the rest of the girls while I'm at it."

"There's a line cabin not too far away that we fellow Long Hunters use when we're in the area. We can leave the horses there," Lupita said.

"I'll even watch them for you," Adalyne chirped. "Lupita doesn't want me with her on this scout anyway. Says she has a bad feeling about it."

I nodded. "Sounds like a plan."

Once we left the main route that connected the two settlements, the ground quickly became choked with tree roots and undergrowth, forcing us to lead our horses. Babs, Greta, and I led our mounts, while Lupita and Adalyne helped with the packhorses.

We walked through the night and reached the line cabin just as dawn broke, lightening the jungle for us in increments. The cabin turned out to be an earthen dugout sunken into the ground. A roof of wooden poles covered with red clay and moss stuck above ground. There was a rude corral also made of wooden poles and covered with a grass roof to shield livestock from the frequent deluges that hit the rainforest set up in the clearing. The clearing was mostly red clay with grass half-heartedly sprouting up in random patches. Howler monkeys bellowed high in the canopy above, marking us as intruders in their territory. I glanced at Lupita. "Quite a relaxing place you have here."

She grimaced. "They migrated into this territory recently. It's quite irritating, really. They make it impossible to listen for threats. If we were here more often, it might be worth it to chase them away. But as it is," she shrugged.

I hitched my sword and ax into place. "Shall we?"

Lupita shook her head. "We're not quite ready yet. Let's tie some strips of cloth around anything you have that might make noise. Also, we're going to have to darken up your skin. Greta, you especially will glow like a ghost out there."

It was a good idea, so we followed her suggestions, including smearing some dark colored mud Lupita had collected by the river over the exposed parts of our skin. Cool at first, when it dried it itched like crazy. "I'll lead the way. I shouldn't have to remind you to watch your footing or tell you how slick it can get under the canopy, but I'm going to tell you anyway. If you're not sure about your woodcraft, follow in my footsteps."

With that she took her boots off. At our questioning looks, she replied, "It will be easier for me to feel where I put my feet. I'll be less likely to give away our position by stepping on something."

We filtered out of the clearing into the jungle. We moved fast at first as we were still a ways away from Sanctuary, but nevertheless we moved quietly. You don't complete the Trials to become a Sister without learning woodcraft and how to hunt, but as quiet as Greta, Babs, and I were, Lupita was a ghost, flickering in and out of our sight and pushing our pace. She led us down game trails, avoiding the worst of the underbrush that claimed any space where sunlight managed to filter down through the thick canopy. That kept our speed fast and our noise down, which was good. Nothing announced someone's presence like hacking through undergrowth. It carried a risk however. There were other predators that called the jungle home, and coming face to face with one of them was bound to be noisy too. Luck was with us, though, and we encountered nothing.

It was two hours past noon, and the sticky, smelly air quieted to an oppressive stillness, no doubt in anticipation of our daily thunderstorm, when Lupita suddenly stiffened and froze. We froze as well, wondering what was going on. We didn't have long to wait as the same lethargic air that moved past Lupita's nose now hit our nostrils, bringing with it the unmistakable smell of death. I motioned for her to continue, and she moved out, moving more cautiously than she already had been. We followed carefully, hands on weapons.

We found what we were looking for in a small clearing. The ground had been gashed and torn by many clawed feet. Gobbets of flesh were strewn about, and blood splashed many of the surrounding leaves, giving off that peculiar iron-rot smell that spilled blood had. Small scavengers scuttled away from what they had been feeding on into the brush at our approach, their banquet interrupted. Babs, Greta, and Lupita silently spread out, searching for threats, while I knelt by the remains. There were only a few scraps left. It looked like whatever had done this had carted off the choicer bits to feast on later, but it was enough. I bent down to a patch of honey blond fur, my nose close to the reeking mud and blood mixture of the soil, closed my eyes, and inhaled deeply.

It was Willow. She had been one of the Sisters stationed in Sanctuary. Memories cascaded unbidden through me in a rushing torrent. Willow as a young girl, in blond braids and homespun dress dashing barefoot down Serenity's hard-packed dirt street giggling uncontrollably with her gaggle of ne'er-do-wells as they played some game incomprehensible to us adults. Her face, covered in mud and exhausted, yet unbowed as she struggled through the Trials. Then later, her expression radiant and proud, when she became a full Sister. I remembered her following me and Alex around, asking us a million questions as we performed some necessary but mundane chore. Tears gathered at the corners of my eyes, and a sob threatened to erupt out of me, but I choked it down. There would be time for mourning later. I straightened up, then began a slow circle around the clearing, sniffing, trying to pick up clues as to what could have done this to her. Despite the undeniable hazards of this forest, there were only a couple of things here that could actually kill a Sister, at least away from the water, and certainly nothing that left claw marks like this that hunted in a pack.

From what I could tell, there were at least half a dozen scent spoors that had been left behind. Some of the blood splashed so liberally on the foliage belonged to them. I felt a brief surge of savage satisfaction. Good. At least Willow hadn't gone down without a fight. Though fairly young, she had quickly proven herself to be one of our better fighters. It looked like she had been overwhelmed with numbers.

I motioned to the others. "This was the culmination of the fight, not its beginning," I murmured. "Let's start backtracking. No unnecessary noise from here on out."

It was an easy trail to follow. Both scent and broken vegetation pointed us in the correct direction. It led us to another, bigger clearing. A huge snarling battle had taken place here. Discarded weaponry and clothing lay in the center of the clearing along with several bodies, the place where our Sisters had made their final stand. Slowly, carefully, silently, we crept through the clearing, studying and scenting as we went, collecting clues, assembling a picture of what had happened here. We completed our circuit and knelt by our fallen Sisters in the clearing center. They had all Changed into their Other forms before the end, fighting to the last. They didn't die alone. Next to them was the almost complete corpse of one of the things that had attacked them. Large and furred, with a partial muzzle frozen in a rictus of pain and carnivore teeth, he looked like a cross between a normal human and one of us in our Other forms. Unlike us, he had kept his basic humanoid shape. His knees still bent like a normal person's and his feet were of normal size, although clawed. Something had reached up into his chest cavity and ripped out his heart. Once upon a time he had been human. No longer.

"It was Marie, Ciandre, Shar, Coraline, and Selena. It looks like they were hunting something and were ambushed here," Lupita whispered

"It looks like Marie and the others tried to fight a rearguard action here to buy Willow enough time to go get help," Babs murmured.

I nodded. In addition to this beast, I had recognized the signs of at least six more attackers that our Sisters had killed. They had given a good accounting of themselves. "There's nothing more we can do here right now. There's no telling how many of these things are still out here. Let's gather up Adalyne, head back to Serenity, and gather the Sisters. We'll need a good-sized crew for this."

We melted back into the jungle and started working our way back to the cabin, keeping the muggy breeze in our faces. The last thing we wanted was to run into another ambush like the one that had claimed Marie and the others.

We took a circuitous route to avoid taking the same path twice. It took us longer, and sunset still found us almost five kilometers from camp. Howler monkey bellows drifted across the air currents, reaching our ears, and announcing an intruder in their territory. It came from the direction of the cabin.

"Adalyne!" Lupita cried, and dashed off, with us at her heels. She soon left us behind, knowing the way better than us. We raced along after her, cursing under our breaths whenever a slip or a wrongly placed foot created noise, but there was no help for it. Going as fast as we could, it still took us forty-five minutes to reach the cabin. As we got closer, growling and snarling, interspersed with yelps of pain inflicted, reached our ears.

We burst into the clearing, panting with the effort, our lungs straining, legs burning. Two nightmarish creatures, Adalyne in her Other form, and another figure, were rolling around in a snarling, spitting ball, clawing and biting at each other while trying to simultaneously defend their more vulnerable parts. Adalyne's attacker looked just like us in our Other forms, yet was half again our size. He had managed to pin her under his greater bulk, and she was getting the worst of the exchange.

"Hey!" I screamed, drawing my weapons, trying to distract it from attacking one of my Sisters, a daughter in all but name, my mind racing on how to defeat it. We were not prepared to fight something like us. We needed spears. And silver. Our long dead designers had engineered a severe silver allergy into us. It was the most effective way to kill us, slowing our healing to that of a normal human's. Other than that, the next best way was drowning, or inflicting massive damage that overwhelmed our healing capability.

He, at least I assumed it was a he, looked up, and one of Babs' arrows struck him in the shoulder. He snarled and jerked upright at the sting, and Adalyne used the diversion to try to break free from him. She rolled over and tried to scramble out from underneath him. A big mistake on her part, because she attracted his attention again. His maw gaped, and he fastened down on the back of her neck. She squealed, then went limp as his jaws crushed her spine.

"No!" I screamed as he flung her limp form contemptuously aside and turned to face us. Babs fired another arrow, this time lodging in his neck, and I charged forward.

He rushed me, and I flung myself to the side. We wouldn't fare much better than Adalyne if he managed to bury us underneath him as well. Greta darted in behind him, hacking at his Achilles tendons. It wouldn't stop him for long, but it *would* slow him down until he managed to heal. Babs hit him again. The arrows were just nuisances, but they were distractions.

He changed tactics, stood up on his hind legs, and took a swipe at me with one of his hands. I ducked underneath the swing and chopped at his bicep with my ax. It bit into his arm with a satisfying crunch. I had broken the bone for sure.

That proved pivotal, as right then Lupita showed up. She had Changed into her Other form, which explained her delay in reaching us, and hit him from the side with all the force of a battering ram, knocking him off of his feet, with her landing on top. He could only grasp at her with one arm, kicking at her with his feet, and Lupita was in a rage. *And* she was fighting dirty. She accepted any harm he was going to deal her in order to inflict the most crippling damage she could in return. Her hind legs kicked back, aiming at his genitals, her fangs fastened on his neck underneath his chin, keeping him from biting back at her, and her clawed hands reached for his eyes. She was rewarded for her efforts with a scream of pain that rose in pitch when one of her feet hooked his tender parts and ripped them free. A half second later, she ripped his eyes out, blinding him.

"Hold him! Hold him, Lupita!" I barked as I dropped my weapons and drew my honor dagger. Unlike my other weapons, this one was dimpled purposefully with deep divots and was housed in a specially designed sheath that carried powdered silver in it. Greta, discerning what I was doing, drew hers as well. I darted in on one side, Greta on the other. I slammed the dagger into his chest, then ripped it out, sheathed it to coat it with more silver, drew it back out again, and slammed it into another part of his body, Greta doing the same from her side.

Babs entered the fray then, and grabbed his head, her arms thickening with muscle, her fingers lengthening and growing into claws, digging into his muzzle, holding it closed while Lupita continued to rip at him and Greta and I kept stabbing. That was a trick only the oldest and most disciplined of us could do; changing some parts of our body, while keeping the rest human. It took a lot of concentration, but it was a great way to conserve our bodies' resources. We could manage a full Change only once a month, but depending on how much of our body we changed, we could manage several partial changes in that same amount of time, without the subsequent vulnerability.

His healing slowed and his struggles grew weaker as the silver started to take effect. Lupita, sensing the weakness, began chewing through his neck with single-minded focus. Once she severed the spine, Babs flexed, and tore his head free. It was over. Under normal conditions, one could regrow a head, but the silver poisoning of his body made that impossible. Lupita continued to rip at the body, lost in her berserk fury.

I left them to it and ran over to Adalyne, only to find she had forced a Change back to human, and was lying motionless on her back. "Adalyne! What were you thinking? Why did you Change?" I cried sinking down beside her. Great rents and gashes marred her skin all over her body, and her torso was misshapen, most of her ribs crushed into powder. One of her arms lay at an unnatural angle, clearly broken.

"Too much damage," she gasped, her chest rising and falling shakily as she struggled to breath. "If I stayed in Her Shape long enough to heal, the chances are good I would lose my mind, and you guys would be forced to kill me. I can't put my Sisters in that position."

I nodded, tears falling hotly, spattering the ground. She was right. The longer we stayed in our Other form, especially the younger ones, the more likely we would be to lose our minds and humanity, becoming a mindless beast, one that would live only for the red slaughter. It was *only* a risk, and we might have been able to nurse her through it, but she had made her choice; there was nothing we could do about it now.

A howl rent the air, jerking my attention from Adalyne. Lupita crouched over Adalyne's assailant's corpse, her every fiber trembling with the need to pursue vengeance. I scrambled to my feet, then approached Lupita slowly, my hands held out. "Lupita, listen to me," I said calmly, my hands motioning at Babs and Greta to get away and see to Adalyne. Very carefully, they backed away from Lupita and got behind me to keep Adalyne company. "You can't go off hunting more of these things. You'll only get yourself killed. I need you to Change back. Come on, Lupita, Change back now." I willed my pheromones to start wafting from me, asserting my dominance, and reinforcing my command. She snarled, tensing and crouching down, defying me.

"Change back now," I said sternly. "Lupita, change back. That's an order! Don't challenge me on this, my daughter. Do it! Now!"

She snarled at me again, but obeyed. Crunching noises echoed throughout the clearing as limbs shrank, joints realigned themselves, and a pelt covered in coarse fur changed into smooth human skin. In a few minutes it was over, and Lupita sat before me, naked as the day she was born, sobbing. "Damn you for making me do this, Lyr! I'm useless now!"

I knelt in front of her and took her face in my hands. "You can never be useless to me, my precious one. Even if you could succeed in your quest for revenge, you would be lost to us in the end. I will not accept that sacrifice. I need something else from you. I need you to go to Serenity and get help. If anyone can slip by our enemies, if in fact they are between us and Serenity, it's you. Gather the Sisters, and bring them to Sanctuary. Your vengeance will be realized then, one way or the other, I promise."

I straightened back up to my feet. "Now come, Adalyne needs us."

We sat around our fallen Sister in a circle in the dirt, held her hands and stroked her hair and face until she passed. At least in the end, she wasn't alone.

Although time was of the essence, we didn't hurry to the next part. We buried Adalyne just outside of the clearing by a tree that bore her favorite orchid. It was backbreaking; we spent more time chopping through tree roots than we did digging, but we did it right, digging her grave so deep even the most motivated scavenger couldn't reach her. Even the howler monkeys stayed silent, perhaps mourning with us in their own way.

The next morning we stripped the gear from one of Babs' packhorses. Lupita vaulted up on her back. "I normally don't mess with these silly creatures," Lupita remarked as she gathered a fistful of mane. "I much prefer the feeling of dirt between my toes and solid ground under my feet."

"You're riding a horse without a saddle or bridle. I think you're doing just fine. Be safe, don't take any unnecessary risks, and we'll meet in Sanctuary in time to drink some Skull Hammer from the heads of our enemies."

Lupita grinned, a feral, vicious expression. She leaned down and grasped my forearm. "I'll bring a couple of bottles from Stel's. For Adalyne!" With that she kicked the horse forward and headed off, disappearing quickly from view.

"Come on, let's get ready to go," I said, turning to our horses. We saddled our mounts, and loaded the packhorses in silence, until Greta couldn't take it any longer.

"So what's the plan? Because you know we can't sneak past them with the horses. Are we going to charge in? Try to get past them before they catch us?" she asked.

I shrugged. "Maybe. There can't be that many of them, or our fight last night would have attracted so many this place would be crawling with them. Even if there's enough of them to encircle Sanctuary, they'd have to be spread pretty thin, don't you think?"

Greta looked mulish. "I think we should have gone back with Lupita, and come back in force. That's much better than risking you riding into a situation we still know nothing about!"

"We have Sisters in Sanctuary that might need our help!" I snarled. "I won't abandon them! You know me better than that."

Greta stared at me defiantly for a second, then dropped her eyes, unwilling to challenge me. I laid my hand on her shoulder and gave her a little affectionate shake. "I know you guys love me. But I'm not exactly made of glass. I'll be alright."

Babs, who had been staring off into space, suddenly chimed in. "You might have a point about them being spread thin," she said. "Let's cut some saplings and turn them into lances. A hit with a lance from a charging horse carries a lot of momentum. Even if it doesn't kill them, having a tree stuck through their gizzard will slow them down long enough for us to get past them, right?"

"That's a great idea, Babs. Let's do it."

We cut several saplings to length, sharpened one end to a fine point, and each carried one. We lashed the spares to one of the packhorses. It was going to be really, really awkward to carry a long stick through the jungle undergrowth, but they might make all the difference in order for us to break through the theoretical line of monsters waiting for us.

We started off for Sanctuary with as much stealth as a line of horses in jingling harnesses could manage, hoping the odds would be with us. Belief in any sort of gods hadn't gained a wide hold of the people of Kaler. This world had been colonized by scientists who had believed they were gods, not by people who believed in gods themselves, at least according to legend. There were some religions that were popping up out in the hinterlands, but the denizens of the larger population centers were still very secular. However, if there were gods of chance out there, they were certainly favoring us.

We were riding with the wind in our faces, when a certain pungent odor hit our nostrils. We reined in the horses immediately. "Tuskers!" I whispered, somewhat unnecessarily. Babs and Greta could smell them as easily as I could.

Tuskers were obnoxious little bastards that looked a lot like domestic pigs, except that they were carnivorous, with a predator's teeth and an armored head with a single horn growing out of it. Their favorite tactic was to impale an animal multiple times, then follow it for a distance, letting it bleed out. While not dangerous to us, they could kill our horses, which would be a serious inconvenience. But sometimes two problems could solve each other. I quietly dismounted and motioned for Greta and Babs to do the same. When they crept over to me, I grinned. "I've got an idea!" I whispered.

We wrapped our lances in rags and coated them in pitch we gathered from some nearby trees. Circling carefully into the wind, we located the herd in a small clearing. It was a sizable herd, sprawled in ungainly fashion throughout the plot of scraggly grass and red dirt. Contented grunts occasionally issued from one of the sleeping forms as tails swatted ineffectually at the flies that flitted around them. I looked at Babs and Greta then grinned, feeling like a kid about to commit mischief. We lit our lances on fire, then kicked our horses into a gallop, straight at the herd of tuskers, howling like banshees. The tuskers, who, like most predators, liked to sleep the day away after a successful hunt, bounded to their feet, then milled about uncertainly. Obnoxious and aggressive though they were, like most animals, they feared sudden noise and fire. Grunting and squealing in sudden panic, they broke away from us, towards Sanctuary. We spread out behind them into a rough semi-circle, keeping them bunched and herding them to Sanctuary's walls as best we could. Almost immediately, the herd began fraying as individual tuskers broke off into the undergrowth. This ploy wasn't going to last longer than a couple of minutes. Luckily we were fairly close to the town. We had chased them almost to the walls, when with a sudden snarl, a monster leapt out onto the trail. It looked like us, yet wasn't. Huge, furry, and slavering, saliva dripped in huge ropes from its fangs, as it waited for its prey to run conveniently to its arms. The tuskers split around it like water parting around a boulder in a stream, and I was right behind them. I lowered my burning lance and buried it in its chest. The lance went all the way through its torso and burst out its back as I rode it down, pinning it into the soft earth as I galloped past, releasing the shaft. It screamed in sudden pain and writhed wildly, trying to free itself. I wished it luck.

The tuskers ran right up to the gates, then split off to either side, following the unpeeled tree trunks that formed the outer wall of Sanctuary, trying to escape us. "Open the gates! Open the gates!" I screamed. They swung outward slowly, a couple of my Sisters straining to push them open, and we galloped into safety.

Siege at Sanctuary

We pounded into Sanctuary's compound, and reined in our lathered horses. Babs and Greta threw down the flaming lances they were still carrying. The gates behind us swung closed again, shutting us in.

"Mother Lyr!" The cry drew my attention as I was dismounting and before I could take stock of the situation. A figure jumped down from the wall walk, bounded over, and buried me in an enthusiastic hug. I grunted as all the air was expelled from my lungs, but I let the hug continue for a second before pushing the girl away from me. She was over a head shorter than me, with hair like flames and freckles that were sprinkled across her cheeks and nose. She normally lit up a room with her energy and looked like someone's kid sister, but she was one of us, with all that entailed.

"Discipline, Rose," I chided, but my heart wasn't in it. Truthfully, I had no idea what was waiting for us when we entered the city, for all we knew, we could have been riding to our deaths, and so was intensely relieved to find that the Sisters still held the town.

The outpost of Sanctuary wasn't much yet, just a wooden tower with some simple log buildings built around it and surrounded by earthen ramparts with a log wall built on top. Someday it would be more. It was going to be our gateway to the world, our main trading post, and our first line of defense. But that was a ways away.

"How bad is it, Rose?" I asked.

Her grin faded, her enthusiasm at seeing me draining from her in an instant. "It's bad, Mother. Let's go to the wall where we can see better," she replied. Without waiting for a response from me, she ran to the wall and climbed up the short ladder that led to the wall-walk. The wall-walk wasn't much, just split logs fastened to the fortress wall, but at least they allowed us to see over and defend the wall.

I followed her up and stopped beside her. She was gazing intently out at the forest that started just beyond the kill zone of the walls. The rest of the tusker herd was milling around on the earthen part of the wall, grunting in frustration and looking for a way in. I looked at Rose questioningly. "Wait, and watch," she murmured.

I turned my attention back to the jungle. I didn't have to wait long. Suddenly, a chorus of howls rent the air from beyond the treeline. The tuskers, who had been treated very poorly so far, what with being woken up from a sound sleep and then chased all the way here, all of a sudden found their day going from bad to worse. They milled around uncertainly, growing more uneasy and unsure by the moment. Then, at an unseen signal, they scattered in all directions, trying to make it to safety anywhere they could. It didn't seem to help. As soon as the tuskers disappeared into the forest, growls and snarls sounded, followed by high pitched squeals of fright and pain. After that, I could hear the ripping, tearing, and crunching sounds of large predators eating.

Something moved at the edge of the forest, drawing my eye. A gray form crept up, just out of the light. Yellow eyes like lanterns gazed balefully at me from the gloom. It looked like one of us in our Other forms. I turned away from it and looked down into the courtyard. Some of the Sisters had congregated below us. They were joined by a larger group of women, with some older children and teenagers sprinkled in. I didn't recognize any of that group. I hopped onto the ladder and slid down it. "Navi, Malaika!" I pointed at two of the Sisters. "Take care of our horses, will you? The rest of you follow me into the keep. I need the full story."

We gathered in the Main Hall, around the dining table. Other than Babs, Greta, and myself, there were eleven other Sisters.

"Tell me what has happened. From the beginning," I ordered.

Kamaria, a tall, muscular woman with skin the color of the night sky, began. "Something attacked a hunting group from a tribe of the Lawless at the edge of the plains. The only victim that survived was named Abdul, who happened to be the headman of the tribe and became infected himself. He Turned and attacked his own people. The men of the tribe fought a delaying action, giving the women and children enough time to get away. They made their way here, where we took them in. Some of the men survived, became infected as well, and also Turned. They tracked their women here and encircled Sanctuary. As far as we can tell, they can't change like we can. They're stuck in their beast forms, and those beast forms run in a spectrum from full beast to hairy and almost humanlike. We figure the ones with the least successful forms have been already killed off by their betters before they even got here. Our best guess from observing these things is that there were originally eighteen to twenty of them. After Marie's sortie, we think there's a dozen of them left."

Rose interjected, "They like to sleep during the day and come out at night. The ruckus with the tuskers woke them up. At night there's always one or two that try to climb the walls and get in. They're not very organized, so we've been able to drive them off, but it's a near thing."

"Why didn't anyone try to make it to Serenity to get help?" I asked.

"Marie didn't think there was any need. This is before we really knew what we were up against, and by the time we figured it out, it was too late," Kamaria replied.

I pinched the bridge of my nose with my fingers. I guess I couldn't really blame Marie. We got used to thinking we were the biggest monsters around and we got complacent. It was a lesson that was worth remembering. "It's only a matter of time. Eventually, one of them will make it and the rest will follow. We don't have the numbers to hold the whole fort and we could get overrun if we got split into little pockets defending different structures here. How many refugees do we have here?"

"About forty," Rose said.

"Are they all non-combatants? Are there any warriors in the group?"

Rose shook her head. "You know how these Lawless tribes are. The men beat all the fight out of any women they get a hold of. They were lucky they made it here."

I looked around. "Other than Navi and Malaika, are these all of us?" I meant the other Sisters.

Another Sister, Ophelia, pursed her lips in disapproval. "No. There's Yusi, of course."

"What's she doing?"

"Teaching the refugee children."

I was rendered speechless. Teaching kidlets was all well and good, but we had a bit of a crisis here. Yusi's priorities seemed a little skewed. "All right, here's what we're going to do. Gather up the refugees. Have them round up the horses and bring them to the keep. Break out all of our spears and arrows. We need to stage all the powdered silver we have on hand in strategic spots to coat their heads with. Babs, Greta, and I will be on the roof shooting at anything trying to get in, and tracking where they go in the compound here so we won't get ambushed in the morning when we venture out. The rest of you will split up into teams to guard the windows and doors on the first and second floors. Barbara and Greta, take charge of the weapons, and Rose and Kamaria, can you round up the refugees and put them to work?" They nodded.

"Good. When the time comes, we'll keep the horses on the first floor here and shut the women and children in the cellar. Now let me go see what Yusi's up to."

I found her in the barracks that was slated for new Sisters going through training. As I approached the door, I heard her voice, muffled by the building, followed by the children's voices, lifted in singsong repetition. Opening the door, I saw her pointing out letters to a group of children sitting on the floor, all between the ages of five to ten. They were all, Yusi included, dressed in floor length yellow robes with a sleeveless burgundy robe over the top of it. Behind Yusi and off to the side was a good sized shrine that I couldn't quite see.

Yusi was tall and willow thin, quiet and thoughtful, from what I remembered, with black hair, an olive skin tone and a slanted shape to her eyes common to the residents of Li-Zhang. She was truly young, not young-looking like most Sisters, in her twenties, having recently won her Sisterhood. She caught sight of me and her eyes brightened. "Mother!" she exclaimed, dropping down to all fours and placing her head on the floor. The children hurried to copy her example. I felt my cheeks heat up with embarrassment, and stifled a groan. If Babs, Greta, or any of the other old ones saw this, I would never hear the end of it.

I ignored it and turned to the children. "Class is dismissed for the day, kids. Your mothers need help getting ready for tonight. Yusi, stay here for a moment, please."

As the children gleefully got up and stampeded out the door, shrieking with joy, I bent down, and helped Yusi up. "Yusi, what are you doing?" I asked gently.

She looked puzzled. "Teaching the young ones, of course. I'm setting them on a better path, where they have a chance to truly leave their old ways behind them."

"Ah," I replied. "And this?" I fingered the material of her robe.

"Their uniforms, of course," she replied, grinning. "Children find comfort in structure, and looking like each other helps."

I nodded, somewhat helplessly. "You do know that Sanctuary is in somewhat of a crisis right now, don't you? Is this really the best use of your time?"

Her eyes flashed for a brief instant, before she dropped them again and bowed her head. "I believe the children need structure, normalcy, and something else to think about other than being scared for their lives. I teach them during the day, but I still help the other Sisters patrol the walls at night. I am doing my part, most Honored Mother."

I patted her arm. "I believe you, Yusi. But be careful. If you wear yourself down too much, when the climax comes and your Sisters and these children need you the most, your mind or your body will betray you."

"I hear and obey, Mother," she replied, her head still bowed.

I fought the urge to roll my eyes. I appreciated the loyalty, more than she could possibly know, but I never felt comfortable being put on a pedestal. The higher the perch, the longer and harder the fall, and the more extreme the reaction when the picture that person had built up in their head was shattered. Instead, I wandered around her to get a better look of the shrine set up in such a place of pride. It was built of gray river rock with an arched alcove. In the alcove was a ceramic figurine that had been sculpted with some skill. It was the figure of a woman, tall, strong, with one hand held out, palm up, beckoning. At least it was half a woman. The other half was rougher, blurred as if in shadow. A monster with long, wicked claws and a short muzzle wrinkled in a savage snarl. Its toothsome maw, filled with fangs, stared hungrily at the viewer. The overall effect was terrifying.

"Yusi, what is this?" I asked.

Her head snapped up and she flashed a smile of pride. "That is an effigy of you, Mother. I will teach the children to honor and revere you as the founder of our clan."

"Yusi. This statue isn't going to do anything except teach the children to have nightmares about me every night." I turned away from my terrifying effigy to face Yusi again. My eyes fell to her other arm, the one that was hidden from me when

I entered the room. On her arm was a tattoo. Of my face! "Yusi! What is that?" I asked in horror.

"That is you, Honored Mother," Yusi whispered, completely dejected now.

All right, this whole thing was just... unhealthy. I was understanding Ophelia's earlier disapproval now. "Why, Yusi?" I asked.

"I don't think you understand what you mean to us, Mother. I mean, not really. You've rescued all of us, in one way or another from the very worst time of our lives. You raised us and showed us a different path, one where we're free to make our own choices, and fulfill our destiny fully. For the first time in all of our lives, we're truly free. I love you for that Mother, and I want everyone to feel the same way about you."

I was quiet for a long moment. We in the Sisterhood learned to suppress and control our emotions. It was safer. Our biggest challenge was never attack from without. It was always losing ourselves to our Other. To lose our humanity. It was a war we were always going to have to fight, and not all of us were going to win it. To have someone so candidly share such strong emotions with me was like getting a really hard punch to the gut. It stole my air for a minute.

I enfolded Yusi in a hug. Something I rarely did with anyone. "I hear you, my daughter. But you have to understand something. I am as human as you are. I have flaws like any person, and you're setting yourself up for crushing disappointment if you don't realize that now. I won't be worshiped. I refuse. That's too dangerous. You'll have to get rid of that shrine. I won't countenance that. But I love you, too, as I love all of my daughters." I pushed her out to arm's length, squeezed her shoulders, and gave her a little shake. "Now come. We have work to do."

The horses were tied to hitching posts right outside of the Keep. They would be brought in at the last moment as things would get really crowded and messy really fast with them in the Great Hall. The glue pots were bubbling on the stoves in the kitchen when I walked in with Yusi. Under the direction of Rose and Kamaria some refugee women were busy nailing thick boards across the windows. The goal wasn't to stop the monsters, just delay them long enough for the Sisters to stab them, repeatedly. Buckets of silver powder were set near any potential entry point.

A Sister would stab a creature, dip the spearhead in the bucket of silver, then stab again. Repeat ad infinitum. The more silver got in their bloodstream, the more they would weaken, slow down, and the less dangerous they would become as anaphylactic shock set in.

Elsewhere, under the watchful eyes of Babs and Greta, other women were dipping spears and arrows in the glue, then once the glue got a little tacky, they dusted them with silver powder. One of the refugee women seemed to disapprove of the process. You couldn't tell from her expression because all of the women wore head scarves that covered their whole head and veils that covered their faces, but every line of her body was broadcasting outrage. Interesting. Apparently not all of the fight had been knocked out of one of them at least.

"Is there a problem?" I asked softly as I moved up behind her. She jumped at least six inches off the floor and whirled towards me. She relaxed slightly when she saw me.

"No. No problem," she answered, staring at the ground, refusing to meet my eyes.

"Your demeanor says differently," I replied. "What's wrong?"

She gestured at the silver. "This is such a waste! You're throwing away a fortune here! How can you be sure this will even work?"

Looking at the body language of her companions, I could tell that they didn't like this woman all that much, and wished that she wasn't talking. I'd be willing to bet that this woman wielded a certain amount of influence in the tribe, probably the headsman's wife or sister. She probably had been in charge of the money or inventorying the loot or something. I'd guess that she might have been in charge of the other women to a certain extent, as well. At least the ones that didn't have the protection of one of the men in the tribe.

"Oh, I'm fairly confident this will work. You see," and I loomed over her. "You could say those monsters out there, and we," and I gestured at my Sisters, "are related to each other." She shrank away from me a little. *That's right, you're not in charge of anything any more.* I raised my voice a little so that all of the women could hear me. "Don't worry. Those monsters out there have to come through us to get to you. And it takes a lot to kill us."

* * * * *

Night had fallen. The women and children were shut down in the cellar, and the horses were tied up wherever we could fit them on the first floor of the keep. They worried me more than a little. If they panicked and broke their leads, they could get in the way. A lot.

I was on top of the keep roof with Babs and Greta. We all had our bows, Babs with her warbow, and Greta and I with our hunting bows. Although not as powerful as Babs's one hundred pounder, at seventy pounds draw weight, they still packed a punch. I sniffed the air almost continuously, trying to catch any hint of a scent. The compound was draped in dark velvet; we hadn't left any torches lit outside. Didn't want them to catch anything on fire in the coming excitement. No matter. We Sisters could see in the dark much better than an unenhanced person. The night was normal, so far. Insects made their customary noises. Out in the jungle depths howler monkeys bellowed. A saber-toothed cat coughed quietly on its nightly rounds. Normally they were more confident in the noises they made when announcing their presence, but tonight bigger predators hunted.

"Do you think this will actually work?" Greta murmured.

I shrugged while continuing to scan the surroundings. "It's the best plan I can think of at the moment. We don't have enough people to man the walls, and if we tried, they would eventually pick us off one by one, whittling us down. The chances of us getting anyone through their ranks and back to Serenity to get help are slim. We were exceptionally lucky to break through in the first place, apparently. This lets us concentrate our forces and reinforce each other, while appearing weaker than we are. Baiting the trap, so to speak. It might not happen tonight, but I think that the first one that makes it over the wall will be a signal to the rest, like ringing a dinner bell."

Greta nodded and muttered quietly to herself, "I think *we* have an excellent chance of being overwhelmed up here." She didn't mean for me to hear it, but I caught it anyway. I started to snarl in response, but killed it, regaining control of myself.

The night crept on. Artemis and Chang'e, our two moons, traveled slowly across the diamond strewn velvet. We watched in silence. A couple of hours before midnight, my eyes caught something moving in the darkness. A clawed hand caught the top of the wall. A monstrous form, looking like a horrifying mishmash of big cat, wolf, and human pulled itself quietly over the wall. I nudged Greta. "Track that. See where it ends up." I whispered.

She nodded. I kept watch for more. I didn't have to wait long. A second, then a third crept over the wooden walls and made their way through the town. They moved slowly, sniffing the air as they went, hunting. One found the livestock that had been shut up in the stables. Excitedly it started scrabbling at the siding, trying to force its way in. The animals inside started bawling in panic and throwing themselves against the sides of their pens trying to escape. The thuds of their bodies hitting the wood echoed across the plaza, reaching our ears easily.

Babs drew, aimed, and released in one quick motion. The silver dusted arrow flashed across the square and buried itself to the fletching in the beast's shoulder. It howled in pain and surprise, then whirled to face the keep, trying to find what hurt it. Babs launched another arrow, but this one whizzed right over the top of it, missing. The creature was able to track the path of the arrow, however, and looked across the square and up, seeing us. It snarled, lips curling up to reveal jagged, mismatched teeth. It started to roar at us when I launched my own shot. It struck him right in his ugly muzzle. His roar choked off into a whine, and he frantically brushed at the arrow with a paw, trying to pull it out.

Babs looked at me. "Lucky shot," she joked. I grinned at her triumphantly.

In the meantime the creature had managed to pull out my offending arrow. With a scream it launched itself across the quad towards us. The keep walls didn't even slow it down as it hurtled itself up the wooden siding.

"Incoming!" I barked. "I'll handle this one. Track the others!" I dropped my bow and drew my sword and ax. This would have to be timed perfectly. I moved to the edge of the wall and watched it climb. Honestly, it made a terrifying sight as it scrabbled up towards me. Powerful muscles bunched and released under its pelt. Claws sank deep into the wood, gaining it purchase; bloody drool frothed and dripped from its lips, and its eyes glowed like two baleful lamps. Adrenaline exploded through me like a live wire, and I suddenly had to clamp down on my instinctive response to Change in order to meet this threat. Human reason was the key to this fight. That and silver. It was far stronger and faster than me, but its ability to think was buried under a red haze of hunger, rage, and the need to slaughter. I also had the advantage of position.

Its claws hooked into the top of the parapet, and just as its head cleared the top of the wall, I chopped down with my sword. My timing was perfect. My sword buried itself between its eyes, splitting its skull. All its momentum stopped, and it hung limply from the wall, its dug-in claws refusing to let go. I jumped up on top of the wall to get a better angle. Two strokes of the sword and its suddenly handless body dropped ten meters down to the ground. It would eventually heal, even from those grievous wounds, but it was out of the fight in the meantime.

Suddenly, another beast clawed itself onto the top of the wall, drawing my attention. This one paused at the top, standing upright on its hind legs. It glared malignantly at me, its eyes glowing, then raised its muzzle and howled, a stentorian call to battle. Other howls answered it from the forest, the pack responding.

I studied him carefully, trying to gauge who this was. Was it the source of all my ills, the one who started this whole mess? Or had he been the leader or one of the under-chiefs of the lawless tribe that had been Turned?

Around me Babs and Greta's bows began to sing in earnest as they loosed shaft after shaft at the three beasts that were milling around the courtyard, trying to incapacitate them before the others showed up. Other forms began flowing over the top of the wall. The pack had arrived.

I held the leader's eyes, then lifted my face to the moons and howled in response. I focused, letting just my throat Change. It thickened, deepening my voice. The notes of my song rang over the courtyard, a direct challenge to his authority. I ended it and glared back at him. *Come on, take the bait,* I thought. His eyes blazed at me and he jumped down from the wall. With barks and swipes of his claws, he directed his pack to surround and attack the keep, but kept back himself.

My eyes narrowed. This one had retained more of his mind than the others. He sure didn't believe in leading from the front, though. Coward. Probably a bully in his former life that ruled through intimidation and brutality.

The monsters started crashing into the doors and windows, testing their integrity. My Sisters were about to be tested.

* * * * *

Rose was stationed in the Great Hall by the front door and two of the windows. Ava, Mia, and Kelcee were stationed around the other windows on the first floor. Kamaria was their strategic reserve. A sudden, heavy bang on the door startled her, but she relaxed after a moment. The door was made of ironwood and set into the heavy timbers of the keep's frame. It was almost as strong as the walls themselves, and unlikely to be breached by the monsters milling around outside. Of more concern were the windows. They had done the best they could in the time they had, but they were definite weak points.

Rose could hear the shuffling of their heavy bodies and hear their muttered growls and snarls. She tilted her face a little and sampled the air. The musky rankness of their forms wafted to her nostrils; the stench of furry bodies that eschewed bathing other than getting caught out in the occasional rain shower. A shiver of atavistic fear ran through her. It was a little like the first time she had seen a Sister in her Other form.

A Sister in her Other form was a symbol of destruction and carnage, an almost unkillable machine of murder. Rose took a deep calming breath and tightened her grip on her spear. She knew what they were facing, but there was a vast difference between what she had been and what she was now. She was a Sister herself, one of the elite, one of the very few who had made it through the grueling training and weeding-out process. There were monsters in the world, true, but she was one of them. That thought made her smile and gave her strength to face the coming storm.

A heavy crash jerked her out of her head, and snatched her gaze to one of the windows. The wood splintered under a heavy blow, and then splintered some more under another. It was one of hers and she positioned herself carefully by it. Best case scenario, the beast would tear a hole into the planking and try to force itself through it, slowing it, and giving her a nice target. Worst case, it would tear all planking out of the window and be able to jump through, forcing a breach.

The blows, crashing, and clawing continued. Vaguely, she was cognizant of crashing at other windows, but her focus was narrowed to this single point; her window. With a loud splintering sound, part of the planking broke and was torn free. A grotesque face glared at her, spittle dripping from its fangs in long ropes. Rose made herself hunch down and look smaller, making herself look like less of a threat. She tried to look scared, like prey.

The ruse worked. The creature threw even rudimentary caution to the winds and tried to climb through the too-small hole. Perfect. Rose waited until the last second, then thrust her spear into the spot where its neck joined its shoulders. It howled in pain and she jerked her spear back out. She thrust the bloody spearhead into the bucket of powdered silver then stabbed it again. And again. It shrieked in agony and struggled against the wooden planking, trying to free itself one way or another.

"It burns like a sonuvabitch, doesn't it boyo," she snarled joyously, and stabbed him again. It screamed, sounding almost human in its agony. The wooden beams suddenly bowed inward, almost completely giving way under the creature's weight. Suddenly, there was another snarl, higher pitched in tone, and another furry figure entered the fray. It was smaller, with a light chocolate-colored fur, but better proportioned, but no less fierce for its smaller size. It latched onto the monster stuck in the window, sinking its fangs into the back of the monster's neck and yanked it in and down, bearing it to the ground.

"Damn it, Ava, this isn't part of the plan!" Rose shouted. She started stabbing in a frenzy, trying to hit as many vital spots she could reach. Then Kamaria was there, wielding a wicked looking ax. She sank it into the invading monster's back, right at the base of its spine. She ripped it free with a sickening sucking sound, and sank it in again, trying to separate the creature's legs from the rest of its body. The monster's struggles got weaker as it absorbed more damage. Finally, Rose, with a freshly silvered spear, managed to sink it into the thing's heart. With a long sigh, the monster gave up the fight, and went limp.

Rose and Kamaria straightened up, gasping for breath. Rose dashed sweat out of her eyes, and leaned on her spear. "Thanks for the assist, Ava. Can you go help Kelcee now? You're panicking the horses. Mia!" she shouted. "Try to calm the horses down, will you?"

Ava scampered over to Kelcee's position and Rose turned to help Kamaria, who was already trying to hammer the broken planking back in place.

* * * * *

The refugees huddled down in the cellar and listened to the sounds of combat above them as those strange women that took them in battled the things that used to be their husbands, brothers, and fathers. Mothers of the young ones did their best to comfort the really small children with limited success.

"What do you think, Amira?" Ximena asked. Amira being the one that had dared to criticize the large woman that had come in today, acting like a queen.

Amira snorted. "That one's plan is stupid, and we are all going to die." Ximena was one of the few allies Amira possessed. Tribes rose and fell in the Lawless Lands. It was the way things were. The only way to win the game was to survive. When the tribe was still a tribe, and strong, she had wielded the scraps of power she had been gifted harshly. As a result, few of the other women liked her. It was only because of that gifted authority that the women still looked to her in times of trouble. That, and there were always women like Ximena trying to curry favor.

"What do we do?" Ximena whispered.

"We wait. Maybe the strange ones kill enough of the demons that the demons leave, and we can stay here. Maybe we can escape with the dawn when the demons sleep. Worse comes to worst, we throw some of the weaker, slower ones to the demons, especially if we take the horses. That will give us enough time to escape."

Ximena nodded and moved away, huddling in the corner as the battle raged on above their heads.

* * * * *

Ophelia and Yusi were patrolling the hallways of the second floor, spears in hand. Ophelia was in a foul mood. "How did I get stuck being partnered with a deviant like you?" she growled.

"You hit the jackpot, I guess," Yusi snarled back. In addition to her spear, she had grabbed a cleaver from the kitchen for close-in work. A sudden crash interrupted their bickering. As one, they sprinted down the hallway to the room where it originated. They reached the room in time to see one of the creatures getting to its feet, the wreckage of the window planking draped around it. It shook itself, flinging the rubbish off of it, then snarled at them.

"Hello, handsome. Do you have an invitation to this party?" Ophelia asked, right before she lunged with her spear. The monster batted her spear aside, but Yusi was there, and sank her spear deep between its ribs. It howled and bit at the spear shaft. Powerful jaws crunched, and it bit the spearshaft in half, leaving the head buried deep in its ribs. Its distraction gave Ophelia time to sink her spear into its other side. Andraya, the other person who was patrolling the second floor rushed into the room from the other direction, and also stabbed the beast.

"Pin it. Pin it!" Yusi shouted, drawing the cleaver. It was time for some close-in work.

* * * * *

We really could have used another person up here, I thought as I looked down at the courtyard. In addition to the one that I had crippled, two more were down. One from a lucky shot by Babs that had punctured its eye and lodged in its brain. It lay there, twitching, unable to control its body. I wasn't sure if it was going to recover from that injury or not, but it would take longer than the time it had left on this planet if I had anything to say about it. The other one looked like a pincushion; the amount of arrows stuck in it had been enough to overwhelm its system and send it into anaphylactic shock. There were still seven creatures milling around down there and we were almost out of arrows. At least two had broken into the keep, but I couldn't spare more than a fleeting moment to worry about the Sisters there. Young they all might be compared to Babs, Greta, and myself, but they were still tough, smart warriors, and they outnumbered any beast that managed to break in. At some unseen signal, two of the beasts started scampering up the keep's walls.

I readied myself to meet the rush head on, but a thump behind me had me whirling around. The pack leader had climbed up the opposite side of the keep with one of his packmates. They were stalking Babs who was still firing at the other two creatures who were climbing.

I lurched across their path while yelling a warning to my two companions. The packmate was just turning his attention to me when I struck with a backhand cut to its front forelimb with the sword in my right hand, followed up with an uppercut to its throat from the ax in my left. As it sat there choking on its blood I body-checked it off to the parapet to the ground below.

Unfortunately, that meant I ignored the leader too long. I cried out as I felt the searing pain of claws digging into my shoulder and spinning me around. I looked up into the leader's slavering face as his other hand grabbed me around my throat and hoisted me up as if I were a kitten. He roared into my face, and shook me fiercely. He was showing off, toying with me before he killed me, because I had dared to challenge him.

I heard Greta cry out my name, then screamed a scream that started out loud and startled, but faded out quickly. I wanted to cry out myself, but I couldn't get any air. I couldn't match the leader in arm strength alone, even if I Changed. But I didn't have to use just my arms. I dropped my weapons, grasped the hand around my throat with one hand, then brought my legs up around his arm. I crunched my whole body hard and jackknifed, rocketing my forehead into his snout. He roared in pain, and his grip loosened as his eyes watered.

Having milliseconds to spare, I ripped my honor dagger free and rammed it into his chest, right where his heart would be. He howled and dropped me completely.

I fell to the roof, coughing and trying to suck in fresh air. Sparing a precious half second, I looked over at Babs. She was getting the worst of it, caught between the other two wolves. I grabbed the weapons I had dropped and staggered to my feet, intending to hit her, only to get hit by something that felt like a swung log that batted me across the roof. I skidded across the wooden planks, slamming to a stop when I hit the opposite wall. I shook my head, clearing the cobwebs from it and looked up just in time to see the leader charging toward me full speed. I tried to get back up on my feet, knowing full well I wouldn't have enough time to get set before that thing hit me like a ton of bricks. Then a furry blond form shot over the top of the wall and barreled into his side, knocking him off of his feet. Greta was back, and she was pissed.

She swarmed over him like a rabid weasel, clawing and biting. He roared and tried to snare her, to drag her around to his front, where his greater strength could come into play. She was too quick, though, not letting herself stop in any one place long enough where he could get to her. Desperate, he rolled over on his back, pinning her. Perfect. That got her out of the way and exposed his chest and belly to me. I sunk my ax into his sternum with a brutal overhand chop. Ripping it free, I hit him again and again, trying to damage him so much his healing would slow down. Reversing the ax, I hit him with the spike and used that as a lever to pry him off of Greta.

"I've got this now!" I yelled at her. "Go help Babs!"

She scrambled out from underneath him and hurled herself into the fray where the two other wolves had Babs buried underneath them. Levering my monster off of Greta had trapped my ax underneath his bulk, so I let go of that and used my sword two-handed to hack at his back, an ultimately losing strategy as the sword had layers of thick muscle to cut through to get to anything vital. Luckily for me, he thrust himself to his feet and turned to face me. I danced to the side and hacked down at the back of his knee severing his lower leg. He howled in pain and dropped to all threes, the shock of losing a limb breaking through even his berserker haze. I spun and whipped an underhand cut up, cutting off his muzzle. He shrieked and tried to scrabble away, all thoughts of fighting gone. I stalked him closely, and when he tried to climb over the wall, I kicked him off of it. He bayed in fright, then I heard him hit the ground with a sudden thump twelve meters down.

I cursed at our lack of foresight at not bringing any spears up with us. My dagger and ax were gone, still buried in the pack leader. Greta was crouched over Babs's unmoving form, snarling for all she was worth and swiping at the last two wolves anytime they got close. With all their attention on Greta, I was able to scurry up to them before they knew I was there. Four fast two-handed swings, and I had hamstrung both of them. Snarling, they dragged themselves around to face me, but their hindlimbs flopped uselessly behind them, at least for the moment. Greta didn't waste any time, throwing herself on top of one of them, trying to hold it down, while I split the skull of the other one, knocking it out of commission.

Sprinting past them I jerked Babs's dagger out of its sheath and buried it into the side of the beast Greta was riding. I ripped it out, and broke into a flurry of stabbing, while Greta worried at it from the other side. When I heard the other monster start to stir, I whirled and chopped its head off, then I returned my attention to the last one.

After a seeming eternity, but was probably only about a minute, it was over. Both wolves lay dead at our feet. I glanced down in the courtyard. The four uninjured creatures that were left had forgotten their quarrel with us and ripped the leader to pieces. Apparently he hadn't been well liked. I looked at Greta. "Call the Sisters to the Hunt, Greta," I said.

Greta turned her face to the sky, and howled a long, quavering song that rang with notes of hunger, bloodlust, and the joy of the hunt. The wolves down in the courtyard paused in concern, as the Sisters answered her with voices that started out as women, turned into shrieks of pain as the Change overtook them, and deepened into answering howls of craving for the blood. The front door burst open and almost a dozen furry figures burst out in a headlong rush. Greta dove over the keep's wall, not to be left out.

I left them to it. They didn't need me. Instead I dropped to my knees to examine Babs. Her torso was a mass of great gashes, and her arms and legs were shredded like they had gone through a meat grinder. Four great claw marks had gouged across her face, ruining one of her eyes, and a hand was missing, but she had been able to protect her vital organs. We were tough. Anything that didn't kill us outright, we were able to recover from in time. Her eye would regenerate quickly, and she would even regrow her hand, in time.

I cradled her head in my lap, and gently stroked her hair and face. She opened her eye and gazed up at me. "Hey," she whispered.

"Hey yourself," I replied. "It's over. You did well, my daughter. Rest now."

She sighed, nodded, and closed her eye. In a moment she had slipped into a deep sleep while her body began to heal the massive damage that had been done to it. I picked her up and carried her to the trapdoor that led from the roof to the third floor. Getting her down that ladder was going to be a bitch. But when I flung open the trapdoor, Yusi was there.

"Yusi! Why aren't you hunting with the others?" I asked as I handed Babs's limp form down to her.

She grinned as she accepted the weight. "Someone had to stay behind to guard the children, both from our attackers and any of our Sisters that may get too.... enthusiastic."

I nodded as I jumped down, eschewing the ladder entirely. "Good thinking." I left Yusi to take care of Babs with instructions to put her in one of the beds here in the keep, and I made my way downstairs to the ground floor. I paused at the open main entrance before I cautiously made my way into the courtyard. There was danger not only from the invaders but also from a young Sister who had lost control, or... one who suddenly entertained ambitions about deposing me and setting herself up in my place. None of the Sisters here would be able to keep that place, however. Even if they managed to kill me, there were many older ones back in Serenity that would kill them quicker than you could blink. However, caution didn't cost anything except a little time.

I picked my way through the carnage littering the ground to where the pieces of the leader were. I sighed in relief as I retrieved my dagger and ax. Not being armed was worse than being naked. I knelt down and sniffed deeply at his remains, trying to determine his line. The scent wasn't immediately familiar. I got even closer, my nose just about touching one of the pieces, and inhaled deeper. After a while. I straightened back up in frustration. It was familiar, but I just couldn't place it. It looked to me like this pack leader had been made by someone that didn't know what in the Makers' hell they were doing, making these poor mutant abominations.

The scrape of claws against stone brought me springing up to my feet and whirling around. It was one of the Sisters, crouched down, looking like she was about to charge. I sniffed. Navi.

"Navi, Change and report, please."

Navi only crouched deeper, her upper lip beginning to lift away from her teeth in the beginnings of a snarl.

"Stop that!" I growled, standing straighter, making myself bigger. *This pup thought she could challenge me*, I thought, rage building at the affront. That anger made me start to exude dominance pheromones. It was a trait that we shared with w'reaver pack leaders, the horse-sized predators that our Makers designed, and who we were really based on. They used the same pheromones to control their highly aggressive, often recalcitrant charges. "Don't make me paddle your backside until you piddle on the floor. I'm in no mood for any more shit after the night we've had. Change!"

Navi drew away from me as my posture and the pheromones I was emitting broke through her blood haze. She lowered her head in submission, and began to shake. A minute of agony and the sounds of cracking bones and joints later, a naked Navi was kneeling on the ground, forehead pressed against the dirt. "I'm sorry, Mother. I lost control for a moment."

I relaxed my posture, lowering my weapons. "It's all right, Navi. We all slide from time to time. Now, tell me what has happened."

"Some of us chased the ones that could run into the forest while another group stayed behind long enough to finish off the cripples here. I was with Malaika and Gabriella. We chased one down and ripped him apart. Malaika and Gabriella ran off to help any other Sister group still hunting, and I came back here."

"Good. Now go get cleaned up and dressed. I'll wait by the door to welcome the other Sisters as they come in. After that, we need to have a meeting."

* * * * *

It was actually the next morning when Lupita showed up with a dozen Sisters in tow. They were armed to the teeth and looked ready to fight a war. After gathering to examine the bodies, we met around the big table in the Great Hall. Plans had to be made for things going forward. Two Council members made the trip. Alexandra, whom I just called Alex, my second and the first one I made, was here, along with Grace. I always thought Grace's name was a bit of a misnomer, as she was one of the most merciless fighters I had ever met. All the Sisters from Sanctuary were at the table, as well as Babs, who was up and about, the stump of her arm heavily bandaged. Her eye had already grown back, and all but the worst gashes had closed up and mostly faded. The amount of damage her body had taken had really slowed her healing. As a courtesy, I allowed Amira and Fatima, the de facto leaders of the refugees, to attend.

"This is what we know so far," I said, starting the meeting. "And some of this information we have now is thanks to Amira, here." I nodded at her in thanks and recognition. "Someone who called themselves Fenrir walked into your tribe's camp, and managed to get your brother Abdul alone, ostensibly to plan a strike on another tribe. That's when he mauled Abdul and escaped into the night during the confusion. Do I have it right so far?" Abdul apparently was the pack leader we had fought.

Amira nodded, keeping her eyes lowered submissively.

"All right. Even though Abdul was badly injured, he managed to recover. Shortly after that, he began to exhibit unstable behavior. He began to grow claws on his hands, and started to act increasingly more violent. In the course of trying to control him, most of the rest of the men in the tribe also got infected, correct?"

Amira ducked her head again. "Yes."

I nodded. "All right. Ladies, what is the situation now?"

"All of the werewolves that were here in the compound are accounted for. We caught and killed all but one, and that one barrelled headfirst into an army wasp nest. He managed to avoid being eaten and dragged himself away, but we found him again when the wasps had calmed back down."

"Sounds good. So as far as we know, we have this episode contained. We won't let our guard down, though. For the foreseeable future, we're going to do enhanced patrols all around Serenity and Sanctuary. No less than three Sisters on any patrol. If they run into any other wolves, and they don't outnumber them at least three to one, they are to disengage and retreat to either town, sounding the alarm. Understood?"

Everyone nodded in agreement. "Good. Now, we have find this Fenrir and stop him. We can't afford to let this contagion get out of hand."

Amira raised her hand. "Excuse me, your Worship. I don't understand. How is this your problem? You stopped it here. That's all that matters, no?"

I shook my head. "No. This Fenrir is highly infectious and unstable. He has no control and doesn't know what he is doing as far as making more wolves. I'm speculating that he's experimenting, trying to find the right process in order to make more of himself, more like what we are. If we don't stop him, Kaler will likely be overrun with wolves. Regular humans are ill-equipped to deal with this threat, and soon, there might not be any more humans at all, at least not on this continent. It is our responsibility and duty to stop this before it gets out of hand. This takes precedence over anything else. In light of that, Grace, I want you to take Lupita and two more experienced Sisters who are strong fighters, and try to backtrack his trail. See if he's still in the area. I will take Greta and... " I looked around the table, "Yusi." Yusi was young, but she seemed to have talent as a fighter, and had a cool head. Plus, I had absolute confidence in her loyalty. I also didn't want to let her out of my sight. She had shown a rather alarming propensity to put me on a pedestal. A couple of months traipsing around with me should knock that hero worship of me right out of her head. "We'll try to find the places he's been and any other creatures he might have made."

"Alex, I'm leaving you in overall charge of both towns while I'm gone." She didn't look happy about it, but she understood. Of all of the Sisters I trusted her the most to keep things together while I was gone.

"Babs, I want you in charge of Sanctuary. keep developing the pups, and don't fall asleep out here, all right?"

Babs nodded. She would do fine keeping the pups in line.

"Amira," she jerked like I had poked her suddenly with a stick, "you and everyone else are welcome to make your home here in Sanctuary. If you want to strike out on your own, you're welcome to do that, too. As long as nobody is forced to stay or go, whatever the decision is. Understand?"

She ducked her head in that submissive manner she had. I studied her a moment longer. There was something about her that bothered me, but I couldn't quite put my finger on it. Something was… off. I mentally shrugged and moved on. I couldn't spare any more energy thinking about it right now. "Does anyone else have any questions?"

"I understand everything, except why it is you that has to go, Lyr." Alex looked especially mulish.

I sighed. "I can't let this go. If we didn't have two growing communities to take care of, I would gather up all of the Sisters and we would have a Wild Hunt like no other that would sweep all before us until we found Fenrir. But I can't do that. Ultimately, it is *my* problem, my responsibility. I can't stay back and send others into danger. I am the best equipped to deal with this problem. So it will be me going."

"But Mother, you know how important you are to us. How will we manage without you?" This came from Rose, whose eyes glimmered with unshed tears.

And this was another thing that would have to be fixed. This dependence and focus on me was starting to get unhealthy. They needed to learn to live without me. I was a person, dammit, not a symbol or figurehead. I couldn't tell them that, though.

"I understand, more than you know. But I *am* going, and all you guys are allowed to say is 'Aye, aye, ma'am.' Got it?"

"Aye, aye, ma'am," they all chorused.

Two days later I gave Alex a fierce hug before mounting up on Red. Yusi and Greta were already mounted up and ready to go. Yusi had shed her robe and was wearing the typical outfit that all of us wore, a soft black leather shirt and trousers that were designed to split cleanly apart when we Changed. She was also borrowing Babs's mount and gear. The rest of the Sisters and quite a few of the refugees had gathered to see us off. Grace and her three compatriots had already left, backtracking the pack back to the camp and seeing if they could pick up Fenrir's trail. If she lost it, she was to hit the caravan route and head west.

I was heading east. That was where the major cities were on this continent, and it was likely he had either come from there, or was going there. Time would tell.

"Take care of yourself, Mother," Alex said.

"You too, daughter," I said. "And the rest of you, my daughters, keep your eyes open, and your silver close. And behave yourselves!" I winked at this last bit to let them know I was joking. There were a couple of dutiful chuckles, but most of them looked like they were going to my funeral. I bit back a sigh, reined Red around, and started off. I waved as I rode out of town.

* * * * *

Amira and Fatima also waved as the Queen left. "It is good that they let us live here, no?" Fatima whispered.

Amira snorted softly. "They need the labor. Still. Yes, you are right, it is good. I shall learn all of their secrets," she watched as Lyr and her companions rode out of sight, "make them my own, and use them."

The Lawless Lands

S anctuary was nestled behind a series of low hills that hid it from the flatlands that comprised the Lawless Lands. After a couple of hours of riding, we topped a ridge and drew our horses up. Below us, like a rumpled bed sheet, grasslands rippled as far as the eye could see. Herds of wildebeest, bison, zebras, giraffes, and elephants grazed among the islands of trees that punctuated the sea of grass. Their movement churned up clouds of dust, turning the low horizon a burnt ochre, before the normal brilliant blue of the sky reasserted itself. Other animals we couldn't see lived down there as well. Saber-tooth cats, lions, hyenas, quaggas, and giant sloths also made their home here.

"It's hard to believe our ancestors created all of this," I said quietly.

Greta, who had heard this all before, grunted noncommittally, but Yusi looked at me curiously, "What do you mean, Lyr?" she asked.

I peered up at our sun, a blazing white disk in the sky. "Apparently our star is too young for complex life to have developed on its own. When our ancestors settled this planet, it was a blank canvas, and they were master painters. They developed all of this, different ecosystems separated by natural barriers, then sat back and watched it all to see if it would settle into equilibrium."

"How do you know all of this?" Yusi asked.

"Jack told me once, before he left for Earth," I replied.

"Fascinating," Greta grunted with a decided lack of enthusiasm.

I glowered at her. "You're like a bear with a sore tooth. What's your problem?" I demanded.

"Nothing," she grumbled. I said nothing, just continued to stare at her until she finally relented. "It's really nothing. I just have the Shift hangover."

I nodded in understanding. After a full Change, while we still kept most of our strength, our bodies' reserves were low, and our healing slowed to little better than a normal person's. It left us feeling... vulnerable; an unfamiliar, unwelcome feeling. And the older we were, the worse it was because we went through most of our life feeling invincible. "I can sympathize," I said. "But that does bring up a good point. You're still vulnerable. We need to plan around that."

"I can take care of myself," Greta muttered sullenly.

"I know you can, honey," I soothed. "I just don't want anything to happen to you." I pondered for a moment, then grinned, a thought popping in my head that amused me to no end.

"Say, this gives me an idea. Why don't we pretend you're in charge for the next couple of weeks or so. This way we can protect you without it seeming strange, and it will add another layer of anonymity for me. You can be a wandering baroness, and we are your loyal bodyguards," I said.

Greta scowled. "I think that's a terrible idea. We're supposed to be protecting you, not the other way around. Putting you at the tip of the spear is foolishly risky." Yusi nodded in agreement.

I smiled again. "Well, it looks as if we have two nos, and one yes. Good thing this isn't a democracy. The yeses have it." I straightened and studied the terrain a bit longer, looking for the easiest path, as well as potential places we could be ambushed, by man or beast. I shook out Red's reins and kicked him forward. "Look alive, ladies. This is the first step of a journey into a wider world, where we will hopefully see wonders that delight, many splendorous things, and meet new and exciting animals and people."

"And kill them," Greta said, chuckling to herself.

I gave her a slow, fierce smile. "Better them than us," I replied.

* * * * *

Waryn reined his horse to a stop at the crest of a low rise, surveyed the wagon train he was charged to guard, and tried to think of a way this wouldn't end in total disaster.

The caravan creaked its way across the Lawless Lands at a glacial pace, looking for all the world like the world's largest arthritic snake. Waryn glared up at the sweltering sun hanging in the pale blue sky doing its best to cook all the water out of him, mopped his face, and took a swig from his canteen to cut the dust that he'd been chewing on for the last several hours.

He watched the wagons filled with grain file slowly past his position and swore for the thousandth time. His boss was usually pretty smart when it came to business, rising to become one of the richest merchants in Newar, but this latest venture was insane. In the past, on his trips to the city of Li-Zhang, he limited himself to spices, which had a high value in relation to their volume. While he had no doubt the grain would have value in the world-city, it seemed to him that too much could go wrong.

He looked down at his two nearest guards and grimaced. He wished that Levi wasn't so cheap when it came to hiring people to protect his person and property. These two, for instance, proved Waryn's point painfully. One of them was small and twitchy, with dirty blond hair and rodent-like features. His name was Scot, but nobody called him that. They called him Snot, because his finger was always buried knuckle deep in a nostril looking for who knew what. The other one was average size with greasy dark brown hair, and a real troublemaker. Waryn didn't even remember his real name. He had been called Snags for as long as he could remember because of the rotten teeth that grew in his mouth like poisonous black mushrooms.

A slight movement in the corner of his eye broke his reverie. He snapped his head around, trying to recapture in his field of vision whatever had made the movement. There were many predators here, lions and hyenas being but a couple, and a long slow wagon train was a particularly vulnerable target. *There*! Off to his right and down, some distance away in a slight gully carved by flash floods during the wet season, were six horses, moving at a right angle towards the caravan. Immediately he spurred his horse into a gallop towards the train.

"Snot! Snags! On me!" he yelled at the two closest riders that formed part of his meager security force. He was able to gather up a few more riders on their way, and they approached the spot where the gully entered the plains proper with weapons drawn to find the party already expecting them. Three mounted women with three pack horses were drawn up, calmly waiting, their hands resting casually on their pommels, away from their own weapons.

Waryn jerked his horse to a sudden stop, stunned. Women traveling alone through the Lawless Lands wasn't just unheard of, it was inconceivable. The only people living in this unforgiving place were widely scattered bands of outlaws, some of whom had been here for some generations. But in all cases, women were property, kept for breeding and maintaining the nomadic campsites while the men were out fighting, hunting, and pillaging. He supposed it was possible some could be used as a distraction or potential spies, but he'd wager not only everything he had, but everything his boss had, that this wasn't the case here. They wore worn sleeveless leather jerkins and pants sewn up the side with wide leather thongs. A petite blonde sat between two taller brunettes, one of which sported odd tattoos on her arms that Waryn couldn't make out from where he sat.

Their weapons looked similarly worn, but well cared for. Waryn knew beyond a shadow of a doubt that women couldn't be warriors, but his instincts screamed that these women were dangerous. Beneath their apparent tranquility there was a tense watchfulness that he'd seen in too many veterans to count.

Snags, apparently, didn't possess those same instincts. He rode his horse in a circle around the group, trying to intimidate them. Snot just sat next to Waryn, rested his hands on his pommel, and leered. The women appeared to ignore Snags, but Waryn would have bet his wages, and Snag's life, that they knew where he was at all times.

"Hello, and safe passage to you and yours," the little blond one said. "We are traveling in the same direction as you and were wondering if we could join your train. We have some skill as guards and scouts, and traveling with such a large group would make our journey safer as well."

Snags, who had been riding in ever tightening circles, pulled up next to the largest one, crowding her. "I say we let them ride with us, Captain. We ain't never had whores travel with us, before. It sure can get lonely on the trail."

Waryn inwardly groaned as the woman glared at Snags. Menace wafted off of her like heat waves in the desert. "Back off before I hit you so hard you'll be gumming your food even more than you are now, worm!" she growled.

Snags placed his hand suggestively on her thigh and began running it up. "Come on, Sweetness. I'm sure we can come to some sort of arrangement."

Quicker than Waryn could follow, her elbow slammed back, catching him full in the mouth, hard enough to throw him out of his saddle and onto the ground. In a flash she followed, kicking her feet free of her stirrups and vaulting clear over the back of his horse to hit the ground on top of him. A knife flashed and she dug it into his throat. Snags lay very still, afraid to even breathe.

"Is this the kind of behavior we can expect from your men? If that's the case, then maybe we shouldn't ride with you, because you won't have any men left by the time we reach your destination," she growled, looking up at Waryn with brilliant green eyes while crouched over Snag's prone form.

Waryn rolled his eyes. "Snags is dumber than dirt and more undisciplined than most. Don't judge all of us because of the actions of one. I don't do the hiring or firing on this train. That would be my boss, The Honorable Arthur Levi. I can introduce you to him, however, and he can decide what he wants to do with you. You better not damage Snags anymore, though. It won't help your case."

With a little shove, the woman released Snags and climbed back on her horse and nodded at Waryn. Without a backward glance at Snags, Waryn wheeled his mount around and started riding back to the caravan.

* * * * *

As we followed Waryn to meet his boss, Greta leaned over to me and whispered, "That went well, didn't it?"

I shrugged. "He's still breathing, isn't he? I didn't damage him any more than he deserved, and we're still getting to meet this Levi person, so I think it went great. A little demonstration, and word will get around. Maybe I won't have to break any bones."

The Honorable Arthur Levi was a stout man going to fat with a florid skin tone, russet hair, magnificent mustachios, and a well trimmed pointed beard. He was dressed head to toe in burgundy, wearing a burgundy felt cavalier hat with the feather of some large unknown bird stuck in it, his tunic and overcoat were burgundy embroidered with gold thread, and his pants were actually leather dyed burgundy. Completing this flashy ensemble were a pair of burgundy knee high boots, that had little gold spurs fastened to them. He was seated on a beautiful large black horse bigger than Red, the only part of his outfit I liked. He was striving to look prosperous and fashionable, but I thought he looked ridiculous.

Waryn trotted up to him and respectfully touched his hand to his hat. "Milord, these ladies would like to join our caravan. They say they can act as scouts and warriors for us."

Arthur's eyes measured us, slowly sweeping up and down our entire lengths. A look of disgust flashed across his face, almost too quick to be recognized, but he smiled and swept his hat off in a flamboyant gesture, and sketched a shallow bow from his saddle.

"My ladies! I'm pleased to make your acquaintance! I'm sorry I can't use your… services." His expression carried the utmost regret, and his tone was so smooth it would have been easy to miss his implied insult. "But I would never be so ungallant as to leave you unprotected in lands that are as fraught with danger as these, so you have my leave to travel with us under my protection." His manner was magnanimity personified.

I managed to keep my tongue behind my teeth, and not tell him what I thought of his condescending attitude, but it was a near thing. Actually I was rather proud of my self restraint. Greta, who had adopted an air of supercilious superiority as soon as we caught sight of Waryn, nodded back at him swiftly, probably worried that I would say something that would ruin his offer for us. "Thank you for your generous offer, Mister Levi. We will accept, she said, effecting what I believed was an aristocratic tone. I had no idea if it was accurate or not, though. "I am Baroness Greta of the barony of Serenity." Arthur perked up at those words, his snobbish manner relaxing a little. "These are my ladies-at-arms. Lyr," she nodded in my direction, "and Yusi," she concluded, pointing her chin in Yusi's direction. She said it so smoothly that one would never guess she was lying. And just like that, we were in.

The wagon train trundled on until dusk. The wagons were formed into a square, the horses unhitched and picketed. Campfires sprang into existence and the cooks started cooking dinner. Arthur invited Greta to dine with him, as she was the only one worthy of the honor, but she begged off, pleading exhaustion, and ate with us instead. All the guards and drovers were congregated around the largest campfire, and a sorrier lot of men I don't think I've ever seen outside of a bandit camp. We were sitting next to Waryn, when another figure strode out of the darkness into the flickering firelight. He was tall and muscular, with broad shoulders and narrow waist, and had hair as black as a starless night that fell in a braid halfway down his back. Dressed in the leather clothes of the Lawless Lands, he stalked into the light, a tiger surrounded by dogs.

Greta leaned over to Waryn and murmured, "Who is that?"

"That's Berand, my scout. He's the one guy I was able to hire myself. He has quite a reputation as a warrior, but more importantly, he knows the Lands. Unfortunately, being a native of this place, he isn't really trusted by the rest of the company. They leave him alone for the most part, though."

"Why?" Greta asked, her eyes never leaving Berand's form.

"They've seen him in action, and they want no part of him. He's incredibly fast with those blades of his. There's not a one of us that can touch him."

"Hmmm."

I couldn't resist. I leaned in close to Greta and whispered, "Mmm, so pretty. He looks delicious, doesn't he?"

"He sure does," she murmured dreamily, then snapped out of her reverie. "Uh, what?"

"Oh, nothing," I said, smiling.

Right about then, Snags separated himself from the rest of the group and started ambling over. A very, very large man followed him. They stopped in front of us. The man following Snags was huge, a head taller than me and half again as wide. Dressed in a sleeveless leather jerkin, he had long coarse brown hair that seemed to extend to his shoulders and arms. His features were thick and rough-hewn. I couldn't put my finger on it, but something seemed a bit off about him, like he had something in him that wasn't quite human.

Snags jerked a thumb at the big guy. "I was telling Skam here about what you did to me, and he doesn't believe that a woman could fight like that. We were wondering if you would like to give us a demonstration?" He gave us an oily smile.

Greta pretended to stare at him for a few moments, then turned and gave me a brilliant smile. "Well?"

I pretended to ponder the two idiots in front of me, but I was really thinking of ways to get back at my traitorous friend. She would pay, oh yes she would. After a couple of seconds, I shook my head, "I would break him."

Snags snorted, and grinned, showing off his rotted stumps in all their blackened glory. "I thought not. It's one thing to hit me when I wasn't expecting it, but now faced with a real man you back down. Typical woman."

I didn't have anything to prove to these losers, but I was about to get up and give them a pointed lesson in why you don't mess with a Sister, when Yusi piped up. "I would be honored to spar with Skam. Her head was bowed, and she spoke softly, as was her want, but I hid my grin. She might be acting submissively, but it was all a facade. Yusi was deadly when she got going.

Greta cut in, "These will be the rules. Unarmed combat only. Fighting will continue until the loser submits or can no longer fight." There was no objection. When Greta spoke in that tone of voice, it would take a stalwart soul to defy her.

Snags grinned even wider, if that was even possible. "Sure! Should we place a little wager on the outcome? Say, if Skam wins, do we get the pleasure of her company for the night?"

Never going to happen in a thousand years, worm, I thought. "And if Yusi wins, do I get the pleasure of cutting your balls off? I would be doing a favor for the whole human race," I retorted.

Snags started to laugh, until he saw that I wasn't joking. The smile left his face in a blink, and he shuddered. "Uh, perhaps not."

The word spread quickly, drovers and guards surrounding the contestants, forming an impromptu square in anticipation of some after-dinner entertainment. Confidence that us uppity bitches would be put in our place ran high, and money began to change hands as rampant betting ran amok, mostly on how fast Yusi was going to lose. Nobody was betting on her to win. I got up and moved through the crowd, betting a couple coppers here, a couple there, on Yusi to win. I was getting terrific odds, but I made sure to keep the bets small. If I cleaned everybody out of all their money, that might make things awkward, and we were going to be traveling with them for a couple of months. I completed my circuit and sat back down next to Greta.

"You're incorrigible," she murmured, her mouth barely moving. I didn't bother to reply, just smiled and leaned forward, resting my chin on the palm of my hand, studying the combatants.

Greta called out, "Rules are, fight until someone can't continue or taps out. No one interferes, got it?" A general sound of agreement murmured through the crowd and the two contestants nodded. "Begin!"

Skam immediately charged her, trying to bury her under his weight, but Yusi danced to the side and hammered a blow into his ribs as he rushed past. The other onlookers might not realize the power of that punch, but Yusi was stronger than most men, as were all of us. The pain should have dropped him then and there, but he sucked in a breath and turned back towards her. She danced back and he approached, more cautiously this time. They settled into a rhythm of punch and counter punch, Skam trying to set her up for a big knockout blow, which was his only path to victory whether he knew it or not, and Yusi guarding against that same blow, patiently waiting for her opening. It came faster than expected, Skam, starting to look tired, suddenly feinted a jab, then knocked her hands aside and closed in a clinch. His hands closed on her throat, and he lifted her up in the air to the cheers of all the onlookers, her hands clasped around his wrist. Showing off, he let go with one hand, and shook her a little, roaring in triumph.

Then, almost too fast to follow, she hooked one leg over his elbow and jerked, bringing her in closer to him. The other leg slid around the back of his neck, then using her first leg, she completed the clinch, leaving his arm trapped. She snapped her body violently back, bringing him to the ground with her, both hands clamped on his arm. She heaved with her body, applying just enough pressure to almost break his elbow. Frantically he tapped her leg with his other hand, and just like that the match was over. Stunned silence fell over the camp, and I grinned and rose to collect my winnings.

We settled into a pattern after that. The wagon train averaged about twenty-four kilometers a day, and we rode with it. Sometimes we rode out on sweeps with the scouts, sometimes we stayed close to the train. Since we weren't officially part of Waryn's crew, we slotted into anywhere we were needed most. Greta started to ride with Berand more often than not, and Skam, who had developed an almost puppylike devotion to Yusi, followed her around whenever he could, much to her chagrin. Since that meant he was in my company as well, I got to know him. He turned out to be surprisingly sweet, if really, really dim. Days turned into weeks, and I watched the moon change with concern.

"We're going to have to leave the train for a few days. Talk to Berand and Skam. Reassure them that we'll be back, and make sure they don't follow us," I said one night at dinner. Greta and Yusi didn't reply, just nodded. They knew.

The next day I rode beside Waryn for a short while. "We've got something to take care of. We'll be gone for a couple of days, and then we'll be back."

Waryn gave a short nod. "Got no say in what you do or where you'll go. I will say this, you've more than pulled your weight. You'll be missed."

I gave him a playful punch in his shoulder. "Don't worry, we'll be back."

We left the train right then and rode away at a right angle from the train's direction. We rode fast, trying to put as much distance between us and the train as possible. We found a place to camp on a plateau that gave us a good view of the sky and picketed the horses as far away from us as we dared. We started a fire, but kept it low, mostly to warn away the predators that weren't human that inhabited the plains, to stay away. Then we waited for night to fall and the moons to rise, sitting next to each other, so close we were touching. First rose Artemis, the first and lesser of Kaler's two moons. Goddess of the hunt, she glowed silver, her pockmarked face sporting spots of a darker gray. Anticipation built in our veins, as we awaited the appearance of Kaler's second moon. A couple of hours later, Chang'e made her appearance. Her face glowed pink, purple, green and blue, with higher clouds of white alternately scuttling across or veiling her face. The sight of her called to us, her song felt by us deep in our blood and bones. The long dead scientists who designed my maker built this into us, to force us to Change and help us learn to control it. That is why a new Sister couldn't roam free from our settlements. Their control wasn't good enough to fight Chang'e's wiles. Greta, Yusi, and I could control ourselves, but she still called to us, a siren song. As one, drugged by her sight, we raised our voices and sang back to her, a wordless love song somewhere between a croon and a howl, each voice singing their own unique song. We continued our vigil through the night, swaying and singing, until she dropped from sight, as the first rays of dawn broke, lightening the sky.

We slept then, woke up late in the afternoon, then repeated the scenario a second time, and a third. By then Chang'e's face was hidden enough by shadow that it broke her spell over us, and we were able to continue on with our lives, our monthly ritual concluded, leaving us a little drained, but feeling complete and recentered.

It took us two days to catch back up with the wagon train. Skam's brutish face lit up when he saw Yusi. She gave a long suffering sigh, her eyes rolling skyward. Greta's eyes, however, were darting back and forth, clearly looking for something. Or someone. I waved to Waryn when I saw him, and cantered up. "Hey! Good to see you again, Waryn! Where's Berand?"

Waryn gave a sharp, irritated shrug. "I don't know. He disappeared not long after you did. I haven't seen him for a couple of days, which I'm not happy about, I can tell you."

As a matter of fact, Berand joined us that night. As he rode up to the fire, Waryn looked up sharply. "And where in the nine circles of hell have you been?"

"Scouting," Berand said shortly, but his eyes fell on us and lingered on Greta. I propped my chin on my hand and studied him carefully.

I leaned over to Greta "I find his timing suspicious. See if you can find out where his 'scouting' took him. I have a feeling he was spying on us."

"Really?" Greta replied.

"Well, you, to be more specific. See if his behavior changes around you at all. If he saw what we were doing, he might find that strange, and treat us differently. If there's a potential problem, I want to know about it, so it doesn't blindside us."

The next day dawned like any other, but by midday, clouds were gathering with extreme rapidity on the horizon. Lightning flashed and thunder rumbled, depressingly often, as the storm front rushed towards us. We dug our long coats out of our packs and donned them just as we got hit. Visibility dropped to nothing, and we slogged forward, our heads down. There was no chance for sweep riding or scouting, and I hated the lack of security. My only solace was that not even the bandit clans would be insane enough to be out in this weather.

The storm lasted for two solid days, and our progress slowed to nothing as the teams' hooves slipped in the mud and the heavy wagons bogged down. There was zero possibility of starting a fire, which led to a couple of pretty miserable nights, huddled in a circle, our hands clutching our coats and our heads bowed as the rain beat a brutal tattoo on us.

It was with relief bordering on a religious deliverance that we greeted the sun the next day. While conditions were still muddy and slowed travel considerably, we bent about our tasks with a lighter heart. That only lasted until we hit the next river. The storm had swollen the river considerably. Fording it was impossible. We all rested as The Honorable Arthur Levi, Waryn, and Berand clustered together to discuss their options. They stood a little apart from everybody else, obviously not wanting anyone else involved in their discussion, but I could hear them easily enough. Waryn and Berand wanted to wait until the river subsided and cross then, but Levi was adamant that they find a way to continue. Waryn warned him he could lose half his wagons this way. Their discussion got more animated until everyone could hear them. Snags and Skam were having their own conversation a little ways away. That seemed to go better, because Snags mustered enough courage to interrupt his superiors.

"Excuse me, your worship, but Skam here says there's another fordable part of the river a day and a half that way." He pointed north.

Berand narrowed his eyes. "I know of no other fordable spot on this river."

Snags sneered. "Well it just goes to show you don't know everything, do you, Pretty Boy? Skam says he's from this area, and he can guide us."

"I don't think we should stray from the known route..." Waryn began, but stopped when Levi raised his hand.

"We can't afford to lose the time. We'll let Skam guide us."

Snags smiled in triumph, unfortunately, because we got the full treatment of seeing his rotten mushroom mouth. Waryn walked away, shaking his head. After a second, Snags followed him.

"What do you think?" I asked Berand when everyone else was out of earshot.

He shrugged. "I haven't been where they are taking us. I think we need to be ready for anything."

"Agreed," I said.

The train swung immediately north, Skam leading the way. We began a slow, steady climb. By dusk, the landscape had changed, from the wide open grassland to a drier, rockier terrain punctuated by twisting canyons. Waryn stopped the caravan, and ordered everyone to set up camp.

I sat in the saddle, studying our supposed route. I didn't like it. It smelled wrong, a place ripe for an ambush, but I couldn't figure out why. This was a high bulk, low value train. Not normally a target for the bandits that roamed these lands. Turning Red around, I returned to camp.

The next morning, when the train set out, Berand, Greta, Yusi, and I rode ahead, scouting, much to Skam's chagrin. The cream colored canyon walls rose up around us, ever higher, hemming us in. By midmorning, we came to a place where the canyon forked. We stopped, considering our choices.

"Greta, you and Berand take the left fork. Yusi and I will take the right."

"I thought Greta was the Baroness," Berand said.

I looked through him. "You're not a dumb man, Berand. You've had to have figured it out by now. Let's go." I kicked Red forward.

The further I rode into this fork, the less I liked it. It was still, silent, except for the wind that softly played the nooks and crannies that pocked the walls everywhere, creating its own haunting, creepy melody. An hour in and I started to catch whiffs of something new. A musky, alien scent hung in the air, tantalizing, but impossible to nail down.

"Do you smell that?" I asked.

Yusi nodded, and tightened her grip on her spear. The farther we rode in, the stronger the scent got. We could now pick up different variations, as if from several different beings, distinct but related, but we still couldn't localize it.

At this moment, hoofbeats sounded a rapid pattern behind us, approaching fast. We spun our horses around, readying our weapons. Skam and Snags appeared, galloping towards us. Skam was waving frantically. "Not safe! Not safe!"

He shouted. At this moment something struck me hard in the back of the head. I felt myself falling off of Red, saw Yusi falling off of her horse, and then everything went black.

* * * * *

Yusi's eyes fluttered open, then quickly shut again, and she tried to place where she was. She had a blinding headache that was making it hard to focus, but she made the attempt anyway. It was cool, moist. Crackling sounds and the smell of woodsmoke let her know that there were torches or a fire in this space. Her nose quested, trying to pick up other scents. One jumped out at her, the acrid, biting odor of man-sweat. A scent familiar to her. Her eyes flew open of their own accord, and fastened on the person in front of her. It was Skam.

"What did you do?" she whispered.

"I take care of family," he answered unhappily.

* * * * *

I woke up slowly. The first thing I noticed was that my head was killing me and that I was tied to a chair. The second thing I noticed was that I was in some sort of cave or tunnel. The light was dim, flickering, the air cool and moist. The walls were of rough stone, but looking like they were carved by nature, not man. Junk and garbage were scattered haphazardly across the floor. A heavy, musky, pungent smell hung in the air, saturating everything. I slowly raised my eyes and stared my captors in the face.

Kaler was colonized because the scientists that settled it wanted freedom to conduct experiments without any pesky restraints like laws or any ethical code that wasn't written by them themselves. The result was almost unrestrained tinkering on any and all lifeforms, including humans. One of their projects was to develop a strain of human that was stronger and tougher than normal humans. One that could work harder and longer at menial labor while remaining content. One that would be better suited for colonizing planets with a harsher or more deadly environment than normal humans with less support. They ended up with a humanoid almost three meters tall and covered with coarse, reddish brown hair. Their derogatory name was Squatch, or Beastmen, and they were subjected to more than their fair share of persecution and bigotry, but they were still human. Not quite as sharp as a normal person, but human, with a human's desires and emotions. I'd had dealings with some, and I had found them gentle and easy to get along with. They just wanted to be left alone, generally.

These beings looked different, devolved somehow. Their features were brutish, their foreheads shallow, like an ape's. Their scent had a feral, rank edge. There were three of them, all male. Two of them were about the same height and weight, but a half head shorter than what I assumed was the leader. His long brown hair was graying, and he was half again as broad as the other two. They were all staring at me. I settled myself down in the chair.

"So, what's the plan?" I asked.

* * * * *

"What do you mean?" Yusi whispered.

Skam shrugged. "Family need food. Family need breeders. I bring. I bring grain, I bring you. I bring Lyr. Make family happy."

Yusi touched her tongue to suddenly dry lips. "Listen to me very carefully, Skam. You've made a huge mistake. Your family is in terrible danger. You must let us go, now!" she said urgently.

Skam shook his head.

"Skam! Listen! You captured Lyr! It's the one thing she pounds in our heads from the very beginning. 'Never let yourself be taken captive because then you can't control the situation.' If you let us go right now we'll walk away. Your family will be safe, I promise. But if you don't, if your family tries to harm her in any way, she will kill all of you. Every man. Every woman. Every child. I won't be able to stop her. Please listen. You must convince your family to let us go!"

* * * * *

The big guy spoke. "Need breeders. You breed."

I shook my head. Being restrained was bringing back memories from my distant past that I had buried deep down in my psyche. Now they were coming back, a dark upwelling of coldness and poison. Panic threatened to set in, but underneath the panic, there was the hot lick of lava that was my rage rousing from the caged slumber I normally kept it in.

"That's a bad plan," I gasped, trying to maintain control, holding on to my chain of rage with sweaty hands, and feeling it slip away, link by link. "Here's a better plan. You let me go, and I won't hurt you." I knew he wouldn't. Something like me was completely out of his experience, and normally I could take that into account. But right now I was fighting my situation, my past, myself, and my future humiliation, and I was losing. My Rage roared in my mind, drowning my panic and everything else like magma welling from the ground, fully awake now. The Change threatened.

He shook his head. "You breed! You breed now!" He nodded to his two flunkies. Without a word, they grabbed my wrists, untied them from the chair, then dragged me across a narrow, padded table with frightening power. Apparently they'd done this before. Another mistake.

* * * * *

"You will all die! Please!" Yusi begged. Then, from deep in the complex, hoarse, howling screams of pain rang out. She closed her eyes. "Too late," she whispered.

* * * * *

I started with my hands and feet first. Talons burst out of my boots. My fingers lengthened, strengthened. Claws sprang out where my fingernails used to be. Talons dug into the table legs, claws dug into the tabletop, and I used it as leverage to launch myself across the table at one of my captors that was holding my wrist, wrenching my left arm free from the grasp of the second. I sought the first one's embrace like I would a lover's. He stumbled back, trying to get away from me, but I clung to him, claws digging into his flesh. He howled in pain as my clothes split, muscled flesh covered in fur spilling out. My face shifted, a short muzzle forming and fangs ripping out from my gums, my human teeth falling out and pattering on the dirt like hail. My feet dug into his belly and ripped downward, eviscerating him, and I sank my teeth into his throat, ripping it out in a shower of bright red blood. I sprang past him and spun, facing the other two and putting space between myself and my tormentors while I completed my transformation.

I ripped the remnants of my clothes from my body, howled, and charged. The chains I normally bound myself with were gone, and I was completely free. All that there was in this world was the hunt, the killing of prey, and the bright, sharp iron tang of blood.

* * * * *

When Yusi heard the howl, she jerked sharply on her bonds. The rope held, but the arms of the chair came apart, and she surged to her feet. She grabbed Skam's ear and dragged him down to her level. "Where are your women and children? We need to save as many as we can!" she shouted.

It was a race then. Skam led her through the complex, to the living areas, where they grabbed everyone they could and brought them to one room. Howls, screams, and the sounds of combat echoed through the tunnels, coming ever nearer as Lyr worked her way toward them. Yusi turned to the motley, inbred remnants of the family they managed to bring together. "Stay here. Do not try to run. Make yourself look small and non-threatening. Keep your eyes on the ground and do not look at her. Most of all," she looked at Skam, "Do not try to fight. That will seal your fate. I will do what I can to stop her."

They waited. The crashing and screaming grew louder and closer, growing to a crescendo, then falling to silence, broken by the sound of claws clicking on stone, and deep raspy breathing. A shadow appeared in the doorway. "Look down! Look down!" Yusi hissed, reminding them. She then stepped forward, spreading her arms wide and very carefully not meeting Lyr's eyes. She didn't want to do anything that could be misconstrued as a challenge.

A rumbling growl sounded. Yusi took a deep breath, sublimating her fear. "You know me, Mother. I am your daughter. These people are not a threat to you. They are children, babies, and their mothers. You are safe now."

The shadow took a step into the room, claws clicking on the stone, revealing itself. Lyr in her Other form was a waking nightmare. Shaggy dark brown fur wet with blood covered a body sheathed in ropy muscle designed for speed and power. A short muzzle contained a mouth full of vicious fangs, perfect for cutting and tearing. Long, needle-sharp claws tipped fingers and toes, with the thumbs and big toes outsized, the better for ripping. All of this was tethered to an indomitable will, a force of nature. Glowing green eyes focused on the people kneeling across the room, their eyes downcast, and she took a second step into the room, then a quicker third, building momentum. Yusi stepped in front of Lyr, blocking her path, keeping her eyes down.

"Please, Mother, don't do this. This isn't right. Let them go. Let it end now." Quickly she stepped forward and wrapped her arms around the monstrosity in a gentle hug, burying her face in the gore-soaked fur. Clawed arms reached around Yusi and dug in deep, eliciting a wince from her, and the horrific head came down, ready to tear into the back of her unprotected neck. But then the grisly nostrils flared as they inhaled her scent, and the monster paused. Slowly the claws eased out of her back, shrinking back into nails. The monster diminished, turning into just Lyr.

* * * * *

I faced the survivors. My eyes landed on Skam. I felt my lip lift in the beginnings of a snarl. The urge to kill him was almost overpowering. The fact that I was naked, unarmed, and powerless was the only reason he was still breathing. "Where's Snags?" I demanded. He had a reckoning coming his way, yes he did.

"Father killed him. He wasn't family. He didn't know plan."

I looked at him, and at the pitiful remnants of his clan. "I get that you have to take care of your family, and that's the only reason you're alive right now. If I ever see you again, I'll kill you." I gestured to Yusi. "Come on, let's find my equipment." I followed my own scent back through the tunnels to where it began. They were daubed liberally with crimson, and littered parts and pieces; a collection of the wreckage of human lives.

Yusi, walking next to me, noticed everything. "They were all adult males, or armed," she commented.

I nodded and stopped, wincing. I had no memory of what had happened, which was a bad sign. It was common in young Sisters, recently Turned, but I couldn't afford to lose control like this. "There must have been a small part of me still in there, after all. At least that's something." I turned to her, "You showed a lot of courage, back there, but it was incredibly dangerous for you. I could have killed you. You shouldn't take chances like that."

"There was no one else, Mother, and I couldn't stand aside and let you slaughter innocents. The guilt for both of us would have been unbearable."

I turned away and started walking down the tunnel again. "We're not built to feel guilt," I said coldly.

My equipment was stacked in the corner of the room where I had been held. Apparently they couldn't even wait long enough to distribute my weapons before they got down to the all important task of breeding me. I found the pieces of my clothes, and was able to tie them back together with strips of cloth torn from the clothes of the dead in the room. Then Yusi and I walked back into the light.

Amazingly, the fork that Berand and Greta took led back to the river. It wasn't fordable here either, with sheer stone walls on both sides, but it was also far narrower. Narrow enough we were able to build a crude bridge that would support the wagons, after a couple days of back-breaking labor. I don't know if Levi saved any time; I rather doubted it.

Once we had crossed the river and made it back onto the regular route, I commented to Yusi, "You know, in the future I can see us setting up waystations along the most traveled route a couple days apart with teams of fresh horses and oxen to replace worn out mounts, and a safe place to stay at night. The Sisters could even provide roving guards to shepherd wagon trains from station to station, and we could establish a town at the halfway point between east and west where merchants could trade so they wouldn't have to make the entire trip. Pretty exciting, huh?"

Yusi rode in silence for a little while. "I can't stop thinking about Skam's clan. You single-handedly destroyed it. Do you think that was really necessary? You were in control, after all. You didn't have to do what you did."

I thought about it for a while, trying to order my thoughts. "That's the thing. I wasn't. I haven't been that out-of-control since I was a young one myself. The fact that any of them survived is because of you.

You've now witnessed one of *my* flaws. The one thing I can never be is a victim, or seen as weak. You know us. The Sisters are a violent and hierarchical order. Any sign of weakness will lead to others challenging me for leadership, and I can't have that. It's accreted into me, blood and bone, and I can't change it now."

"But no one will ever know."

"You will. Greta will. That is enough."

Yusi gave a little shake of her head. "Still doesn't seem right."

I shrugged. "Possibly not. But it is what it is. One of the negatives of being who we are."

We rode in silence again. Yusi laughed shortly. "Do you think Skam can successfully lead his clan?"

I snorted. "I wouldn't wager any money on it."

"That's my thought as well," she whispered, her shoulders drooping.

I sighed. "What would you have me do, Yusi? Offer them sanctuary?"

"They need help. Isn't that what you say our vision is? To offer anyone a place, free from oppression?"

"And how do you suggest I do that? There's no way that family would ever find their way safely across the Lawless Lands. And I am not going back to act as nursemaid. I would probably end up killing Skam anyway. I don't think I could help myself."

"I could guide them," Yusi said reluctantly.

My eyes roamed around, finally lighting on Greta and Berand, once more stuck together. I grinned. "I have a better idea," I said, and kicked my horse into a gallop. Greta looked at me as I approached. "I need you to escort Skam and his family to Sanctuary," I said without preamble.

Her eyes flashed. "Why me?"

My eyes cut over to Berand. "Because I think you'll be leaving soon, anyway. This way I'll have at least one Sister watching my back. And it will give you more time to figure out your relationship with Berand. I'm sure he'll follow you across the length and breadth of the Lands if you let him. If after you get Skam's clan settled, and you want to find us, I'm sure you can catch up, eventually. And if not," I looked deep in her eyes, "I release you from my service for the rest of Berand's life."

Greta looked like she was going to protest for a second, then nodded in acceptance. "It shall be done, Mother," she said.

I leaned over and hugged her tight. "I shall miss you, my daughter. Come find me when you're ready." With that I reined Red around and rode back to Yusi.

"It's taken care of," I told her. I brushed a bit of moisture from my eyes. "Onward."

The Ripper

The world-city of Li-Zhang lay before me. We had been traveling through the ricelands needed to sustain it for the last day and a half. I turned in my saddle and glanced back at the long line of wagons creaking behind me and grimaced. We were still with Levi's caravan, and the horror of bringing those wagons up The Wall, the unbroken cliff face that separated the Lawless Lands from the city-states that lived on the Altan Plateau, still gave me nightmares. Berand and Greta weren't with us. They had taken their leave before we ascended to go collect Skam's family and bring them to Sanctuary. Who knows what lay before them after that. Maybe they would come find us, but I doubted it.

Our caravan was just one in a long line of people, carts, wagons, draft animals, and even other caravans all headed to the same place. Yusi and I crested a small rise and finally got our first look at the world-city in all its glory. Or at least its wall. The gray stone stretched before us in either direction as far as we could see, hiding most of its architecture. Here and there the curved roof of a taller building peeked above the wall's top. Brightly colored purple rectangular flags set atop the battlements at regular intervals rippled in the breeze. A monstrously wide gate split its otherwise unrelieved monotony exactly in its center. Clustered in front of the walls of Li-Zhang like children gathered for story time, was a collection of brightly colored tents that stretched for a kilometer or more in any direction around it. I adjusted Red's gait so I casually ended up riding next to Waryn. He looked at me sidelong as I rode beside him, but didn't shy away. I was pretty sure he thought I had killed Snags when I went missing in that cave almost a month ago, but despite that we had still managed to become friends. "What's up with the tent city?" I asked.

"Li-Zhang doesn't like outsiders. Non-natives are restricted on pain of death to the Merchant's Quarter, and there's too many merchants for everyone to fit in the quarter. Only a small percentage of permanent residents have set up shop there. It's easier for the rest of us to set up right outside the walls and trade that way. Cheaper too. We avoid the registration and licensing needed for doing business inside the city, as well as dealing with the Trade Mandarins. Just a couple of well placed bribes to the right individuals and we're left alone. The city's native merchants buy from us, then sell the wares in the city proper. After a handsome markup, I'm sure."

I nodded. "So, what does the World City offer in entertainment to us poor outsiders?"

He grimaced. "The citizens of Li-Zhang don't offer shit to us foreigners, so it's up to us to entertain ourselves. There's inns and taverns spread throughout the Quarter thick as fleas on a dog, but there's not room for much else other than drinking or listening to musicians play. However, out in the Tents there's a wide cleared space where caravaners and the people who prey on them gather every night. There's music, dancing, fortune telling, and anything else you can think of designed to separate us from our money."

I nodded. "Thanks. Good to know. Yusi and I are going to get settled in The Quarter, but maybe we'll make an appearance there tonight."

Waryn arched an eyebrow. "Maybe?"

I shrugged. "I like to keep my options open. Maybe we'll get distracted sightseeing. Who knows?"

He chuckled and shook his head. "You'll be by. I'll keep an eye out for you."

I laughed and softly punched his shoulder. "Be seeing you, Waryn," I said, then kicked Red into a canter towards the city.

* * * * *

We joined the line that snaked endlessly back and forth like a hungry serpent trying to breach the gargantuan walls to reach the tasty human snacks inside, and waited. And waited. And waited some more as the snake ever so slowly slithered into the Merchant's Quarter. A short eternity later we ended up at the front of the line and saw what was taking so long. What appeared from a distance to be one huge gate was actually seven gates that pierced the wall, and at each gate a table was set up. Richly robed men sat at each table, and the endless line behind me split into seven separate streams, like the mythical hydra's heads, and formed at each table. There would be a series of questions, the robed person would make some notes on a scroll, then hand it to the person he was questioning, sometimes with instructions. The person would then be allowed in, the next one in line would step forward, and the process would repeat. It was a good thing I was practically immortal, otherwise I might die of old age before I made it to a table.

By the time it was my turn, my blood pressure had risen to dangerous levels, and I was a little surprised I hadn't pulled out all the hair on my head. As I stepped up to the table, the man sitting behind it glanced up at me, and up. Apparently I was taller than he was expecting. He was clothed head to toe in rich emerald green from the round cap perched on his head to his velvet robe and trousers, and finally to his shoes with their upturned points. Gold piping accented everything in elaborate, swirling designs, adding to his high style. I felt positively shabby in my travel-stained sleeveless leather jerkin and leather pants.

"Name?" he intoned.

"Lyr."

"Reason for soliciting admittance?"

"Looking for a room for my companion and myself, and a place to stable our horses."

He looked annoyed. "What is your reason for being here?"

"I just want to experience your fair city."

He looked skeptical at that. "Length of stay?"

"I don't really know. Less than a week, I'd expect."

He nodded, scribbled some characters on the sheet of paper in front of him, poured some wax on it, and stamped it. He rolled it up and handed it to me. "Take this. Head down the Way of the Golden Lotus for a block, turn right down White Lily Way. Go into the second building on the right. You will need to register there."

"What building is that?"

He looked me up and down again. "The Ministry of Prostitution of course. Anyone wanting to whore here has to be examined and licensed."

A red haze suddenly obscured my vision, and I imagined slapping him so hard his head would face backwards. Instead I took a deep breath and dropped a gold nugget the size of a finger joint on the table. "Just tell me where I can find a good inn and maybe you can keep all the teeth in your head."

His face turned red and he spluttered incoherently. Apparently he wasn't used to anyone talking to him like that. The gold disappeared quick enough, however. "Go four blocks over and three blocks down. You're looking for the Jade Dragon."

I jerked on Red's reins and walked past, nose up in the air, not even deigning to look at the little weasel. We found the Jade Dragon easily enough, and after promising them my weight in gold or my firstborn child, whichever came first, I secured a room for Yusi and me and stabling for our horses.

"Come on," I said, dragging Yusi out with me. "Let's go find that party that Waryn was talking about."

* * * *

It had been a long, fun night in the caravaners' tent city outside the walls of the world city Li-Zhang. My mind was still pleasantly befuddled by memories of pipes, guitars, fiddles, and drums beating out a lively tune while feet stomping in time to the music raised little clouds of dust in the dance square. Yusi and I had danced all night, and I had even stolen some kisses and fondles from a handsome guard who had traveled with a different caravan like a lovestruck teenage girl. But as the sun started breaking over the battlements of the city, painting streamers of pink, purple, and orange over the canvas of blue sky, it was time to head back to our dearly bought room in the merchant's quarters of the city. We leaned on each other for support, singing softly the tunes our ears had heard as our feet stumbled slightly, perhaps protesting being forced to the mundane task of walking when the dance was ever so much more fun. We were halfway through the labyrinth of cobbled streets that comprised the Merchant's Quarters when Yusi abruptly stopped.

"What is it?" I asked, then caught it myself. A thread of a scent separated itself from the dusty, feces and urine-laden soup that made up the bulk of smells in any city. The iron scent of a lot of blood spilled. As one, we turned and followed the scent's trail. It led us deeper into the quarter's warren, the poorer section, where the alleys and streets grew narrower and more twisted, the buildings looming ever closer, blocking off the clean light of dawn.

We found her, discarded like so much refuse, in a rare open spot by an abandoned warehouse, where the buildings were a little farther apart, giving us some light and air. She had been young, and pretty once. No more. Her skull looked misshapen. The amount of blood which pooled under it meant she had been bludgeoned. Her brown hair, which had been brushed and braided earlier, was now mussed and matted with blood and other things. Her light brown skin was spattered with her own blood, and her eyes stared sightlessly into the sky. Violent death was not uncommon in the cities; predators and prey weren't limited to the wilderness. It was the savagery of this death that marked it as unusual. Her dress had been ripped in two, exposing her for all to see, and she had been torn open from her loins to the bottom of her throat, her intestines pulled out and tossed out of the way.

I crouched down next to her, careful to touch nothing, to get a closer look. It took some concentration to block out the sewer stench of ruptured intestines, but I needed to see. There was nothing surgical or precise about her butchery. It looked like she had been clawed open by a great cat.

"Her liver is missing," Yusi said in a carefully detached tone.

I nodded. "Fastest way to recoup energy," I replied clinically, keeping my emotions under control with an iron hand. "This is a mess. Everything here is sloppy and savage. She looks like she was mauled by a lion. However," I pointed at her genitals. Her pubis and labia were also missing, but she looked like she had been skinned, the edges of the skin around that area looked sharp, like it had been cut with a knife. "The killer kept a trophy, so there was emotion as well." I leaned down closer, and inhaled deeply, trying to sort out the scents beyond the obvious ones of shit, piss, blood and fear, to get the scent of her killer. It was there, tantalizingly close, yet out of reach. However, I could detect traces of a rank and feral odor that told me beyond a shadow of a doubt what had killed her, if not whom.

I straightened up and took a step back, to get a wider perspective. Her dress said all too clearly what she had done for a living. It was made of a fine cotton, dyed scarlet, and low cut, exposing more skin than was considered proper in this place. She had worn a black corset made of leather with bamboo strips used for boning. Everything was of fine quality, but not the sort of quality a lady might wear. I studied her for a while longer. A slow anger kindled deep inside and began to build. I've lived a long time, and seen and dealt death more times than I could count, but most animals kill without passion, in order to survive. This kill was obscene. There was malice here, and contempt. All throughout history, the strong preyed on the weak, and women had borne the brunt of it. I was so tired of it all, and wherever my influence held, I would make it stop.

I looked over at Yusi. "This was done by a shifter, and not one of ours either. A male, and not too tightly wrapped. Go and get the guard, I'll stay and watch over her."

I used the time waiting for the guard to cast a wider circle around the body, trying to catch the killer's scent and the direction he left. The trails of both led in the direction Yusi and I came from. It was pretty clear that they had come here for a bit of privacy, he killed her, and then left the same way. He wasn't expecting to get caught, because he left the same way he came in. I then stood vigil over her body, until I heard the whistles of the guard announcing their arrival.

Dealing with the guard was an ordeal. They came in running like there was a fire somewhere, swords drawn and whistles blaring. The response time was impressive, I had to admit. Problem was, they seemed to regard me as their primary suspect. They started shouting at me in their own language, of which I understood none. I slowly backed away from the body with my hands raised, keeping them away from my weapons. I'm sure this act had intimidated more than one visiting merchant, but I'm not most people, and I sure wasn't going to give up my weapons. Yusi arrived before things could get out of hand, and luckily, she spoke their language, so was able to calm everyone down.

That didn't alleviate the watch sergeant's suspicions though. I think he would have been happier if he could have arrested me as the murderer and gone back to the station house in time for lunch with everything neatly wrapped up. As his men bustled about, taking notes and wrapping her body up in sailcloth, he stood right next to me and entertained himself by glaring at me suspiciously every few minutes.

"How did you find the body?" he asked.

I shrugged, silently cursing him. He could speak perfectly good Common when he wanted to, the bastard. "We were headed back to our room at the Jade Dragon but got lost and ended up here. When we saw the body, Yusi went to find you, and I stayed behind to make sure nothing happened to the scene." I watched as a couple of the guards unceremoniously dumped her body onto the cloth and rolled it up like they were making the world's biggest smoke. Then they picked her up and literally tossed her into a wagon. I ground my teeth together so hard I thought I might break one. "Maybe I shouldn't have bothered. Who was she?"

It was his turn to shrug. "Just another whore. Probably tried to rob her customer and he killed her for it. Served her right."

I saw red for a second, and it took every ounce of self control I had to not grab him by the throat, lift him up and shake him like a rat until his neck broke. For a full thirty seconds I focused on my breathing until I regained enough self control to not kill him out of hand. "Is there someone who might know who she was?"

He turned to me and looked me slowly up and down, taking in my sleeveless leather jerkin, and the leather pants that hugged my form. Then he looked at Yusi, who was wearing the same clothes I was. "Maybe you know her. All whores know each other. Did you register with the Ministry of Prostitution when you arrive?"

I saw red again. I'm sure a blood vessel popped in my forehead. "We're done here." I gestured to Yusi and we left.

"They're not going to do anything, and this is beyond them anyway, so it's going to be up to us," I said as I stalked away. I glanced up at the sky. It was well into morning, the sky clear and blue, but not far enough advanced for the morning chill to burn off. "All the bawdy houses will be closed and all the working girls abed. We'll start our hunt at dusk."

* * * * *

We started our day at the same time as the lamplighters, drifting from tavern to tavern, buying a tankard, and just listening, trying to catch any undercurrents of fear in the populace, or if anyone had even noticed that a girl had been brutally murdered the night before.

"I'm not hearing anything, Lyr," Yusi told me as we were leaving our latest tavern.

I nodded. "I hear Madame Butterfly's is around the corner. Let's see if she'll tell us anything."

Madame Butterfly wasn't much help, and none of the other bawds I talked to knew anything, either. That meant most likely this girl worked the street. Luckily though, that meant she most likely had a territory, a small one that wouldn't have been far from where she died. So we at least had a place to start.

"We should split up, cover more ground faster," I said.

"Isn't that dangerous? We won't be able to support each other," Yusi asked.

"It's a little risky," I agreed, "But, he's going to be looking for prostitutes, someone he can get alone and take his time with. We're armed, and aren't vulnerable. If he's hunting tonight, I wager he'll pass us by."

"As you command, Mother," Yusi bowed, and strode off into the night.

Yep, Yusi wasn't happy with me, I thought as I continued on the direction we'd been going. I went through the area, street by street. The first several yielded no results. The women either wouldn't talk to me, or said they didn't know the girl, but they had all heard of the murder. The fear and nervousness in their demeanors gave it away. I got lucky, eventually. It was a dark, narrow, twisty street perpendicular to a main, brightly lit street that housed many taverns along its length. A stable of girls was lined up, waiting for any patrons to come looking for a good time. Overseeing them all was a character flamboyantly dressed in a crazy outfit. It was a teal silk jacket and pants paired with a frilly silk shirt and ruffled cravat. He wore impractical shiny leather shoes with polished brass buckles on his feet. An impressive hat crowned his head with lavender ostrich feathers cascading down from the brim in a waterfall effect. If the lighting had been just a bit better, he would have gleamed. The only thing that struck an incongruous note about the whole ensemble was the worn stiletto dagger and serviceable cudgel hanging off his belt. Good for either protecting his assets, or robbing his clients, I'd bet.

His hands went towards those weapons and he glared at me as I approached. "What do you want?" he demanded. "You can't have any of my women. The Ministry of Prostitution has banned same-sex love, on pain of imprisonment or hard labor. You want to work? You too big to make much money as prostitute, but maybe I could find some men for you, men with specific tastes." He ran his eyes up and down my body in a speculative fashion. I felt like someone had just dumped a bucket of eel slime on me.

I stopped a pace out of his reach. "I'm not here for any women, and I'm not looking for work."

He grinned, a few of his teeth gleaming gold in the flickering torchlight, and relaxed a little, his hands coming away from his weapons. "So, are you looking for a good time? I'm not an escort normally, but if the price is right, I could entertain you. My girls have no complaints." Out of the corner of my eye, I saw a couple of his girls flinch, and a couple more rolled their eyes. My opinion of him slipped a couple more notches, from the gutter, down into the sewer. I felt my lip curl in disgust, and had to tamp it down. I glanced up at the sky. Chang'e hung pregnant in the night. She was only a day away from being full. No wonder my control was fraying a little.

"I only want to talk," I said.

His smile vanished. "If you not here to spend money, then leave. I have a business to run."

"There was a girl murdered not too far from here last night. A working girl. Was she one of yours?"

His cudgel came off his belt in a flash, and he stepped towards me, trembling in outrage. "Are you saying I can't protect my girls? Off with you! Before I beat you and turn you out to work for me."

One quick step forward and I laid him out with a right hook that began from down by my belt all the way up to end at his jaw. He never saw it coming and measured his full length in the street, ruining that pretty suit. I looked over at his girls, who shrank away from me. "He offended me. Now, can you tell me what I need to know?"

I left the alley five minutes later. Yes, they knew about the string of brutal murders. They called him The Ripper because of the way the bodies were torn apart. It only ever happened to girls that worked the Quarter, so the powers-that-be ignored it. No, they didn't know her personally, but they knew that she was an independent that worked a couple of streets down. With a definite destination I increased my pace. The hunt quickened. The alley in question was narrower, darker, and in an even poorer section of the Quarter. Here, there were fewer lights, spaced more widely apart, and fewer taverns. This was not prime territory. In the mouth of the alley, hiding in the shadows, someone lurked. I pretended not to notice her, and leaned against the closed workshop that stood on the corner of the alley with my back partially turned towards her. It was really hard not to tense, preparing for a stab to the kidney. I would recover, but it would still hurt like crazy.

The half-expected thrust never came. Instead, I felt a little fluttering touch at my belt, like a moth's wings brushing my face. Instantly my hand flashed back and grabbed onto a too-thin wrist. Effortlessly I hauled her out in front of me, her weight next to nothing. The expected knife appeared in her other hand and punched towards my midsection, but I slapped it out of her hand. "Now, now, let's have none of that, little rabbit," I chuckled. I'm not going to harm you, even though you tried to rob me just now. I just want to talk." She was young, barely older than a child, with smudged white skin, black hair and bitter chocolate eyes. She barely came up to my chest. She should still have been with her parents, not out here.

"Let me go!" she shouted, pulling at her hand as hard as she could.

I grabbed a fistful of her wrap with my other hand and gave her a bit of a shake. "Stop that," I growled. "Or do you want me to call the guard and tell them you tried to kill me? Answer my questions and I'll let you go on your merry way. I'll even pay you for your time." I let go of her wrap, pulled a ten yuan coin out of my purse and held it in front of her. Her eyes widened. That was as much as she could expect to earn from turning at least five tricks. She nodded.

"I'm going to let you go now. Just know if you try to run, there's nowhere you can hide from me. I will find you." She nodded again and I slowly released her wrist, ready to grab her again if she bolted.

She rubbed her wrist a little resentfully. "What do you want to know?"

"What's your name?"

"Daiyu."

I nodded. "Daiyu. That's a pretty name. Yesterday, not too far from here, a girl like you was murdered. I was told she worked this territory. Did you know her?"

She gave a jerky nod, her lip trembling. Big fat tears started to well up in her eyes, and run down her cheeks.

"Who was she?"

"Her name was Chen Xia. She was kind, and pretty, and gentle. She looked out for me, as much as she was able. She was my friend. We stuck together when we could."

"Did she have any family?"

"None that claimed her. She came from some village outside the city. Her family kicked her out when she wouldn't marry who they chose for her, so she made her way here. She tried to find other jobs, but you have to know somebody in this town to find respectable work. Or be able to bribe a bureaucrat with the right connections."

"Did Chen Xia have any regulars?"

Daiyu shook her head. "We've only been doing this a little while, and the customers we get don't make enough money to visit us regularly."

I exhaled in exasperation. This was beginning to look like a dead end. I started to ask another question, when a scream rent the air. I flipped the coin to Daiyu and took off sprinting. It sounded like it had come from the direction that Yusi had gone. I found the street she had gone down and tried to follow her scent, with scant success. The everpresent odors of urine and feces, both animal and human, confused my nose. I hit more than one dead end in the damnable crazy patchwork of streets and buildings that had no business being where they were. I finally caught a hint of her scent down an alley even narrower and more piss-soaked than the others. I hurled myself down it and was rewarded with her scent growing steadily stronger, and fresher. I burst out of that alley into a larger, more open street. Brick buildings walled off both sides. Other than the narrow passageway I had squeezed out of, there were no other cross alleys. Under the circle of a single lamp, two figures lay, one on top of the other. I could see the one on top was Yusi. I rushed over and knelt down beside them. Yusi was unconscious, and her back looked like it had been shredded. I ran my hands over her head, fingers questing through the hair matted with blood. She had been bludgeoned, like Xia, the back of her skull feeling mushy and gravelly. I let my fingers rest there for a minute. Already I could feel it firming up, reforming as her skull grew back into its proper shape. I rolled her gently off of the other body. Yusi had been shredded from the front as well, defensive wounds. As I watched I could see them start to close up as well. In our human forms we weighed over twice as much as we would appear, part of our gift that let us transform into our beast form and back again. We could take our body weight in damage and still survive, unless silver was involved. I left her alone for the moment and turned my attention to the other person.

She appeared to be a prostitute as well, dressed in clothing that was more revealing than any respectable woman would wear. She was young, couldn't be more than sixteen, and covered in blood, but alive. I sighed as I watched her chest faintly move with shallow breaths. Carefully I pried apart the shredded remnants of her dress. She bore claw marks from neck to knees. I leant closer and inhaled deeply. There were three scents mixed and intermingled on her form. Hers, Yusi's, and her would-be killer's. There was also Yusi's blood and the killer's blood mixed in with hers. I took another deep breath. There, in the ruin that was her neck I could smell the killer's saliva.

I sat back. This complicated things. This girl was covered in the blood and saliva of two Kindred. That by itself wasn't enough to guarantee she would get infected, but there was a chance. There was always risk in trying to create another Kindred, and there was a spectrum of success and failure. The simplest and perhaps most merciful solution would be to kill her now, but that wasn't a decision I had to make right away. She might not Turn, after all.

A soft groan directed my attention away from the girl and I looked over at Yusi as she dragged herself to a sitting position, breathing heavily. "What happened?" I asked softly.

"I found them just as he was starting on her. She was already unconscious, and he was clawing and biting at her. I barrelled into him, knocking him off of her and we fought. He had changed his hands into claws. The only thing I had was my honor dagger. I cut him a few times, which drove him berserk. He picked me up and threw me. My head made contact with the lamppost, hard. I fell on top of her. Things got fuzzy after that. I think he was trying to pull me off of her and I was holding on to her as hard as I could. That's when he started clawing my back. Then you showed up, and he ran," she paused and gently probed her head, wincing. "I think," she finished.

My head snapped up and I inhaled deeply. So stupid of me to forget my surroundings in my concern for the two victims. "Stay here with her," I said. Yusi nodded, although she wouldn't have been able to get up anyway. I rose up and walked a slow, widening circle, scenting as I went. I caught his stink fairly quickly and followed it, making sure he wasn't still hanging around. The trail led straight down the street with no deviations, and no attempt to hide it. I followed it at a jog until the street ended abruptly at a high wall. The scent trail continued up it. I looked up, considering. This was the wall that separated the Merchant's Quarter from the city proper. Foreigners weren't allowed into the regular city, on pain of death, which meant our killer was most likely a local, and had scaled the wall and disappeared. I turned away to return to the girls. He wouldn't be back tonight.

When I got back, Yusi was on her feet, leaning against the lamppost for support. "Let's get back to our room." I glanced down at the girl lying on the cobbles. "We'll bring her with us."

It was no mean feat sneaking her past the innkeeper and the other patrons. We kept it simple, pretending she was dead drunk and we were simply helping her across the floor and up the stairs. Being the only one that didn't smell of blood, I left Yusi to watch the girl and went down to speak to the innkeeper. Five yuan bought me his forgiveness as well as a bowl of water and some linen towels. I bribed the maid into giving more towels that I could use as bandages, along with some needle and thread. Arms full, I managed to make it back to our room without spilling too much of the water. I deposited everything on the side table next to the bed. "All right. Let's get her undressed and cleaned up."

Thankfully the girl remained unconscious as we carefully stripped her bloody clothes off of her body and carefully cleaned her. Gashes crisscrossed her torso everywhere, but luckily he hadn't had time to tear into her deeply. She had lost a lot of blood, though. We pressed the flaps of skin back into place and sewed them up. If she didn't get infected enough to Turn, she was going to be horribly scarred the rest of her life.

When we finished with her, Yusi cleaned herself as best as she could with the bloody water, then passed out on the other bed. I sat in one of the room's chairs and watched our patient for a while before falling asleep myself.

Sunlight streaming through the window and hitting me square in the face woke me. I put my hand up to block the light blinding me, then straightened up with a groan. Falling asleep on an unpadded straight-backed chair was enough to make even my muscles complain. Yusi was already up, had gone downstairs, and brought back a huge platter of steamed buns and a pot of congee for us for breakfast. We didn't speak as we dug in. Yusi, especially, ate a ton, having to recover all the energy she spent healing last night.

"What do we do with her?" Yusi asked after we finished.

I shrugged. "We wait. We're not even sure if she's going to live, or if she's infected. If she is, then I will have to give her a choice. We might be stuck here for a while."

"The guy we're hunting, the killer. I think he might be an aberration. He changed his hands, but nothing else. I'm not sure he can. What are we going to do about him?"

I tapped my finger on my chin thoughtfully. "It's better if we assume he has exceptional control rather than being an abomination. However, I suppose we could test that theory. If he is an abo, then he'll have less control, and the moon is almost full. A smart person will lay low for a while, but if he doesn't have control, he won't be able to help himself. He'll have to hunt. We can take advantage of that."

I left Yusi with the girl, who was still unconscious, and went shopping. I needed some very specific items. I found the large cloak easily enough, but the rest of the costume was a lot harder. Luckily, Li-Zhang was the Crossroads of the World, and you could find almost anything for the right price. It took a while, but I finally found what I needed, and headed back to our room.

Yusi looked up when I entered the room. "She's been stirring, but she hasn't woken up yet."

I nodded, set down my bundles, then went over to the bed. She looked to be sleeping peacefully. I put my hand on her forehead. She was warm, but not excessively so. I peeled back the blankets and unbuttoned the nightgown we had put her in to check her wounds. Nothing looked infected or angry. In fact, she was healing very nicely, which was worrisome in its own right. The cooler air hitting her skin caused her to shiver involuntarily. Her eyes fluttered, then opened.

"Wha, where?" she saw me, then startled.

I didn't understand what she said, because she didn't say it in Common, but I read her body language easily enough. "Shhh. Easy there, Little One. You're safe now." I put my hand back on her head comfortingly, and also to gently hold her down so she wouldn't bolt.

She made an effort to switch languages, "Where am I?"

"You're in our room at the Jade Dragon. You were attacked and badly hurt. We rescued you. Do you remember anything about what happened?"

She shook her head. "No, not much. He was average size, not huge like you foreigners. He come up to me, I thought he was potential customer, but all of a sudden he jump on me. My head hit the rocks, and everything went black."

I nodded. He was a Li-Zhang local, which meant he wasn't part of my Maker's original crew. Which also meant we stumbled onto our quarry's trail.

"What's your name?" I asked.

"Zhong."

"Zhong, huh? That's a pretty name. No family name?"

She shook her head. "It means Middle. I was second girl born. Unwanted. I'm dead to my family."

Well that was horrible, but not unexpected. It also made things easier for us. "Tell me, Zhong, how long have girls gone missing around here?"

Zhong shrugged, then winced. "Probably two, three a month killed like that for as long as I've been here. Drop in bucket, though. Girls always missing around here. Die in childbirth, or sex diseases, or killed by pimp or jealous customer. No one cares. Always new girls coming in from country villages."

I grimaced. Apparently I had inadvertently stumbled onto the perfect hunting grounds if one wanted to hunt humans. Well, I was going to cull one of those predators soon. The rest would be taken care of in due time. "Thank you, Zhong. You can rest here in our room for as long as you want. We have plenty of food here. Is there anyone I need to talk to on your behalf, let them know that you're alright? A loved one, a Madam, or a pimp?" Zhong shook her head. Good for us. I stood up. "Rest. We'll have a long talk when you're feeling better."

Yusi and I went hunting that night. We left Zhong alone in our room with plenty of food available in case she got hungry. We also made sure to take any clothes and money with us down to the stables where we stashed it with our horses' gear. If she suddenly got the urge to leave, the only piece of clothing available to her was the nightgown she was wearing. I hoped it would help deter her. I didn't want to have to track her down again.

I was wearing my man-getting costume tonight. It had started out as a harem outfit, but I altered it by cutting away every nonessential scrap of clothing in order to show as much skin as possible, so it was little more than a bra and underwear. I did sew in a panel of silk running diagonally from the top to the bottoms of the outfit, in order to hide my abdominal muscles. Working girls didn't have my abs. I was larger than ninety-nine percent of the women walking the streets, which worked against me, so I would flash as much skin as possible, trying to short circuit any man's brain that saw me into overlooking my size. The cloak I purchased was voluminous, large enough to completely cover me from neck to feet, useful in case I ran into any guards. I wasn't registered with the Ministry of Prostitution, and I didn't feel like spending time in what passed for their prison. It also completely covered the ax I had strapped to my back and my honor dagger. Yusi was my shadow tonight. It probably would have been better if she could have been the bait, but he probably already had her scent and would avoid her. She was going to hide, but always be close to me, in case it took both of us to take him down. She was also going to be the one to stop him from escaping if it came to that. I looked up at the night sky. The moons were going to be full tonight. I grimaced. My Other would be wanting out tonight, and if I got into a fight, it would be even harder to keep her caged in with my adrenaline pumping and rage aroused. Oh well, it couldn't be helped. It would also make it nearly impossible for him to not hunt tonight if his control was unsteady.

I chose a street between where the two attacks happened and parked myself next to a handy lamp with an unlit alley behind me so I could disappear into the shadows in case any guards showed up. I leaned against a wall of the nearest building and opened the cloak all the way to show off my assets. I had also brought a large gourd of rice brandy with me as well. I spilled some of it on me and took swigs of it from time to time, letting some dribble out of my mouth and onto my body. Anything to make me look more vulnerable. Plus, glistening skin equals sexy skin, or so I'd been told. Yusi hid somewhere downwind of me, far enough away to not spook our prey, but close enough to come to my aid. She also acted as lookout, ready to signal if any guards showed up. I was banking on the fact that he would position himself upwind of me before he attacked. Any hunter worth their salt would do that.

The night passed slowly. It was too quiet. The streets were dead, which was unusual. At some point Yusi drifted up to me. I sent her on a quick patrol to other streets, just to see if I picked a poor one. She came back a little while later to report that the other streets were not as busy as usual either, then drifted away again. Apparently the local populace was more sensitive to the undercurrents of fear running through the Quarter than I had given them credit for.

The night ground on. I saw nobody, potential customers or otherwise, which was good I guess. I sank down onto the cold cobbles, acting like someone who had drunk too much to stand, and was trying to keep warm. I let my mind wander a little and gazed up at the sky, watching Chang'e march slowly across the sky. A slight scuffle and an acrid scent was the only warning I received before a clawed hand reached around from the alley at my back, hooked my shoulder, and dragged me into the shadows with frightening strength.

I grabbed onto my attacker's wrist with one hand, and fumbled for my honor dagger with the other. It came free just as his other hand latched onto my throat and I slammed it into his forearm. He screeched as the silver dust that was carried in the dagger's pits were released into his bloodstream and burned him like acid. While he was distracted by the pain, I grabbed him under the armpits, dropped my hips, twisted, and flung him into the street where I could see him better.

He hit the ground rolling and spun back up to his feet, facing me. He was a small man, barely coming up to my chest, slightly built, with straight black hair, brown eyes, and toffee skin. He looked like any average Li-Zhang citizen. Totally unremarkable.

He glared at me as he pulled my dagger out of his arm and dropped it onto the ground with a clatter. Blood continued to well up out of his arm in a constant stream, healing retarded by the silver dust. "Buurrnss," he growled.

I bared my teeth at him in a feral grin, looking straight into his eyes, challenging him. "It sure does, doesn't it sonny?" I chuckled. I wiggled my fingers at him in a come-hither gesture. "Come on, runt, bring it."

He howled, and charged at me, shockingly fast. I spun to the side out of his way, and when he stopped, I sunk my fist into his ribs. "You're not fast enough, Junior."

He roared, and began swiping at me with his claws, beyond any thought of strategy, and fighting on instinct. I survived this furious assault by dodging, dancing out of the way, slapping his claws out of line, and taking the hits I couldn't avoid on my arms and legs. My strategy was to wear him out. I wanted him alive to answer my questions. I wanted him, but I wanted his maker more. He kept on swiping, indefatigable. My feet kept moving, I kept dodging, until he overextended one too many times. I grabbed his arm and yanked. He flew past me, and I raked my nails down his back as he went. He screamed in shock and pain as he rolled back up to his feet and looked at me in disbelief. I showed him my own clawed hand, gnarled, with thick brown fur sheathing it from fingers up to my elbow.

"Oh look, I can do it too," I said. "Can you change completely? Come on freak, show me your beast form. It's the only way you can beat me." I reached behind me and unstrapped my ax.

He snarled at me and charged. As I stepped in to meet him, I noticed his incisors had lengthened into a set of fangs, but that was it. He launched a huge overhand swing at me. I used the flat of my ax to deflect it, then chopped down at his arm. There was a split second of resistance as my blade hit the bone, then it was all the way through and his arm dropped free.

He howled again, not noticing his missing arm yet, and swung his other at my face. His claws tore through my cheek and across my ear, puncturing my eardrum and severing my earlobe. It was my turn to snarl in rage and pain, and I punched him in the throat. He bent over, choking, and I sank my ax into his spine. All the air escaped from his lungs with a whoosh, and as he fell to the ground I ripped it free with a brutal tug. It released with a sucking sound, and I slammed my foot down on his back, keeping him down. I swung at his other arm, severing it at the elbow. He screamed in pain, and flung me off. He got to his feet, his spine obviously healed, and tried to escape from me, only to impale himself on Yusi's spear. Blood escaped from his mouth in a great gout, and she tore her spear out and swung it at his legs, sweeping his feet out from under him. He fell to his back onto the ground, and with a brutal swing of my ax I amputated one of his legs. We could heal from a lot very quickly, but regrowing limbs took quite a bit longer. He screamed in agony and started blubbering.

I sliced a strip of cloth from his tunic and used it to gag him. I hoisted him onto my shoulder like a bag of meal, and nodded at Yusi. "Let's get rid of those limbs and take him somewhere we can question him." She nodded, gathering them up and my dagger while I started jogging quickly, the Ripper's torso jouncing on my shoulder, causing him to grunt in pain with every bounce. I threaded my way quickly through the maze of streets and alleys, not wanting to be caught with a limbless torso in my possession. I had a certain destination in mind, and thank the gods the streets were nearly deserted at this time of the night.

I found my way to the deserted warehouse where this whole adventure had started. I paused for a second, looking at the spot where I had found Xia's body. She would never know it, but she was about to get the justice she deserved. The main double doors were chained shut, but around the side of the warehouse, I found a man-door. I kicked it open and went inside with my burden. It was completely empty, its floor the same cobblestones that formed the streets outside, except these had accumulated dust from long disuse. I carried him to the center of the room and dumped him unceremoniously onto the ground, causing another muffled squeal of pain. Yusi followed me in and quietly closed the door. She tossed me my dagger and leaned against the door. I caught my knife, sheathed it in one smooth motion, then crouched down, ripping the gag from his mouth.

He worked his jaw a little, then started screaming invectives at me in his own language. I understood none of it, but judging by the way Yusi stiffened, it wasn't complimentary.

Ignoring him, I studied him carefully from his head to the end of his leg-stump. His wounds had scabbed over, and his arms and leg had almost completely grown back. Impressive healing. He was still screaming at me, and it was starting to hurt my ears a little, so I gave my honor dagger's sheath a little shake, making sure that the powdered silver in the outer sheath filtered through the holes in the inner sheath enough to coat the dagger's blade again. Then I drew it and jammed it into the end of his stump closest to me. His invectives cut off in a howl of agony, and tears began to stream down his cheeks. I wiped my blade on his pants and resheathed it.

"I have questions, and you will answer them," I said in a quiet, conversational tone. "Now, this can go easy, or it can go hard. Your choice."

He shook his head defiantly and spat on me. I sighed. The hard way it was. In one motion I drew my dagger and sliced his ear off. He wailed again. Then I started methodically beating him with the pommel of my dagger. That was the problem with our kind. We were mostly immune to poisons and drugs, and we could handle a lot of pain and take a lot of damage. That meant I was going to have to be brutal.

When I stopped, his face was a mass of bruises, one eye was missing, and the other was almost closed. His face was lumpy and misshapen from broken orbital sockets and cheekbones, and I had dislocated both of his arms. Normally I didn't like doing this, but I didn't mind so much in this particular case. I left his mouth and jaw alone, though. He still had to talk.

"Let's try this again. We'll start with something easy. What's your name?"

Exhausted, the fight knocked out of him for the moment, he mumbled something in his own language.

"He says his name is Jaw-Long," Yusi said quietly.

This went back and forth. Eventually I found out he belonged to one of the great bureaucratic families in the city, one step below the nobility, worked in the Ministry of Prostitution, and he hated all women in general, and women of ill repute in particular. He had been killing at least three women a month for at least five years now, but he had only been Turned for a couple of months. My stomach was churning by this point. I was finding out my limits for how much damage I could inflict on another being without it damaging my soul, but this was too important to stop.

"All right, final question, and the most important. Who was your Maker?"

He gibbered out a series of words as fast as his mouth could form them.

"Jaw-Long says he never learned his name, only that he was a foreigner like you, tall, with long black hair and brown eyes. He says he was chosen to cleanse this city of its wicked ways. He says the Master left. He doesn't know where he went."

I groaned inwardly. That wasn't enough information, but I knew that the Jaw-Long well was dry. I would have to do something that I didn't want to do.

"Hold him," I told Yusi, then began to shift. I needed my Other's nose, but I didn't want to leave myself vulnerable for a month by shifting fully. This was going to require focus and some delicacy. I triggered it by letting my control slip, picturing myself slowly changing, starting with my skull. I groaned quietly as I felt my bones shift, teeth falling out, muzzle forming as the front of my face grew at an accelerated rate. Fangs burst out, drooling saliva and blood. My hair fell out, to be replaced by fur. It started spreading faster, moving down my body. My arms thickened and lengthened, claws erupting from my fingers. There, that was good. I snarled as I halted my transformation, chaining my Other in this halfway state. I imagined her howling in rage and frustration as I wouldn't let her completely off of her chain, then I pushed the image down. I couldn't afford to be distracted now. When I was stable, I opened my eyes. Jaw-Long was petrified with terror. I smelled the sharp ammonia smell as his bladder released. I brought my head close to his face and inhaled deeply, catching his breath, then closing my eyes and focusing completely on his blood, smelled again. There, deep down, locked in his DNA code, I caught the unique signature of another Kin. I had the scent signature locked now.

With a sudden shriek of terror, The Ripper broke. He flung Yusi off and ran towards the door. Big mistake. Never run from someone who's predatory nature was so close to the surface. I was on him before he took two steps. My claws hooked into him, biting deep, and I rode him down to the ground. My jaws opened and fastened on the back of his neck, biting down on instinct, crushing his spinal cord and tearing through his flesh, severing his head.

Lifting my head from my kill, I sang to the moon, a song of triumph, joy, and thanksgiving at a successful conclusion to the hunt. I flopped down on the dusty cobbles, satiated, and slowly changed back. While I was doing that, Yusi flipped the body over and drove her honor dagger straight into his heart. Without a lethal dose of silver, there was a possibility the body could regrow a head. I looked up at Yusi.

"It was Fenrir," I confirmed, then shook my head, puzzled. "He smells like he's from my bloodline, but I've never Changed a male. That's a violation of the Second Law."

Yusi shrugged, just as confused as I was.

The sun was peeking over the top of the wall by the time we made it back to the Jade Dragon. Jaw-Long's torso was left in the warehouse, and his head and limbs were deposited in several outhouses on the way back. Being one of the bureaucratic families, he might be missed, but it was unlikely anyone would ever figure out his murder.

It was a challenge to drag my carcass up the stairs. I was so tired. I opened the door and stumbled into the room, stopping when my eyes fell on the bed. It was empty.

"Well, shit," I said.

The Lost Lamb

I sighed, heavily, looking at the empty bed. Weariness and the partial Change I had gone through sapped my strength. "We're going to have to go get her."

* * * * *

Zhong trudged through the empty streets of Li-Zhang in nothing but a night-shirt towards where she kept her pallet. It was the witching hour and Chang'e hung in the air, lighting her way better than the lamps that dotted the streets sporadically. She had a change of clothes there and a few coins. She appreciated the foreigners' help, but she didn't trust their motives. No one did anything in this city without some kind of angle, and she wasn't going to stick around to find out what theirs was. Also, it had been way too long since her last smoke, and she was starting to feel twitchy. As soon as it was light, there was a place she could go.

Morning found her dressed in actual clothes, and hurrying through the now packed streets to her destination. It was a nondescript door deep in the slums, not too far from the wall that separated the Merchant's Quarters from the City Proper. Next to the door was a black triangle with three gold dots in each corner. She knocked, and a small portal in the door slid to the side. After a moment, it slid shut again, and she could hear the clacking of several bolts being slid open. With a creak of unoiled hinges a burly guard with a head completely shaved save for a single scalplock swung the door open, and Zhong stepped inside. She walked down a dim hallway and descended a small flight of stairs. The space opened up into a large room. Candles and lanterns guttered fitfully, casting a wan, shadow-filled glow. Tables were scattered randomly throughout, and every one was occupied by people playing poker, mahjong, pai gow, and sic bo. She ignored this, and threaded her way towards the back, where the money cages were set up. She went up to one of the clerks working behind the barred windows and said, "I need to buy passage into the city, and some smoke."

He said nothing, but his head twitched up and down in a "show me the money" gesture. Hesitantly she spilled all of her money onto the counter.

He gave it a quick glance, assaying the amount in a split, expert second. "That's not enough."

"Please! I was attacked just the other day, and I think they're still after me! They're foreigners so I can get away if I can just get into the city. You know the ministers; they won't let me in unless I have a writ or someone to vouch for me! Is there someone I can talk to? Maybe I can work out some kind of a plan with him?" She let some tears well up into her eyes and run down her cheeks for added effect. Maybe she could appeal to his sympathies.

He stared at her coldly, then shrugged. "I'll talk to Chen Qiang. If he decides to speak to you, you can plead your case with him." Shaking his head, he walked away, leaving her standing there uncertainly.

After about five minutes a dark green door set to the right of the cages unclacked, and swung open, revealing the clerk. "Follow me," he said. Zhong followed him past closed doors and open offices. She passed by men lounging around, idly smoking cigarettes, counting money, or portioning out balls of opium paste onto waxed paper. The clerk led her down to the very end of the hallway, and stopped at a closed door. He gave it a couple of raps and opened it, motioning her inside. Zhong stepped into an office. It was a small windowless office, dominated by a large, dark brown desk. Behind it sat whom she presumed was Chen Qiang.

He looked to be in his twenties, richly dressed in red and gold silk, and his head was also shaved, except for a single dark scalplock that was braided and hung down to his waist. He was very handsome, with well-defined cheekbones and a chiseled jawline, but his brown eyes were flat, soulless; eyes that could order someone's death with less emotion than his dinner.

She stopped a pace away from the desk and stood quietly, her hands clasped in front of her, and kept her eyes on the floor. A nice, submissive posture. The clerk left, quietly closing the door behind her.

He gazed silently at her for a second, then leaned forward. "So, you have two foreigners after you. Why?"

Zhong kept her eyes downcast. "They saved me from the Ripper, then treated my wounds. They were kind to me, but something seems wrong about them. Nobody does anything for nothing, and I just know they have plans for me. I felt it was safest if I left. They can't follow me into the city."

"As you say, nobody does anything for free, and you don't have enough money to pay for passage. What do you propose?"

Zhong fell to her knees. "Please, Most Honored Chen, sir, I'll do anything you want! I'll work for you until my debt is paid off! Any job you want me to do!"

Qiang kept her in suspense for a long moment, then leaned back, smiling thinly. "Sure. We're always here to protect our people from the depredations of those wicked outsiders. We'll arrange your passage right away, and don't worry about your debt. I'll think of something for you to do." His smirk told her that he had already figured out what he was going to require of her. Normally, that might have worried her, but the pain and the chills that were steadily increasing in strength and frequency drowned anything else out.

"Oh, thank you, Most Honored!" Zhong leaned forward and pressed her head to the richly patterned carpet. A little obeisance couldn't hurt. "Also, could I have a little smoke? It's been a while, and I'm starting to hurt."

Qiang's smirk widened into a grin, teeth gleaming whitely, and pulled a cord by the wall. "Of course! Here, follow my man Cheng here. He'll get you set up." The door opened and a small, nondescript man shuffled in. "Cheng! Take the young lady down to our private room and take care of her will you?"

Cheng nodded and led Zhong out of the office through another of the hallway's doors. After several twists and turns he opened another door and took her down some stairs into the basement level. Here the floor was bare dirt, and the walls were orange brick. He took her down a narrow hallway bordered by narrow doors. Opium smoke leaked out from the cracks of the poorly fit doors to hang in a pall near the ceiling. He led her to the last door on the right and ushered her in. It was a bigger room than most, unusual in that it seemed private. It was also bare, devoid of all decoration, other than a lit oil lamp that hung near the ceiling, and a pallet on the floor, next to all of the paraphernalia needed to smoke opium. He directed her to lay down, then squatted down next to her, lit the spirit lamp, and busied himself preparing her pipe. When it was done, he handed it to her, then silently rose to his feet and left, closing the door behind him. Zhong inhaled deeply from the pipe, exhaled, then inhaled again. She did that until all the opium was gone, then let the pipe drop from her fingers. Just as the opium was taking effect, the door opened and men started filing in, customers from the gambling room as well as most of the Triad that had been lounging around doing nothing. Zhong smiled dreamily and giggled a little. Apparently Qiang had already thought of a way for her to work off her debt. Then the Opium Dream rose up like fog in her mind, and dragged her down into darkness.

She woke up to the sensation of lying on cold wet hard cobbles, and rain striking her face. She was soaked to the bone, and her whole body hurt. Even worse, the opium seemed to be wearing off because she felt hot and yet chills wracked her body. Gasping in pain, she struggled up into a sitting position and looked around. Walled compounds and planted greenery blocked most of her view, but it was obvious that she was no longer in the Merchants' Quarter. The Triad had kept their word at least. She shivered harder. She was alone now in the city, not knowing anyone, and with no money. She wanted to cry, but she hadn't cried since she was a small child. The sound of slippers scuffing on the cobbles made her look up. A pair of women were walking toward her. They were wearing large rice straw hats that kept most of the rain off of them, but it was obvious they weren't wealthy or highborn ladies. One of them wore the practical leggings and long overtunic favored by the factory ladies, and the other wore a low cut, figure-emphasizing silk dress, hinting that she was a fairly successful entertaining lady of some type, either a singer/dancer or high-end prostitute. They stopped and looked at her miserable sodden mass huddling on the ground.

"Qiang?" the well dressed one asked. Zhong nodded.

"He's such scum," she snorted. She held out a hand. "Here, come with us."

* * * * *

We didn't waste any time following her. Yusi left her spear and her bow and arrows in the room. They wouldn't do any good where we were going. She did pause at a weapon seller's booth long enough to pick up a kukri; a vicious, backwards-curved knife that was deadly in close quarters. Then we followed Zhong's trail. It was difficult at first, frustrating and time-consuming; being hours old and crisscrossed by hundreds of people. We had to backtrack a couple of times, but as it led further off the path, the scent got stronger and easier to follow. It led us to where she had slept, a filthy, meager pallet inside a makeshift hovel fashioned from scraps of wood. From the looks of it, she had abandoned it as soon as the sun rose. Yusi squatted down and picked up a small square of wax paper. She sniffed it, then held it out to me. "Opium," she said.

I nodded and looked away. It didn't surprise me. If this was my life, I'd try to escape it any way I could, too. "Her scent leads off this way," I said. We followed it deeper into the rat warren that formed the poorer sections of the Merchant's

Quarter. The alley grew ever narrower as the buildings grew closer together, the overhangs of the second and third stories almost touching, conspiring to choke out any sunlight that tried to reach the cobbles. Half-seen people peered out at us from the shadows of their open doorways, no doubt curious as to why two strange foreign women were foolish enough to encroach on their territory. I knew without a doubt that eventually some of them would grow bold enough or desperate enough to try their luck. Only our confidence and the quality of the weapons we carried gave them pause so far. If they only knew it wasn't the weapons we carried that made us truly dangerous.

Her trail ended at a plain, charcoal-colored door set in a forgettable wall. Emblazoned on it was a black metal triangle with three gold dots set in it. I pointed at the sign. "What does that mean?" I wondered aloud.

Yusi chewed on her thumbnail for a minute, deep in thought. Suddenly, she brightened. "I remember my mother telling me stories about places like this when I was little, and she wanted me to go to sleep. This is a place where people go to play games like mahjong. She told me there's even a secret knock and everything!"

"Why would they need a secret knock? And why would your mother tell you stories like this? Why didn't she tell you normal children's stories?"

"I don't know. It was a long time ago. Maybe she didn't know any. Maybe she did and I got bored easily and wanted something different. What does it matter?" Yusi said defensively.

"You're right, I'm sorry," I replied. I pointed at a narrow alleyway across from the door shrouded in gloom. "Let's go skulk over there for a while and see how the locals do things." We jammed ourselves into the alley, little more than a crack between two buildings, and narrower than the breadth of my shoulders. Why the builders didn't have the buildings touching like everywhere else on this street, or have an alley wide enough to actually use, I had no idea, but at least this alley was too narrow for the residents to use as a bathroom or a garbage dump. The only thing we had to contend with, other than getting to know each other much more intimately than I would like, was the odd rodent corpse.

Luckily we didn't have to wait too long, which my rapidly cramping muscles were thankful for. This place seemed to be popular with the working class, and we were able to catch the knock pattern they used after the first couple of patrons. At the first break in the stream of locals entering the place, we hurried over to the door ourselves. Yusi knocked on it in the correct sequence, and a small portal slid open, and the face of a heavyset, mostly bald man popped into place. "I don't know you. What do you want?" he snarled.

She handed him a large gold nugget. "I have a tourist here who wants to have a little fun, and we hear this is the place to get it. She's got a lot more where this came from. In fact, why don't you keep this for your trouble?" There was a noncommittal grunt, and the portal slammed closed again. Latches unclacked, and the door squealed as it was pulled open. Beefy Boy stepped aside and waved us in.

"Downstairs," he grunted, his piggy eyes nearly disappearing into the fleshy folds of his face as he squinted at us.

We edged by him and walked through a moldering hallway with peeling paint and down a short flight of stairs. I caught faint traces of Zhong's scent under the stronger scent layers of mold, mildew, and smoke. We stepped into a large room with red painted walls trimmed in cheap gold paint. Rugs, faded by time and worn almost through by countless feet, covered the floor, and tables of various sizes filled the room, barely leaving room for patrons to squeeze around. A pall of smoke lingered in a thick gray layer from the ceiling down to the patrons' heads, almost obscuring their features from my view. Muttered conversation mingled with the clicking sound of tiles being set down, the riffling of cards being shuffled, and the muted thump of dice hitting felt. The whole place reeked of tobacco, marijuana, opium, and desperation.

I followed Zhong's scent to the back of the big room. A series of barred cells separated this space from the rest of the room. A number of men were working behind the bars, and Zhong's scent led straight to one of them. He was organizing and stacking an assortment of clay chips when I walked straight up to his booth and knocked on the counter. "Excuse me. I'm looking for a friend of mine and was wondering if you could help me?"

He ignored me completely, continuing to arrange the chips. Pursing my lips, I blew out a piercing whistle. All activity in the place stopped. The muted chaotic sounds cut off as if by an executioner's sword. His gaze jerked up to meet mine, shocked. I smiled innocently at him. "I require assistance."

He looked at me blankly, then jabbered something back in a completely different language. His tone and expression said that he didn't understand me, but his body language broadcast that he understood me perfectly well and didn't want to deal with me. He probably figured if I thought he couldn't understand me, I would just go away. The urge to pull those cheap brass bars apart and show him he wasn't as safe as he thought was overpowering for a brief moment, but I let it pass. Wrecking the place wouldn't get me any cooperation. I would play his game. For now.

I turned to Yusi, gesturing for her to try.

She sighed, then rapped out a question. He shook his head vehemently, then replied in a short burst. "He says he doesn't know what we're talking about."

It was my turn to sigh. I dug in my pouch and held up another large gold nugget. I was going to run out of them at this rate. "Tell him we need to speak to his boss," I said. Yusi unnecessarily translated. The clerk's eyes had lit up with avarice when he had seen the nugget. He nodded, reaching out eagerly for the gold. I pulled it out of his reach, shaking my head. "Uh, uh. After you introduce me to your boss."

An unhappy, furtive look crossed his face, but then vanished as a sly smile split it. It looked especially stupid on him, and I mentally prepared myself for the inevitable double cross. Unobtrusively, in his mind at least, he yanked a pull cord under his desk then walked around his colleagues and out of the cage. A second later there was the sound of latches unlocking, and he motioned us through with a big subservient grin that didn't manage to conceal the smirk plastered across his face. We strode through and waited while he closed and relatched the door, multiple locks slamming into place with finality. He then led us down a very long hallway, past a number of doors both open and closed. About halfway down, a couple of shadows stepped into the hallway behind us, and followed us silently. The clerk led us all the way to the end of the hallway, before it made a sharp ninety degree turn, where a closed black door sat shut, the same gold symbol on its surface that decorated the door in the alley. He knocked on the door in a specific pattern, then waited for the muffled response before opening it, and scurrying in, shutting the door behind him, leaving us alone in the hallway with our two shadows. A muted conversation began, barely audible even to my ears. I turned my head and studied our bodyguards. They were both larger than me, broader and taller, which was rare in this city, from what I'd seen so far. Unlike the elegant silks the clerk wore, these two were dressed in a pants and tunic outfit made of a sturdier denim material dyed brown. Their tunics were quilted and had brass studs, making them almost like a gambeson. Decent protection without being cumbersome. I raised an eyebrow at them, inviting someone to say something. They said nothing, staring back at me flatly, my existence obviously an irritant to them. At that moment the door opened, and the clerk beckoned us in, bowing low.

In a windowless office dominated by a brown desk sat a man dressed in an elegant red and gold silk outfit. His was a pretty face, with sharper, more defined angles than most of the denizens of Li-Zhang possessed, until you saw his eyes. Flat, almost reptilian, they were the eyes of a killer, one that could remove someone's fingernails before dinner, then sleep dreamlessly through the night. I recognized the look. I smiled and held up the gold nugget to the clerk, handing it to him openly in front of everybody. Looking embarrassed, he nevertheless snatched it from my hand quickly enough before scurrying out of the room. Idly I wondered how much of that gold he was going to be allowed to keep.

The man behind the desk studied us coldly for a moment, then said, "You requested this audience, how may I serve you?" He didn't sound as if he wanted to serve us at all.

We're looking for a girl, and her trail led us here. We need to find her," I replied.

"She is not here," he replied coolly.

"Then if you could point us in the direction she went, we'll be on our way," I said.

"That's not possible. She went into the City, a place that doesn't allow foreigners such as yourself admission."

I stroked my chin with my hand thoughtfully. "That's unfortunate. She was showing symptoms of the plague when we were treating her. How did she manage to get into the city looking like she did?"

"I saw no symptoms when she was here. In fact, she said that you were chasing her. I was doing my civic duty protecting one of our citizens from two foreigners with shady motives. As far as how she got into the city, that is none of your concern. Too much curiosity about that on your part can prove dangerous," he said, a hint of menace creeping into his tone, warning me to drop the whole thing.

I ignored the hint. I can do obtuse really well, when I want to. "Well that's too bad," I said. "I guess we'll have to report to the Ministry of Health that there's a possible plague-bringer in the city, and that we last saw her here. Even if they don't investigate this right away, they'll have a record of it, and when the plague starts ripping through the city, they'll know exactly where to start."

He glared at me. "What makes you think that I will let you out of here alive to go spreading such wild tales?"

I stared him down, letting ice creep into my own gaze. "Because I'm capable of unimaginable violence," I cautioned softly, letting menace seep into my own tone. "From one killer to another, I suggest you heed this warning." I didn't know if his arrogance and overt misogyny would allow him to listen to me. Time would tell. The tension ratcheted up in the room immediately. I decided to defuse it a little, and give him an out.

Reaching into my pouch, I pulled out a handful of nuggets. Back in the jungle, we had access to a lot of gold. It was in the streams there, and in some locations, grew on special trees. We also had trees that grew silver needles, and others that extruded iron.

"Tell you what. Get my friend Yusi here into the city. She'll find Zhong and bring her back here, while I stay here and behave myself. We'll take Zhong out of the city before she can infect anyone else. You get to protect the city and your interests, and make a little money in the bargain. It's a win-win for you."

He stroked his face, thinking. It didn't take him long to make a decision. "Fine. We will show your companion the way into the city. But that is as much help as we will offer. Success or failure for finding the girl will rest on her shoulders alone. That is the only deal I will offer. Take it or leave it."

"Done," I said. I dumped the nuggets on his desk. He nodded sharply to one of his chunky boys who gestured for Yusi to follow him out. "So what's your name?" I asked when they left.

"My name is Chen Qiang, but you can call me 'Sir.' Now, you may wait out in the common area. Try your hand at some of our games. You may find them entertaining," he replied.

"That's all right. I don't gamble. It seems to me to be the fastest way to find yourself in someone else's debt. Is there somewhere else I can wait? Maybe somewhere I can sleep for a bit? It's been a busy couple of days."

Qiang slammed his pen down, irritated. "Fine. You may wait in the room Zhong stayed in before she went into the City. Now if you don't mind, I am a very busy man, and you've reached the limit of my patience."

I could feel my face getting red and hands begin to shake as rage threatened to overtake me. The urge to reach across the desk and knock all of his teeth out was almost overpowering. I concentrated on my breathing, trying to bring myself under control. Qiang watched me the whole time, smirking as he watched my reaction. That was like a bucket of ice water being thrown in my face and calmed me down quickly. He was just the type to use my emotions against me. I lifted an eyebrow, inviting him to make the next move. He nodded to Chunky Boy Number Two, who motioned me to follow him.

I followed him down a long hallway, through many twists and turns, into the basement. There were several rooms built down here on either side of the hallway. As we passed them I could smell the scent of many different customers in each room. Opium smoke wafted out under the doors, creating a pall near the ceiling. Chunky Boy led me down to the last room on the right, opened the rickety door, and motioned me in. I stepped in and he shut the door behind me. The room was barren save for a pallet against one of the walls. A lamp and pipe were set up next to it. I strode over to the pallet, then stopped, jerked up short. I smelled Zhong on it. I also smelled opium and the scent of many, many men. The air positively reeked of sex. My vision darkened to almost nothing as a red haze dropped over my eyes.

* * * * *

Yusi

I was blindfolded and led through what I assumed was a secret route through the city. They led me down stairs, my footsteps muffled on the stone, through hallways where the sounds of our passage echoed off wooden walls, and down more stairs into a basement. That led into a tunnel system. The scent of damp, musty soil filled my nostrils, and I could feel the clammy earth under my feet start sticking to the soles of my boots. They took random turns and even looped back on our path a couple of times, trying to confuse me so much that I would never be able to find my way back. A futile endeavor, really. I would be able to easily find my way back by following my old scent. In fact, I could even smell Zhong's faint scent whenever we crossed it as they led me around in circles. Apparently they took her on a more direct route. Useful to remember later. The only thing that really concerned me was if they tried some kind of an abduction scheme or tried to take advantage of me in some other way. Killing them all would prove to be.... awkward.

Luckily for them, however, they remained professional. Or as professional as a couple of thugs could be, at any rate. Of course, it could have had something to do with the fact that the first time they let me stumble when they led me across a patch of rubble strewn earth, I made sure to "accidentally" stomp on one of my handler's insteps as my foot wobbled on the broken masonry. He had barked in pain and turned the air blue around us with his stream-of-consciousness profanity. It was actually impressive. I apologized profusely of course, and his companion's loud guffaws at his friend's predicament redirected the guard's anger away from me. Win-win. After that they were much more conscientious in their duty, and there were no more mishaps.

Finally, I was led out of the tunnel system through another basement, then up a narrow flight of stairs into a large open space. It felt like my boots were striking a wooden floor. I actually couldn't hear my footsteps because of the noise around me, drowning everything else out. There was the creaking of wagons, thumps from burlap bags being thrown around, jokes, shouting, and laughter from dozens of different voices. Dust from rice, wheat, oats, and rye hung heavily in the air. It would have clogged my nostrils save for the fact that the blindfold I was wearing covered my nose and filtered out a lot of it. Nobody seemed surprised to see a blindfolded woman being led through what was obviously a warehouse. Either this happened on a regular basis, or some other pressure was being exerted.

The smell of dust dropped dramatically as I was led out of the building, and the timbre of my footsteps changed, going from wooden floor to cobblestones. My handlers led me down the street for a couple of hundred meters and through several alleyways, making sure they switched direction several times. They finally jerked me to a stop, and yanked the blindfold off of my head. Bright light stabbed through my eyelids, and I scrunched my eyes closed as tight as I could, fighting against the glare. Slowly, I tried opening them, then shutting them again, in phases, as I slowly adjusted to the daylight.

As I was blinking painfully in the light, one of the men leaned into me. "You will say nothing of this to anyone," he growled menacingly. "If any rumor of a secret way into the city gets back to us, we'll know who to search for."

I ignored him, eager to get on with the hunt. There was a lost child to save. I sampled the air around me, trying to get the barest hint of Zhong's scent. Something didn't feel right, and I knew that these criminals wouldn't go out of their way to be helpful.

"She wasn't left here," I said, absolutely certain about it as soon as I said it out loud. "Where was she dropped?"

That's your job to figure out now, isn't it?" The second man chuckled. I turned and studied them intently, truly studied them for the first time, absorbing their essences and what motivated them. The first one, the one that threatened me, was a stone wall. His was a cold essence. He followed his orders, whatever they might be, with no more emotion than an automaton. A useful trait in a soldier. The second one was ruled by... hotter impulses. His was an essence of flame, unpredictable and destructive. I smiled at him, my teeth snagging on my lower lip. His gaze locked on it.

Got him. I slid over and pressed myself tightly up against him. "Can you tell me where she was left? Please?" I whispered breathily into his ear, giving his earlobe the slightest little lick, more imagined than felt.

"The Lotus District. Ten blocks that way," he gestured, stammering a little.

"Thanks!" I said brightly, moving away from him. Or at least, I tried, but his arm had circled around my waist, holding me tight.

"I can think of another, more personal, way you can thank me," he grinned, his breath, sour and overladen with the scent of sake, washing over me.

I relaxed into his embrace, sliding my arm around the back of his neck, shielding his body from the first guy's view, and whipped out my little belt knife, pressing it into his groin. He stiffened and tried to pull away, but I held him tight, jabbing the tiniest bit harder with my knife. I put my mouth close to his ear and whispered again. "Now, normally, I charge for this procedure, but in your case I could make an exception. Do you want me to proceed?" He shook his head, a quick, nervous jerk.

"Good. Now, let me go. I have to find Zhong, and I'll be here in the city for as long as it takes. And you want me to succeed as fast as possible. The longer I'm delayed, the greater the chance your boss will say something stupid to, or try to take advantage of, Lyr in some way. When that happens, she will paint the walls red in his blood, and use his entrails as garlands for the New Year. And none of you will be able to stop her. Believe me when I say this, because I've seen her do it before. Listen to me, and it will save your life. That is all the thanks you will get from me, and it's undoubtedly more than you deserve." I pulled free from his slackening grip, stepped back, and gave them both a saucy grin. "Thanks for your assistance. I have to go now!" I gave them a little wave and bounced away. Men. So easy to manipulate. One just needed the correct lever.

* * * * *

Zhong

Zhong was on fire, and every fiber in her being hurt. Sweat poured from her body, completely soaking her clothes and the pallet beneath her. She groaned as her stomach cramped sharply, gripping her abdomen in an iron grasp. She turned on her side and vomited uncontrollably. She hadn't eaten much in the last two days, so nothing came up except froth, but the violent contractions made her even more miserable. Moaning, she rolled onto her back.

A hand, icy in comparison to her skin, gently touched her forehead, gauging the temperature of her feverish brow, then left, only to be replaced with a cool, wet cloth that felt even more freezing.

"Smoke. I need my smoke," Zhong moaned, as another wave of pain washed over her.

"Sorry, girl. That isn't allowed here. You're going to have to ride it out. Survive or not, it's up to you." The voice was soft and not without sympathy, for all the iron that lay behind the words. Silk rustled as the body belonging to the hand and voice got up and left, leaving her alone in her misery once more.

Huimin closed the panel behind her. The girl's stifled whimpers and groans carried through the thin paper. Meilan, the house's owner and mistress over all of the women that lived there, was waiting for her.

"How is she?" she asked.

Huimin shook her head. "Not well. She's been hurt severely recently, and if that wasn't bad enough, she's going through opium withdrawal right now. I'm not optimistic."

Meilan nodded. "Do what you can. If her fever worsens, we'll put her in a cold water bath. That will guard against her brain burning up, anyway."

Huimin bowed. "As you say, Mistress."

Meilan nodded, and padded away, her indoor slippers whispering against the bamboo floor.

* * * * *

Yusi

The Lotus District was a conglomeration of neighborhoods surrounded by factories. The stench of tanneries on the far end of the city still reached my nose depending on the wind direction, adding to the rich mixture of dung, both animal and human, garbage, and human sweat as people toiled about their daily routines. It was a little overwhelming, and made it impossible to find Zhong's scent, which would have been a challenge anyway. Still, there was more than one way to track prey. As hurt as she was, she wouldn't have been able to get far on her own, so I started making my way through the district, mapping it in my head. I found the alleyways and ad hoc shantytowns of the street people, and explored them all. Normally a lone woman walking through those places would be taking her life in her hands, but one look at the weapons festooned around my person, as well as the fact that I was walking around looking like I owned the place, kept the predators huddled in their hovels.

Once I eliminated those places, I hung around places where people gathered, like markets, food vendors, and tea houses, and just listened. When in a city this size, I figured it was best to break it down into neighborhoods. And a neighborhood in a city this large was like a small town unto itself. Any new person was an item of interest, and people being people, liked to gossip. I didn't hear anything about Zhong, but listening to peoples' conversations and complaints about their various ailments gave me the idea of wandering around the apothecary shops as well. If Zhong was getting as sick as I figured she was getting, somebody trying to help her would most likely come around.

I was unlucky, however, and a day of wandering around brought me no closer to Zhong. As night fell I decided to try to find the girls that worked the streets at night. One of them might have heard of Zhong. A tour of the district ended in complete failure. Apparently prostitution was only allowed in the Pearl District. I cursed the damnably efficient and organized bureaucracy of Li-Zhang, and found myself somewhere to spend the night. I didn't want to get too far afield on my first day in the World-City. Every instinct I had told me Zhong was close by. I found an out-of-the-way corner in the middle of a bunch of walled compounds and settled down for the night. It wasn't the first time and it wouldn't be the last time I spent a night under the stars.

The night passed slowly. A cold, soaking rain fell in the middle of the night, wetting me through and completely ruining any chance I had of sleeping the night through. At least I didn't have to worry about hypothermia. Because I was a Sister, my body had all the resources it needed to keep my temperature somewhat normal. The predawn chill settled into my bones, making me shiver and lowering my mood even further. After a seeming eternity, dawn finally broke over the buildings, bringing its light and hope to the streets. In the distance I could see two women walking in my direction. Both wore large, floppy straw hats, although one wore a linen tunic and trousers, and the other wore a beautiful green silk dress embroidered in gold thread. On their way home from a night of work, most likely. I figured they would ignore me and pass right by, but they saw me and adjusted their course until they were standing in front of me. I watched them dully from where I was squatting, tired and wondering what their game was.

"Oh, look, here's another one in as many days. What is Qiang thinking? If he smuggles too many people in here, it will draw the attention of The Guard," the one in the linen tunic said to her companion.

My fatigue vanished in an instant and I shot to my feet, startling the two women. "What did you just say?" I demanded.

* * * * *

Lyr

I don't know how long I stood there trying to get myself under control, to keep myself from breaking out of that room and teaching all the men in the building a lesson they would never forget, at least for the last ten minutes they were still breathing. It took a while. I focused on my breathing. In and out. In and out.

"I won't lose control. I don't slaughter people out of hand. I'm not that kind of monster. Don't give in to my urges. That gives control to my Other." I repeated it over and over to myself while I focused on my breathing. Eventually I calmed down. It was good that no one came in during that time, because they would never have left the room alive.

When I had myself under control again, I went and flipped the stinking pallet to its other side. I wasn't a fastidious sort normally, but I couldn't bring myself to sit down on that revolting brew of scents, and there was no other furniture in the room. I didn't know if the other side was any better, but at least the smells wouldn't be as...fresh. Gingerly I settled myself down on the pallet and settled in to wait.

There was no way for me to track how much time passed in that subterranean room, and there wasn't anything to do, so I dozed fitfully. A timid sounding knock startled me into wakefulness. "Yes?" I called.

The door cracked open, and a servant bowed his way into the room. "Qiang sent me to ask if you wanted some smoke?" he asked diffidently, bobbing his head.

"I don't smoke. Anything," I clarified, afraid he would suggest tobacco or devil's lettuce instead. I would like some food and water, however."

The servant bowed, then scuttled out the door. He arrived about half an hour later, by my rude estimation, with a linen covered platter and a wineskin. He set them down on the ground in front of me, and whipped the linen away, revealing a plate of chicken gong bao and rice, then bowed again, a jerky, nervous gesture. "I'm sorry, we don't have water available for you, so please accept this wine in its place, with my compliments." He bowed himself out, closing the door behind him.

Not trusting these types too much, I brought the chicken gong bao up to my face and inhaled. The heavy scent of spice pretty much overwhelmed everything else, but beneath the waves of capsaicin, I could barely detect a different scent. I set the food aside, uncapped the wineskin and took a small sip. There was a strong bitterness mixed in with the usual flavors one got with fermented grape juice.

"Opium," I grunted. They had laced everything with opium. Apparently they wanted to put me in a more agreeable mood. I wasn't sure how it would affect me. Because of our regeneration, we Sisters had an extraordinarily high tolerance to any kind of drug or poison. I mean, my favorite drink back home was Skull Hammer, which was a mixture of pureed fruit, pure alcohol, and laced with army wasp neurotoxins that would paralyze or kill a normal person. It gave me a nice, tingly feeling. Besides, I was ravenous. Despite how stupid it seemed on the face of it all and the risk it posed, I ate everything. I ate slowly, however, taking a half dozen bites, then waiting a handful of minutes, trying to figure what its effect on me would be. The food would be followed by mild waves of contentment and satisfaction, but I felt little else. I grinned. Whoever came into this room next was going to be surprised.

After I ate, I lounged on the smelly pallet, and waited. After what felt like an hour, I heard footsteps scuffling in the dirt outside. I leisurely rose to my feet as the door opened. Qiang came in, followed by two of his goons. I could see several more men clustered in the hallway behind them.

"Whatever it is you gentlemen have planned, you'd best rethink it," I said pleasantly.

* * * * *

Yusi

The two women, Taolei and Jing by name, brought me to the House of the Plum Blossom, the same place they brought Zhong. It was owned by someone who had been a high courtesan in the Royal Palace back in the day. When she retired, she bought this place and rented it out to working girls of all castes. It was a large place, three stories tall and built around a central courtyard.

Inside was nicely appointed, with polished cherry floors throughout, giving a dark, rich tone. Paper partitions separated the various spaces. They brought me upstairs to where Zhong was staying. Jing slid a partition aside and gestured me in. Zhong, unconscious, her skin glistening with sweat, lay on a pallet in the center of the room. Another woman was tending to her, laying a wet cloth on her forehead as I stepped in.

"Huimin, this is Yusi. She was searching for Zhong here and thought she might be able to help her," Taolei said.

Huimin nodded, her expression lightening in relief. "That's good," she said.

I knelt down beside her. "May I?" I asked, gesturing at Zhong. Huimin nodded.

"I've helped many girls break free of opium's grip," she said as I peeled away the sheet covering Zhong. "But many I've tried to help have chased The Dragon into ruin as well. Zhong, I'm afraid, is part of the latter category."

I nodded as I drew the sheet down to her feet. She was dressed in a simple nightgown that was soaked through with sweat. She shivered as if she had chills, but her skin was burning hot to the touch. I rucked up the nightgown, exposing her injuries. They were, to a one, red and inflamed, the tissues straining the stitches, pus leaking out around the edges. I gently poked one, even that light touch causing her to whimper, unconscious though she was.

"How did she receive those injuries?" Huimin asked softly.

"She was attacked by The Ripper," I replied absently, my mind racing as I frantically tried to think of a way to fix this. I could only think of one solution, and I knew that Lyr wouldn't like it.

All three women gasped. Apparently, even here in the city, the Ripper was known.

"It's such a disgrace. I don't know why the Guard can't seem to catch him and put an end to this," Jing said hotly.

"The Guard won't go to the trouble until a noble or rich merchant gets attacked," Taolei retorted. "As long as it's whores, or just women getting attacked, they won't put in the effort to end this scourge."

"He's a scourge no longer," I said, still staring at Zhong.

They gaped at me. "Are you serious? How?" Jing asked.

"My mother, Lyr, killed him," I said.

"She sounds formidable," a new voice said, entering the room.

I turned to look at the newcomer. She must have been one of the premier beauties of her generation when she was younger. Even as an older woman, she was still handsome. Her face still appeared unlined, but I could see skillful application of cosmetics had been used to conceal any wrinkles. Her dark hair was pinned atop her head in a neat and stylish bun, and she was dressed in a dark green silk cheongsam that hugged her body. Various birds and flowers were embroidered on the dress, adding to its beauty.

"She is that," I replied, sketching as much of a bow as I could from being on my knees. "Meilan, I presume?" Jing and Taolei had told me about the mistress of this house when we were walking here. They, and the other residents of this house seemed to hold her in as high a regard as we did Lyr.

She bowed back, a slow and graceful gesture. "How is she?" she asked, obviously worried.

I shook my head. "Not good."

"Is there anything you can do?"

I shook my head again, and sighed. "I can't do anything. But Lyr could. The trick is getting her to agree to try."

* * * * *

Lyr

Qiang stepped forward. "I see you have quite enjoyed our hospitality," he said smoothly. "My companions and I feel some recompense is in order."

I snorted. "I paid you in gold. Much more than this shitty room and the food and wine you laced with opium are worth."

He smirked. "We disagree. But don't worry, I think we can come to some sort of arrangement." The two goons that stood next to him leered at me.

I didn't waste any more time on words. Some people only understood one language. I took two quick steps forward and hooked a punch into the nearest goon's liver. I'm as strong as most men, and my bones, covered in a crystalline matrix of concentrated cellular energy and amino acids that allowed me to change shape, were over twice as thick as a normal person's. Getting hit by me, or any Sister for that matter, was like getting hit by a club. He crumpled, receiving my knee in his face on the way down. While everyone else stood still in shock, I spun around Qiang and hooked a punch at goon number two's chin. The strike was perfect, and he collapsed, unconscious.

Ignoring Qiang was a mistake. Taking care of his bodyguards gave him enough time to react. He snapped a kick to my head, rocking me back. I stumbled back, my legs suddenly made of rubber, and my sight blurred. Qiang followed up, unleashing a flurry of kicks and blows, trying to get past my suddenly desperate defenses, not wanting to give me a chance to get set. It was a valiant effort, but he couldn't get me down permanently in those first couple of seconds, and his window of opportunity closed. Adrenaline surged, and my system kicked into a higher gear. My vision cleared, and I could think again. I blocked his strikes more effectively, settled into a rhythm, and waited for an opportunity. It came with a kick he didn't pull back quickly enough. I trapped his leg then swept his other out from underneath him. He hit the ground hard and I gave him a good stomp on his testicles. All of his breath whooshed out of him, and thoughts of fighting left him as his hands involuntarily covered his groin. My gaze lifted to sweep the rest of the room. The two goons were still out of action, but some of the other men had started to filter into the room.

"Stay back," I warned. "Or I'm going to start damaging him permanently, and then I'll turn my attention to you. If you continue, this will begin to get a lot more bloody." I wrenched his foot brutally sidewise to make my point, eliciting a howl of pain from him. I dropped his foot, grabbed his hand, and yanked him up to his feet, drawing my dagger as I did. I wrenched his arm behind his back, and set the dagger to his neck. "Leave! Now!" I barked, putting a deeper growl into my voice as I did. Everybody left swiftly, some stumbling over the still prone guards.

"Now," I purred softly, "Let's go to your office and wait for Yusi together, shall we?" I pigeon-walked him all the way back to his office. He hopped a little bit, unable to put his entire weight on one of his feet. Apparently I had sprained his ankle a little bit. I couldn't bring myself to care.

When I got to his office, all the serious Triad members were there, just waiting for me to drop my guard. "I don't want to be disturbed by anyone except Yusi," I warned as I kicked open the door and shoved Qiang inside. "If any of you geniuses try to break in, I'll kill him, and then go through all of you like a tiger eating goats." I slammed the door closed. Apparently, Qiang wasn't a trusting soul, because there were half a dozen locks on the inside of the door, as well as a thick wooden bar. I dropped the bar in place and turned to Qiang. He had sat down in his chair and regained his oily composure, sneering as he looked at me. One of his hands was hidden below his desk.

I drew my sword in a blink and rested it on his throat, directly below his Adam's apple. He froze. "Whatever you were thinking about doing, I'd advise you to reconsider, at least until you know all the facts about me," I suggested mildly, letting my sword rest just a hair heavier on his neck. "And that's now my chair, for the rest of the time I'm here. So let go of whatever it is you have a hold on underneath that desk, and get up." I pushed a little harder, causing him to fall over backwards as he tried to get away from my sword. He scrambled up and backed away from me, the merest rivulet of blood trickling down his chest.

"You won't get away with this!" he blustered, swiping angrily at his neck. "You can't fight all of us, and I'll make sure you suffer in ways you can't even imagine before you die!"

I set his chair back upright and spun it so its back rested against the wall with one hand, keeping my sword pointed at him with the other. Now I could keep an eye on him and the door at the same time. I sat down in the chair and rested my sword on my lap. "I wouldn't be too sure of that. I assume you're familiar with The Ripper cases?"

"What?" he demanded, confusion replacing the angry expression on his face.

"The Ripper cases. You know, all those poor street girls getting torn to bits over the last several months?"

"Yes, of course I knew about that, but I didn't think about it too much. It wasn't my concern," he replied.

"Well, let's just say that he and I are related, so to speak. Only he was a pale, weak shadow compared to me." I lengthened the fingers of my left hand, fur sprouting through my pores, fingernails growing and morphing into claws. I raked my hand across his desk, gouging deep furrows on its surface. "Believe me when I say I could kill you and everyone in this building, and there's nothing you could do to stop me."

He cried out in sudden terror and scurried as far away from me as he could get, pressing himself into the corner of the room. "What are you?" he whispered, his voice trembling.

I grinned at him, a feral, joyous grin, and half-rose out of the chair. "Something you should do everything in your power to keep happy until Yusi gets back," I cackled roughly at him, trying to sound as menacing as possible. So we waited, and that's exactly how Yusi found us, me still in the chair, and Qiang still huddled in the corner of the office. I had kept my monster hand, and occasionally I would scratch it on his desk when he looked like he might start scheming, or if I got bored.

There was a polite knock on the door, and I lifted the bar of the door. Yusi stepped through, noticed the deep gouges in the desk, Qiang pressed in the office corner, and raised an eyebrow. "Have you been amusing yourself?" she chuckled.

"Yes I have." I saw no reason to elaborate.

"Well, at least he's still breathing. I wouldn't have bet a yuan either way as to whether this place would be occupied by people or corpses by the time I got back."

"I don't know what you're talking about. I was on my best behavior the whole time."

She gave me a rather severe look. "I may not know you as well as some of the other Sisters, Mother, but I've been travelling with you long enough to know how you can react when you run afoul of a certain type of person." She stared Qiang down. "Your response can be quite... energetic."

I snorted and she laughed quietly, then stepped aside to make room for someone else to enter the room. Another woman moved into the room. She was dressed in a beautiful red dress embroidered in flowers and birds. An elegant white straw hat sat on her head, with a sheer silk veil attached to it, covering her face. White gloved hands reached up and carefully removed both the hat and the veil. She was an older woman, still pretty, and carried herself with grace and assurance.

"This is Meilan, Mother," Yusi said respectfully. "She owns the house that took Zhong in. Meilan, this is Lyr, Mother of our people."

Meilan bowed deeply. "I'm honored to make your acquaintance, Lyr."

I bowed back. "As am I, Meilan." We straightened up and looked over at Qiang as he stirred from his corner.

He looked at Meilan appraisingly, one corner of his mouth lifted in a sneer. He seemed overfond of that expression, I thought. I much preferred an expression of horror on his face. It had been most delicious. "Meilan. I should have known. You're the one who's been helping these... women?" His tone made it seem like calling us women was a stretch.

Meilan looked at him coldly. "Chen Qiang. I am merely cleaning up your mess, as usual. These ladies believe they can help that poor child you left abandoned in the streets, and I am expediting their efforts."

"The fact that you're assisting them... displeases me, and I have a very long memory. Just remember that." Qiang's odds of living through the day continued to go down, I thought.

"I served the Emperor for many years before I retired, Chen Qiang. We loved each other. He still talks to me weekly, did you know? The bureaucracy may run the city, and you may have the bureaucrats in your pocket, but the Emperor is still revered, and if he takes a dim view of your operation, The Guard will make an example of you and your Triad, much to the delight of your many enemies I'm sure. If a whisper of the Emperor's interest in you reached your bosses' ears, what do you think their reaction might be?" She paused, arching an eyebrow.

"Something to think about. Now, if you'll excuse us, we have a matter of urgency requiring our attention." Meilan turned and left, Yusi following close behind, guarding her.

I waited until they left the room, then slammed Qiang up against the wall, pinning him with my body. I buried my nose in the crook of his neck and inhaled deeply. Then I grabbed his chin and wrenched his head to the side, exposing his cheek. I ran my tongue up the side of his face, making it as wet and gross as possible. "I have your scent now, Qiang. And your taste. I have eyes and ears everywhere. There are fifty women just like me that answer to me alone. If anything happens to that lady or the girls that live with her we will find you. We can reach you anywhere you can think of to run to or hide. And when we find you, you'll be the guest of honor in our ensuing hunt. There won't be enough left of you to put in a jar. Do you understand?" He nodded frantically, his breeches darkening with a liquid stain. I released his face. "Good."

Apparently Meilan knew the correct people to bribe, because she was able to smuggle me into the city proper with little trouble. She just dressed me in her hat and veil and marched me through the main entrance. She was a formidable woman.

She led me to the House of the Plum Blossom and up to Zhong's bedroom. Zhong lay still and quiet on her pallet, unconscious. There was another woman there, scarcely more than a girl, attending to her. She took a cloth off of Zhong's forehead, dipped it in a bowl of water, wrung it out, then placed it back on her.

"That will be all, Li. Thank you," Meilan said as we entered. Li sketched a small bow from where she knelt, got up, and left.

I took Li's place by Zhong and lifted up her nightgown. What greeted me made me hiss in surprise. All of her wounds were infected, inflamed and oozing pus. I gently laid the back of my hand on Zhong's cheek. She was burning up. I shook my head and leaned down to inspect her wounds more closely. I took a deep sniff, trying to get a clearer sense of her condition. Underneath the pus's putrid odor, there was another scent, a bitter metallic tang. I sighed, shaking my head again, and looked up at Yusi and Meilan. "I don't know what you expect me to do," I said.

Meilan waved at Yusi. "She thinks you can cure her. She was pretty adamant about it, in fact."

I glared at Yusi, angry at her presumption. "She's not a good candidate for that."

Yusi fell to her knees beside me. "Please, Mother! I know you can save her! You have to at least try," she begged.

"Why does this matter to you?" I asked. "You barely know her. People die all the time, Yusi. You can't save everyone. It's impossible. And even if you could, you shouldn't. Dying is a part of life for everyone. That's a lesson you need to learn, if you yourself are going to survive the long years you have ahead of you."

"She reminds me of someone I knew, long ago," Yusi whispered, shivering a little, upset. A tear welled up out of her eye and crept slowly down her cheek. She dashed it angrily away. "And I *have* seen death. More than I care to think about or remember. That's why I vowed long ago that I would fight it, in any way I can. I may not save everyone, but I *will* try. It's all I can do. And so I'm asking you, Mother, to save Zhong. Please."

I shook my head at her. "She's dying, Yusi. The Ripper has infected her. Not enough to actually help her fight the other infections she has, just enough to pile on one more thing that her body has to deal with. Even without all of that, she would have a less than-even-chance of survival.

"Plus, she hasn't gone through The Trials. I know nothing of her, of her will or character. And she's unconscious. She hasn't given me her *consent*, which is even more important. How can I force our condition on her, without her even knowing about it? It's immoral."

Meilan cleared her throat. "If I may?"

I nodded at her.

"I understand about choice. I also understand that we women are all too often forced into paths not of our choosing. Whether it's slavery, or an arranged marriage, or being abandoned by our families because we have no worth in their eyes and they can't afford to feed us. I've seen girls like Zhong before. She's a survivor. Can't you see she's fighting even now? All I ask is that you give her the ability to choose her own destiny. But she has to live first."

"Do you understand, really understand, what you're asking of me? I'll have to take her to the point of death, then try to keep her alive while her body fights the changes that will be thrust upon her. The chances are great that I will kill her outright trying to do this. And even if she manages to survive, she will then be locked in a battle of wills with a monster that will be trying to get out for the rest of her life. If she loses that battle, she will also lose her humanity, and I will be forced to kill her."

Meilan thought about it for a long moment, then nodded sharply. "She is a fighter. She should be given the chance at least to choose her fate. I have seen so many, many girls have that choice brutally ripped away from them. I would not see it again here."

I looked at her, then looked at Yusi, gazing at me hopefully. "Dammit," I sighed. "All right, I'll try. While I'm doing this, have the kitchen start preparing some broth. Zhong is going to need it."

* * * * *

Zhong

Zhong opened her eyes. The first thing that came to her notice was a cool breeze wafting through the room. It ruffled the white drapes gently before caressing her cheek with its gentle touch. A hand touched her forehead. She followed it up and blearily focused on the face it belonged to. It slowly swam into focus, coalescing into a pair of bright green, almost luminous eyes. The strange woman, Lyr.

"Welcome back," she said.

A Monster in the Dark

It was a no name hamlet in the northern reaches of the Taurish province inhabited by a collection of families eking out a simple existence through forestry and herding. The houses were made of logs chinked with mud and topped with grass thatched roofs. Chickens and pigs rooted through the muddy streets for food, while goats, or if a family was particularly well off, a milking cow, were tied off by the houses. Community vegetable gardens were dotted throughout, and a wall made of two rows of sharpened logs driven into the ground with dirt packed in between the rows encircled the town, protecting the villagers from the occasional raid from less-than-friendly neighbors or even the odd attack from one of the Lawless Land bands. Outside of the walls, fields of wheat were plowed in the springtime, while sheep and cattle were allowed to run free. Sheep being sheared in the spring and cattle rounded up in the fall. It was one of hundreds of such hamlets scattered throughout the Altan Plateau, the inhabitants being sturdy, independent sorts, distrustful and hostile to outsiders, and not above launching an occasional raid themselves. However, unlike those other villages, this one harbored a secret.

* * * * *

Zhong cursed silently as cold rain hammered down, plastering her hair to her head, running off of her braids in rivulets, and flowing down the back of her neck in a small river. This was as miserable as she'd been in a long, long time. For the life of her, she couldn't figure out how her life had taken such a dramatic, surreal turn. Sure, she could retrace all the steps that led to this moment, but it still made absolutely no sense to her. She squinted through the downpour, barely able to see the figure riding in front of her. Another one rode behind her, neatly boxing her in. There wasn't a lot of love lost or trust between her and her erstwhile new companions yet, it seemed. She couldn't blame them, she supposed. She'd always been a loner.

A separate tiny stream of water managed to find a part of her body not already chilled and pinched her with its icy fingers. Zhong cursed again, out loud this time, and nudged her horse into an awkward trot to pull abreast of the leader of their little band. "What are we doing out here?" she demanded. Lyr turned her head and stared at her, and Zhong shrank down under the weight of that emerald green gaze. Frankly, she didn't remember too much of how they met two months ago. It was all a jumbled mess of hazy memories in between bouts of unconsciousness and the Opium Dream. Apparently she had been attacked and infected with *something bad*. Lyr had given her a choice: submit to her control, or death. Easy choice at first, but now she wasn't so sure. One thing she was sure of, these two women she had fallen in with frightened her more than anyone else she had ever dealt with; guard, pimp, customer, or bureaucrat. "Sorry," she mumbled.

Lyr held her gaze a moment more, then turned her face up to the pewter sky. Rain ran down her face in runnels. She looked at Zhong again. "We are looking for a secluded, safe place to hole up. This is a pivotal moment for you, Zhong. Your initiation into the Sisterhood. For the next three days, Artemis and Chang'e will be full. During one of those days, you will Change, your Beast will be free, and you will kill anything and everything that crosses your path. We're going to help you, so you won't do something we'll all regret later."

Zhong shivered, and it wasn't just the cold rain water making its way into every single crevice on her body. She didn't really believe what they said, even now. It sounded too fantastical, and she wondered if maybe she had fallen in with a couple of crazy people. Well, she would just bide her time, and when the moment appeared, she would make her escape.

They climbed out of the small swale they were riding through, and topped out on higher ground. A small village walled with timber slowly appeared out of the mist like a bashful bride. Lyr reined in her horse and stared in disbelief. Blowing out an exasperated breath, she said, "That's unfortunate."

* * * * *

Most of the time Kai Ottoson enjoyed being the village headman. It was a job that wasn't too onerous and came with a lot of prestige. This was not one of those times, however, as he squelched through ankle deep mud to one of the poorer huts situated away from the more prosperous center of the town and closer to the wall. And he really wished that Seig, the village priest, wasn't accompanying him right now. Seig was a zealot, and oftentimes made Kai's job harder. Dressed in undyed woolen robes and gripping a gnarled staff as tall as he was, his eyes seemed to burn with a feverish, inner fire.

Kai slopped up to the hut in question, the mud sucking at his feet, and hesitated. Taking a deep breath, he banged on the rough wooden door, paused for a moment, then banged some more. Slowly the door opened, and the portal was filled with the imposing figure of Solveig Mathildesdottir. She towered at least a head over him, dressed in undyed woolen leggings and tunic, filling the doorway with her body. If she had been a man, she surely would have been a warrior of great renown, likely matching the exploits of the legendary Conan, whose own adventures stretched back into the mists of time, passed down faithfully to regale each new generation, but she was just a woman, and thus fated to a life of quiet obscurity. Still, she could be fierce, and she made Kai nervous.

She didn't look fierce at the moment, however. Her blonde curls framed a wide face whose bright blue eyes were red from weeping.

Kai cleared his throat. "It's time."

"Please," Solveig said, her voice hoarse from weeping, "She's all I have left."

Kai winced. The village had lost her husband, Gunnar in an abortive raid last year, and the year before that, the couple had lost their son as he tried to protect the village flock from a pack of wolves. "I'm sorry, Solveig, you know the law. Astrid's name was drawn, and that's all there is to it."

Solveig's expression hardened, and her massive, work-reddened hands clenched into fists. "Over my dead body."

Seig's eyes narrowed. "It is Odin's will that Astrid join His Valkyries in Valhalla. Will you defy his will?" he declared loudly.

Kai sighed and put his hand on Sieg's shoulder, silencing him. "Be reasonable, Solveig," he begged quietly. "Don't make this harder than it has to be. Don't make me gather the menfolk to do this and make a big scene that will upset everyone."

A faint scuffle sounded as a foot brushed against the hard packed dirt floor of the mean hut, and a shadow separated itself from the interior gloom and squeezed past Solveig. The shadow resolved into Astrid as she appeared into the light, taking her mother's hand. She was slightly shorter than her mother, slimmer, with braids of chestnut brown hair pinned up around her head. She had always favored her father, with his hazel eyes and whipcord lean body.

"It's all right, Mamma. I am ready," she said. She tried to sound confident and brave, but Kai could see she had also been crying. Her eyes were red, the skin around them puffy.

Solveig opened her mouth to speak, but whatever she was going to say was lost as one of the wall guards hurried up. "Jarl! Three strange women are here asking about finding shelter! I thought maybe you should talk to them."

* * * * *

I cast a worried look up at the sky, trying to gauge how much daylight we had left, a difficult proposition on this overcast day. We had to get Zhong as far away as possible, before night fell. With any luck, the sky would stay overcast and she wouldn't get a glimpse of the full moons. She was as difficult to deal with as any whiny teenager right now. I couldn't wait to see what she would be like when The Change hit her. Funny thing was, I doubted she would have even been selected as a candidate under normal circumstances. Ever since I created the Trials, candidates had to earn their chance. Most failed. It was rare for someone to have the required traits of mental toughness, emotional stability, pain tolerance, and being a never-say-die survivor to become a successful Sister. The only thing Zhong had going for her was her do-anything-to-survive attitude. Hopefully the rest would develop in time.

The gates suddenly swung open and two men hurried out. One was rather prosperously dressed in a high quality linen tunic dyed in a rich blue, decorated with fancy gold embroidery and woolen trousers. The other one was dressed in undyed woolen robes that reached to his feet. The fancy man stepped towards us, with his hands held out wide like he was going to welcome us into his village. However, the two guards on the top of the wall with arrows nocked in their bows ready to draw and fire at a moment's notice painted a somewhat different picture. I raised my hand before he could launch into any sort of speech. He looked like someone that liked to talk. No doubt that's how he got his way most of the time, wearing people down until they got tired and gave up.

"I don't mean to take up any of your time, and we don't want to stay in your village, lovely as I'm sure it is. I'm just wondering if there's any shelter to get out of the weather about a half day's ride from here?"

Fancy Man rubbed his chin thoughtfully. "Yes, actually, if memory serves. The founder of this town, old Olaf Gundersson had a gold mine about two hours from here as the crow flies. However, the ground between here and there is pretty boggy right now and there's danger of your horses getting stuck, so if you head west into the forest, there's a ridge that curls around in a northeasterly direction that will lead you right to it. You should reach it about nightfall."

I nodded. "Much obliged." With that we turned and rode away.

* * * * *

As the three women rode to their deaths, Seig turned to Kai. "What are you doing? With those three in the way, we can't move forward with our sacrifice! You risk bringing down Odin's wrath on us all!"

"You ever stop and think that maybe those poor women will serve as the sacrifice instead?"

Seig snorted. "They are not of us. I doubt that Odin will accept them as a sacrifice. I shall go read the portents, and then we shall see!" He whirled dramatically and stalked back into the village.

Kai watched him leave, shook his head, and sighed. Seig occupied an important role in the village, but he reveled in his position and took pleasure in any drama he could whip up. He created more problems for Kai than any other five villagers combined.

* * * * *

The forest was composed of mature fir and spruce trees interspersed with oak and maple. The trees closed in around us as we rode in, cutting out the light and muffling the sounds we made. It was hushed as we rode through, as all such forests tended to be. The most common sound was the sighing of the wind through the tree tops, the surprisingly loud sounds of heavy water droplets hitting vegetation, and the creak, sighs, and rustles the trees made as they swayed back and forth, dancing to the eternal tune the wind played. Moss and ferns carpeted the soft ground of the ridge the horses trod, while off the ridge on both sides the earth became nearly impassable, with large boulders and fallen trees laying in a jumbled jam. Birds sang as they set up nests and fought for territory. On one side a stream picked its way between some of the rocks, adding its own part to the concert. Everywhere smelled of wet moss, earth, and rotting wood. If I focused, I could hear the rustling sounds of small creatures scurrying through their homes.

The ridge led us around, just like Fancy Man said it would, and as twilight stretched its shadowy fingers through the trees, we found the hole in the hillside that was presumably Olaf's mine. For a long abandoned mine it was suspiciously clear of vegetation around the mouth of the mine. Ferns and moss clustered around the mouth of the mine and scrawled thickly up the hill, but the area directly in front of it was clear.

I dismounted from Red and cautiously scouted around. The area directly in front of the mine mouth was undisturbed mud, except for a couple of three inch holes in the ground about shoulder width and a half apart. I approached the mine cautiously, and peered into its mouth. A trench dug on one side of the tunnel floor acted as a drain, pouring out its contents and keeping the mine floor dry-ish. The trench looked maintained. Inside the tunnel, there was a smell I had never smelled before, but carried a suggestion of carrion. This whole thing smelled like a trap. I backed carefully away from the mouth and turned back to Yusi and Zhong. "We'll set up camp out here."

Yusi accepted it stoically, swung down from her horse, and started setting up camp, but Zhong thrust her lower lip out and stared at me mulishly. I held her gaze, and raised an eyebrow. "Well? Get going."

We got the horses picketed, set up a shelter, foraged some dry wood, a not insignificant accomplishment in this weather, and ate dinner. When we were finished, we settled around the fire. Zhong stared sullenly into the flames, Yusi sat facing out the way we had come, and I faced the mouth of the mine. Something about that place raised the hackles on the back of my neck.

I took a deep breath and gave myself a little shake. "Zhong!"

She looked up, startled. "What?" she asked.

I settled myself into lecture mode. "Pay attention. It's time to introduce you to the Mysteries of our Sisterhood. Where we came from. What we are, and what our place in this world will be. Understand?" Zhong nodded.

"All right. The first thing that you have to know is that Kaler is not humanity's birthplace. Our homeworld is a planet named Earth, out there, somewhere in the stars." I gestured at the night sky, dark and boring now, but which I knew to be velvet covered liberally in diamond chips on a good night. "Our ancestors came to this place searching for a new home. They called themselves scientists, whatever that means, but what they really wanted was to set themselves up as gods and tinker with the very fabric of life. This world was a blank slate with no life of its own, perfect for their needs. They settled far to the south of here, on a completely different continent, and set this one aside as a laboratory and preserve. They seeded this land with plants and animals both from Earth, and ones they created from nothing, observing which would survive and thrive, and which would perish. This land is also where they decided to tuck away some of their more controversial experiments; ones which some of their more moral citizens might object to. We were the results of one of those programs."

Zhong pointed at Yusi and me. "You mean you two personally?"

I chuckled and shook my head. "No, not us personally. They were trying to make perfect spies. People that could pass through any kind of security, yet take infinitely more damage than a normal person and always be armed to boot. However, I've seen some of the weapons they used at the time, and let me tell you, we don't compare to those machines. But machines break down, and they wanted to create something that wouldn't. Something that could live on its own for weeks and months with no help and come out fine." I paused to take another breath. "The program was both an unmatched success, the pinnacle of all of their expertise, and a complete disaster. All the effort they put into making us blend into society failed because we weigh twice as much as we should. Any machine that could accurately weigh something would expose us instantly. Yet we are still the only humans ever created that can change our shape completely to another form, and then back to ourselves.

"They used men originally. Men Turned like us are hyper-aggressive and un-stable. They can't control their rage, which means they can't control their Beasts, and they degenerate into monsters. Always. They also couldn't be controlled, so the people in charge of that program decided to freeze them, literally. That was actually a blessing for them because another star system took offense at what our ancestors were doing. Called it an affront to God's plan and declared war on them.

Not a great idea to declare a holy war on people that know how to manipulate the very fabric of life. Apparently we "won" and sterilized our enemy's system, eradicating all life there, but they were able to fight their way here and hit Kaler with a single warhead that killed everyone on the southern continent which was where ninety-nine point nine percent of people were living. The only people living here were scattered teams of researchers, who had to start from scratch. All their fancy tools failed within a generation, and they had to start from the very beginning, banging rocks together.

"Meanwhile, the failed experiments who were frozen slept through it all; the catastrophe, the mega deaths, the survivors rebuilding everything from nothing. The equipment holding them eventually broke down. They woke up about seventy-five years before I stumbled across them. Seventy-five years of inflicting pain and suffering on the people around them before my friend Jack and I put them out of everyone's misery. That's why one of the first laws I laid down when I started the Sisterhood was there could never be male Kindred. It's forbidden."

I figured that was enough for one night. Her initiation into the Mysteries was going to be unorthodox, to say the least. Normally, we would have a class of candidates fighting to become Sisters, and only the ones that demonstrated the necessary tenacity, mental stability, and character would be Turned and admitted. They would learn all of this after we had broken them down and started rebuilding them. I had no confidence that Zhong would have made it through the weeding out process, or would even have wanted to become a Sister in the first place. But here we were.

Zhong straightened. "Is that it?"

I nodded. "For tonight."

She took a deep breath. "Well, I have to say… that is the dumbest story I've ever heard! Everyone knows that the world was created by Pan Gu, the mythical giant who separated chaos into its opposites of earth and sky. You're insane! I've let a couple of crazy bitches take me away from my life and everything I've known to end up here in the middle of nowhere!"

Yusi shot to her feet, but I waved her down. "You had a choice," I said quietly, trying to hold onto my rapidly fraying temper.

Zhong snorted. "Some choice! Life following you around, doing what you tell me to do, or death. Well, I'm tired. I'm tired of being cold and wet, and I'm tired of doing your bidding, Your Majesty! I mean why are we out here in the rain and wind when we could be nice and dry in that cave over there! In fact," she jumped to her feet, grabbed her bedding, and stalked into the mine adit. "I'm done! I'm done taking your orders! From now on, the only person giving me orders is me!" She cast down her sleeping roll and glared at me defiantly. A split second later a shape like a giant tube separated itself from the darkness making up the roof of the cavern, shot down, and swallowed Zhong whole.

"Holy shit!" I screamed, jumping up, ripping my sword from its sheath, and sprinting over to whatever the fuck it was that just gulped down Zhong like an appetizer. It was still hanging there wriggling like some obscene cocoon as it fought to pull itself back up to its hole while keeping ahold of its meal. As I got closer, I could see it more clearly. It looked like a giant, dark gray and purple grub. Bumps and nodules studded its surface, and smooth tentacles fluttered and undulated around its body like it was swimming through the ocean.

"Why in the names of all the Created Hells would the Makers create something like this?" I shrieked as I swung my sword down as hard as I could on it. I gaped in astonishment as it bounced off the tough, rubbery skin, barely scratching it, then a tentacle whipped around, hitting me in the chest and knocking me off of my feet.

* * * * *

It was dark all around her. Slime coated her skin, and something was squeezing her on all sides. She couldn't breathe. All she knew was she had to get out. She had to find a way to breathe. She began clawing ineffectually at whatever it was that held her. Panic struck and her fight-or-flight response kicked in, releasing a slew of chemicals and hormones into her bloodstream, triggering her Change. She let out a soundless scream of agony, wasting more of her precious air as it felt like every bone in her body broke at the same time. Her face was breaking, dissolving and changing, and she sobbed as she was sure she was being digested. She began to claw more frantically, trying to get out, and her fingernails lengthened, hardened, became claws that started ripping and tearing. The squeezing became worse as she felt like she was swelling, but with that came extra energy and strength. Her clawing and scratching redoubled.

* * * * *

The Grub of Death convulsed suddenly like something had stung it and began shivering and shaking spasmodically. Its mouth opened again and I threw myself to my feet, yanking my ax out. "Get me some rope!" I yelled at Yusi, and charged the grub. I swung again, but not with my sword and not at its tough outer hide. Instead, I buried the curved beak of my ax into its open mouth, burying it to the haft. A deep, booming croak erupted from deep within its body and the grub whipped its whole body up out of the way of a second strike. Tentacles whipped around wildly like whips, trying to drive me back, one striking me on the face with a crack, leaving a welt across my cheek, and another feeling its way toward its mouth, trying to find and pull out the thing that hurt it. I hacked at that tentacle with my sword, slicing it in two. Thank the Makers for small favors, I thought. Apparently the tentacles weren't as tough as the body.

I had its full attention now and more tentacles shot out toward me, trying to wrap me up. I exploded into action, spinning away from a couple, parrying a couple more, then spinning back in with a wide sweeping slash to sever a half dozen at the root.

Yusi rushed in, rope in hand. "Tie it off to the ax handle, then use the horses to keep this thing from crawling back into its hole," I gasped as I continued to hack at the tentacles, trying to give her cover. Yusi threw a couple of half hitches on the ax handle with one end of the rope, then sprinted back to her horse, vaulting up into the saddle. She wrapped the other end around her saddle pommel, then kicked her horse into motion. The rope snapped taut, and began pulling the monstrosity out of its hole. It lasted for about a second, then the ax came free, slipping out of the grub's mouth, and went flying back towards Yusi, crossing at least two thirds of the distance back before tumbling to the ground. Yusi kicked her feet free from her stirrups and sprinted to pick the ax back up. I retreated out of the creature's reach and held out my hand. "Ax!" I shouted. She tossed it back to me and I slipped the rope free from the haft and clenched it in my left hand before charging back into the fray. I built up some momentum, gathered myself, and sprang onto the top of the worm.

It went mad and bucked like an untamed horse, trying to throw me off. Tentacles whipped around, trying to grab me as I scrambled around the hard, knobby body, collecting more than a fair share of cuts and bruises as parts of me would catch on the sharp bony knobs. I fell off the other side keeping a hold of the end of the rope, and rolled underneath the grub dragging the rope with me. Jumping to my feet I grabbed the other side of the rope hanging off the creature and tied a quick slipknot. I yanked the noose tight and waved at Yusi, who, anticipating me, had climbed back on top of her horse. She nodded, and kicked her horse forward carefully. The rope tightened further, this time holding, caught on the worm's bony knobs.

I chopped down at the grub again, but this time with my ax. I had better luck with this and my ax blade sank about halfway in. I ripped it out, and readied for another strike. Strength. I needed more strength.

* * * * *

She couldn't see, couldn't breathe, but she was having success tearing through this soft, squishy material. Suddenly, she broke through one wall and her nose was in a small open space. Air kissed its tip and she reflexively let out the breath she was holding and inhaled as deeply as she could. Nasty, moist air filled her lungs, but at least it was fresh oxygen. She sucked in another breath and redoubled her efforts, following the thin trail of fresh oxygen reaching her nostrils.

* * * * *

The grub twitched again, as if something else was hurting it, and I let my Other off of her chain. I grew taller as my feet lengthened until I balanced on my toes, claws bursting from them. My hair fell out, fur burst from my pores, and my nose and jaw lengthened, turning into a short muzzle. My teeth fell out, pushed aside by the fangs of a predator that grew in their place. My hand, larger now and tipped with claws, moved up my ax haft, where it was twice as thick as it was near its butt. I growled and swung down again, rewarded with the ax head burying itself out of sight. Blue blood splashed, and its rank, acrid odor hit my nostrils. I yanked my ax free, howled in triumph, and chopped down again and again, faster and faster and faster, momentarily lost in a frenzy of bloodletting.

* * * * *

She was still clawing, biting, trying to get free. The brief burst of air had rejuvenated her, but that was fading and she was starting to weaken. Suddenly, what appeared to be a spear of light stabbed her slime-smeared eyeballs, and she reached for it with all the desperation of a drowning woman. There was a flash of pain, and she screamed as she felt two fingers shear away, but she didn't let it stop her.

* * * * *

The sudden shock of my ax hitting something other than rubbery flesh startled me out of my fugue. I stopped, and peered at the giant gash I had made, trying to figure out what was going on. The creature took advantage of my distraction. Two tentacles latched onto my ax, trying to tear it free from my grasp, while a dozen more wrapped around my limbs and torso, trying to restrain me. I snarled in rage and yanked back, trying to break free. The rubbery tentacles stretched, tightening down on my limbs, but I wasn't without weapons. Growling, I dragged an arm close to my mouth and bit down, shearing them as heavy scissors cut through sailcloth. Bitter acid blood flooded my mouth, but my arm was free. I jerked back and forth even harder as I tried to keep the grub off balance while I worked to free my other arm.

Astonishingly, a slimy arm sheathed in black fur and missing two fingers thrust itself out of the gash I made. Like an abomination being birthed from a horror, a Sister in her Other form and covered in disgusting mucus tore free from the worm and sped into the night. A long, wavering howl drifted behind her, advertising the direction she was going.

Quick as thought, Yusi kicked free from her horse and chased after her, changing as well, leaving me alone with my adversary. I turned back to it in renewed fury. I had a child to catch.

* * * * *

She was running; running away from whatever it was that tried to hurt her. Her clawed feet tore at the soil, offering excellent purchase, while her heart pumped blood effortlessly to her powerful limbs. She snorted intermittently as she ran, trying to clear her nostrils of the cloying, stinking slime that clung to them. If it wasn't for that, she felt as if she could run forever. She stopped briefly to scrub her nose against some grass and blew the last of the mucus free from her nose. Her ears pricked up and backward as they caught a sound. Something else out there was running, and closing fast. Instantly she was off again, legs pumping, her spine flexing to add extra power to her hindquarters. She didn't know how long she hurtled along the ground, but whatever it was kept pace with her. Being chased didn't sit well with her. She could feel the wiry power in her body, and knew without a doubt that she was the strongest thing in this forest.

She stopped suddenly and whirled to face her tormentor. Rage and adrenaline boiled in her veins like the headiest of nectars, even better than the opium she used to smoke. She would show whatever was chasing her who the true predator was. She roared her defiance and hate as another body crashed through the underbrush to face her. It was another one like her, a female, larger and longer, but still lean and covered in brown fur. She made no move to attack, but waited, brown eyes watching her calmly. Zhong crouched lower to the ground, hind legs tamping down, digging into the ground, and snarled her defiance, lips rippling and contracting back from her teeth, displaying them in all their glory. The creature like her did nothing but give a little shake of her head, warning her.

Zhong snarled again, tensing, then howled, charging across the clearing with freakish speed. She leapt, claws spread wide, ready to expel this interloper from her territory. Her enemy rose to meet her, but at the last second shifted her weight to the side. Paws grabbed her foreleg, claws dug into her side behind her ribs, a little twist and throw, and Zhong kept flying, straight into the trunk of a tree.

She felt ribs snap, and hit the ground hard, a little dazed. She climbed to her feet, shaking her head to try and clear it. Her opponent still did nothing, just waited. She shrieked in rage and charged again.

She was halfway to her enemy when something else hit her in the side with all the force of a battering ram. Over and over she and her new foe rolled, with her kicking and biting desperately, trying to free herself. When they came to a stop she found herself pinned, her assailant's teeth latched onto her throat. She panicked and started to thrash around, trying to escape, but those jaws tightened on her throat with frightening power, threatening to cut off her air, and the massive body didn't budge, holding her down with ease. She stopped struggling for a second, and felt the jaws loosen a little. Zhong forced herself to stop and think, beating down the feelings of rage and bloodlust. Growls gave way to whines as jumbled thoughts cascaded through her mind, racing around like a runaway cartwheel, but lacking any sense of cohesion. What was happening, where was she, and most importantly, what was she? Sounds reached her ears from distances that she normally wouldn't be able to hear, and even more significantly, her nose was gathering a gargantuan amount of scents, and flooding her brain with an overabundance of information. Slowly she was able to narrow her focus on the creature that was holding her down. She became aware of the heat radiating off of both of them, and the musky odor they emanated. Something else entered her nose, not a scent per se, but it nevertheless exerted a calming influence on her. She stopped struggling completely, and just submitted to her fate. Abruptly the pressure from the jaws around her ceased, and the weight pinning her down disappeared. She scrambled to her feet and faced her attacker, huddling as close to the ground as possible. Uncontrollable shivers raced up and down her body as she faced what had pinned her down. It was yet another creature like her. While her first attacker had been slim and built for speed, this one, while undeniably still female, was built for power. She was taller through the shoulder than Zhong, and had to be at least twice as wide through the chest. Confidence and authority radiated off of her in waves. Brilliant green eyes glared at her from a monstrous face. She was the most awesome, frightening thing Zhong had ever seen, and it terrified her. She gathered herself to run away, but a tensing of muscles and a warning growl that rumbled up from the depths of the creature made her settle back down, almost against her will.

Green eyes glanced at the first creature. Something passed between them, and the first creature nodded slightly. She shivered, almost a seizure that wracked her frame, then seemed to melt. Fur fell off of her in great clumps, her short muzzle shrank back into her skull, her claws retreated back into her fingers, and her hips and spine realigned. In a remarkably short time, a naked Yusi sat before her.

"Listen to me, Zhong," Yusi said in a calm, soothing tone. "You've taken your first step into the Sisterhood. Now it's time to take the second. I need you to visualize yourself as you were, a human woman. Fix that image in your mind."

Zhong tried to do that. It was hard. The bloodlust and anger were still there, like simmering soup in a pot that was threatening to boil over past its lid. With a stubbornness she had possessed in full measure for her whole life, she closed her eyes, steadied her breathing, and shoved the rage back down, gaining a measure of calm. She imagined herself as she had been, a petite woman with a round face, and otherwise unremarkable features, brown eyes, and brown hair cropped shoulder length, like many other inhabitants of Li-Zhang. When she had the memory of what she looked like firmly in her mind, she nodded at Yusi.

"Good. Now, open your eyes. I want you to look at yourself as you are now, and imagine yourself turning back into what you were. Your body will know what to do from there."

Zhong looked at her arm covered in coarse brown fur, her elongated knobby fingers tipped with wicked claws, and gasped in horror. The image of herself shattered, and she was overcome with what she had lost, and what she had become. She tried to cry, but all that came out was a series of whining barks. A clawed paw grasped her arm and she looked up into a pair of green eyes gazing at her in sympathy. She gave Zhong a little encouraging nod, and Zhong took a deep breath, fixed herself in her mind, and willed herself into the girl that she was. There was blinding, cramping pain as *things* shifted around in her body. She could feel parts and pieces fall off of her, while others retreated back into her body with intense itching sensations. After what seemed an eternity of pain, but was probably only a couple of minutes, she found herself sitting, panting from exertion and naked, in the middle of the forest covered in sweat and forest detritus.

She looked up and saw Lyr sitting across from her, also naked. "Welcome, Sister," she said.

* * * * *

Dawn found us, dressed again, sitting around our campfire. Changing always left us tired and drained, but at least we wouldn't feel the moons' pull as strongly over the next couple of days. I looked over at Zhong. "You know we are the most vulnerable, the most *human*, after we change." I drew my belt knife, and drew the edge across my palm, gashing it. I held my hand up to her, so she could see the blood running down in rivulets. "It will take about a week before we will start healing and regenerating like we normally can, and a month before we'll have built up our reserves enough to be able to Change again. And that's *if* we can eat enough. If we can't then it can take longer." Zhong nodded somberly, and I continued. "Demonstrating your Other form is the first step of your journey. Now, you must learn the discipline to properly control Her. Discipline and control must be your mantra going forward if you want to survive. It will be a constant struggle for control with your Other, and if you lose control to Her and stay in that shape too long, you can lose yourself completely. Zhong will die, and the only thing left will be the Monster. Understand?" She nodded, and I clapped my hands. "Good! Now, we'll wait here for a couple of weeks, then explore that mine and make sure there are no more of those monstrosities lurking about. Try not to get eaten next time, all right?"

* * * * *

One Month Later

The cart creaked along slowly, wheels squeaking, even though its burden was light. Astrid rode in the back. A couple of poles, as thick around as her arm, rode with her. When they got to their destination the poles would be driven into the ground, and she would be lashed to them, an unwilling sacrifice to the Monster that lived in the dark. A quartet of guards walked alongside the cart, with Kai driving. They couldn't risk their sacrifice escaping. Seig marched with them, staff in hand, and a self-satisfied smirk on his face. That smirk slowly dissolved when they reached their destination. Three women sat on their horses facing them. One, long and lean, held a bow, arrow nocked, in her hand. Not one of the three looked happy.

The one that had done all the talking earlier leaned over in her saddle, arms resting on the pommel. "Are you happy to see us?" Her voice could have frozen a river.

Kai froze for a second, then forced himself to relax. "Why, hello!" he said, smiling as wide as he could. "I'm surprised to see you here! Did you find the mine? Or did you end up sheltering somewhere else? And why are you still in the area?"

The leader smiled thinly, but the smile didn't reach her eyes. "Oh, we found the mine all right. We also found out what lives there. And its brood. They didn't survive the experience, unfortunately."

At this, Seig exploded. "You lie! No mortal can kill a Handmaiden of Odin! Only a witch, or a sorcerer of Loki can kill a Chosen of Odin! He decrees you must pay the price, and so you shall!" He gestured grandly at the guards. "Kill them!"

Kai half stood up in the cart. "No! Wai..!" but it was too late.

The second the command left Seig's lips, Yusi drew and fired. A feathered shaft materialized between Seig's eyes, and he dropped like his legs had been cut out from under him. The four guards charged on foot, and Lyr spurred her horse at them, drawing her sword.

It was over in seconds. Kai closed his eyes, and opened them again to find Lyr's sword pressing against his throat, the hot blood that used to belong to his fellow villagers coating the blade and wafting into his nostrils. "It was your notion to send us to our deaths, was it not?"

Kai nodded, ever so slightly. "I saw a chance to save one of my people, so I took it."

"And yet, here you are," Lyr replied, her icy gaze flicking to Astrid and then fixating back on Kai.

Kai swallowed nervously, his Adam's apple making painful contact with the tip of Lyr's sword. "Olaf Gundersson found it, right before it ate him, the poor old bastard. Seig's grandfather, who was the priest at the time, declared it a sign from Odin. He was the one that came up with the idea of sacrifices to appease Odin. We were allowed to substitute prisoners captured in raids, in the beginning. It wasn't until Seig became priest that he insisted on using our own people, specifically our young women. Our village is dying because of it, but Seig had the support of the warriors and the more superstitious among us. I couldn't defy him and keep my place as headman."

Lyr barked a short, unamused laugh. "Nice story. However, I don't really give a..." and she tensed, about to thrust.

"Wait!" Lyr halted at the sound of Astrid's cry. She looked over at the young woman, standing up in the cart, clasping her hands, until her knuckles were white from squeezing the blood from them. "If you kill him, I'll never get to see my mother again," she sobbed softly.

"Is this true?" Lyr asked Kai.

He nodded frantically, willing to grasp at any lifeline, no matter how threadbare. "Technically, she's already dead, at least in the eyes of many of the villagers. They might consider her to be one of Odin's Valkyries come back to Earth. They wouldn't want anything to do with her, and probably wouldn't even open the gates to her. You'll need me."

Lyr stared him in the eyes for the longest moment, then withdrew her sword a hair. "No matter. I can always kill you later."

* * * * *

"Hallo the gate!" I called cheerily from the bed of the cart. I was standing there, Kai in front of me with his hands bound in front of him. Yusi, Zhong, and Astrid stood on the ground next to us, holding the horses. We were well out of bowshot range. Heads poked cautiously over the wall, then popped up farther like a savannah ferret's in surprise when they saw us. "Your turn," I murmured to the traitorous bastard standing in front of me, poking him lightly in the back with my dagger.

Kai gulped. "Open the gate! Astrid and these two fine young ladies are going to collect Solveig and some of their things and then they'll be on their way! I'll just wait right here until they come back out!" he called.

"Are you sure, headman? Do you need us to come get you?"

Before Kai could respond, I jabbed my dagger in his back, a little harder this time. "Be very careful how you answer that question," I warned.

He frantically shook his head. "No! Everything's fine! Hurry up!"

The guard shrugged, and motioned at someone on the ground. The gate started cranking open. My trio disappeared inside.

"They're prime examples of warriors," I said sarcastically. "No wonder you're sacrificing little girls."

Kai's face turned as red as an apple. "Mind your manners," he hissed. "One word from me and those gates will shut, trapping your girls inside. I wouldn't wager too much on their chances after that."

I twisted his collar in my fist, choking him. "You'd die first, remember? Also remember that we're the ones that killed that worm, something your whole village couldn't do. Your warriors would barely slow Yusi down, and I could climb that wall of yours in a flash. Nobody in there would like what would happen next." I poked him again with my dagger to make my point. He shut up after that.

Fifteen minutes later, the gang returned, Astrid and who I presumed was Solveig in front, carrying their meager possessions in a pair of burlap bags with Yusi and Zhong following behind. Solveig was large, taller and wider than me, with a blocky muscularity that her rough woolen dress failed to disguise. Her sky-blue eyes were framed by a wide, round face roughened by wind and work. She stumbled along in a graceless shamble, those blue eyes vacant with shock. First, she was absolutely sure that her daughter was dead, then that same daughter comes back from the dead, and convinces her to leave everything she ever knew behind. Almost anybody would have a hard time adjusting. I muscled Kai out of the cart and onto the ground. Solveig's eyes snapped onto him. Her face quivered a little, and then her ham-like fist cocked back and slammed him in the face. I chuckled. Apparently Solveig had some fire in her.

Kai flopped onto the ground, clutching his broken nose with his bound hands. As he rolled around on the ground, I cut the nag free from the cart and helped Astrid and Solveig onto him. I swung up onto Red and looked down at Kai. "Don't try to follow us. You wouldn't like the consequences. We'll turn this bag of bones loose once we're safely away. It should make its way back to you."

"What are you planning on doing with them?" Kai managed to spit out.

"I'm going to give them something you never did," I replied. "A choice." With that, I clucked to Red, and turned him south. We needed horses, and Fenrir was still out there.

A Haunting at the Herder's Bazaar

"Does that sky look like snow to you?" Liam asked anxiously. He was a slight man with a nervous manner whose fine orange hair had started to desert the top of his head some years ago and relocate south to form a fringe around the side of his skull. It then morphed into a set of muttonchop sideburns and a big, bushy, orange mustache. He was the owner and proprietor of the general mercantile store in the sleepy little town called the Herder's Bazaar, and it was about time for the herds with their herders that were the lifeblood of this town to make their migration from their summer pastures in the north to their southern winter pastures.

His wife, Maeve, always the calm pragmatic one, cast a practiced eye at the slate gray sky that seemed pregnant with anticipation. She stepped outside onto the porch and inhaled deeply. The air, colder than it had been just a day before, scratched her sinuses and tickled her throat and lungs. If she squinted she could almost see the crystalline snowflakes start to form. She went back inside. "Any day now," she said confidently.

Liam rubbed his hands briskly together in excitement. "Excellent!" Then he paused. "I hope they don't tear the town up too much this time," he said, worried again.

* * * * *

It was raining again, and I tilted my head up briefly, letting it hit my face. It was colder than it had been, cold enough to start being dangerous. I glanced behind me. Solveig was huddled miserably atop Red at the moment, while Astrid was shivering on top of Yusi's horse. Neither one of them was outfitted correctly for a life on the road, something I was going to have to fix soon, before one or both of them caught their death. I sighed and removed my slicker, then slowed my pace a little. As Red drew abreast of me, I handed my coat to Solveig. For a second she acted like she wasn't going to take it, but at a stern look from me, her will crumbled and she put it on, sighing gratefully as she was now protected from the rain, and warmed a little from the residual heat of me wearing the jacket.

"But what about you?" she asked. "Won't you freeze now?"

I shook my head. "Not as bad. We're built a little differently than you and Astrid." Our bodies had access to magnitudes more energy resources than theirs did. We could generate a lot more body heat to keep warm than a typical human.

"Do you know if there's a settlement nearby?" I asked. "We need to get you and Astrid properly outfitted for traveling or you're going to be well and truly miserable."

Solveig deliberated silently for so long I was beginning to worry that I had broken her brain, until she finally spoke. "I think there's a village somewhere to the northeast of us. I remember Gunnar telling me about it. It was a target for raids in the past. He said something about there were good times and bad times to raid this settlement, but I can't remember why."

"Hmm. Well let's head that way and find out why."

* * * * *

Chyanne was mucking out Prince's stall when her brother, Adriano strode into the barn. Tall and athletic, with the grace of someone who had spent most of his life in the saddle, he had broad shoulders, a mane of wavy brown hair and bright hazel eyes. Having had to listen to her girlfriends gush about him many, many times in the past, she knew he was considered handsome, gorgeous even. Unfortunately, in Chyanne's opinion, his personality really messed that attractiveness up.

He leaned on the gate and watched her fork more shit into the wheelbarrow. "The nomads should be traveling through here, soon. When they get here, I'm going to be looking for a husband for you."

Chyanne dumped her forkful of crap in the wheelbarrow. The urge to stab him with it was almost overpowering. "You're not in charge of the ranch yet, and Da would never allow me to be married to anyone I didn't want to be married to."

Adriano's lips pulled back from his gums in an impressive sneer. "You don't have to remind me that he always doted on you. But he's slipping away fast. Soon he'll be gone and then neither of you will have a say." With that, he spun on his heel and left.

Chyanne stood there for a full minute, her hands twisting on the handle of the pitchfork over and over, shaking in fury. Dropping her fork, she went to saddle Prince. She needed a ride to clear her mind, and Prince needed the exercise.

Adriano swore as Chyanne burst from the yard, her stallion running flat out.

"That girl's sure enough a firecracker," a voice rasped beside him.

Adriano cast a sidelong look at Dougal, the ranch foreman and the one who had spoken.

"She'll calm down quick enough with a wedding crown on her head and a couple of babies in her belly," he replied.

Dougal nodded and spat a stream of tobacco juice on the ground. "I 'spect. You got anyone in mind?"

Adriano shrugged. "One of the Nomads will do the job well enough."

Dougal looked a little startled. "Nomads, huh? The Boss won't like that. You know how he adores her. He always wanted her to get married and settled down here on the ranch."

Adriano grimaced. "Don't remind me. But Da's not going to be around forever. When he's gone, look to your hole card, Dougal, and remember who's going to be in charge."

* * * * *

The rain had stopped a couple of days ago, but though dryer, the temperature had plummeted. Now the sky held a promise of something else in the air. Solveig looked up at the leaden sky. "Smells like snow," she commented.

"Snow?" I was a little startled. I thought back. The last time I had seen snow... When I was ten, a rare winter storm had blown through Newar's streets. For one wondrous day, the city had been covered in a clean white blanket. The city had reasserted itself quickly, though. After a day, soot from thousands of chimneys had turned the white a dirty gray. That had to have been... sixty years ago, I'd guess. "Well, in that case, Solveig, let's pick up the pace a little and find that town of yours. None of us are outfitted correctly for that kind of weather."

We arrived in town as the first flakes of snow began swirling down. The town was a random collection of buildings mostly built along one main street. In the middle of the street there was a well. The street had been widened all around the well, forming a courtyard of sorts. The buildings were all of wood, and for some reason the walls facing the street were taller than the other walls. It made them look grander, I supposed. A raised boardwalk had been built in front of all the buildings so the residents wouldn't have to tromp through the muddy street on a regular basis. Posts stood out in front of every building so you could tie up your horses. There seemed to be about half a dozen places dedicated to selling just alcohol, a couple of inns, and three or four general stores, judging from the signs.

We stopped in front of the nearest store and tied our horses off. There was a magnificent black stallion, probably one of the prettiest I had ever seen already tied off. The other girls piled into the store, but Yusi and I paused to watch the snow swirling down. For some reason I couldn't explain fully, watching the individual flakes swirl down filled me with anticipation and excitement.

"I've never seen snow before," Yusi said in wonder.

"This is only my second time," I murmured. "The first was in an entirely different life."

When we finally entered the store, we walked into a welcome wall of heat. A strange contraption built entirely of iron was placed as close to the middle of the room as possible without impeding progress to the goods. Astrid, Solveig, and Zhong were huddled eagerly around it holding their hands out. The only other customer in the store looked on with amusement. She was of average height, with pale, pale skin, midnight black hair, and eyes so blue they seemed to glow. She wore brown leather pants the color of chocolate that hugged her figure, boots of the same color that reached almost to her knees, a black leather vest and white long sleeved linen shirt. I'd wager from the casual way she was standing there that she was a regular customer, and I'd also have placed a bet that that magnificent horse out front was also hers. She was standing in front of a counter that ran almost the whole length of the store. Standing behind the counter was a twitchy little man whose fiery orange hair seemed to have migrated from the top of his head to frame his face. I assumed that was the owner.

Before I could say anything or introduce myself, I heard the sound of galloping horses approaching like a roll of thunder, accompanied by whooping, shrieking, and hollering. The girl curled her lip in disgust, leaned against the store counter, and just waited. The sound of hard-soled boots thudding against the boardwalk towards the store made me and Yusi move over to the side of the door into some convenient shadows that pooled there. We had no wish to get run over. My hand came to rest on the pommel of my sword, however, in case this invasion wasn't friendly. The owner's twitchiness seemed to increase, which I wouldn't have believed possible, but there was an eagerness there, also, so I assumed everything was going to be alright.

Four men burst in wearing strange woolen skirts that reached down to their knees. The dresses were dyed a muted blue color with burgundy and green lines woven through it, making a unique pattern of squares. They also wore wool hats in the same pattern as their dresses where one side flopped over the side of their head. They were loud and boisterous, one in particular, and his eyes lit on Astrid, who had ignored the four men and was still bent over, warming her hands. His eyes lit up with a mischievous gleam and he walked over and smacked her on her ass, hard. She jerked up with a shriek, then turned and punched him in the chest as hard as she could.

"Hey! Don't touch me, you pig!" she said.

He laughed, obviously not hurt, and enfolded her in a great hug, squeezing her hard, and trapping her arms between them. "Don't be like that, little darling. I can see you're new here. Let me take you out, feed you up a little, and show you the sights." His friends laughed also, and one of them started towards Zhong. The glacial Look of Death she shot him stopped him in his tracks. Smart man. And the fact that Zhong wasn't afraid to stand up for herself made me proud. I took the temperature of the room in an instant. Solveig was standing there, frozen and mute, with her big hands clenched into fists. The girl by the counter looked angry but resigned, like this sort of thing was normal, and the shop owner just looked scared.

"Let her go." I sunk a lot of steel into that command.

He looked up from the struggling Astrid and noticed me for the first time. He looked me up and down, then sneered. "I would say wait your turn, darling, but you're not my type. Maybe one of these gentlemen here would be willing to accommodate you, but I'd doubt it."

I didn't waste any more time talking. Some people only understand one language. I stepped up and smacked him on the back of the head, hard, knocking his cap off of his head. There are some people that nothing infuriates them more than a good smack, and I was guessing this guy belonged in that category.

He did. He let go of Astrid and turned to face me, his hand raised, and his features twisted in anger. I didn't wait for that hand to fall. I gave him one hard jab in the teeth with my left hand, and followed it up with a short, brutal hook to his jaw with my right. He went down like he'd been clubbed. He was lucky I pulled my punch. I could have shattered his jaw without effort. Instead he only lost a couple of teeth. A fair trade.

The other men looked at me in shock. "D'ye know what ye've done? Ye've struck one of the Gwynedd!"

"His momma should have raised him to treat women better. No means no, boys. He's lucky he's not sucking his food through a straw for the rest of his life. Now, pick him up and get him out of here."

"And if we decide to teach you a lesson instead?" he sneered.

I raised an eyebrow. "It'll take more than the three of you. Now leave, before I raise those skirts of yours, paddle your behinds like your parents should have done, and make you my bitches, you dress wearing sissies."

They started forward anyway, but the sound of a spear butt thunking onto the floor brought them up cold. Yusi had just admonished them that she had a spear out and ready for use. They glared at us. They weren't scared, but they knew that if they escalated the situation, someone was going to get killed, likely one of them. Instead they hoisted their comrade's limp body up and half dragged him out of the store.

I walked over to the counter. The little shopkeeper looked even more scared, if that was possible. "You hit one of the Gwynedd," he said.

I shrugged. "Couldn't have been the first time."

"That was a very foolish thing to do," he insisted. "They will retaliate, you know."

"Well, then, you had better fix us up with what we need so we can be on our way before they get back, now shouldn't you?" I looked over at the other customer. "Was he helping you first?"

She shook her head, still grinning from all the entertainment I had just provided her. "Nope. I just finished. You go right ahead."

I purchased winter clothes, long oilskin jackets like what Yusi, Zhong, and myself had for Astrid and Solveig, as well as a sword, knife, hand ax, and spear apiece for them. It was time they started learning to defend themselves. It relieved me of a goodly amount of the gold I had brought with me all the way from Serenity. I was going to have to start budgeting, or we were going to have to find some way to make money if this continued. As we were heading out the door to our horses, a finger tapped my shoulder. I looked behind me into the blue eyes of the girl.

"You know, old Liam wasn't wrong. It won't be long until those boys round up some more of their friends to come hunting to teach you a lesson. I have a ranch just to the south of here. I would be delighted to offer you a place to stay out of sight for a bit and treat you to a bit of supper."

I smiled at her. "Why, that sounds really nice. I haven't had a meal in forever that one of us hasn't cooked." I held out my hand. "I'm Lyr. What's your name?"

She grabbed my hand and shook it vigorously. "Chyanne. Chyanne Campbell."

The ranch turned out to be half a dozen buildings of varying sizes surrounded by a timber wall. Fenced paddocks were randomly strewn about outside the wall, that obviously usually contained whatever stock they had, but were conspicuously empty at the moment. Yusi and I were riding double on poor Red next to Chyanne while Solveig and Astrid were astride Yusi's horse. I hated to use the horses like this, but I was assured it was a short ride and Chyanne wanted to get us out of sight before the men of Gwynedd got organized.

"Why are all the paddocks empty right now?" I asked.

Chyanne shrugged. "We always pull the horses in when the clans come through in the fall and the spring. There's less chance of unfortunate incidents involving a clan 'accidentally' gathering up our stock with theirs. I'm not implying that it has or would happen, just that it could."

I nodded. "Makes sense."

We rode through the open gates into a spacious, hard packed dirt yard. Chyanne jumped down from her stallion, Prince, and ran to close the gates. Yusi jumped off of Red, allowing me to dismount and I ran over to give her a hand. We maneuvered the heavy gates shut, and put the locking bar into place.

"There! That ought to do it," Chyanne said with satisfaction.

I noticed movement out of the corner of my eye and turned my head to catch it fully. A man was stalking towards us. He was tall, with wavy brown hair partially captured by one of those wool caps. He moved with assuredness and grace and I paused for a moment to enjoy the view. "Who is that?" I asked.

Chyanne scowled. "My brother, Adriano."

Adriano crashed to a halt before us, his brows drawn together in anger. "Chyanne! How many times do I have to tell you to not race your horses out of the compound? Try to act with a little decorum! How am I going to find you a husband with you acting like a wildcat all the time?" His gaze fell on me. "Who is this?" he demanded.

Chyanne linked her arm in mine. "This is my guest, Lyr. She and her companions just rode into town and I invited them here to stay for a couple of days."

Adriano looked like he was about to explode. "How dare you? You don't know anything about them! They could be from a raiding party sent to gather information about us. Or whores looking to make quick money and distract our hands. Or any one of a number of sneaky things."

I stiffened at the whore comment, but before I could lay him out, Chyanne cut in. "I extended them Guest Right!"

"I could revoke it," Adriano replied hotly.

"You're not in charge brother. That authority is not yet yours. Shall I take this matter to Da?"

For a second there, I thought he might actually explode, then he turned on his heel and stalked off.

As he was walking away Chyanne leaned closer to me and said, "I'll bet you think he's good looking, don't you?"

I shook my head. "Not anymore."

Dinner turned out to be an all inclusive affair, with both family, hands, and servants gathered around three large tables. I thought it was going to be awkward, but Adriano managed to be civil. The head of the house and Adriano's and Chyanne's father, Cian, was even wheeled out to join us. His mind was spotty. Sometimes it was here in the present, and sometimes it wandered in the corridors of his past. Still in all, it was a pleasant time for everyone, with a lot of jovial banter being traded around the table between the Campbell employees. Adriano and Chyanne also joined in, the exchanges managing to humanize Adriano. Chyanne gave as good as she got, her quick, tart, verbal ripostes displaying an agile mind and fiery nature. There was steel in that one, all right.

After dinner we were shown to the barracks that housed all the unmarried female workers. We each settled into unclaimed bunks and turned in for the night.

* * * * *

Llewellyn, Chief of Clan Gwynedd, sat astride his horse, surrounded by his sub-chiefs, and gazed at the town with an acquisitive eye. This was the next step, he thought with a certain amount of satisfaction. The first step had been hammering all of his family members' clans and family groups into one cohesive tribe that dominated the summer grazing grounds, and by the time he was done, he would have a kingdom of the north. Maybe, someday, he would be able to challenge both Dragon and Primus far to the south for dominance, with all the rich grazing lands that came with it.

"Let's get this started. Call them out," he told his herald, Conor.

Conor nodded, and lifted his horn to his lips. Taking a deep breath, he blasted out a brassy challenge. And again. And again. Slowly the townsfolk began shuffling out, wondering what all the noise was about.

"Hear ye, hear ye!" Conor bawled. "We are pleased to once again enjoy the warm embrace of your town. However, this year, the Clan Gwynedd will not be trading with you. Instead, we will require a tribute of ten percent of your goods and services. In recompense for this, you will enjoy our protection from the other clans, or any raiders or other outside forces. That will be all!"

* * * * *

Dew kissed the grass of the field outside of Campbell's walls, and light tendrils of fog danced over the grass. Chyanne was planning on taking us on a tour of their operation, and, more importantly, showing us her horses. If Prince was representative of what the farm produced, I fully expected the others to be equally outstanding. But, we got interrupted, and were now hanging out just inside the gates, which had just been opened. A group of men were waiting on horses just outside of bow range. Adriano and a couple of Campbell retainers had stepped out to meet them.

"Good morning," he said pleasantly, holding his arms out wide in greeting. "Who might I have the pleasure of speaking with?"

"My name is Nechtan, of the Clan Gwynedd," the apparent leader of this small group said.

"Welcome, Nechtan. Have you perhaps come to parley for some horses? You know we have the finest breeding stock anywhere around."

Nechtan shook his head. His horse moved under him impatiently, and he calmed it with a touch of the reins. "We will do no trading. As we have told the town, as the dominant clan on the plains here, we now expect tribute of ten percent the value of your horses in either coin, stock, or some combination thereof."

I couldn't see Adriano's face from where we stood, but I could read his body language easily enough. He stiffened in shock and anger, then slowly his stiff posture relaxed into a semblance of his normal stance. He brought a hand up to his chin, and thought. "Would a brokered marriage with a bride price also be acceptable?"

Chyanne gasped in outrage and would have marched out there, but I grasped her arm firmly, and held her in place. "Quiet!" I hissed. "Let's see how this plays out."

Nechtan thought for a second and said, "If the bride price is deemed acceptable, then a marriage in lieu of tribute can probably be arranged. Not that it matters, but it might generate more interest among the clan if we knew what the bride looked like."

Adriano looked back and gestured peremptorily to Chyanne. She shook her head and would have refused, but I gave her a little push. "It's all right," I said. "I won't let anyone do anything to you that you don't want to do. But we have to play the game right now, so your brother stays relaxed and happy. If he starts to get suspicious, he'll watch all of us more closely."

Chyanne thought about it, then nodded. I let her go, and she slowly edged out past the gate. She was a stunning woman, and Nechtan nodded in approval.

"Aye, she'll do," he said.

Afterwards, Chyanne and I walked around the property. Yusi followed closely behind us, my own silent shadow. "Is this Clan Gwynedd thing new?" I asked.

Chyanne nodded. "Aye. Before now, they were just one of the many Nomad families. They all traded with us, same as the other clans. They weren't anything special."

"Where are the other clans?"

She shrugged. "They'll be along. They're most likely in pastures further north. It'll take them a little longer to get here, that's all. Gwynedd themselves will be moving south into fresh pastures as soon as they complete their little deal," she scowled at the thought.

I pondered for a moment. "I think I might have a solution to your problem," I said, grinning.

* * * * *

Zhong was in a foul mood as she and Yusi disrobed for their assignment that night. She looked up at the rope that was still dangling down the outside of the wall. She only hoped that it would still be there when they got done.

"I don't know why it has to be us," she grumbled. "Why can't her High and Mighty do this instead?" then gasped as a pair of Yusi's fingers latched onto her ear, and twisted, hard.

"If you want to live a long and fruitful life, you will never utter those words around another Sister again. One of the older ones would kill you quick as thought for such disrespect," she hissed.

"I understand! Please forgive me," Zhong squeaked.

Yusi stared at her a little longer, then released Zhong's ear. She glared at Zhong until she was certain that Zhong was properly contrite, then relaxed a little.

"That's better. Now, to answer your question, Lyr is our reserve. If, in the unlikely event we are captured, it will be Lyr that will rescue us. If she were captured, we might fail. She won't, even if she has to slaughter the entirety of Clan Gwynedd in order to rescue us. Understand?" Zhong nodded and Yusi continued. "Plus, Lyr's Other would have far less patience with your disrespect than she does, and your control isn't that great. If her beast thought your beast was challenging her, you wouldn't survive the night, so be thankful."

Zhong nodded again, rubbing her ear, and Yusi clapped her on the shoulder. "Good! Now look at this as an exercise in Changing into your Other, followed by a good run."

The next morning it dawned calm and quiet. Adriano threw open the gates, then spent the greater part of the morning pacing around them, waiting for Clan Gwynedd's emissary to come claim their tribute. As the morning wore on, he became more and more nervous and angry. Finally, his patience snapped, and he strode off, looking for Chyanne. He found her in the stables. "Saddle Prince," he snapped. "And follow me."

* * * * *

They rode off, Adriano with Dougal and a couple of other retainers, and Chyanne. I rode with them. "This doesn't concern you," Adriano snapped at me.

I smiled beatifically. "I'm just along for the entertainment," I said.

Chyanne smirked at me. "Are you going to enjoy some entertainment, or are you the entertainment?"

I shrugged. "Whichever," I replied.

We arrived at the spot where Clan Gwynedd and their herds had encamped. Empty fields and wrecked tents greeted us. One hundred meters away, the entirety of Clan Gwynedd gathered. There seemed to be a lot of shouting and finger pointing going on.

"What's going on?" Adriano wondered.

"Looks to me like they're having a spirited discussion regarding the challenges and consequences of leadership decisions. They might even be talking about changing said leadership," I observed. "Very entertaining." I grinned widely.

"Looks like there will be no deal today, brother," Chyanne laughed.

"Then I will wait," Adriano snarled. "Today, tomorrow, or when another clan of unwashed Nomads comes, it makes no difference."

"And it makes no difference if I will it yea or nay," Chyanne murmured.

"None!" he snapped.

"What did I ever do to you, in this life or another, to make you hate me so?" she whispered.

"You're just in my way," he replied.

"Well! Let me fix that for you, brother!" she yelled, eyes glistening. She wheeled Prince around with a jerk and galloped off in the direction of her home.

"What does she think she's doing?" Adriano muttered.

"If I had to guess, I'd wager she's going to say goodbye to her father and start packing her things," I drawled.

He glared at me. "Over my dead body. Dougal! Patty! Fetch her back will ye? It's time and past she acknowledges my authority. Maybe a taste of the strap will change her attitude."

"Stand fast, boys," I warned.

Adriano sneered at me. "You have no authority here! After I teach her a lesson, mayhap I'll turn my attention to you. Go!" he snapped at them.

I spurred Red over to him, grabbed him by the throat, and half dragged him out of the saddle. "Hold!" I shouted, in a voice practiced in thirty years of barking orders at rebellious Sisters on the training grounds.

They stopped and looked to see me holding a dagger to Adriano's throat. "You've lost one Campbell already today. Don't make it two by being stupid." They carefully sat still, not wanting to make any sudden movements that might trigger me.

"See? I carry my authority with me, as far as my will extends," I told Adriano.

He struggled, without success. "Your fingers are like steel bands," he gasped. "What are you?"

I leaned down and breathed in his ear, "I'm all woman. Do you want to find out?" I purred throatily, licking his cheek playfully. I chuckled in delight as his eyes widened in fear and shock. Frantically he shook his head.

"That's all right. I prefer real men, and you're just a little boy playing at being a man. Don't let that little boy's ego drive you into losing more than you're already going to lose today," I growled, my humor vanishing in a blink.

* * * * *

Despite my bravado, I didn't breathe easier until we left the compound a couple of hours later, Chyanne mounted on Prince and with a dozen good brood mares and fillies following along behind her, her inheritance from her father. Solveig and Astrid were mounted on their own horses, so at least that problem was fixed. I had figured it was a fifty-fifty chance as to whether Adriano would stay cowed, or react badly with only me to handle it. Yusi and Zhong were spent, Astrid and Solveig were liabilities, not help, and I didn't know what Chyanne was capable of.

I hadn't needed to worry, though. When Cian learned of his son's brilliant plan, he hit the roof. In an apparently rare moment of clarity, he had rounded his hands up, reminded them he was still in charge, and proceeded to tear a long, bloody strip off of Adriano. At Cian's direction, the hands wrangled the horses that belonged to Chyanne, and he saw her off with a teary farewell, and an admonition to take care of herself. I think he knew that he couldn't protect her much longer and the best thing for her was to let her go.

Yusi and I moved into the lead with Chyanne. Zhong, Astrid, and Solveig kind of encircled the rest of Chyanne's horses, keeping them bunched.

"So, what's the plan? Where are we going?" Chyanne said once the ranch disappeared from sight.

"We continue our hunt," I replied.

"What are you hunting?"

"Monsters. We're hunting monsters like ourselves."

Chyanne snorted. "You're no more monsters than I am. Really, what are you hunting for?"

I chuckled. "Even so. We're hunting someone moving through the world, and where he goes, death and destruction follow. Have you heard any rumors of something like that? Families gone missing, villages slaughtered, anything like that?"

"All the time. But those are usually because of raids from other settlements. Hells, Dragon and Primus account for most of those, not monsters out of legend."

"Then I think we'll go south. Thanks anyway, Chyanne." Out of the corner of my eye I noticed one of the horses separating itself from the herd, and reined Red around to drive back into the bunch. Yusi followed me.

"Well," Yusi said to me as Chyanne turned south. "We managed to collect another one."

There was a strangely satisfied note to her voice, and I looked at her quizzically. "I suppose so," I said finally. We rode in silence for a while. "You know we're going to have to train everybody now, right?" I said. "There's too many for us to protect now, and Zhong, while her control is coming along, doesn't know how to actually fight."

Yusi smiled broadly. "We'll manage. We always do."

Shattered

We noticed the smoke first. It rose lazily into the air like black fingers trying to claw at the clouds in the sky and drag them to earth. "Halt," I called to our small column, and reined Red to a stop. I leaned on my saddle pommel and tried to think. Since our little foray in Chyanne's homeland, we had been bearing steadily south, trying to escape winter, as much as anything. The further south we went, the more time seemed to reverse, the early winter of the far north changing back into autumn. Despite the time pressure, we'd been traveling slowly, with lots of time spent weapons training, trying to hammer at least a basic knowledge of self-defense into the heads of people that never had to think of it before. Of them all, Solveig had been the biggest surprise. Apparently, she had been a member of the Homeguard back in her village, tasked with its defense while the men had been raiding. She already had a basic knowledge of how to fight. It was now a question of expanding on it.

"What do you think it means?" Astrid, who had been riding next to me, asked. It was a reflexive question. She knew. We all knew. She just wanted some reassurance, or for me to tell her that her supposition was wrong.

"Nothing good," I replied.

Yusi, who had been riding rearguard, came up next to us. "We're going over there, right?" she asked. "There may be people there who need our help."

I sighed. This was not a decision I wanted to make. "Everyone, stay here a moment. Zhong, keep a nose out will you? There's no telling who or what may be lurking around. Yusi, follow me." We rode away from the group until I was sure we were out of hearing range.

"This is a bad idea, Yusi. You know that, right? The only sure thing we know is that whatever is down there is going to be awful. We don't even know if there are survivors down there. There still might be soldiers hanging around looting and pillaging, or worse. Anything more than a platoon, you and I will have trouble dealing with."

"There's Zhong..." Yusi began.

"Zhong is learning fast, but she's still just a pup. Not only that, but she hasn't gone through the regimen like a normal Sister would have. Her loyalty is still questionable. Plus, she is a survivor, as in survive before all else. There's no guarantee that if things get dicey, she won't cut and run to save her own skin."

"What if we left the others here and just went down there ourselves?"

"They won't be any safer here. There's always foraging parties combing through the countryside, like fingers running through hair. If one of those found the girls, Zhong could get overwhelmed pretty easily. It wasn't that long ago that you both Changed. I'm not sure you could again so soon. The safest thing to do is give those places as wide a berth as possible. Don't forget, we still have our primary mission. We have to find Fenrir and eliminate him before he causes any more problems."

"But there may be children down there!" Yusi said, a desperate note in her voice.

"We can't save everyone!" I snarled. "We have to look to our own first before we can save anyone else. For all intents and purposes, it is just you and me right now."

Yusi took a deep breath, gathering her thoughts. "I love you, Mother, but sometimes your focus is a little narrow. There is no 'Us and Them'. There is just Us. One People. The only 'Them' are the ones that hurt those that are weaker than them. We have been given a gift, Mother. We should use it for good."

I closed my eyes and fumed for a moment. Unfortunately, Yusi had a valid point. "We'll ask the others. It's not fair for us to demand that they risk their lives against their will."

* * * * *

"So that's the whole of it," I said to the group. " We don't know what we'll find down there, but it will most likely be horrifying. The safest play would be to bypass this entirely and go somewhere else. Yusi however," and I smiled at her, "Thinks that if there's anybody down there that needs help, we should help them. Now, since we don't know who is down there, the danger level's high. I'm not going to put everyone's life in jeopardy without talking to them first. Who thinks we should leave, and who thinks we should try to help?"

Zhong shrugged. "It's not our problem. I think we should leave."

"I think we should see what we can do to help," Chyanne said, raising her hand.

"I agree with Chyanne and Yusi," Astrid said, very carefully not looking at Zhong.

"Solveig?" I asked.

She looked tired. "I remember once, before I was married, I saw the aftermath of a raid. It's going to be bad, young ones, really bad. I wouldn't want to wish those sights on any of you. Having said that, however, I wouldn't be able to sleep at night without giving solace to anybody that might have just lost everything."

Zhong looked mulish for a second, then sighed and nodded. "I'll go with the group."

"All right. Here's the plan. Yusi and I will scout ahead. You ladies hang back. If there's more soldiers there than we can handle we'll signal, so you can disengage and run away. We'll fight a delaying action if necessary. When we emerge onto that plain, no more unnecessary noise, got it?"

Although I was almost a century old, I had never seen the aftermath of a major battle. I had seen the aftermath of a group of marauders that had overwhelmed one of the tribes in the Lawless Lands more times than I would care to count. It was how the Sisters came into being after all. It was all the same. Only the extent of the wreckage differed. This hadn't been a major battle, merely a skirmish. But still.

Bodies of soldiers littered the battlefield outside of the village, swelling in the weak sun. Some of the village buildings were still smoldering. Nothing moved. We rode cautiously toward the village, weapons in hand. I tried sampling the air for any telltale scents, but the pall of woodsmoke drowned everything else out. Apparently the combatants' main bodies, at least, had left the area.

We rode through the village's main street, the horses' hooves sinking ankle deep in the churned mud. The human wreckage was everywhere. Men. Women. Children. The children especially were hard to look at, every wound inflicted on them a desecration. I dismounted from Red, my boots squelching in the mud. "Chyanne and Zhong, stay with the horses. Yusi, you go with Solveig, and I'll take Astrid. Let's start clearing houses. If anyone runs into any trouble, call out."

We went house to house, making sure that nobody was hiding and in need of help. There was no one. The dead ruled over this place. Then, at my direction, we stacked all the bodies in one of the bigger houses, piled it high with straw and whatever dry wood we could find, and lit it on fire. The soldiers' arms and armor we stripped off of the corpses and set aside. There was no telling when they might come in handy. As the bonfire blazed in the night, we stood, hand in hand, with heads bowed.

We were exhausted both emotionally and physically when we retired to the manor house, a silent and somber group. The house had been looted, but it was the only building in town where the miasma of death didn't linger. We had just finished nibbling on our rations when there was a pounding on the door. Sword in hand, I yanked open the portal and ended up looking cross-eyed at a spear thrust in my face. Behind it were a pair of furious chocolate eyes set in a dark brown face.

"Who are you, and what are you doing in My Lord's House?"

* * * * *

Her name was Winda, and she was a warden for the local excuse of a lord. Her job was to manage and keep track of the wild game that lived hereabouts, and keep the peasants from hunting them. Winda had been out in the forest, which is how she had been spared. She had managed to find and hide some people who had also been outside the village limits: some shepherds, farmers out in the fields on the other side of the village, away from the invaders, women gathering herbs and mushrooms in the forest, people like that. Twenty in all. She calmed down when she found out we weren't robbing the place, and had in fact taken care of all the victims, saving the survivors quite the chore, although some of them wouldn't have the closure of being able to say good-bye to loved ones. On the brighter side, their last memories could be happier ones, spared from seeing the ruin that their relatives had become in their final moments.

After everyone was settled, with some villagers at the bonfire, which was still burning brightly, holding their own remembrance ceremony, and others having retired to their own houses, I stepped outside to get some air and think. In the distance, wails, and cries of grief reached my ears, brought to me by the ever-so-helpful wind. Winda appeared next to me, materializing out of the darkness with Andrew, a shepherd and one of the five surviving men. Silently we stared at the orange glow from the bonfire in the distance.

"What's the plan now?" I asked.

Andrew and Winda looked at each other for a moment. "We rebuild and wait for Lord Rodrick's return," Andrew said.

"And when might that be?" I asked.

Winda shrugged. "Spring, maybe? Maybe he'll show up for a mid-winter hunt, or to get away from his wife and his responsibilities at court. We really don't know. This place is just his seasonal hunting lodge. The rest of the village are the year round caretakers. We exist at his pleasure."

"How wonderful," I said dryly. "How about you people? Are there enough stores set aside for you after this raid?"

Andrew looked somber. "They fired the granaries and took all of the cured meats. We have some cattle and sheep that were held away from the village proper that we can gather up, but those belong to milord, and we can't take too many of them. He won't begrudge us a few, but if we kill too many, he'll most likely take a whip to us."

Winda looked thoughtful. "There's the stores in the manor house cellars. We stocked almost half the harvest there. The soldiers didn't find those."

Andrew looked shocked. "Those belong to Lord Rodrick! They're the taxes from the harvest! If we touch them, he'll do more than whip us!"

"He would care more for those stores than his own people?" I asked.

Winda nodded slowly.

"Sounds like a real charmer," I said. "Without those stores, what are your chances of survival?"

"Assuming the soldiers from Dragon don't come back to finish the job in the first place? Not good," Winda said.

Andrew looked like he wanted to argue, but couldn't.

"Well, it sounds like you have a choice to make. You can do what you're supposed to, and most likely die, if not quickly by the sword and spear, then slowly through starvation or disease. Or you can do what you must to survive, and deal with Rodrick's displeasure some time in the future."

Andrew's features screwed up in displeasure. "*Lord* Rodrick. He's a baron," he said.

"He's not *my* lord. Let me know what you decide." With that I turned and went back into the manor house.

The next morning I stepped out to face the survivors. They seemed to be split, with Winda and the vast majority on one side, and four others standing on the other side, well apart. Andrew was in that group, as well as another man dressed in gray robes. A large yellow sun was emblazoned on his chest. The group of four looked less than happy.

Winda stepped forward. "We will do what we must to survive," she said.

"Good," I said. "Let's get to work."

I split everyone into teams. Winda I sent out to hunt with a couple of her fellows, Yaa, and Jakob, over the protests of the four overruled people. Astrid and Chyanne were placed in charge of butchering and smoking what was brought back. The vast majority of us I set to the backbreaking task of erecting earthwork fortifications around the town, again, against the protests of the minority. I ignored them. As it stood right now, you couldn't defend the village against a stiff wind, much less any invaders or even raiders from another settlement. The guy in the robes flat out refused when I told him to dig.

"Who are you, anyway?" I asked, holding onto my temper with difficulty.

"My name is Bard," he replied.

"And what do you do, Bard?"

He drew himself up proudly. "I am a priest of Apollo. My job is to ensure that there is a bountiful harvest, as well as tending to the emotional and spiritual needs of my flock."

I sighed. He was going to be difficult to deal with. "Fine. You can take inventory of all the foodstuffs, clothing, wood, etc. Anything we'll need to get through the winter. Bring the tallies back to me, along with a report of potential shortfalls."

"I don't take orders from a woman!" he shot back.

I leaned in closer to him. "If you don't work, you don't eat. And since my Sisters and myself are sitting on the largest cache of food in the village, we can make that stick. Your choice."

"Fine," he huffed, and flounced off.

And so began the laborious task of trying to save these people, with the small but vocal minority of people acting as millstones around our necks. We started by digging a trench around the entirety of the village and using the dirt to start constructing ramparts. Luckily for us, on the second day of our excavation, a group of refugees, thirty strong, from another village showed up. In contrast to our rather haphazard mixture of skin tones, these people were much more uniform in their color, all being a rich mahogany. I dropped the shovel I was using and strode out to meet them. They stopped en masse, their spokesman taking a half step forward and removing his cap, kneading it nervously.

"Hello," I said.

"Hello," he said diffidently. "Our village was attacked, much like yours. Only ours was razed to the ground. It was only by the Makers' own grace that we were away helping with Milord's harvest at his ancestral home. We came back to nothing but ashes. If we left right now, we might make it back to his home before winter sets in, but he doesn't have enough room to house us or food to keep us through the snows.

"We noticed the smoke from here, and started over here to see if maybe we can join you? We bring nothing but our strength, our skills, and a willingness to work as hard as we can to survive the coming winter."

"Yes," I said with relief. The amount of work I was envisioning with the amount of people we had was daunting, to say the least. "All are welcome."

"Wait!" I heard a voice behind me. I groaned inwardly and turned my head to see Bard come panting up behind me. "We have no desire to share our meager stores with outlanders. You must rebuild yourselves, as we are forced to do."

I raised an eyebrow at him. "Are these poor people not wayward sheep to tend to, much as you have described the people of this village?"

He shook his head stubbornly. "They are not of us," he declared.

"Fine," I snapped. I picked my shovel off of the ground and thrust it at him. "Then you can dig!"

He changed his mind. Things went more quickly after that, even with the extra pressure on the food stores. I sent more people out foraging and hunting. Nuts, mushrooms, and wild grains were found and stored, as well as more game being brought in. After we finished the trenching and ramparts, I determined that wasn't going to be sufficient. Luckily, there was a substantial grove of oak and maple trees close by. We were able to cut them down, drag them over, split them in half, set them in the trench we had just laboriously dug, and repack in the dirt we had just dug out. In the final analysis, we had a tiddly little wall by the end. Foraging and hunting continued apace, as we raced against the coming of the snow. Winda assured me that this area got plenty of snow in the winter time, even this far south.

We were able to house the new refugees easily in the remaining empty houses. My group stayed in the manor house, much to Bard's dismay. He had been living in a small church close to the manor house, but I got the impression he would have preferred to move up in the world, so to speak, and move into the manor himself. One night, after dinner and having cleaned up after a long day of playing in the mud, Yusi and I were lounging by the fire.

"So, what's the plan?" she asked me.

"For a change, I really don't have one. I don't know how long we're staying, or how much responsibility I have to take for this group of virtual strangers. Despite the tragedy they've just experienced, they're already in a better position than they were just a week ago, despite risking their lord's ire. I have the Sisters to think of as well as finding Fenrir and dealing with him. The longer I'm away, the more chances things have to go wrong back in Sanctuary and Serenity. Plus, Alex and the rest of the Sisters are probably worried about us being gone so long. How much time can I really spare here?"

"I don't know the answer to that. And there's another thing to consider. Fenrir may be making more monsters as we speak. As it stands, there is only you, me, and Zhong to deal with that. Even if we find him, how are we going to deal with him, just the three of us?" Yusi asked softly.

I heaved a big sigh. "I don't know," I said heavily.

She took a deep breath, and said carefully, "You might want to think about making some more Sisters while we are here, since we're likely to be stuck here for a while. There's a promising group of people out there, surely a few of them could pass the Trials. I have a premonition that we could use more help."

I didn't like that idea at all. I hated making more Sisters, and only did it as a last resort. Back at home, it was under controlled conditions away from any outsider's prying eyes, and the candidates knew what they were getting into. I didn't like setting more monsters loose in this world.

"It's a risk. You never know how people will react when they find out our secret. The plan this whole time was that we would keep a low profile. That we would be safer hidden."

Yusi nodded. "I know. But have you thought about what would happen if we find him and fail? How long until the Sisters find out what happened to us, if ever? Or find him again? How much damage can he do in the meantime?"

I sighed. "You have a good point. We have to start training all the able-bodied to defend themselves soon, anyway. We'll see if there are any good candidates then." It would have to be done with delicacy. We would have to make friends, recruit, make sure they were more loyal to us than to the people they had lived their entire lives with. I'm not sure it was even possible.

We started weapons training the very next morning. I had the first group of men and women assembled, holding staffs that would serve as spears until they learned the basics. One of the men raised his hand, trying to get my attention.

"Yes, Dip?" I asked.

"Why are there women here? Women have no place in combat," he said.

"You do know that you're talking to a woman, right? One that is about to start training you how to fight?" I replied.

He shrugged, his expression making it clear that he didn't think I should be fighting, either.

"Tell you what, why don't you, Babur, Farid, and Govinda try to defeat me? Let's not damage each other too much, so a light tap on a vital organ will count as a kill. I'll give you a minute to strategize."

They stood in a circle, talking animatedly while I waited. Then, as one, they rushed me, staffs raised, trying to take me off guard. I dove to the side, rolling to my feet in one fluid movement. This put me behind them, and to one side, and I took advantage, jabbing Govinda in the ribs, putting him down. The other three faced me, stabbing wildly with their staffs. I danced around, tapping their tips out of line, keeping them from touching me, until I could work to one side of them. Instantly, I knocked Farid's staff into the two others, tangling them up, and opening up Farid's side. I stabbed him in the stomach, hard, then pushed him further into the other two with my staff, knocking them off balance. I stepped behind the other two, jabbed Babur in the kidney, then whacked Dip on the back of his head. All three went down, howling in pain and rubbing at their affected body parts.

"Well, Dip? Did we learn anything today?"

He nodded. "At least one woman can fight."

"Do you want me to set you up against Yusi? Or Solveig maybe?"

He thought about it a moment, then shook his head.

"Congratulations! You can be taught!" I said. "Now, get in line. Let's begin."

We trained in rotations for a month while off-rotation groups continued with hunting, foraging, and otherwise prepping for winter. We taught them how to use spear, knife, and sword. How to properly form a shield wall, and fight as a team, both in large groups, and in trios and pairs. They had gotten to the point where I was no longer afraid they were accidentally going to stab themselves or their companions. Several of the men, as well as some of the women like Solveig, Winda, and Yaa were turning into decent soldiers, ones that could hold their own against regular infantry. Chyanne, while competent dismounted, was much better astride a horse. I'm sure she would make an excellent scout and cavalry officer, but I didn't know anything about cavalry tactics, something I would have to rectify.

I was still no closer in trying to figure out how to broach the subject of letting potential candidates learn our secrets, but that problem got solved for me. On a cold star-filled night of the first full moons, Yusi and I took Zhong out away from the village, ostensibly on a scouting foray. We tied our horses to some brush and continued away on foot, putting distance between us and the horses. We built a fire and sat cross-legged, preparing ourselves.

"Now, Zhong, you've never actually experienced normal full moons. You Changed before they rose the first time, and you and Yusi had recently Changed before the second rising, when you scattered the Gwynedd clan's herds. It didn't have the same pull on you as it will tonight. So think of this as an exercise in control. The moons will test you tonight, trying to call you to Change. Don't let them."

Zhong took a deep breath and nodded.

I smiled encouragingly. "Good. Let us begin. Close your eyes. Empty your mind. Focus on your breathing. In, and out. In, and out." Yusi and I mirrored her, focusing on our breathing, sinking into a meditative trance, letting the moments wash by. When I opened my eyes, Artemis was breaking over the horizon.

"Open your eyes, Zhong," I whispered.

She slowly opened her eyes, and gazed in wonder at the moon. "She sparkles," she breathed.

"Yes she does. Do you feel her pull?" Zhong nodded. "Resist it. Focus on your breathing. Your instincts will tell you it's time to Change. Push that thought down. You are the one that's in control, not your instincts." Zhong nodded again, breathing deeper, trying to achieve calm.

She did pretty well as Artemis continued her hunt across the night sky, until Change'e chose to rise. The prettier of the two sisters, she rose in her dress of many colors; pink, purple, green and blue in pastel hues. White veils of higher clouds scuttled across her face. I held my breath. This was the moment of truth. Change'e exerted a strong influence on us. Even experienced Sisters such as Yusi and myself felt her pull like a drug. Zhong stared at her, transfixed.

"Zhong!" I said urgently. "You must fight Change'e's wiles. She is the seducer. Let her call wash over you and pass you by. I know the urge is strong. You must fight it!"

Zhong stared, unable to tear her eyes away. Her breathing deepened, quickened. She began to shake violently, a thin tendril of blood starting to wend its way out of her nostril.

"Shit!" I spat, jumping to my feet as she fell to the ground, convulsions wracking her frame. "Get ready," I told Yusi unnecessarily, who had already jumped to her feet, hand on her honor dagger. Zhong's hair fell out as coarse, short black fur grew in its place, covering her entire body. Her feet lengthened and elongated, turning into a wolf's hocks while her toes also grew, sprouting wicked claws, perfect for finding purchase on the earth. Fingers and arms also grew longer. Zhong's body thickened, adding 25 kilograms of muscle in what seemed like an instant. Her clothes ripped apart along the seams and fell cleanly off of her. Her nostrils and mouth lengthened and enlarged, forming a short muzzle, creating more room for her predator's fangs to burst through her gums. She finished changing and rolled to her feet, giving herself a quick shake and stared at me, eyes glowing slightly in the moons' light. I tensed, but waited. It was important to remain calm. Any sign of fear could result in an attack.

"It's all right, Zhong. We'll try it again next month," I said quietly.

She looked at me a moment longer, then turned and dashed off into the night, away from the village. I let out the breath I had been holding, and looked at Yusi. "Yet another tense full moons. Come on, let's follow her; make sure she's not going to get into any trouble." We started off at an easy jog, tracking her by scent and light. We found her three miles away. She had brought down an elk and was busy tearing at its corpse. We stopped, giving her plenty of distance, and settled down to wait. A slight rustle in the underbrush made us jump right back up again, hands on our weapons. Winda stepped out of the concealing shadows. We all stared at each other, unsure of what to do while Zhong fed.

"Who are you people?" she breathed.

I paused, gathering my thoughts, torn between the need to keep our secrets, and the overwhelming urge to explain things before Winda panicked and ran away screaming, triggering an unmitigated disaster. The urge won out, and I took a deep breath, before launching into an explanation.

"We are the products of a weapons program the Makers made before The Fall," I began. "They were trying to develop a perfect covert operative. Someone who looked human, could pass through an enemy's security system, yet be fast, strong, incredibly resistant to damage, with heightened senses, appear unarmed, yet make their own weapons when needed. I was changed by one of the original generation, and I made the Sisters, two of whom you see before you. Why don't you sit down next to us and wait? It'll be safer for you."

Winda slowly and carefully stepped over and sat down next to us. "Don't make any sudden movements, and keep your voice to a whisper. Zhong is still new, and her control isn't the best, especially tonight."

"I think she's wondrous," Winda murmured.

"That's not the reaction most people have when face to face with a Sister in her Other form," I chuckled softly.

"What happened to the others? The ones that made you?" she asked.

"They're dead," I replied. "They were all men, and men can't handle the stresses of their Beast very well. It's the higher levels of the hormone that makes them men. It doesn't react well, and it drives them mad, eventually. That's why I don't Change men. It's too risky, too prone to going catastrophically wrong."

We sat in silence for a while, listening to a large predator feed.

"You know, we're always looking for people to introduce to The Mysteries, and you seem promising. I can tell you more about it, if you're interested," I said after a while.

"Yes, I think I might be," Winda said, never taking her eyes off of Zhong.

We discussed things throughout the night. Winda knew a place outside of the village we could meet, an old crofter's house, abandoned for years. She also agreed to pass the word around to other women about forming a 'Secret Society' of women dedicated to supporting and helping each other out. Zhong gorged herself, then fell asleep, changing back into her human form. She woke many hours later, when the sun was well up, disoriented, holding up her hand to block her eyes from the sun. It was understandable. Waking up naked, covered in blood, next to the cold carcass of an animal you had killed the night before, and having no memory of how you got there, was a disorienting experience. During the night, Yusi had thoughtfully tied Zhong's clothes back together with some spare thongs we kept for just such a purpose. I took those clothes over to Zhong, and crouched down beside her, holding them out to her.

She took them from me, looking down at the ground in shame. "I failed. I'm sorry," she said.

"We all fail, from time to time," I said, putting my hand on her shoulder. "Don't worry, we'll keep working at it. That's the key to success, in the long run, anyway. Come on, let's get you home."

We started the Sister's Society slowly. We took those women that were showing the most promise in fighting aside for more training at night, after everyone else had gone to bed, and met at that abandoned crofter's cottage. Whereas before we had focused on group tactics and fighting as a team, now we focused on teaching them one-on-one fighting techniques, especially facing foes that were larger and stronger than they were. We drilled them mercilessly, working on breaking them down mentally while building them up physically; training techniques that had held up for centuries. Anyone that wanted to quit could, at any time. They were even allowed to hang out at the hut while the rest trained, making food for, and feeding the aspirants when they were done training for the night. We were looking for a very specific type of person. Single women only, but women with kids were allowed. Loyalty to a mate was a major point of conflict when we wanted their primary loyalty to be to us, at least in the beginning. Once a Sister had been a Sister for awhile, and demonstrated complete control, I had no problem with her finding a mate. Kids were different. A mother protecting her child would fight all the more fiercely for that child. We were looking for a person that wouldn't give up, no matter how bad things got. Physical strength wasn't as important as mental. Being a Sister was a never ending fight for control against the baser instincts of their Other. Mental toughness was paramount. In my experience, the ones that acted toughest failed, their personalities too brittle to survive the Change.

We started with forty-four, including Astrid, Solveig, and Chyanne. It was a sizable percentage of the village. At the end of two months, in the deep of winter, we were down to ten, with about six more still hanging around for the fellowship. Surprisingly, Solveig had dropped out, although she was one of the hangers-on. While she excelled at all of the physical tests and in fighting, she lacked the drive and competitive streak that was needed. She was slightly too laid back. Even more surprisingly, Astrid was still competing. When I first met her, she had been quiet, submissive, relying on her mother to take the lead. Through the trials, she had discovered a deep wellspring of strength within herself. It was a delight to watch her develop and evolve. Chyanne had also made it. The ranch girl possessed a fire and a stubborn strength a kilometer wide and fathoms deep. Winda had also made it. She didn't know the meaning of the word quit, and unlike everyone else, she knew what the prize was at the end of it all.

So here we were, nineteen of us gathered together in the dead of a snowy night on the Winter Solstice. Fitting.

"Welcome to tonight's meeting of the Sister's Society," I began. "I just want you to know how proud I am of all of you for making it this far. You should be proud of yourselves, too. And now we come to the final test to become a full Sister. Pass this, and you will share a kinship with Sisters you haven't even met yet, ones that are a half a world away. These final tests are tests of will and choice. The first is: Can you keep and bear our secrets? Make no mistake, your very lives depend on your ability to pass this test.

And the final test is a Test of Choice. Will you choose to take the final step, to become a full Sister? But, before you choose, you should know what that choice will entail." Yusi stepped forward, draped in a cloak that covered her from head to toe. She dropped it to the ground, revealing her nakedness underneath. Without ceremony, she dropped to her hands and knees. Immediately she began shaking, making little sounds of pain. Some of the women, including Solveig, stepped forward to help.

"Stop! You must stand and watch. Don't move, and don't run away. You must never run away from one of us. It attracts our attention and makes you prey. You must remember this."

Meanwhile, fur began to sprout over Yusi's body. Limbs lengthened, claws and fangs sprouted, and in a couple of minutes, Yusi in her Other form slowly straightened, rising to her feet. I looked around at the aspirants, both the ones that had passed the trials so far, and the ones that had failed. A few looked horrified, ready to bolt, biting down on their hands ready to keep from screaming. Winda and three of her friends looked eager, their eyes shining in the firelight. I had a feeling she had tipped them off as to what was going to happen. No matter.

"This is us. This is who we are, and what it means to be a Sister of the Moon. If you choose this, know that you will never get old, and you will never get sick. You have the potential to live forever, if you don't get killed, but know that your family around you that aren't Sisters, including your children, will get old and die while you remain young. Also know that there is always a risk with this process. Not all women can successfully make the transition. You might not survive. Take as long as you need to make this choice, because once you make it, you can't unmake it." I nodded to Yusi, and with some whimpers, she changed back.

"Now, we have a feast all prepared for you. Go enjoy it. You've earned it. Feel free to talk amongst yourselves or ask us any questions you might have, but say nothing of this to anyone not here tonight, on pain of death." The cracking of bones and joints shifting was a pointed accompaniment to the otherwise silent gathering. When Yusi was done, Zhong stepped forward and handed her her clothes, which Yusi took gratefully. When she was dressed, she moved to stand next to me.

"I hate the after," she said.

"The after?"

"You know, feeling weak and vulnerable," she said.

"You mean human? It's always good to be reminded of how we were before. It lets us keep our perspective and reminds us that this should always be a last resort."

"I've been reminded of that an awful lot lately. You know, you could have done it this time," she shot back.

I looked at her, weighing whether or not I should rebuke her for the insolence. I let it pass, because I liked this Yusi better than the one that was unthinkingly, slavishly devoted to an idea of me.

"No, I couldn't, and you know why," I finally replied. If any of the women chose to become Sisters, it would fall on me to Change them, a process that was almost as draining as Changing, depending on the number being Changed.

"How many do you think are going to go forward with this?" she asked.

"Winda, Yumna, Amari, and Yaa for sure. I don't know about the rest. Chyanne and Astrid have been with us for a while now, but they've never seen this side of us before. This will definitely be a break between Astrid and Solveig. All children leave the nest eventually, but this is a more extreme way than most. And some people struggle with the idea of immortality as much as others struggle with mortality. Come on, let's join the party. Make ourselves available."

We headed over to join the group. I tore the leg off of a turkey that had been slowly turning on a spit for most of the evening and took a bite, burning my mouth in the process. Winda's group was standing off to one side, plates full, looking relaxed. Chyanne and Zhong were huddled together with the other major group, women that hailed from the refugee village. Astrid and Solveig were off to the side, having an intense discussion. Solveig looked especially upset, her ruddy face flushed with anger. Astrid looked unhappy but adamant, her arms crossed across her chest. Solveig shook her finger in Astrid's face, and Astrid shook her head. This agitated Solveig more. She caught sight of me, and marched over, shaking off Astrid's restraining hand.

"You! This was your plan all along, wasn't it?" she demanded.

I shook my head. "No. I don't normally do things this way, but circumstances are forcing my hand. I'm hunting someone like us, someone very dangerous, and I will need soldiers to help me fight."

"Liar!" she screamed, and clumsily tried to slap me in the face with a wild swing from one of her tree trunk arms.

I took a half step back and slapped her hand out of the way. "I taught you better than that," I scolded. "Use your brain."

Solveig brought her hands up, properly this time, and settled into her stance. She unleashed a flurry of jabs at me, trying to set me up for a finishing strike. I danced away from her, slapping her hands out of line, keeping her off-balance.

I wanted to tire her out. Tired people made mistakes. And she did, eventually. She overcommitted to one of her jabs, overextending and ending up off-balance. It was only for a second, but it was long enough. Instantly I twisted out of the way, wrapping her arm in mine. I yanked it behind her, kicking her feet out from underneath her at the same time. She fell to the ground face-down with me on top of her. I hooked her legs with mine, wrapped her in a full-nelson, then rolled underneath her, pulling her on top of me. With me applying pressure on her head and neck, she was helpless, unable to move.

"You were always going to lose your daughter," I said quietly into her ear. "Whether she got married to someone else, or died from illness or childbirth, you were always going to lose her. Even in a perfect world, you would still have died before her, and lost her that way. At least this way it is *her* choice. And keep in mind, you can always try to complete the Trials again later. Now, are you done acting foolish? Can I let you up now?"

Solveig tried struggling a little bit more, but I had all the leverage and held her easily. Eventually, she quieted and her body relaxed. I could feel her as she gave a little nod, as much of one as she could, anyway. I let her up. "Come on, let's go get a drink." I draped an arm around her shoulder and led her off, Astrid following us, worry written all over her face.

I started with Astrid. In the old crofter's hut, she sat on the bed while I sat on an old milkmaid's stool next to her. I changed my hands in my Other's, but only the hands. "This is how it's going to work. My claws contain a contagion that will spread throughout your body and convert it into a Sister's." That wasn't quite true. It was actually a gland at the base of my thumbs that produced the retrovirus that infected a person's body, but I didn't tell any of my aspirants that. This was my final secret, the one that only I knew. I didn't want anyone else but me to produce Sisters. There was too much that could go wrong. The stakes were too high for there to be competing bloodlines out there.

"Now, to give you the best chance to have a successful transformation, I have to claw you over as much of your body as possible, and go as deeply as I can. It will be excruciating. After that, you will get very sick as your body fights the contagion.

This is the most dangerous part. Not everyone survives. You have to want to live even as you feel the worst pain you've ever felt in your life. Yusi, Zhong, and myself will watch over you through this process, but you'll be unconscious throughout most of it. Now is the time to change your mind. There is no shame in backing out now. Are you sure you want to go through with this?"

Astrid took a deep breath, then nodded.

"Why?" I asked.

"Because I don't want to be at anyone's mercy again. Not any priest, husband, man, or woman. I want the ability to make my own choices and live my own life."

"You will still be at my mercy, and the mercy of the Sisterhood," I warned, then relented. "But even after you become a Sister you can still marry, have children, and do a range of things depending on your interests. You can farm, or become a scout or warrior, or healer, or anything that interests you, as long as there is some need to fill."

"Whereas before, my only choices were to be wife and mother, or a sacrifice," Astrid said bitterly. "I'll choose something that gives me options. And time."

I had her stand up and disrobe, tied her hands to a beam overhead, and put a gag between her teeth. "All right. Time to be brave," I said, kissing her tenderly on her forehead. "Let's begin."

And so it went, throughout the winter. I would take one aspirant to the cottage, infect them, then nurse them through the crisis they experienced as their body at first fought, then lost, to the contagion that changed them forever. It all became a blur to me as I pushed myself to my absolute limit, both physically, mentally, and emotionally, as I first almost killed, then tried to save, each young woman. There was also the chance that the process wouldn't be one hundred percent successful, that their bodies would survive, but they would lose their minds, or that the process wouldn't succeed all the way, and we would end up with the type of failed Others that we faced back in Sanctuary all those many months ago.

Surprisingly, we didn't lose even one, which was an honest-to-Makers' miracle. By the time winter was starting to lose its grip on the land, we had welcomed ten new Sisters into our family. They weren't out of the woods yet. They still had a fierce fight ahead of them as they adjusted to their new bodies, and had to learn how to deal with violent new urges and emotions that whipsawed from one extreme to another. That's why the Trials were so rigorous. We had to weed out the aspirants that weren't mentally or emotionally strong enough to handle these things.

Each month when the moons were full, we would take the new Sisters and Zhong out into the woods, coax them through their Change, and then teach them to control it. They all managed it, another minor miracle. The weapons training also continued apace both with the new Sisters and the other aspirants that hadn't successfully completed the Trials, until they got to the point where I would pit them against any normal army of a similar size in the entire world. I now felt confident we could hold the village against any bandit or raiding group that might show up. That belief would shortly be put to the test.

It was the very end of winter. Snow still lay on the ground, but I could feel a Chinook, a warmer, drier wind, coming. The Thaw would soon be on us. It was almost time for planting, which was good. Our stores were almost gone. Some of the villagers were out tending the animals beyond the walls, while others were patrolling those walls, on the lookout for trouble. I was walking with Bard, inventorying the stores. We still didn't like each other much, but had learned to work alongside each other. The sound of a horn suddenly reverberated through the town, interrupting us. I sprinted to the wall, leaving Bard panting along behind me. I scurried up the ladder to the wall-walk, where Dip was energetically sounding the alarm.

"What's going on?" I asked.

He pointed off in the distance. I looked in the direction he was pointing. Several hundred meters away, I could see a group of mounted horsemen riding towards the town. From here it appeared that their armor was black and red.

"It looks like Dragon Skirmishers," he said grimly.

"Let's hope not. Hopefully it's a group of bandits or raiders masquerading as Dragons," I replied. Dragon Skirmishers were the elite warriors for the Dragon city-state. They were highly skilled in combat, scouting, sabotaging enemy resources far behind their enemy's front lines, and ambushes. Of all the forces we could meet, they were one of the last ones I would want to face. Twisting around, I could see the village herders sprinting to the relative safety of the walls.

"Apollo!" Bard, who had just made it to us, exclaimed. "What are we going to do?"

"Fight," I said shortly. I looked down as the full available fighting force of the village assembled below. Everyone except the new Sisters had donned the armor we had stockpiled so very long ago.

"Take your places on the wall!" I bellowed. "Sisters! To me! As soon as our people are inside, close and bar the gates!" That last order probably wasn't necessary, but I didn't want there to be any mistakes.

We were all battened down when the force brought their horses to a halt in front of our gates. Their leader leaned back in his stirrups. "Hallo! We require housing and board for us and our horses!" He called, directing this to Dip and Bard, the only two males on the wall facing him. Bard looked nervous and was about to reply, when I raised my hand, forestalling him.

"We're sorry. We don't have enough stores to feed your men and still survive until our next harvest. You'll have to try your luck somewhere else," I replied pleasantly.

He stiffened as if struck. "I'm not in the habit of being told no. Or dealing with a woman. In my experience they're only good for one thing. Now, this place dared to defy me last year. I taught it the error of its ways, or so I thought. Are the peasants of this shithole so stupid, they need to be taught such an object lesson again?"

Rage and a cold wave of adrenaline washed over me, like an incoming ocean tide. I turned to Dip and Bard. "Take everyone to the Manor House and barricade it against attack. I'll be counting on you to protect your flock. The Sisters and I will handle this. Now go," I told them gently, but firmly.

Bard looked confused. "Sisters? What are you talking about? I don't understand."

"And you don't need to. Just heed your calling and protect those people who can't protect themselves. Do you think you can do that?"

Dip spoke up. "You can count on us Lyr."

"Good. Now go."

When I saw everyone who wasn't part of our little club retreat off the wall and out of earshot, I turned back to the Dragon leader, who was waiting with growing impatience.

"By what name do I call you, soldier?" I asked.

"My friends call me Tiberius. The soldiers under my command call me Centurion. You can call me Master. In fact, it's better if you don't talk at all, and open these gates before I lose patience and burn this miserable hovel down around your ears!" he snarled.

"I saw the aftermath of your 'object lesson.' In fact, I had to clean up your mess, so forgive me if I don't trust your men's discipline or sense of mercy."

Tiberius smirked and leaned back in his saddle. "If you saw our handiwork, then you know what we're capable of. If anything that should encourage you to do whatever you have to to keep me and my men happy."

Out of the corner of my eye, I saw that Winda had moved next to me. Her hands were gripping the wall in front of her so hard, they were shaking. She was glaring at Tiberius with a naked, volcanic hate. I covered one of her hands with one of mine, trying to calm her a little. The time wasn't right, not yet. "I also saw that you lost most of your command that day, striving against this one little village. Well done! However, you've forgotten two things. One, the village didn't have me last time. I'm the difference maker."

He looked bored. "And the other?" he drawled.

I stood up straight, grinning a rictus grin. "There's always a bigger monster in the dark, waiting just outside of the light, Tiberius," I said, triggering my Change. My Sisters, taking their cue from me, Changed as well, Winda's growls of pain morphing into a series of short barks. She was laughing, the joy of finally being able get justice for all of her slaughtered people supplanting her pain. Our other Sisters weren't laughing. Rage and hate guided their voices, and they bayed their hate and their lust for blood as we flowed over the wall like rainwater escaping from an overfull barrel.

Tiberius's smirk vanished, and he sat frozen, his mouth hanging open in astonishment as we raced towards them. Even through the noise we were making, I could hear a horrified moan involuntarily escape him. It wasn't a memorable battle. It was a slaughter. Most of a cavalry's advantages lay in their momentum, the shock as they hit an opponent's infantry line, shattering their formation. We denied them that, swarming over them before they had a chance to react, and not a one of us felt an iota of mercy.

When it was finished, there wasn't a single Dragon soldier breathing on the battlefield, when we Changed back and lay, panting and naked on the torn ground, like so many nymphs out of ancient myth. We couldn't get dressed if we wanted to. We had left all of our clothes on top of the wall when we shifted. Eventually, I dragged myself to my feet, and stumbled over to the gates. Banging on the timbers as hard as I could in my weakened state, I shouted, "Open the gates! Let us in!" Silence answered me. The other Sisters wearily got to their feet and joined me in a big group as I continued to pound on the gates with the palm of my hand.

Suddenly, Bard's face appeared above the gates. "Why, hello," he said, smiling. "What are all of you doing outside the gates?"

"I'm in no mood for games, Bard. Open the gates and let us in, or I'll make you regret it," I growled.

His smile vanished, like a blown out candle. "I don't think so," he said. "I've had my suspicions about you from the very beginning, and now I've seen you as you really are. Witches from the blackest pits of Hades's Underworld." He raised his hand and Andrew and six other men appeared next to him, bows in hand, and arrows nocked. "This is where I send you back to the House of the Dead, you immodest whores. Give Hades my regards."

The seven men raised their bows and I tensed. There was nowhere to run, nowhere to hide, and in our current condition we were as vulnerable to injury as any normal human. Maybe I could dodge some of the arrows, for a while at least.

I hoped Alex, at least, would be able to carry on my vision for the Sisterhood. I spared a brief second to mourn the loss of our new companions. I would have liked for them to have had enough time to fully live their lives. I fixed my eyes on Brand's smirking face. One way or another, he would pay, of that I had no doubt. If I didn't punish him, someone else eventually would.

"Stop!" Yusi cried. The bowmen paused. "If you do this, there will be no salvation for you. We are not the only women like this. There are other Sisters out there, and they will come looking for Lyr. When they find out it was you who harmed her, they will exact retribution on you and everyone you know in ways that will make this," and she gestured at the field of corpses behind us, "Seem gentle and merciful. You will all die screaming as you are torn apart slowly, piece by piece. Think about it. Picture it. You won't get another chance."

"Don't listen to that handmaiden of Hades!" Bard screamed. "Shoot them! Now!"

The sound of pounding footfalls on the wall's walkway distracted them again. The rest of the village's militia approached Bard and his men from two sides at a trot, Dip in the lead on one side, Solveig and her contingent on the other. Bard looked triumphantly at me. "Now you will see, Harlot of Hades, the power the righteous wield when they fight together," he crowed.

His smug demeanor shattered however, when Dip barked an order and the militia pointed their spears, not at us, but at Bard and his men. Solveig loomed next to Andrew, hammer in hand and tense with a rage that was almost brimming over.

"Drop your weapons, or we'll add your corpses to those others laying in the field out there," Dip growled. The men in question dropped their weapons with alacrity.

"Sorry it took us so long, Sisters," Solveig called down. "They barred us inside the manor. It took us a minute to break out."

"That's all right, Solveig," I called back. "Can you open the gates and let us in? We're freezing our tits off out here."

* * * * *

We didn't throw Bard and his ilk out in the snow like we should have. We did, however, strip them of anything they could conceivably use as a weapon. Andrew and the others were expelled from the militia, and Bard lost all of his flock with the exception of three or four people, and the influence that came with it. He was forced to actually work like the rest of the village, or not be allowed to eat. It was good for him. Maybe it would even build some character and empathy. Maybe not. Some people were incapable of developing those traits. Only time would tell if Bard could apply those lessons.

Spring was well underway, and I was getting antsy to be back on the road. There was no telling how much mischief Fenrir could be getting up to with this reprieve he was getting, not that he even knew we were hunting him. Everyone had completed the spring planting at both village sites, and now Dip and his people were rebuilding their village, with our assistance. That's where the Sisters and I were, helping out, when, faintly, a long distance away, I heard the ringing of a bell. Dropping my ax, I whistled, a long, ululating tone, and dashed off in the direction of our village, my sisters and the rest of Dip's people hot in pursuit. We got to the village with the gates still open, thankfully. Bard was standing in the middle of the square, directly outside the front door of the manor. Each wrist had been tied to a rope that was being held by two different mounted warriors, stretching his arms wide. His shirt had been ripped from his back and hung down in tatters from his waist. A burly man with a thick brown beard and dressed in a tunic and hose of surpassing quality was folding his sleeves back, holding a nine stranded whip. His intentions were brutally transparent.

"Hold!" I shouted. "Don't even think about it," I continued in a low growl when everyone turned towards me, shocked expressions plastered on their faces.

"Who are you to tell me what I can and can't do?" the man with the whip demanded. "This is my land. This is my manor, and these people belong to me. I can do with them as I wish."

"Ah. Lord Rodrick, I presume," I said, motioning to everyone who had followed me. Quietly they began filtering out around me, disappearing behind the houses and other buildings. "I've heard a lot about you, and not been impressed with any of it. Where were you, when this place was attacked, your people slaughtered? Where were you through the winter when your people fought starvation? Where were you when your people were attacked yet again by the Dragon soldiers?"

Lord Rodrick scoffed. "I was in Primus. This place is merely my hunting lodge away from home. And these peasants exist and serve me at my pleasure. I have the prerogative of deciding whether they live or die, not that I have to explain myself to the likes of you. Now, I will show you the breadth and depth of my mercy by allowing you to leave with what you have on your backs. Anything else you own is forfeit."

I laughed. His arrogance was astounding, as was the fact that he thought I would just meekly pack up and go away. I was playing for time, trying to keep their attention on me for a little while longer as my militia slowly filtered into strategic positions, readying their weapons. "That's right. You were gone. But I was here. I cleaned up the dead, rebuilt the town, and kept everyone alive through the winter. From where I stand, this place and these people belong as much to me as they do you, and I say you won't do this." I made a sharp gesture and suddenly everyone appeared, surrounding Lord Rodrick and his retainers, spears lowered and arrows nocked in bows. "Now, keep your hands away from your weapons, and you just might survive this day."

We disarmed Lord Rodrick and his people and shoved them in the manor house while we gathered everything up. When we were all ready to leave, I met with the irate lord one last time. He sat in his chair in the Great Hall with a flagon of ale in his fist, fuming. When I entered, he looked at me, fury turning his face an ugly purple color. "I'll see you hanged for this, you know!" he spluttered.

I sketched a short, mocking bow. "Well, I guess I better take my leave then, milord. We'll leave you to your pleasures." I turned to leave, then twisted back to face him. "Oh, by the way, everyone is leaving with me. They're relocating to the next village over. Apparently the lord of that demesne is a more decent sort than you are, and actually cares for his people. And there's the added bonus that he's a duke, while you're merely a baron. Don't try to make trouble for them. I added a wall around that village as well, and everyone here knows how to fight at least as well as your knights. You probably wouldn't survive the experience. Farewell, and enjoy bringing in your land's harvest by yourself, as well as all the other jobs that need to be done around here to keep you in the manner of lifestyle you're accustomed to. It will be good for you. A little hard work builds character, I've been told." With that I left.

We barred them in the manor by propping a large timber against the door. They'd eventually be able to get out, but it would give us time to get away without having to slaughter the whole lot of them. Dip and his people went back to their own settlement, taking Rodrick's people with them. I followed them for a bit, then turned aside. My Sisters and I had our own mission to complete. Yusi moved her horse next to mine. We rode in silence for a while, then she said, "Well?"

I sighed. "You're right. We do have more to offer this world. This path will be much more risky. We'll become a target, you know that."

She shrugged. "Perhaps. But think how many more people we can help in the meantime. We'll make such a difference in this world!" She grinned from ear to ear.

I smiled too. I couldn't help myself, Yusi was that infectious. "Come, my daughter, let's go find Fenrir," and I spurred Red into a trot.

Nosferatu Nocturne

Fenrir's trail was colder than the Northern Glacier Fields, so we switched up our tactics and started by tracking down stories and rumors. That was how I found myself sitting in a no name tavern somewhere in the Kingdom of the Bull enjoying a watery beer. There were whispers of monsters in a dark forest near here. Maybe it was Fenrir and whichever unlucky bastards he had managed to Turn. I took another sip of my drink and grimaced. Well, enjoying was a bit of a stretch. This stuff was barely a step up from barley flavored water.

The bar itself was a low ceilinged, dimly lit affair built from haphazardly squared off logs, the gaps chinked halfheartedly with mud. A large, circular fireplace took pride-of-place in the center of the room, merrily blazing away and contributing a much welcomed warmth to the place. Muddy rushes, in dire need of being changed out, covered the floor, their once piney, pitchy scent long since vanished. Mud, thrown by years of tromping boots, spattered and daubed the chinked walls, making the bottom forty-five centimeters of the walls thicker than the rest.

At least the music was good. There was a quartet, three men and one woman dressed in rough working clothes, and seated on stools on the low stage, barely more than a step up off the floor, playing a lively tune. The woman was playing a slim instrument laying across her lap and singing in a lilting, slightly nasal tune while the men accompanied her.

Winda, Amari, and Aadhya were sitting at the table with me, each with a flagon of wine in front of them. It appeared as if they had made a better choice than I had regarding their drinks, although not by much. From where I was sitting, I could smell that the wine was one misstep away from turning into vinegar. Another table was occupied by a couple more of our Sisters. Chyanne was out taking care of the horses with Zhong, while Yusi and the rest of our group were seeing what this little hamlet offered in the way of shopping.

Winda and Amari were holding hands underneath the table. They had been in a secret relationship when they were serving Lord Rodrick, and now that they were free of him, they were more open about it. I sighed and scanned the room, looking for any of the bar's patrons that might object and cause trouble. I didn't give a shit who chose to love whom, but most men on Kaler took a dim view of same-sex relationships, especially between women. Some viewed it as some sort of upset of their imagined natural order of things, and others took it as some sort of challenge to change the poor women's minds. Normally I wouldn't care if they shouted it to the world, but I was tired after a month of living in a saddle, and wasn't in the mood for brawling. Especially not stone cold sober on watery beer.

Aadhya eyed them for a second, then turned to me. She was beautiful, with skin the warm reddish brown tone of a crying bloodwood tree framing large expressive eyes the color of coffee. She was blossoming in this life of hers, free of the constraints of her previous life, and reveling in the freedoms available to her now. She was also turning into a fierce fighter and a natural leader. I had high hopes for her. Actually, I had high hopes for all of my new Sisters. I had gotten unbelievably lucky with this group of women. "So, Lyr, what's the man situation like back in your hometown?" she asked.

I grimaced. "Pretty sparse, if I'm being honest. Most of the residents of Serenity and Sanctuary are girls and women that were rescued from Lawless Lands' bands. Most of the men in the Lawless Lands are barely deserving of the name. The *only* reason they can technically be called men is because they possess a pair of testicles. If you want a good man, you have to find one out here and somehow convince him to drop everything and join you there."

Aadhya sighed. "I was afraid of that," she said.

"Relax. You literally have all the time in the world to find love," I soothed. "You aren't under the same time limits that the vast majority of women have to deal with. You'll find someone, eventually. I promise."

"Hmmph," Aadhya replied, and turned her attention back to her cup.

The tavern door opened, throwing a bright swath of light in the otherwise dim tavern. Yusi came in, trying to appear casual while hurrying at the same time. She was failing miserably, I thought. Leaning down, she murmured in my ear, "I think there's something outside you're going to want to see."

I followed her outside, leaving my other Sisters to enjoy their questionable drinks and the better music. There were two open wagons with four horses apiece parked in the street. They hadn't been there when we arrived, and the red mud caked on the horses' legs and the sides of the wagon said that they'd been traveling awhile.

Clustered around the two wagons were eight women and four men. Judging from the way they were walking and stretching their bodies, they were trying to loosen up muscles stiffened by a long journey bouncing over rough terrain. I studied them for half a minute. Nothing seemed out of place; everyone's body language broadcast nothing out of the ordinary.

"So? I don't see anything wrong," I said.

Yusi grimaced. "I was in the store when four women came in, escorted by another of the men. I overheard one of them talking about going somewhere she had never been to marry someone she had never seen. She seemed a little nervous about the whole thing."

I stroked my chin, thinking. "I see. That does change things a little. Maybe we should strike up a conversation with the leader of this little party and see what's going on."

We wandered over to the party hanging out by the wagons. One of the men saw us approach and stepped up to meet us, raising his hand.

"Sorry, ladies. We're full up," he said cheerfully. "You'll have to wait until the next round before you can apply."

"Apply? For what?" I asked pleasantly.

"The Marriage Mart of course," he said, a little perplexed by the fact we didn't seem to know what he was talking about. "Isn't that why you came over here? I mean, everyone around here knows about the Marriage Mart. Any young woman without family or prospects can apply and be married. We only take a few women each cycle, so I understand it's pretty competitive."

"Ah. Well, we're not from around here, as you might have guessed by now. Who's in charge of this little endeavor?"

"That would be William. He's with the other girls shopping for some supplies, but he should be back shortly."

"Good. I think I'd like to chat with William; see if I can find out any more about this program he runs."

He shrugged. "Suit yourself," he said, and headed back to the wagons.

I turned and murmured in Yusi's ear. "Gather everyone up, but make sure it's done unobtrusively. I don't want to scare anybody I don't have to, but I have a feeling we'll be leaving soon." She nodded and took off.

While I waited for William to show and Yusi to gather everyone up, I held myself apart from the group by the wagons, not wanting to intrude, but watching for any indication of unwillingness to be there on the part of the women, or any intimidation or coercion by the men. Other than the usual tiredness of people on a long journey and nervousness of normal people being in a new place, I saw nothing. The women talked quietly among themselves. The men stayed a little apart from them, either talking to each other or quietly inspecting the horses and harness, the sorts of unconscious actions that evolved from routinely doing them over a long period of time. The women themselves seemed to be a mix from towns and cities all over the plateau, but all were wearing the same kinds of clothes, sturdy woolen dresses, with softer underdresses.

Eventually the four ladies who had been shopping returned, carrying packages and chattering amongst themselves, followed closely by William. He was of average height and build, a full head shorter than me, face somewhat shadowed by the large leather hat he was wearing. He was wearing brown leather pants, good for life on the road, and a brown and white spotted cowhide coat unbuttoned and gaping open, showing the blue woolen shirt he wore underneath. A sword with worn leather grips was belted at his side.

As he approached, the teamster that I had talked to called out, "Hey, boss, this lady here wants to talk to you."

William looked up at me, revealing a face of regular features, browned by exposure to the elements. He smiled at me, a quick, practiced flash of even white teeth. He held out his hand. "Pleased to meet you. I'm William!"

I grasped his hand and shook it. It was warm and calloused, much like mine. "Lyr. So, I hear that these women are headed off to something called the 'Marriage Mart'?"

His expression took on a slightly puzzled look. "Yes. Why? We don't have any room on this trip, so if you're interested, you'll have to go through the application process like everyone else."

"What's involved in this application process, William?"

He looked even more puzzled. "Well, a lady responds to our advertisement, and goes through an interview process. We ask them a series of questions, seeing if they're right for the Marriage Mart, and we go from there. Are you interested in applying yourself?"

I shook my head. "Not exactly, William. See, my Sisters and I have some experience with people exploiting women, and we tend to take that personally. So if we find out that any of these women are here unwillingly, we'll be removing them from your tender care."

His puzzlement gave way to anger. "Now see here, all of our girls are here willingly. We've even got a waiting list! And even if they weren't, I don't see how it's any of your business, anyway!"

I leaned closer, crowding him. "It's our business, because we make it our business, William. We've seen too many women victimized over the years to turn our backs any longer. So if *we* decide that you're taking advantage of these poor women, we're going to stop it, and there won't be much you can do about it." I snapped my fingers. The champ of horses and the clink of metal harnesses and bits made William look up. My Sisters surrounded the group, silent save for the occasional horse stamping its feet. "And before you can say, 'You're just a bunch of women,' be aware that this group of women wiped out a Dragon raiding party not too long ago."

He swallowed, looking around. "We're legitimate, I swear," he spluttered.

I smiled and took a step back. "Wonderful! Then you won't mind if we come along then, will you? We'll just see you safely to your destination and then we'll be on our way."

He paled and seemed to shrink down upon himself. "You can't! They don't like visitors, and I don't want to be responsible for any misunderstandings."

"Who doesn't like visitors, William?"

"Our customers. They keep to themselves and don't like outsiders, other than the women they order. I can't promise your safety if you come along."

"You let us worry about our safety. We're coming along anyway. Who knows? Maybe they'll thank us for protecting their future wives from any bandits in the area."

"There are no bandits where we're going. Our customers don't allow it. But suit yourself. It's your funeral," he grumped and turned back to his group.

"Winda!" I called. She was in charge of hunting and scouting for the group. "I want you to set up scouting for us once we're underway. Keep them close. I want them in sight of each other and us at all times. It will decrease our effectiveness, but lessen the likelihood of something slipping through a gap if they manage to take out one of our girls. I have a feeling our sightlines won't be great anyway if we're going where I think we're going." She nodded once and ran off to organize things. It was unlikely that anything human would be able to incapacitate one of us, but we were hunting monsters, and there was always the chance we would run into something even worse than we were.

"Astrid!" She jogged up to me. "I want you and Riya staying close to the women in the wagon. Get friendly with them. See if they'll open up to you two, and get their stories. I want to make sure this is all on the up and up." She dropped a slightly mocking curtsy, grinned at me and ran off. I grinned, too. Both Astrid and Riya had a gift where random people would meet them and immediately tell them their life stories. It was an ability I lacked utterly. My gifts seemed to lie more in the direction of intimidation and direct violence. I shrugged. Oh well. One must work with the gifts one has.

The two groups formed up and headed off with commendable efficiency, considering we had never traveled together before, but it wasn't too surprising. We had all been living on the road for months, after all. We held off until we saw the direction William was headed, then flowed seamlessly about the wagons, Winda and her scouts forming a shallow shell around us. I rode up alongside William so I could relay directions to Winda. The rest of our band surrounded the two wagons, the bulk splitting into a bastardized foreguard behind William and me and in front of the wagons, while the rest formed a rearguard riding behind the wagons.

William ignored me, riding beside me in silence, jaw muscles rippling as he clenched and unclenched his teeth. He was still pissed. I let him stew for a while, then piped up. Eventually he would talk to me. Anger was hard to hold onto as it used up too much energy, and boredom tended to loosen tongues.

"If you tell us where we're going, we'll have an easier time protecting you," I said.

He sighed and shook his head. "I'll tell you again. We have no need of any protection. Until you people came along, nobody dared to harass us. The reputation of our clients is well deserved, and they would respond in a devastating manner."

"Well, I'm not from around here, and have never heard about your clients. Who are they anyway?"

"They are people that like to keep to themselves and be left alone. They are very dangerous people that are not to be trifled with." He sighed in exasperation. "Listen, I understand what you're trying to do, but it's not necessary. You're putting your people in danger for no reason whatsoever. You should just leave us alone and continue on wherever you were headed before you met us. I promise we'll be alright. Our clients will protect these women and take good care of them."

"Well, now you've piqued my curiosity, William," I drawled. "By the way, what name do you go by, anyway? William, Will, Willy, Bill?"

His jaw clenched again. "My friends call me Will. You can call me William."

"For now," I said cheerily. "You'll get to like me eventually. I'm going to grow on you. Like a fungus."

"I had that happen once. It ruined my favorite coat," he muttered, kicking his horse into a trot and pulling ahead of me, ending the conversation. I grinned after him.

It took a couple of hours, but we slowly left the plains of the plateau behind us, and started slipping into the forest that loomed ahead of us. We passed the treeline, and headed carefully in. The trees closed in around us, slowly blocking out the light until only fingers of it reached us from above and from the treeline behind us. This was an ancient forest, comprised of towering firs and spruce trees. They blocked all light, inhibiting undergrowth. A deep carpet of evergreen needles covered the ground, muffling the animal's footfalls and contributing to the eerie quality of the forest.

I had dropped back into the rearguard and was riding beside Chyanne for now. The fiery horse princess had only grown more intense after her transformation.

In sparring, she fought with a fierce aggressiveness that was brutally effective and won her most matches in the first pass. That hot-blooded nature sometimes caused friction within the group, however, with the predictable result that left her isolated more often than not. I kept an eye on her. Other than being a bit bitchy, her control over her mercurial emotions was good enough for a pup. I could handle that. She would find her place and make more friends when they discovered that fierceness encompassed loyalty to, and defense of, her newfound family.

We rode quietly in companionable silence, listening to our surroundings and getting acquainted with the heartbeat of the forest. "Creepy," she finally offered.

I nodded. "I can see that. But one might call this peaceful, as well."

Chyanne snorted. "And they would be wrong, too."

I chuckled and we continued on without talking.

I waited another hour or two, enough time for Astrid and Riya to talk with the 'applicants,' then casually rode up to the wagon. I gave the two Sisters a pointed look. they nodded, and the three of us drifted to the back of the party.

"Well?" I asked.

Astrid shrugged. "They're here of their own free will, Lyr. It's been a long journey for some of them, and they're tired from getting jounced around in that wagon for weeks on end, but that's about it."

Riya nodded. "She's right. They're tired, but actually seem excited that they may be nearing the end of their journey. Plus, I'm not getting a whiff of fear-smell from them when they're around the men. In fact, they seem to be more nervous around us."

I nodded, stroking my chin, and thought about what they had just told me for a minute.

"This doesn't change anything yet," I said. "William could be a very convincing liar. He could also be innocent, and the clients are lying to *him*. It's too early to tell, and I wouldn't feel right leaving innocents to a potentially horrible fate."

Astrid and Riya nodded in agreement. Yusi's idealistic nature seemed to have infected the rest of us, I mock-lamented to myself.

We camped that night in a clearing that I could tell had been expressly cleared for that purpose. It was wide, with enough room for both wagons and fodder for the teams. There wasn't quite enough room for our horses, so we had to rope them together. There also wasn't quite enough fodder in the clearing for all of our horses, so we had to strap on the nosebags and feed them from our grain stores. We all gathered around one large campfire and shared the labor of preparing a meal for so many people.

"So how long is this trip going to take?" I asked after dinner was finished and cleaned up.

"Six more days. Unless something breaks and costs time," replied Lucas, who was one of the wagon drivers. Then he looked abashed at answering when William glared at him.

"Why are you really here?" William demanded. The several conversations running around the campfire in waves between pockets of people stopped as if cut off with an ax. "As you can see, as you've seen all day, nobody is being mistreated here. There is no good reason for you to be travelling with us, and every reason for you to go. Yet you stay. Why?"

I stared at him for a long moment, sizing him up, then relented a little. There was no reason for not telling him at least a piece of what we were doing, and a good reason for getting his cooperation. Or at least mitigate some of his hostility.

"Do you know where I make my home, William?"

He shook his head.

"Our home is at the very southern edge of the Lawless Lands. A place where the males that live there are more beasts than men and the women are property, not people. I have seen whole bands of people wiped out, babies ripped from their mothers' arms and their skulls caved in before the women are taken away. What I haven't seen, I've been told tales of rape, murder, and abuse by women and girls who I've rescued over the years.

"And since I've been travelling in the wider world, I've noticed that things aren't a whole lot better in these more 'civilized' kingdoms.

"We rescued Astrid, there," and I pointed at her, "from being sacrificed by her village. And Chyanne over there was going to wedded off against her will to a stranger by her brother.

"So I hope you'll understand that we don't have a lot of trust when it comes to the good intentions of other people. In our experience, it's rare.

"I understand your frustration. You're upset at being forced to do something you don't want to do. In your place, I would be furious, and it does look like everyone is here of their own free will. However, we know nothing of these clients of yours, or how these women will be treated once you leave. The fact that you're making these trips on a somewhat regular basis is concerning, to say the least. You're also correct in the fact that we have something else to do. We're hunting a very dangerous man, one who has the ability to set free a plague the likes of which this world has never seen. But his trail has gone cold. We're reduced to hunting rumors of monsters, and the only rumors we've heard pertain to this forest. So, we *will* persist in hunting down these stories, and find out if there's any truth to them before we move on. Protecting some vulnerable women so far from everything they've known their whole lives is a satisfying bonus. If your 'clients' treat people with respect, then everything will be fine, and we'll be on our way. All right?"

William sat pondering my answer for a while then gave a short nod. "It will be six days through this forest. The last two days I want you to pull in your patrols. They will do no good and might antagonize our clients. I want there to be no misunderstandings. Can you at least do that for me?"

I nodded. "Sure thing, William."

For the next five days we rode through the unchanging forest, in a perpetual state of dusk, sounds muffled by the deep carpet of needles. The peculiar stillness of the woods inhibited conversation, with everyone riding in perpetual state of wariness. But other than that, the trip happened without incident, until the fifth night.

Camp had been set up and we just finished eating dinner, when a scent reached my nostrils, carried by the gentle night breezes. I raised my nose, trying to catch it more fully, and noticed most of my Sisters doing the same.

"Company," I called softly. William and his group looked up at us while my group reached down, surreptitiously loosening weapons in their sheaths, while we waited.

"What is it?" he asked.

I shook my head. "I'm not sure, but whatever it is is downwind from us and getting closer." I tried to get the scent again. It seemed familiar, but it was hard to pin down because of the fickle, eddying night air.

We didn't have to wait too long, five minutes maybe, when a voice bellowed out, "Halloo the camp!" It was deep and booming, coming from a set of lungs and a throat much larger than a normal human's.

"Come in," William replied, his tenor voice sounding downright high and thready in comparison.

Eight figures loomed into the light thrown by a campfire. The adults were huge, towering over the largest of us, and covered in thick, reddish brown hair, almost, but not quite, fur. Four adults, four children. A family group of Beastmen. The youngest, a young girl who looked to be about five, clutched a dog-shaped fur doll in her arms, and warily watched us from behind the safety of her mother's legs.

"Sit down. Make yourself comfortable by our fire. You're welcome to spend the night with us if you wish."

The largest male shook his head. "We dare not. Something is disturbing the peace of this forest. We're heading southwest, trying to keep ahead of it. There's not enough of us to keep the young ones safe. We saw your fire, and decided to warn you."

"Do you know what it is? It's not the residents of the valley, is it?" William asked.

He shook his head. "No. We know of them, and they know of us. We leave each other in peace. This is something different. It feels like a predator that the forest isn't used to. Animals are moving through our hunting grounds as if they were fleeing a forest fire. We don't know when or if whatever is driving them out will end up here, but we can't take that chance with our children. I would advise you to leave, and quickly. Head back to your human towns where you might be safe."

"We can't. We're expected," William said.

The Beastman shrugged. "It's your decision. I've done what I can, but we must go." He tipped his head at his family and they moved out, headed southwest.

I squinted after the departing family, then looked in the direction they had come from. *Interesting*, I thought. I looked over at William. "If you left now, tried to make it to town, do you think you could make it?"

He snorted. "With the wagons? No way. We're closer to our destination, anyway. I have the utmost confidence in our clients to protect us."

"Beastmen are tough. And what they can't fight, they can hide from, at least if it's human. They wouldn't have picked up and left because of a raiding party. *And* they left soon enough it gave them a two day head start. Do you have any idea what they might be running from?"

He shook his head. "I don't have the first clue."

I stared in the direction they came from. "I don't either, but it concerns me."

We made all haste the next morning, trying to beat whatever it was that had the Beastmen spooked. We were rewarded for our haste. We made the mouth of our destination valley by the time the sun hit the horizon. A torii framed the entrance, not a gate exactly, more of a territory marker, letting us know something lived beyond it.

"We will go no farther tonight," William said, looking like he wished with all his being that the opposite was true.

"Why not? Are you worried about your benefactors?" I asked, half curious, half sarcastically.

He shook his head. "No. The path winds up into the mountains. It's narrow, with a lot of sharp switchbacks. Trying to navigate it in the dark is to invite a tragedy. We'll start off at first light." He looked around again. "I'm more afraid of what the Beastmen were worried about."

I nodded, then murmured to Yusi, who was almost always standing next to me, "We'll set extra guards tonight."

We had just finished dinner and were settling in for the night, when Aadhya suddenly whistled a warning. Those of us not on guard duty sprang to our feet, weapons in hand. A figure suddenly materialized out of the dark just beyond our campfire. It was bundled in strange, mottled clothing, face and head covered in a balaclava of the same pattern. I got the impression that it noticed everything about us that it needed to in a split second, then turned to William and bowed.

"Temperate moons to you and yours, William. We bid you welcome." He looked at those of us that were clearly not part of William's usual entourage. "We are a bit confused by the amount of people in your party. You have brought many more females than we have agreed to."

William coughed uncomfortably. "Yes, well, about that. All of the women dressed in riding leathers are not part of our group. They sort of invited themselves along. There wasn't much I could do about it."

I stepped up to stand beside William. Time to do some damage control before things deteriorated further. I sketched a shallow bow. "Greetings and temperate moons to you and yours. My name is Lyr, and I am the leader of my people, far to the south of here. We are on a hunt, and heard of your people. I thought it would be a good idea to take a brief pause, meet you, and maybe create a diplomatic channel. Maybe someday we could be allies, or at least trade goods between our peoples."

The figure held himself stiff while I was talking, then reluctantly bowed his head. "I don't think trading is in our futures. We have everything we need, and hold ourselves separate from other people because it's our choice. We just want to be left alone. However, allies are better than enemies, and far be it from me to offer insult to the leader of another people by denying them entry to our lands. That is for our council to decide." His balaclava moved, like he was smiling. "Besides, I doubt I could stop all of you myself. Come along, but be sure you come in peace. Treachery will be rewarded harshly." With that, he turned and left, melting soundlessly into the night's embrace.

"That went well," I said to William.

He snorted. "It will be easier for them to deal with you in their town, should they choose to do so. You've simply put your head in the lion's mouth now."

We crossed the plane of the torii the next morning, entering the territory of these enigmatic people. There was a clear path ahead of us, not a road so much as a maintained track that led into the narrow valley. True to William's word, it began to climb sharply, switching back sharply on itself to make it possible for teams and wagons to make the ascent. We made it to our destination in the late afternoon, a couple of hours before dusk. It was a well laid-out town, following the natural contours of the forested, gently ascending valley, cobbled streets snaking leisurely throughout. Wooden buildings nestled among the evergreen trees, brown with orange trim, their roofs upturned at the corners like the buildings at Li-Zhang. Cultivated plots of land rose behind the town in a series of terraces. Compared with some of the towns we had been in recently, hovels thrown together in pits of mud, this one broadcast organization, peace and serenity. I looked around and felt a sharp pang of envy. This town made my towns look like garbage dumps. These folks obviously could teach us some things.

William brought the wagons to a large building in the center of town. A middle-aged woman dressed in a simple but well-made woolen dress, stood waiting, hands clasped in front of her. When William dismounted and walked toward her, a pleased, gentle smile creased her face and she held out her hands to him.

"Will! It's so nice to see you again!" she said, grasping his hands and pulling him into a warm hug.

"It's nice to see you too, Sarah," he replied, returning her embrace.

I dismounted from Red and walked forward. William released Sarah and gestured toward me. "Sarah, I want you to meet Lyr, the leader of our self-appointed guardians on this trip," he said, an unmistakably sour note in his voice.

Sarah gave me a little bow. "We welcome you and your companions, Lyr. Marcus, one of our Council members will be happy to meet with you, but not until tomorrow night. Tonight belongs to us women and our younger children. We'll meet the men tomorrow night."

"And why is that, Sarah?" I asked, a little suspicious at this continued secrecy.

She shook her head, still smiling that same serene little smile. "All in good time. We like to acclimate our prospective brides into our society slowly, so as not to overwhelm. It has worked well for us for generations, so we see no need to change our customs, not even for unexpected guests."

I smiled thinly and nodded, acknowledging the barb. I had been a hunter for as long as this woman had been alive. I could be patient.

Sarah led us inside. A large common room greeted us. It was covered in wooden planking, sanded and sealed but not stained, giving off a warm welcoming buttery yellow vibe. A wooden ceiling soared high overhead, painted a darker brown. Cushions had been piled strategically around the room, making it natural to break into smaller groups, the easier for more intimate conversations.

Sarah waved a hand at the cushions. "Make yourselves comfortable ladies, but please leave a couple of cushions open for us to join you later. We're finishing up with dinner and will join you when it's time to eat."

We drifted naturally to the different parts of the room and settled down into the cushions. It was an odd arrangement, but not uncomfortable. I found myself sitting with Solveig and Liesl, one of the prospective brides. She was a pretty brunette, with pale skin, an aquiline nose and bright hazel eyes, typical of some of the settlements of the Bear Kingdom. She gazed around excitedly, taking in the room's appointments.

"This is so exciting!" she gushed. She ran her hands appreciatively on the floor. "Real wood floors! These people must be rich!"

"It is nice," I replied. "Of course, this might be the only building in the town that has floors like this. Time will tell."

"From what I've seen so far, this place looks nice, Lyr. Maybe you shouldn't be so negative," Solveig said, somewhat disapprovingly.

Heat flooded through me as my temper spiked and I had to restrain myself from smacking Solveig down for the perceived challenge. Our relationship had mostly healed after Astrid's Change, but Solveig had since been more willing to disagree openly with me. I took a deep breath, and forced myself to calm down. Breaking Solveig would accomplish nothing save making me look like more of a monster than I already was, and scaring everybody here would wreck any kind of diplomatic relationship I might try to build before it could even get started. Not that I actually intended to. This place was a continent away from our stomping grounds, but that might change, in due time.

"Not negative, Solveig, merely cautionary. We've only seen this building so far. This might be the fanciest building in the town for all we know. I'm sure we'll find out more once dinner is served, and the other women join us."

Solveig gave a grudging nod, acknowledging the point, while Liesl looked slightly uncomfortable. I bit back another sigh. It seemed I was best suited to dealing with the Sisters of my acquaintance. We confined ourselves to meaningless pleasantries after that, until a gong rang from behind the wall. Partitions slid open, and women began streaming out, carrying covered pots and platters of food, which were set in the middle of each group of cushions.

The food placed in my group consisted of a big pot that when uncovered looked to contain ramen. Thin slices of raw beef were placed next to the pot, making my mouth water. There was also chow mein, fried rice, and some kind of stuffed dumpling. In addition, what looked to be a venison roast was put down, and some fresh bread. It all smelled heavenly.

Half of the women left, while the other half took whatever empty seats were available, two of them joining us. They carried a plethora of tableware with them, and plopped a stack of plates, bowls, and silverware among our food, settling into the remaining cushions.

"Hello! I'm Ashlyn!" one of them chirped, taking my hand and shaking it. Her hands were almost as calloused as mine, but I'd wager her callouses came from work, not sword-handling. A vivacious air hung about her, energetic and happy. She had an open, friendly face, with sandy blonde hair and a smattering of freckles sprinkled across her nose. She was young, late teens or early twenties, I was guessing.

"This is Madi," Ashlyn continued, waving at her companion, a plump young woman dressed in a dark blue woolen dress that closed at her throat, covering her body. She waved shyly at us, then busied herself distributing plates and bowls to the group. "Madi's shy and doesn't like to talk much. That's all right, because I talk enough for both of us, right Madi?" Madi ducked her head and grinned, but didn't say anything.

Liesl, Solveig, and I introduced ourselves in turn, then Ashlyn told us to grab a plate or bowl and help ourselves before the food got cold. We dug in with me making a grab for some of that venison roast that had been calling my name ever since it had been set in front of me. There was little talking for the next few minutes as we concentrated on eating our food, but Ashlyn kept darting surreptitious looks at Solveig and me. I hid a smile. I could guess what was coming.

When the rate of eating slowed as we got full, and the pressure in Ashlyn had obviously built to the point of explosion, she piped up, "Why are you two wearing leather?"

Madi's face looked a little pained at her friend's outburst, but I chuckled. "We've been on the road for the better part of a year. Leather holds up better than fabric."

"Your ties are a little loose," she was referring to the fact that the leather strips holding my outfit together allowed a large gap in the seam. "You're showing an awful lot of skin. Doesn't that cause problems with some of the people you run into? And isn't it cold?"

"It's a choice on how we tie our outfits. As you can see, Solveig has hers tied tight, not showing anything at all. You get used to the cold. I run a little warmer than normal anyway. And I don't concern myself very much with what other people think," I replied.

"Is that why you have those tattoos?" She pointed at my arm. "And why does it say you're the baddest bitch on the planet? Doesn't that cause trouble?"

Madi's face went from slightly pained to bright red in embarrassment. "Please don't mind Ashlyn. She tends to be a little blunt is all. She doesn't mean to offend you," she glared at Ashlyn, willing her to shut up.

"It's all right, Madi. I don't mind. I tend to be a little blunt, myself." Solveig snorted in amused agreement, but held her peace. I looked back at Ashlyn.

"Well, Ashlyn, I wear this because I have yet to meet a bitch badder than myself. I call it my little warning label, telling people that if they want to mess with me or mine, they better be ready to go all the way."

"Does it work?" she asked, unabashed.

I thought about it for a second, then burst out laughing, shaking my head. "I suppose not. But at least I tried, right? And I like it."

Ashlyn stared at me for a second, then burst into giggles herself, bursting the tension that had begun to gather in our little group. It was at that moment that a little figure burst out from behind one of the partitions and ran towards Ashlyn. "Mama!" it piped, crawling into her lap and burying their head into her neck. A dozen other figures ran into the room finding their respective mothers as well, interrupting whatever conversations had been taking place.

I looked at Ashlyn's baby. I didn't mean to stare, but they required a good long look. Their head was fully covered in a wrap of some kind, but their skin was pitch black, even darker than Winda's dark chocolate, and contrasting sharply with Ashlyn's peaches and cream complexion. Their eyes were much larger than a normal person's and seemed overlarge in their tiny face.

"Who is this, Ashlyn?" I asked gently, not wanting to spook her baby.

She smiled proudly. "This is my little Gallus. My little rooster who crows at the sunset every night, waking me up. Isn't he precious?" she cooed, rocking him a little. Mighty Gallus looked at me, then jammed his fist into his mouth, chewing busily, and buried his head back in his mother's shoulder.

"Yes he is," Solveig said firmly, as if she was afraid that someone might disagree. Liesl looked a little uncertain, but I nodded my head as well.

"He is at that." I looked over at Madi. She had one of her own in her lap. The enterprising little kid was busy trying to open the buttons of Madi's dress with a single-minded purpose. "Yours?" I asked unnecessarily. She nodded, a shy smile creasing her face, and began opening her dress, helping the little blighter out.

"This is Atticus," she said, once he was settled and suckling happily away. He was also wearing a head wrap and shared the same pitch black skin with Gallus. I looked around. Most of the women that shared the meal with us had children of varying ages that had joined them. Despite the babies' unusual appearances, they were behaving like any other children of that age, at least as far as I could tell. My experience with young children was limited, to say the least.

The little ones' appearance had been a success, as far as I could tell, with everyone's bellies full, watching the children's antics had a soothing effect on everyone. I suspected it was on purpose, a carefully crafted scene meant to put everyone at ease and prepare them for the appearance of the men tomorrow. I had to hand it to them, they seemed to know what they were doing.

"Would you like to hold him?" Startled out of my reverie, I looked up at Ashlyn, questioningly. "Would you like to hold Gallus?" she repeated.

I held up my hands and shook my head. "No, that's all right. I'm not very good with children." I mean, I didn't really know. I could be the best person in the world with a baby, but I'd never held one in my life, if one could believe it.

"May I?" asked Solveig, holding out her arms. Ashlyn smiled in delight and gleefully deposited her little bundle in Solveig's arms. She tenderly cradled Gallus, almost burying him in her warrior's arms. "I just love babies," she cooed, rocking him gently and smiling beatifically. "I haven't really gotten to hold one in quite a while, not since Astrid."

"Didn't other women in your village have babies?" I asked gently.

She shook her head. "Not as many as you'd think. With the men off raiding, and the annual sacrifices, we didn't have a whole lot of women of child bearing age." A tear built up at the corner of her eye and tracked down her cheek. Angrily she rubbed it away with her shoulder. "Yusi killing Seig was one of the best things ever to happen to that misbegotten place, and having killed that monster, maybe the village can have a more normal existence."

"Maybe," I replied. I figured there was maybe a fifty-fifty chance of that. It all depended on who stepped up to occupy Seig's power vacuum, or how long it would take them to figure out that the manpower drain from raiding was unsustainable for a village that small. Either way, it wasn't my problem.

I looked over at Solveig entertaining Gallus. She was cooing at him and making strange faces, trying to get him to smile. He was staring back at her quizzically, but lost it when she started playing the ancient game of 'peek-a-boo' with him. A huge grin split his face showing the barest tips of his incisors, and he chortled in delight. This only encouraged Solveig to try harder, and the chuckles turned into shrieks of laughter. The whole table couldn't help but smile at their antics, including me. He really was a cute kid, I thought. His huge eyes reminded me a little of the small nocturnal creatures called bushbabies that lived back in our jungle.

Cloth rustled as Sarah, who had been seated at another table across the room, got to her feet. She picked up a small bell and rang it. "You will all spend the night here. We'll bring pallets out for you. In the morning, we'll take you on a tour of the village so you can see some of the houses and meet some of the women you haven't had a chance to meet yet. I ask that you stay here and don't wander off tonight. I don't want there to be any accidents or misunderstandings. Thank you." As one all of the other village women got to their feet, picked their children up, and left. They reappeared a couple of moments later and began clearing the dishes. When that was done, everybody reappeared dragging down-stuffed mattresses with them. The rest of us stood up to help, rearranging the mattresses to suit us.

The next day dawned bright and beautiful, painting a palette of pastel oranges, blues, yellows, and lavender across the sky. True to her word, Sarah took us on a tour of the village after breakfast. It was a very orderly village, so much so it made the haphazard collection of huts we had in Serenity look like we squatted in squalor. The disparity between the two places had me gritting my teeth in green-flamed jealousy more than once. I vowed that I would make some changes to Serenity posthaste when I got back.

It was also confirmed, much to Liesl's delight, that all of the houses in the village had split plank wooden floors, a huge improvement from the stamped dirt floors many of the poorer dwellings I'd come into contact with in my travels had. One thing I noticed, however, was how unnaturally quiet the village was. There were a few older women out and about, doing household chores or tending to their gardens, but there was a noticeable hush to the surroundings.

"Where is everybody, Sarah?" I asked at one point.

She smiled at me. "Most of us are awake at night, and sleep through most of the day. You'll start to see more people stirring around late afternoon. Our men and children, especially, are nocturnal in nature. It's probably one of the biggest adjustments you prospective brides will have to make," her gaze swept over the group of young women, who looked a little nervous. "But you'll do just fine."

By the time the sky began to darken, my anticipation at finally meeting the lords and masters of this place had built to a point where I was actually nervous, a fact I didn't like admitting, even to myself. We were once again gathered in the community hall, where rows of pews had been placed for our comfort. We were joined by some of the ladies who had been with us last night and their children. After the ensuing chatter had died down a little, Sarah appeared at the front of the room. She raised her hands for silence.

"Good evening, ladies. Tonight is the night where you meet the rest of the community. I would like to introduce Gaius Marcus, the Chairman of the Town Council. Let's give him a warm welcome, everybody."

We all clapped politely, a sound that died a swift death when Marcus stepped out from behind one of the partitions. Gasps sounded from several members of the audience at his appearance, mostly from the mail-order brides, but from a couple of my Sisters as well.

Marcus was a large man, taller than me, and muscular, obvious even through the loose fitting robes he was wearing. He moved with the confident, assured grace of a warrior at his physical peak. I hadn't seen the like since Berand in the Lawless Lands, a year ago. Like Gallus and Atticus, his skin was night black, his face also dominated by over-large black eyes that gleamed in the lantern light. Unlike the children, his head wasn't covered. Ears reminiscent of a bat's crowned his head, giving him an alien look. He smiled at the crowd, showing off large fangs. The smile was a rueful one, as if he was very familiar with the effect his appearance had on people.

"Temperate moons to all our guests, both invited... and not." His gaze flicked to mine, and his smile turned into a wide grin, letting me know he was teasing. *Cheeky fucker.* "We welcome you here to New Haven in peace and goodwill.

Tonight you will meet everyone you haven't already met, including all of our eligible bachelors and we will hold a celebration to welcome you officially to our community. So come, let the celebration begin!" With that he led us all outside where a large area had been cordoned off, forming an ad hoc courtyard. Lanterns hung on cables strung between trees, outlining it and giving it a warm, yellow glow. The rest of Haven's men were already there. Some were black like Marcus, some were white, and others ran the whole spectrum of skin tones, but to a man they were all built like Marcus, muscular and toned with over-large black eyes and batlike ears. They also all moved with the same tightly contained grace and power.

In one corner of the space a quartet of them looked like they were preparing instruments. Off to the side a couple of tables had been set up and were laden with all kinds of food and drink. Some of the village women were behind the tables drawing mugs of drink from tapped barrels. I wandered over, accepted one and took a sip. The taste was sweet yet had a sharp tang that nipped at the taste buds. It was hard cider, and good.

Once the band had tuned their instruments, they struck up a lively tune. Immediately some of the men grabbed what I assumed were their wives and propelled them onto the dance floor where they began twirling them, giggling, around the quadrangle. Haven's women that weren't dancing, mostly middle-aged and older, started clapping enthusiastically, keeping the beat. There was a group of men that also weren't dancing, standing off to one side. They looked younger than the men that were dancing, about the same age as the group of prospective brides that had just made the trip, and positively exuded nervousness. A couple of them split their time between glaring at us Sisters, as if our presence somehow offended them, and watching the recently arrived ladies. The brides also looked unsure, alternately looking longingly at the dance floor where the couples continued to stomp happily around the square, like they would love to be invited to be out there as well, and nervous at their partner choices.

"Once again, the courtship dance has begun," an amused bass voice said in my ear.

I nearly jumped out of my skin, then cursed myself for my apparent lack of attention, letting someone sneak up on me without noticing. Something like that could get me killed one day. I looked over at Marcus, who had managed to move next to me like a ghost.

"Do you do this often?" I asked, trying to act casual and not like his silent appearance had affected me at all.

"Every time a new generation of us reaches manhood," he rumbled. "Sometimes we'll do it once a year, sometimes five or ten will pass before we ask for more women. But the dance is always the same. Brave young men and women terrified of meeting each other. I assume it's the same everywhere."

"I wouldn't know," I replied, a little sad. That part of my life had passed me by a long time ago. I glanced over at one of the young men that had recommenced glaring at me.

"What's his problem?" I asked.

Marcus snorted. "He is young and suffers from that same condition that all young men suffer from. He thinks he knows everything, and doesn't have enough experience to know that no one ever learns everything, which makes him foolish. He belongs to a somewhat more conservative faction in Haven that believes in sharply defined roles for our men and women. He thinks women must be protected and can't be warriors. I imagine you threaten his worldview a bit."

It was my turn to snort. "What do you think?"

"I think that there are many kinds of strength. The state of your clothes means you have been traveling a great distance. I know how dangerous it can be outside of our valley. The mere fact that you made it here means you are survivors, however you managed to do it, which makes you dangerous and not to be underestimated."

I nodded. "That's very astute of you Marcus."

My gaze wandered over at the children tearing around outside of the courtyard, chasing each other in and out of the lanterns' light, giggling madly. "I don't see any girls. Why is that?"

He looked at me sharply, then seemed to ponder some question silently for a moment. "Are you really the queen of your people?" he finally asked.

"Queen might be a bit of stretch. I am however the leader of my people, and the founder of our community. I call my people my sisters, although it might be more accurate to say they are all my daughters."

Marcus seemed to come to a decision and nodded. "Let's go take a walk where it will be easier for us to talk," he said, turning and striding off.

I shrugged to myself and hurried after him until I caught up and matched his stride. He walked deceptively swiftly, yet his soft soled boots made almost no sound on the path as he glided along.

"How much do you know of Kaler's history?" he asked as a preamble.

"More than most," I replied, thinking of my own experiences and secrets.

"Good. That will make it easier to explain. My kind was developed as an elite soldier class before the Fall. They designed us to be faster and stronger than a regular human, with an affinity to operate at night, as I'm sure you've noticed. We can also regenerate and heal from most wounds that would kill a normal person. Our histories tell of a special serum that our Makers developed that would activate and boost this regeneration ability. We've lost that, but we've discovered that ingesting blood works almost as well.

"They also designed us to be expendable. We were never meant to have children. But they made a mistake in their design." He looked fierce when he said that, an anger towards the designers that decreed that his kind weren't human enough to seek or want their own lives that had been passed down through generations. "We *can* have kids. However, we can only sire boys, and what we are is dominant. Every child we have is like us. And that is why you don't see any girl children and why we have to bring in women from outside of our community in order for our kind to continue."

"Thank you for your honesty, Marcus," I said, nodding my head in acknowledgement. "I wonder why the candor, though. Chances are good that when my Sisters and I leave, we will never meet again, so why bother?"

"Because it is information that will be of little use to you, in the end. And you strike me as a bit of a crusader. Who else would follow a bunch of strangers through a haunted forest in order to see them safely to their destination? And we have never heard of you or your nation. You could be just the two dozen people we see before us, or you could have a nation as strong and vibrant as Primus. There is a potential that you could cause problems for us if the latter is true. People fear what they don't know, and hate what they fear. We are great warriors and soldiers, but we are few, compared to the world at large, and we prefer peace. If a ten minute conversation with you is the price of a peaceful relationship with you and your kin, then it is a small cost.

"Although maybe you can repay me in kind. What are you really doing here? Surely you and your kin don't ride all over the countryside looking for maidens to rescue?"

"No, you're right about that. We're hunting someone; a relative of sorts who leaves a trail of destruction wherever he goes. His physical trail went cold, so we were hunting him by following stories and rumors of monsters. That led us here, a rumor of a dark forest haunted by monsters." I smiled wryly. "That, and safeguarding those maidens you mentioned." Marcus chuckled, which caused me to laugh along with him.

"You and your kind are not welcome here!" a voice interrupted angrily behind us.

Marcus, unsurprised, turned casually to face the interloper. "Ignatius. What a surprise," he said mildly.

"Tell her! Tell her she is unwelcome here, Marcus!" Ignatius spat out as he approached.

Marcus' gaze hardened. "You are not a member of the council, Ignatius. Do not presume to speak for *us*."

"Not yet. But I will be. Many of the men my age agree with me." Ignatius shot back.

"*If* you someday make it onto the council, then of course your opinion will be listened to. But until then, you have no business here. Go back to dance. Have fun. Court a bride. That is what is appropriate for you."

"I'm making it my business. These whores' very presence is offensive to me. Worse, their tawdry dress and behavior could influence our women. I will not stand for it!"

I probably should have stayed out of it. This was most likely some kind of dominance showing or power play on the part of the young one. But I wasn't going to be a pawn in whatever game he was playing. "Fuck off, boy! The adults are talking here!" Master of Diplomacy, that's me.

Ignatius' answer was an attempted backhand slap. "Speak when you're spoken to!"

I dropped into a crouch under the blow. Just barely, he was wickedly fast, and slammed a fist into his crotch. Mighty warrior he might be, but there are few men that can shake off a blow to the gonads.

He lost all of his wind and sank down to his knees, hands clutching uselessly at his abused parts. "I demand...sat... satisfaction!" he finally managed to gasp out.

Marcus was unsympathetic. "You struck first. And to a diplomatic envoy, the queen of her people, no less. She was merely defending herself. Your request is denied."

"I appreciate that Marcus, but if this boy wants to fight, I'll be happy to give it to him!" I spat, my own temper raised.

Marcus sighed, looking at me like he was disappointed. I glared back at him. I might look like someone's younger sister for the rest of eternity, but I was the oldest one here, damn it. I wasn't going to be made to feel sheepish by anyone.

"Fine. Let us adjourn to the caves. You two can spar there. No weapons, and the match ends when one person is rendered unconscious, or taps out." He led us up the path where it wended back and forth, snaking around groves of trees or small islands of flowers. The path led to the mouth of a cave, then descended down into it, continuing its sandy path until it opened up into a large cavern. Sand had been piled up in the center, creating a softer landing spot than hard packed earth or bare ground.

"This is our training grounds, where the young ones learn martial arts, and us old ones continue our journey. Ignatius, go warm up. I would like a word with Lyr here."

Ignatius sneered at me then moved to the far end of the sand, where he began exercising, warming and limbering his limbs up in the cold cavern air.

"I'd like you to reconsider. We aren't like normal people. We have enhanced strength and reaction times. It's not going to be a fair contest between you two. It isn't a fair contest between one of us and one of Dragon's elite warriors. Ignatius isn't going to hold back. He wants to humiliate you."

"I appreciate the concern, Marcus, but I'll be fine, I promise." I stepped away from him, ignoring his sigh and began loosening up my own muscles in the chilly air. We squared off in the 'ring', dancing from foot to foot in the soft sand.

"Begin!" Marcus called.

Ignatius tried rushing me, burying me under his greater mass, but I danced to the side. He really was quick. He straightened up and tried again, but I had the timing down this time and snapped a side kick into his midsection, stopping him cold. He wasn't expecting that and that made him rethink his strategy. He raised his hands, assumed more of a boxing stance and moved in confidently. I matched him, expecting him to throw some combination of punches, then was surprised when he kicked me in the thigh with his shin. It made a loud smack when it hammered into my leg, and pain blossomed up and down its whole length. I grimaced. Kicks like that would incapacitate someone over time, when the leg got too bruised to hold a person's weight, but he was in for a surprise if he thought that would work on me. I answered it by shifting my weight to my back leg, and hammering a front kick into his stomach. Getting kicked by a Sister, with our thickened bones, was like getting hit by a small tree. That knocked him back a step and it was his turn to grimace.

He reset himself quickly, though and unleashed a flurry of blows at me, and it was all I could do to dodge, duck, and mitigate any damage he was trying to do.

His freakish speed was bothering me, I wasn't ashamed to admit. I was faster in my Beast form, but I wasn't doing that here. It allowed him to get close to me and get me in a clinch, where he promptly tried to throw me. It was his turn to be surprised again, because although I looked like I weighed about one hundred and thirty pounds, I was easily double that. He grunted with the effort, but I was able to turn with it, and jumped on his back instead, riding him to the sands. I ground his face in the sand for good measure, then hopped back off, motioning for him to get back up.

He rolled to his feet, face twisted in rage, and launched himself at me, in an all-or-nothing rush, and succeeded in getting me in a clinch again. This time he used his momentum to climb up on me, and twisting around he captured one of my arms with his whole body. His entire weight hanging off one of my arms did force me to the ground, and he slammed the pressure to my arm threatening to break it. I didn't want to admit it, but he had me, so I tapped his arm, signifying an end to the match.

He ignored me tapping his arm and wrenched back, dislocating my elbow. I screamed as the blinding agony hit me.

"Women can't be warriors," he whispered smugly in my ear as he released my arm and rolled to his feet, strolling over to Marcus.

I got to my knees, holding my arm. Marcus was yelling something at Ignatius, but I couldn't hear it through the roaring of blood in my ears. Adrenaline spiked and my rage built into an overwhelming tsunami. I snapped my arm back into place as my body's healing kicked off like a runaway horse. It took all my will to hold off my Beast as my rage threatened to drown me. Panting like I had just finished a twenty kilometer run through the forest, I held her off, and triggered a partial Change. It took the utmost focus and control to change just a part of our bodies; only the oldest and most experienced of us could do it. My right arm, back, and leg swelled as I built up muscle mass in a matter of seconds. My clothing tightened and threatened to split, the rawhide ties stretching to their limit. When I had changed as much as I could, and was sure I wasn't going to keep shifting,

I got to my feet and stumbled over to where Marcus was continuing to upbraid Ignatius, who wore a slightly bored expression.

I tapped him on the shoulder with my left hand. "Ignatius?" I cooed. When he turned around in surprise, I hit him as hard as I could with a wicked hook. My punch connected with his jaw, shattering it, and laying him out cold. The effort broke my ties and split my clothes all the way down the right side.

I looked up at Marcus' shocked expression, still panting like a horse after a two kilometer race. "I'm not normal either," I finally managed to gasp out, still trying to beat my anger down the rest of the way.

"I see that," Marcus managed to say, struggling to maintain his decorum.

I finally managed to calm the rest of the way down, and reverted back to normal, feeling my body shrink down. I hated to Change. It was always my last resort, and now I probably wouldn't be able to do it again safely for at least a couple of weeks. If it had been a full Change, I wouldn't have been able to manage it again for a month.

I looked down at Ignatius, still out cold. "Is he going to be alright?" I asked, feeling just the slightest bit guilty. I hadn't meant to hit him quite so hard, but one broken bone deserved another.

Marcus knelt down and checked his jaw. "It feels like you broke it in three places and knocked out some teeth, but he should recover. He will need blood, though."

"He shouldn't get a wife. From what I've seen his kind tend to be abusive towards those they have control over."

"Just so you know, we don't assign wives to our men. We merely arrange the meeting. It's then up to the men and the women to find each other. Sometimes the women can't get over our appearance, and ask to leave, which we then oblige. Sometimes our young men don't see anybody they have chemistry with and wait until the next group. Despite our appearance, we're not monsters. We're people, and we want love like everybody else."

He straightened back up. "But I agree with you. This was a test for him, one he failed the moment he followed us. He is young yet. Perhaps in time he will gain some wisdom and will be considered appropriate to find a wife. You should go back to the dance. I will take care of young Ignatius here."

Before I got back to the party, I stopped and fixed my ties as best as I could. It wouldn't do for me to show up half-naked. When I finally got there, Yusi, Chyanne, and Winda were lying in wait for me. They pounced as soon as they saw me.

"Where did you go? We were about to start searching for you," Yusi began without preamble.

"Are you alright? Your ties are broken," Chyanne interrupted.

I held up my hands. "Easy, girls. Everything's fine. I was having a conversation with Marcus, then had a little sparring session with Ignatius that got out of hand. But everything's good. Nothing to worry about. Now, did I miss anything?"

"Just that," Winda said, nodding towards the dance square. I looked over, and my jaw dropped all the way to my feet. Out in the middle of the floor, Solveig was dancing with one of the village men. Not any of the young ones either, who had finally gotten up the courage to start dancing with the young women, this was a fully mature man, standing head and shoulders above her, and half again as broad. He was dancing a jig, his feet beating a furious tattoo upon the stamped dirt. Solveig, face red with exertion, and grinning broadly in delight, was matching his pace, her feet flying as she kept up with him. I had never seen her so happy.

I looked for Astrid. She was standing off to one side of the square, hands clapping in time to the beat. She was smiling, but I could see unshed tears in her eyes. I hoped she wasn't jealous of the attention Solveig was getting.

"His name is Scipio. Apparently he's a widower. His wife died in childbirth some time ago, and he hasn't shown an interest in any woman until tonight with Solveig," Chyanne supplied.

"How do you know all this, Chyanne?" I asked, surprised at how quickly she was able to gather that amount of gossip.

Chyanne shrugged. "Ashlyn," she said.

"Ah," I replied. Mystery solved. I watched the dancers for a while. The brides, perhaps fortified by the excellent cider, seemed to have gotten over their initial hesitance, and were now, to a woman, dancing. From the smiles on their faces, I could tell they were having fun. Same with their partners. I felt a weight slide off of my shoulders. Everything here was going to be alright. There were no monsters in this forest. At least, nothing worse than us.

Marcus suddenly appeared beside me. Damn, that man was quiet.

"Everything alright?" I asked, raising an eyebrow.

He nodded. "Everything's fine. Ignatius has been put to bed, and given a dose of blood. It might take him a few weeks, but he will be fine. Hopefully he has learned some lessons tonight. Time will tell."

"Well, I want to thank you for your hospitality, Marcus. I appreciate the welcome you and yours have shown us, but it's time for us to continue our hunt. We'll be on our way in the morning."

Marcus nodded. "Temperate moons to you and yours, Lyr. Maybe we'll see each other somewhere down the road."

"I'd like that, Marcus, but probably not for a long while. Our lands lay far to the southwest of here, on the very edge of the continent. There isn't much need for us to keep wandering into your territory. But I would like our two peoples to remain friends. Maybe I'll come back someday in the far future. If I'm invited," I finished wryly.

Marcus chuckled. "Anytime you want to visit, consider yourself invited, at least as long as I'm on the council. I'm sure there will always be a young buck or two in need of a pointed lesson."

I smiled back at him and was about to say something witty, when a long quavering howl rent the night, singing about prey found, hot blood, and fresh meat.

Marcus cocked his head as I stiffened in alarm. "What is that?" he asked.

"Remember when I told you we were hunting a relative? This is some of his handiwork. Two nights before we arrived, a family of Beastmen warned us about something invading territory next to theirs. This must have been what they were talking about. Is there a place easy to defend that you can put all of your women and children?"

He nodded. "The caves where you sparred with Ignatius. There is only one entrance. We can hold that against anything smaller than an invading army. Is there anything I need to know about fighting these creatures?"

"They're fast, vicious, and smart as a human, at least when the bloodlust isn't controlling them. They also heal as fast as I did and can regenerate. The best bet is to fight them two or three against one. Do you have spears? Boar spears would be even better, so they can't run up the spear shaft to get to you ."

He nodded, smiling grimly.

"Good. Pin them in place, then I'm afraid you'll have to dismember them. It takes a lot of effort to kill one. Do you have some spears for us? We don't have as many as we should. An oversight on my part, perhaps."

"We can accommodate you," he said.

"Good! This is your home. How do you want us to help?"

Marcus thought about it. "If you could secure the buildings in the town, that would free us up to go on the offensive, hunt these interlopers down. That is what we do best, anyway. I'll leave behind a squad to guard the caves themselves. No offense, but I know how we fight; I don't know how you fight. My men will be happier if their own are guarding their families."

I shrugged. At another time or place, I might have bristled at the implied slight or lack of trust in our fighting abilities. But he was right. He and his men didn't know us. We hadn't had any time to familiarize ourselves with our different fighting styles, or how well we would be able to integrate. Now was not the time to experiment. Plus, the promise of action and potentially ending our hunt tonight was triggering my bloodlust. I felt a rising excitement and eagerness to be about our business, to be on the hunt.

Marcus put his fingers to his lips and blew a piercing whistle.

"The party's over, people. We're going to be under attack shortly. Sarah, gather up the women and children and take them to the caves. Scipio, gather up a squad and escort them. Arm yourselves. Boar spears are to be your primary weapon. Agrippa, hunt up some more spears for our guests here. They will hold the village while we hunt. Let's move. We may only have moments." With practiced efficiency, everyone split up to do their tasks.

I split our group into threes. They didn't have enough spears for all of us, but there were enough that at least one person in each group could be issued one. I gave those out to the strongest in each group. It would be up to them to catch and pin our quarry while the others went in for close up work.

"Remember to use your honor daggers to finish them off," I said. "If you come into contact with any of them, be sure to call out for help. We don't want any one group to get overwhelmed out there. Let's watch each others' backs. Now, to the hunt!" I lifted my voice to the moons in a howl of excitement, the thrill of the hunt, and the call of sweet, sweet blood that was going to be spilled by my enemies. My sisters joined me in my song, a wild, savage chorus to the heavens. After that, we split up, first going to each building in the town, making sure there were no stragglers hiding or hadn't gotten the word to clear out to the caves. Howls sounded in the distance, distinguishable now by timbre and tone as they moved closer. They thought they had found their prey, more fools they.

All the houses were clear, save one. I was with Astrid and Solveig. Solveig might be bull-strong, but she was still human, with a human's reflexes, so I, as our strongest fighter, had her with me, so Astrid and I could protect her. Solveig had the spear. It would be her job to hold any creature we caught down, so we could finish it. We found Ashlyn in the last house, searching it frantically, upending everything.

"Ashlyn! What's going on, why aren't you in the caves already?" I asked.

"It's Gallus," she sobbed, looking under her bed. "He decided to hide from me, and I can't find him!"

I cursed silently. We didn't need this right now, and I was afraid we were going to run out of time. "Do you have anything he wore lately, or that he slept in?" I asked.

"Why does that matter? We don't have time for this right now," she cried.

"Just trust me," I soothed, trying to calm her down. "This will help us find him faster."

"Alright, if you say so," she said, scrambling around. She found a used nightie in a pile of clothes and tossed it to me. I inhaled deeply, etching his scent into my mind, then passed it to Astrid, who sniffed it deeply in turn.

"Let's go," I said. Astrid moved deeper into the small house, while I cast around where I was. His scent was everywhere, as would be expected, along with his mother's and father's, so I moved around, casting about and trying to sort the scents out by freshness. I caught the thread of Gallus' scent, and followed it, crouching down to bring my nose closer to it. It led to a spot on the floor. "Ashlyn," I called, "Do you guys have a basement or a root cellar?"

"Yes, yes we do," she exclaimed, despair turning to hope. She hurried over, stuck her finger in a knothole, and lifted up a trapdoor, revealing a hole in the ground. I slowly lifted myself down, and crouched in the cellar. It was shallow, deep enough for someone like Gallus to run around in, but too short for an adult to stand up in.

"Gallus? Gallus honey? You need to come out now. We have to go," Ashlyn's voice drifted down from above.

I swept my gaze around the cellar, trying to find something that stood out in the gloom. Nothing. So I crept forward, trying to follow his scent through the dust that permeated the air. It led me to a corner of the cellar, where a form, bit by bit, congealed, separating from its surroundings. Gallus. As I got close enough, I could see that his skin had taken on the colors of his environment, like some of the tree lizards that lived in our jungle, or the octopuses that we sometimes found in the tide pools two days south from Serenity. Useful in a warrior, I thought idly. "Come on Gallus. We have to leave now," I said softly, holding out my hand.

He exploded into action, trying to dart around me, but as quick as he was, I still managed to snag him by the collar of his shirt. I reeled his struggling little body into my embrace, but shrieking, he managed to bite my forearm, his sharp little incisors, not quite fangs yet, sinking into the flesh.

I growled at the pain, refraining from giving the little bugger a good shake, and crawled to the opening, handing him up to his mother, who gathered him up, cooing at the little beast. I crawled up out of the hole. "Alright, let's get out of here," I grumbled.

We hurried out of the house, Ashlyn clutching her son to her. Out of our eyesight, beyond the town limits, growls and shrieks of pain announced that battle had been joined. Astrid led our group, while I was in the rearguard position. Solveig marched beside Ashlyn, clutching the boar spear and ready to jump in whether we got attacked from the front or the back. Islands of forested greenery flew by us as we rushed towards the caves, and I cursed under my breath. Beautiful and peaceful they might be, but right now they could hide a thousand attackers and we would never know. All I could do was pray that we would reach the safety of the caves before the perimeter of the town was breached.

Suddenly, Astrid careened to a halt, holding up her hand. We slithered to a halt behind her, and froze silently in place as she raised her nose to the air, trying to reacquire the scent that she had moments before. A rustle of shrubbery was all the warning we got as a shadow burst from the foliage and body checked Astrid clear across the road into another island of plants. It started to bound after her, but a scream from Ashlyn drew its attention to us.

It rose to its hind legs and glared at us intently with red glowing eyes. It was just like the monsters I had fought so long ago in Sanctuary, a horrifying mishmash of animal and man rolled into a nightmarish whole. Slobber dribbled from its mismatched jaws and dripped onto the ground in a soft patter, and a deformity in its spine gave it a permanent hunch that allowed its overlong arms to reach almost all the way to the ground. Black-tipped claws adorned fingers that looked like tree branches in winter, skeletal and long.

Ashlyn shrieked and was about to panic and run away when I stopped her.

"Stop!" I barked, authority from years of commanding my troops infusing my voice. She stopped, against her will, held by my voice. "If you run now, it will chase you, and we won't be able to save you. Stay still. I promise, we won't let it hurt you," I added urgently.

Solveig, meanwhile, had moved, putting herself between the beast and Ashlyn, her spear at the ready. Its attention, momentarily caught by Ashlyn's scream and movement, now focused on Solveig. Angrily it tried batting the spear aside, but Solveig quickly brought it back in line before it could charge forward. I moved beside Solveig, ax and sword in hand, waiting for a moment to strike. "All right, Solveig," I said quietly. "Get it."

With a fierce cry, she began jabbing at it, trying to impale it, forcing it back. It batted at the spearpoint, using its speed to keep her from sticking it. I wanted to circle around and attack it from another angle, but I dared not. I was the last line of defense between it and Ashlyn and Gallus. I couldn't let myself get distracted. I had to be patient.

Solveig and the Beast held each other at bay, Solveig's reach and the beast's speed negating each other. I worried that Solveig would begin to tire. I had no illusions about the Beast. It was Solveig that finally made a mistake. One of her thrusts came in a little low. Like lightning, one of the Beast's paws slapped down, pinning the spearhead to the ground. Growling in triumph, its muscles bunched as it prepared to rush up the spear shaft and bury Solveig under its mass.

I saw this all in a split second as I lunged forward, sword poised to thrust into the side of its chest when Astrid hit it like a battering ram from its other side. Astrid's Other form was lithe and sleek, built for speed above all else. She used it now, swarming over the Beast's larger form like a housecat attacking a bear, biting and scratching. Solveig reacted instantly, jerking her spear back and then thrusting forward with all of her strength, catching it in its chest. It shrieked in pain, ignoring Astrid and trying to grab the spear with its paws to pull it out of its chest. That was a mistake on its part, and Astrid didn't waste her chance. Draping herself around its neck, she wrapped one of its arms in her legs and latched onto its other with her clawed hands. Howling with strain, every muscle in her body stood out in taut relief as she flexed, pulling its arms out wide.

That was my cue. Dropping my ax, I drew my honor dagger and hammered it into its chest, aiming for its heart. I pulled my dagger out and slammed it back into its sheath, coating it anew in silver powder. It howled in utter agony as I ripped it free of its home and buried it in the Beast again, this time in its eye. I repeated the process again and again stabbing in a frenzy until the monster lay still and unmoving, its unnatural healing stilled by the silver. Panting heavily, I stepped away, sheathing my dagger for the last time. I would have to clean it later, sure everything was pretty gummed up with the creature's blood.

I turned to Ashlyn, who was staring at us in paralyzed terror. "Come on," I said quietly, soothingly, "Let's get you and Gallus to safety."

We made the rest of the trip in safety, Astrid this time ranging ahead and to either side of us, scouting for more enemies, always staying in the shadows. We didn't need to freak Ashlyn out any more than she already was. She was barely hanging onto her composure, breaths coming in great, ragged gasps, and clutching a squirming Gallus to her like a lifeline. I could tell she wanted to break down and cry her stress out until she was completely drained, but she was holding it together for her son. I respected that kind of strength.

We handed her off at the caves, Astrid staying out of sight.

"Did any of them get this far?" I asked the guards.

One of them shook their head. "No. You see anything?"

I nodded. "We ran into one of them back there. We took care of it."

He snorted. "They couldn't be that tough, then."

"Not anymore than your typical rabid grizzly bear, anyway," I replied, lip curling in a little sneer. I imagine he would change his tune slightly once he talked to some of his fellow warriors who had actually fought some of these monsters.

"Come along, Solveig. Let's see if we can find any more." We turned and left. Astrid joined us once we were out of sight of the guards. We didn't need her to get attacked by mistake.

We didn't find another one. We joined up with some more of our Sisters. They had run into one of their own, but they had called for help and another trio had arrived in support. Caught between six Sisters, the beast hadn't lasted long, so we retraced our steps so Astrid could retrieve her clothes and change back to her human form. Once she was dressed again, we went back to the caves to await the warriors' return.

The last team straggled in. One of them held his hand up to one of his teammates walking beside him. His skin erupted in light. Bands of red and green color rippled up and down his hand once, twice, thrice, then flickered off and on. His teammate's face flashed back at him in a series of staccato bursts, then sputtered off. I filed that little bit of information away. They had a way to silently communicate with each other. I'd wager half the gold left in my pouch that it was more comprehensive than any hand signal system other armies would use.

The teams huddled around Marcus and his group, who had been one of the first squads to arrive. I imagine they were going through some sort of after battle debrief. I let them have their space. They wouldn't welcome me in their midst at the moment, but I had a feeling they would be asking some pointed questions soon.

I didn't have long to wait. Everybody broke up and went to the caves except Marcus' team. He motioned for me to join him. I strolled on over. His group consisted of mostly mature men in their prime, with one or two that looked old. I guessed this was the whole council.

"How did it go?" I asked.

"We lost one of the young ones. It was his first battle, and he got separated from his unit. He gave a good accounting of himself before he fell. Several more of us were wounded; some seriously enough we required blood," Marcus replied. Two thin blood trails ran from the corner of his mouth to his chin. Apparently he was one of the ones that needed blood.

"We dismembered them as you instructed," another one said. "You were right in that they had unnatural vigor. Their wounds closed almost as soon as we made them. Yet we found the two that you killed. You left them whole, yet they were as dead as any. Why is that?"

I sighed inwardly, silently cursing that they were so observant, but I shouldn't have been surprised, and they had been remarkably forthcoming with me so far.

"They, we, are allergic to silver," I said, drawing my dagger and showing them the bloody mess coated in silver dust. "It halts our healing, and if we get enough of it in our system, it can send us into shock and kill us."

"Why did you not tell us this before!" Marcus demanded angrily.

"There are secrets that we keep close because our very survival depends on it!" I snarled back. "And even if I did share the information with you, what would you have been able to do with it in the time we had? Nobody makes silver weapons for good reason, and the silver in powder form is more effective anyway. Do you have a large stockpile of powdered silver lying around?"

Marcus thought about it for a moment, then exhaled sharply, the tension draining from his body. "Fair enough," he said. "Now. Let's talk about your blood. We drank from some of those creatures in order to heal." He closed his eyes, remembering the experience. Apparently it had been good for him. "So much energy. It healed us at least twice as fast as normal blood. There has been talk among some of us that maybe we should extend an invitation for you to live here, permanently."

I shook my head. "Did you get all of them?" I asked.

One of the old ones shook his head as well. "We did not. We killed four. You killed two. At least six got away."

"Then there's your answer. They are what we are hunting, and now the trail is fresh. We will be leaving in the morning."

"Some people," Marcus looked at his group, "Think that we shouldn't give you the choice."

"What, keep us here against our will, like cattle?" I purred, menace dripping from every syllable. "You faced off against a half dozen of these creatures. If we're in these forms for too long, we lose our ability to reason and become little more than animals. There's thirteen of us here, now, in full control of our faculties. And even if you did somehow manage to capture or kill all of us, there are still Sisters back home. Sisters who *will* come looking for us eventually. And when they find out what you've done, they will raze this place to the ground. I think you should reconsider and ask yourselves if your potential reward is worth the certain risk."

Silence lay like a wet, heavy blanket between us for a long, uncomfortable moment, then the whole group threw their heads back and roared with laughter. "We thought it was a bad idea, too," Marcus said, wiping a tear from his eye. "It was one of the youngblood's ideas. We told him that when he stopped sucking on his momma's titties, we might listen to him." He clapped me on the shoulder. "Relax! Everything's fine!"

I chuckled, but my heart wasn't in it. If Ignatius and this other youngblood was anything to go by, then these people might become a problem for us in the future. I might have to actually set up a diplomatic embassy in this place in the future to avoid any potential conflict. And to remind them that we were formidable in our own right. I sketched a shallow bow.

"Once again, Marcus, I thank you and your people for your generous hospitality. Now, if you will excuse me, I have to go make preparations. We have a hunt to finish, and we'll be leaving at first light."

"Let me walk with you, Lyr," Marcus said as I started to leave. Once we were out of earshot, he said, "I apologize for the joke. It was in poor taste. Some of the other council members thought you deserved a slap on the wrist for not telling us about the silver thing. Ashlyn told her husband about how you protected her and Gallus, however. We know what you can do. Getting in a war with your people would be a losing proposition."

I walked in silence for a while, then said, "Point taken. And you've been remarkably forthcoming about your own people. However, it makes me wonder what you've held back in return. It's not prudent to share everything about you to a total stranger. You never know how that will be used against you in the far future. I'm sure you understand."

He nodded. "I do. Now, go make your preparations. We'll see you're properly provisioned for the trip, as thanks for helping us defend Haven." With that he left my presence.

I made it back to my group, who were waiting for me. Solveig stood a little ways away from us, half hidden in the darkness, Scipio at her side. "Let's pack it up, ladies. We have a hunt to resume, now that the scent is fresh. We leave in the morning."

The group broke up and left, going to turn in. It was going to be a long day tomorrow.

"Lyr? Astrid? Can I talk to you, please?" Solveig called out to us.

We joined her, Scipio looming beside her like the shadow of a mountain. We stood there, waiting, while she struggled to find the right way to say whatever she was trying to say. The silence grew uncomfortable as the pressure continued to build inside of her, until finally she blurted out, "I want to stay here! With Scipio, I mean."

Astrid gasped in shock, and I raised an eyebrow. "It's rather sudden, don't you think?" I asked.

She nodded. "I know, I know! And I don't know what's going to happen when we get to know each other better, but," and she took a huge shuddering breath. "We've been on the road a long time, and I'm tired. All I've ever wanted is a home to call my own and a family to love. Now I have a chance to have that again, and I want to take it. Scipio said that even if we don't work out, I'll have a place here for as long as I want, or I'll be free to leave, to find my way back to you. So that's it. I'm staying here!" she looked defiantly at me, as if she expected me to object.

Astrid spoke up first, embracing her mother. "It's all right, Mother. You've given up so much, everything you've known and loved in order to give me a chance to find my own path. You deserve to be happy. I love you, Momma, and I'll come visit when I can," she said, tears falling freely down her cheeks.

Solveig laughed, in between sobs. "You better. I'm still young enough to have kids, you know. I want you to meet any new brothers or sisters you'll get."

Astrid gave Solveig a tight squeeze, then let her go and stepped back. I stepped up, craning my head up to look at Scipio. "Can you give us a moment, please?" I asked.

He hesitated, as if afraid I might talk Solveig out of it, then nodded and stepped back, melting into the darkness like it was his home.

I looked deep into Solveig's eyes. "Are you sure about this, Solveig? You've only just met him tonight, you know. There's a lot you don't know about each other. You'll be all alone here."

She nodded. "I'm sure. I never liked it on the road, and I've felt alone ever since Astrid's Change. She belongs to you now."

I inhaled sharply, stung in more ways than one. I never meant to take Solveig's daughter from her. In fact, I had thought that Solveig had become part of our extended family. It hurt that she had felt so alone, and even more that she didn't think she could talk to me about it.

"Well, in that case, I give you my blessing to seek your happiness here. We will drop in from time to time, however, to see how you're getting along."

She laughed a little, then broke down into gulping sobs, relief from the unbearable tension apparent.

I gathered her into a tight hug, and whispered in her ear, "My sister, my beloved sister. Did you not think I would never have the strength to let you go? You have always had the freedom to choose. But you will, forever and always, be a part of our family. Never forget that. And never forget that if you need us, we will come."

She squeezed me tightly, threatening to pop a rib. "Thank you, Lyr. I was afraid you wouldn't understand."

"I understand, Solveig. Everyone, young and old, man or woman, wants someone to love, and a place they can call their own."

I picked Scipio's outline out of the darkness. "Temperate moons to you and yours, Scipio. Take care of our Sister."

He ghosted back into the slightly lighter darkness that hovered around us, and put a giant arm around Solveig's shoulders. "Thank you, Lyr," he rumbled, a subterranean bass coming out of that massive chest. "I intend to."

We swung onto our horses as light had barely begun to break over the ridgelines and creep into the mountain valley. There had been many tearful farewells when everyone discovered that Solveig intended to stay, which had surprised her no end. But she was here now, arms around Scipio's gargantuan form for support, tears streaming freely down her face. I sighed, sad that we were losing a Sister, but determined to see our quest to its conclusion, so we could continue our own lives.

"Come everyone. It's time for us to continue our Hunt. Let's finish this."

Showdown at the Argent Mines

We followed the scents of Fenrir's survivors from Haven across the Lawless Lands. I was worried that we would have to go hundreds of kilometers out of our way to find a path that was passable by our horses. The Wall, the upthrust cliff that bisected the continent from north to south, separating the savannahs of the Lawless Lands from the Altan Plateau, was notorious for having very few traversable paths that led up its sheer cliffs. Marcus, however, knew of a route that was popular with outlaws that raided the Plateau from the Lawless Lands, and pointed us in the right direction.

Their scent led us along the northern coast of the savannah that comprised the Lands, on a natural ridgeline just out of sight of the Woods Hole Sea, and just north of the marshes that ran the entire width of the northern portion of these plains.

We had little trouble on this leg of our trek. Most of the outlaw bands that infested the Lands like fleas on a dog, clustered much further south, nearer the main trade route that connected the west to the east. Various lion prides objected as we crossed their territory, recognizing fellow predators and not happy about it. A couple of the big males from a few of the prides thought to challenge us, much to their sorrow. It was a hard lesson for them to learn.

Their trail led across the lush savannah into an area of Kaler I had never been before. Grasslands gave way to drier hills, and the hills began to climb ever further up, changing into mountains. As we climbed higher, bright green grass turned into faded green woody brush, dulling further as the brush gave way to sage, then slowly petered out altogether. The peaks above and around us thrust their jagged summits, like broken spear points, into the sky, as if they were trying to puncture it. The rocky terrain and loose rocks made it difficult for the horses, and we found ourselves backtracking several times as the trail disappeared altogether. Against my better judgment, I sent out scouts. I was afraid of ambushes, but falling off of a cliff suddenly appearing in front of us would be bad, too.

We lost Fenrir's trail in the maze of box canyons, dead end trails, and endless backtracking. We lost our own way, too, as our scents crossed and recrossed again and again, hopelessly muddling up our trail.

Just as I was losing hope of finding our way out of this mess and having to dry camp in this desolate wilderness, a call rang out. Winda had found a trail. Not Fenrir's, but human. It was a winding, snaking thing, seemingly crisscrossing the dry washes at random, but we followed it anyway. Its meanderings eventually led to a wagon track, which in turn led into a town, which was nothing short of astonishing in this isolated location. Even more astonishing, it appeared to be a fairly substantial town. More than a dozen weatherbeaten grey-brown buildings clung to the rocky hillside. There were at least three, from where I could see, brick chimneys at least ten meters tall rising high above the town, belching out smoke. Muffled thumps, barely discernible from where we were, sounded in the distance.

As we rode slowly down the one main street that ran through the middle of town, people began to filter out of the buildings to watch us pass. Apparently a group our size didn't show up in this part of the world on a regular basis. A man stepped out of a small adobe building decorated with barred windows, and walked to the middle of the street in front of us, halting our progress. I reined in Red and stopped, studying him. He was of average height, with a lean frame, his skin had a rich chocolate tone, and a generous beard grew around his face, although apparently it was afraid of his upper lip, which was bare. A number of fine lines crinkled around his eyes, either from smiling a lot, or squinting at the sun, I didn't know. A large black felt hat, upturned at the sides, crowned his head, and there was a silver star pinned to his shirt.

He held up his hands. "Normally I would say welcome, but now is not the time. The town of Argent isn't safe right now. You should turn right around and leave, while you're still able," he announced.

"What's going on?" I asked. "Maybe we can help."

A look of profound skepticism crossed his face. "I'm don't know what's happening for sure. But what I do know is that people have gone missing from the mines and this town, taken by Makers know what. If I didn't know any better, I'd say we were under attack, and I'm not sure how much a bunch of women could help. The menfolk around here are stretched thin as it is. There's not enough of us to protect another twenty people."

"You'd be surprised at the difference we could make," I replied mildly. "Tell you what, it's been a long ride and we're tired. Is there a place where we can water and feed our horses? Then we can find a cool place out of the sun and you can tell us what's going on. If we can't help, we'll be gone in the morning."

He shrugged. "Your funeral. It's a bit of a miracle you even made it into town. My name's Caleb, but you can call me Sheriff, as I'm the law here."

"Nice to meet you, Sheriff. I'm Lyr."

We gathered in the biggest space available to us, which was the local tavern imaginatively named the 'Bucket o' Blood Saloon'. Even so, it still wasn't big enough to hold all of us Sisters plus all of the townsfolk that wanted to participate, so Caleb had to send most of them, including all of the women, away. Apparently a 'saloon' wasn't a place a 'properly reared woman' could patronize. Caleb got a beer for himself, and a beer and a whiskey for me.

"Didn't know what you preferred," he said by way of explanation as he plopped the drinks down on the table in front of me. He sat down across from me. Up close I could see more faint lines gathered around his mouth. This was a face that liked to smile frequently. His dark brown eyes studied me intently as he sipped his beer. They were eyes that showed a quick and lively intelligence.

"Thanks," I said, as I sipped the whiskey. It tasted strongly of oak and burned like fire on my tongue. I tossed the rest back, enjoying the way it seared my insides going down. It reminded me faintly of the Skull Hammer I so enjoyed back in Serenity. A wave of nostalgia for home hit me hard. I mentally shook myself. Now was not the time to get distracted.

"Nice, huh?" he asked. "That'll put hair on your chest."

"I can manage that on my own, thanks," I replied drily. "So, Sheriff, what's the deal here? What could possibly be so appealing that it would attract so many people to such an out-of-the-way place?"

"Silver," he replied shortly. "Silver and lead. This town is the greatest silver and lead producer anywhere around. We ship lead and silver bullion to both Li-Zhang in the east and Newar in the west, depending on prices. We can also refine zinc here, which you need for separating the silver from the lead."

He paused and took a long pull from his tankard. "We have over two thousand people living here, with who knows how many more prospectors crawling around these mountains looking for the next big strike. Now, most of my job is keeping drunk miners from killing each other, or the fancy men who make their living fleecing them at cards. But about a month ago, prospectors that would normally come into town for supply runs or to assay ore, started going missing. Prospectors often cover a lot of ground, and theirs isn't the safest occupation, so if a couple didn't show up, I wouldn't worry, but none of them have shown up lately, which is strange."

He paused to take another drink. "Then, strange things started happening. Now, we have half a dozen mines with who knows how many kilometers of tunnels running through them, so it's hard to keep track of everything. Recently however, in the farthest tunnels in the two mines farthest from the town's center, miners have started going missing. And it's not the usual mine tunnel collapse or them falling down a 100 meter hole, either. They've completely disappeared, or the body is missing, but there's a large bloodstain left behind. In the last couple of days, it's gotten even worse.

"I've ordered all the mines closed until we figure this out, which has both the mine owners and the mine workers, two groups of people who normally hate each other, both screaming for my head.

"Normally I wouldn't give two copper coins about what they say about me; the town hired me to do a job, and I'm going to do it, but I've never seen anything like this before. I don't mind telling you, I'm losing sleep over it. The last thing I need is to get replaced by some village idiot who's going to ignore the signs, open everything up and get a whole lot of folks killed."

A current of excitement, almost giddiness, rushed up through me, starting in my gut and shooting up out of the top of my head like lightning. I quaffed my beer in one large, drawn out gulp, then banged it onto the table. "Show us. Starting with the first mine that you've noticed problems with."

He led us out of town to The Silver Lady mine. I deployed scouts all around us in a thin shell, far enough out to give fair warning, but close enough to be in sight at all times. I didn't need my Sisters to start disappearing like Caleb's miners. It didn't look like much, just a gaping hole in the side of the mountain, braced by timbers, and with wooden rails running out of it to a large pile of crushed rock, tailings from the mine.

"Where do you guys get the wood?" I asked, mildly curious. "This country looks pretty barren, if you don't mind my saying."

Caleb shrugged. "There's some pine that manages to grow in some small amounts around here, but we get a lot of timber in trade with the Bull Kingdom. Every once in a while we'll also get some wagon loads from Ion. They're relatively close, too."

"Hmm." I stepped closer to the portal. Air, markedly cooler than where we were standing, was blasting out of the opening. I looked over at him. There's quite a bit of air movement here."

He nodded. "The miners will sink shafts from the top of the mine all the way down to the bottom for air circulation. The difference in air temperature causes the wind you're feeling there."

I moved more fully into the airstream. Interspersed with the dusty smell of pulverized rock and soil and the various scents of small rodents and reptiles that liked to sleep in the semi-protected spaces of the tunnels, a rank, feral odor blasted out of the doorway. It was unmistakable.

"Yusi! Winda! Come here," I called. "Do you smell that?" I asked when they stood beside me. They both nodded.

Yusi waved a hand in front of her face. "They're here. Or they were."

"That's what we're going to have to find out," I said. I sighed. "Kilometers of tunnels with holes drilled through these hills like a giant cheese. This is going to be a nightmare to clear."

"How are we going to do it?" Winda asked.

"I don't know yet. One thing I'm sure of. No one goes out alone, not even to go to the bathroom. We will break up into groups of three and maintain those groups the whole time. We don't want to get picked off one by one."

I turned back to Caleb. "Well, congratulations, Sheriff. You made the right decision. Closing these mines might have just saved your whole town. We have a pretty good idea of what you're facing. Now, let's go see that other mine. After that, I'm going to need to talk to the folks that know these mines the best."

Next, we went to The Pancake Mine, named after the prospector that discovered it. In Caleb's words, 'Pancake was a salty old coot that lived on pancakes, bacon, and coffee and talked to himself and his mule in equal measure.'

He was one of the first people to go missing. According to Walter Smitty, the mine foreman, the Pancake was the last mine to go from a hole-in-the-ground prospect pit, to an actual underground mine. So far it only had one level, and no ventilation shafts yet, just a number of drifts branching off from the main tunnel. The foul odor I smelled at The Silver Lady was here, too. This one would be easier to clear by far.

"I've seen enough. Sheriff, it's time to meet with all the mine owners and their foremen."

We gathered in the Bucket o' Blood again. Sheriff Caleb and Walter Smitty were joined by Samuel, who was the mine foreman for The Silver Lady. Harold Beauchamp, the owner of The Argent Mine, the biggest mine in town, and his foreman, Jon Driver, were also there. Harold was a fleshy middle-aged man dressed in a snappy yellow and green checked wool suit that gave him a slightly jaundiced look. The expanse of his belly strained his vest and pants, and the goatee on his face did little to direct attention away from his many chins. An expensive gold chain stretched across his vest with several different types of minerals and gems hanging from it like some sort of charm to ward off evil spirits. He carried an air of pomposity about him that shouted he was better than everyone else in the room, and everybody should immediately defer to his obvious genius. He was the one that had been the loudest protesting what Caleb had done to protect the town, and immediately rubbed me the wrong way for some reason.

I began without preamble. "I would like to start off by saying that you owe Caleb here a vote of thanks. His caution and quick thinking has saved a lot of lives. There's been a bunch of creatures running around all over the continent, causing trouble. We've been hunting them for over a year now. Now, what we have to figure out is if they're still here or if they have moved on, which means we'll have to clear out each mine, level by level, tunnel by tunnel. I also suggest we send out patrols to see if any of these creatures are still out there in the hills.

What I do know for sure is that they have been in at least The Pancake and The Silver Lady."

"And how do you know that?" Harold asked, his tone suggesting that I was making all this up.

"I smelled them," I replied shortly. "If you smell their stink once, you never forget it. You've been dropped into a world of shit, but luckily we're here now, and you'll need our help."

Harold dismissed me with an airy wave. "If it's anything, it's a pack of wolves or a bunch of crag cats, maybe a bear. Either way, we can handle it ourselves. I don't see how a bunch of women can help," this last was said with a corner of his mouth pulled up in a sneer.

I leaned forward until I was intruding in his personal space as much as possible, and pinned him with a glare. "You're not facing animals, you overstuffed bag of shit. You're up against things that used to be men, descendents of a military program started by The Makers before the Fall. They're fast, heal from most wounds, and have a viciousness that only a constant craving for blood and flesh can bring about. And although they might have lost their humanity, they're still smart; smart enough to utilize strategy, and lay traps. Without us, you don't stand a chance. Most of you would be slaughtered out of hand. The unlucky few will be Turned, cursed to spend eternity as an animal that once remembered being human. So until you know what you're talking about, why don't you sit down and shut the fuck up."

Harold had turned an alarming shade of red during my speech, and was about ready to lunge out of his chair at me when a shout from Caleb stopped him in his tracks.

"That's enough, Harold. Lyr's right."

Harold dropped heavily back into his chair and turned his piggy glare from me to Caleb. "She's right about what?" he demanded.

"Everything," Caleb said shortly. I smothered a snort of laughter. I don't know if Harold caught Caleb's implied insult, but I sure did.

"What I want to know," Caleb continued, staring at me, "is how you know so much about this."

I didn't say anything for a moment, then asked, "Can I borrow your knife, please?" Wordlessly he handed his belt knife over. I took it, then drew it sharply across my palm, deep, to the bone. Blood gushed, spattering on the table in rivulets. Everybody who wasn't a Sister cried out in shock, and leaned away from the flood, with Harold leaning back in his chair so far, he overbalanced, crashing to the floor.

"Wait!" I barked. "Watch!" Everyone gaped, then cried out in astonishment, as the flood decreased to a trickle, then stopped, the gaping wound closing of its own accord, the flesh and skin growing back together. I swiped my other hand across my palm, wiping away the residual blood and exposing new, pink skin. "How do I know?" I asked rhetorically, raising an eyebrow. "You might say we're related, those creatures outside and us. They are abominations, and we are what the Makers envisioned when they created us all those centuries ago. We've been unreasonably lucky in the fact that the man making these horrors doesn't know what he's doing, or we'd already be buried under an onslaught of these creatures and humanity's cause already lost."

I looked deeply into Caleb's eyes. "There are many monsters in this world, Sheriff Caleb. You've just met one of them, and another one is out there, in the dark. Will you accept our help?"

Caleb's shrewd eyes bored into mine. "Do we have any choice, really?"

I shook my head. "Not really. This is our mission, to eradicate this plague before it takes hold and plunges this world into permanent darkness. But we can help each other out. You could use our expertise in fighting these creatures, and we need your expertise with the mines. It will save many lives in the long run, and give you a chance of surviving this next week. Are you with me?"

Harold had scooted his chair a good four feet away from me and was now holding his hands out, making some kind of strange sign with his two index fingers, forming a cross in what I assumed was a warding gesture. "Witch! Get you gone from my sight!" He looked at Caleb. "We should burn them all at the stake for the demons they are!"

I snorted. "Good luck with that. We would go through this town like a flash flood after a thunderstorm. Don't try it, unless you're tired of living."

Caleb was shaking his head. "Harold, it will puzzle me until the day I die why your daddy left you the mine when he died. You've clearly spent way too much time in that chemical lab of yours. It's eaten away at your brain." He looked at me. "Yes, we will accept your help. What do you need from us?"

I thought about it for a minute. "First, we need to gather everybody and concentrate them in as few buildings as possible, to make it easier to protect them and harder for the abos to pick people off one by one. Then, we'll need to gather all the timber we can lay our hands on. In every mine that smells like the abos we'll block every hole and entrance except for the main one. The mines where we can't find evidence of them we'll completely shut so they can't occupy them. That way we won't have to keep clearing them over and over again. Next, we'll need to make boar spears, a lot of them. That's the most effective way to fight them. Attack them three to one or more, pin them in place, and then kill them.

"I'll give fair warning, it's like trying to hold back a bear. It won't be easy. Now," and I swept my gaze over all the miners in the room, "how much silver do we have on hand?"

Everyone looked at Harold, who, after a brief struggle, seemed to gain control of himself. He thought about it for a while, then shrugged. "Not much, but I should be able to process some of our bullion and produce some fairly quickly. Why?"

"It will be crucial," I replied. "Caleb, let's go talk to your blacksmiths. We'll need those spears right away."

I went with Caleb to talk to the blacksmiths about producing the spears we would need after he broke the townsfolk into different 'action committees.' One group was responsible for gathering the noncombatants, one for organizing the miners so they could start plugging holes, etc. When they were ready, each party would get a deputy and a group of Sisters to smell out which mine contained the abos, and then protect the work party. After telling them what design would work best; a spear with a guard that would prevent our prey from running down the shaft at us, and a shaft as thick as a strong man's wrist; we went to meet up with Harold.

He met us in his lab, which looked like a combination kitchen and forge. To my surprise, he had changed his clothes from his fancy suit to a canvas pair of overalls and a leather shirt. I thought it suited him better, personally. His manner had changed, as well. He still carried that air of pomposity with him, but he looked more comfortable in his surroundings, and somehow I knew this was the place where he was happiest. On a table in front of him were a couple of different rocks, a bar of dark gray metal, and a silver coin.

He looked at me warily when I entered, as if he half expected me to leap at him and tear out his throat, but he kept his composure when I stopped in front of the table. He cleared his throat. "Now, I know you know this, Sheriff, so I'll say this for the benefit of the witch here. Our primary ore is called galena. He held up the first of the rocks, a bluish grey stone that glittered brilliantly, reflecting light in rainbow hues from its many facets.

"This is a lead-silver ore. When refined, it produces primarily lead, with a small percentage being silver. We pulverize it, separating out the ore from the host rock, then melt it down into this," he proudly lifted up the gray metal block. "This is our lead-ore bullion. Now, Li-Zhang is our main customer for this; they use lead in a lot of different things, and this is what we ship to them. The bandits of the Lawless Lands would try to rob us for any silver we carry, but they have no use for lead." He smiled smugly. "At Li-Zhang, we process this bullion further, separating the lead and the silver. We sell the lead to Li-Zhang, keeping the silver."

"Normally we don't process silver here, but we do have that capability." He held up the other rock. It was pale, cream colored, and bubbly all over its surface. "This also occurs in the Argent Mine. We can extract zinc from this and use that to separate the lead and silver. Luckily, we were getting ready to send a shipment to Li-Zhang when all this unpleasantness started, so we have plenty of bullion on hand. I'll get my men to start producing the silver right away."

I nodded, impressed in spite of myself. "Good job, Mr. Beauchamp. I'm impressed. The sooner you can extract the silver, the better. It will work best if it's in powder form." As I turned to go, he raised his hand.

"Excuse me," he stammered. "What do we need the silver for, anyway?"

I hesitated, then looked over my shoulder at him. "They're allergic to silver. It stops their regeneration, and enough of it can kill them outright." I left before he could ask anything else. I didn't elaborate because he was just the sort of person who would slip silver into our food or drink. I had no desire to get poisoned here. He was a smart man and would probably figure it out on his own anyway, but it might buy us some time before the inevitable betrayal.

With most of the townsfolk relocating to the two inns in town, The Grand Hotel and The Palace, we ended up staying in the Bucket 'o' Blood. Unsurprisingly, the second floor of the saloon housed a bordello. The working girls doubled and tripled up in half the rooms, and we crammed ourselves into the other rooms on the sheriff's insistence, much to the saloon owner Leroy's indignation at losing the most profitable part of his business. To be fair, we weren't all that happy about it, either.

"Ugh. This is disgusting," Yusi said, covering her nose with her hand as we put our gear in the room where we were staying.

I could only nod. The room, while as clean as it could be in this remote location, still stank of human sweat overlaid with the pervasive smell of sex and the perfumes and incense used to try and cover it up. Put all together, it was overwhelming. "I can't imagine any of our other Sisters will enjoy this either."

Someone knocked on our door and I opened it up, revealing Winda's dark form. "Does your room stink as much as ours?" she asked as she stepped into the room.

"Take a whiff for yourself," I replied, gesturing to the room.

Winda took a tentative sniff, then grimaced. "Yes," she growled. "Nice to know our Queen isn't afraid to wallow in the same muck as us."

I snorted. "Just let me know when I *don't*," I replied.

Winda laughed. "So what's the plan, Mother?"

"Tomorrow Caleb's going to lead a hunting party, what he calls a 'posse' out to look for abo signs. I want you, Amari, and Chyanne to go with them. If he forms more than one posse, detail some of our better horsewomen to go with them.

"I'll have Aadhya organize some guards for the crews tasked with closing up all the mine portals. Let them know if we find any more mines with abo scents.

"Yusi, I want you to take the last group of Sisters and form up a home guard. It will be your job to protect the townsfolk that can't fight. When everything's ready, I'll lead the first assault. We'll start with The Pancake Mine. From what I understand, it will be the easiest. We'll need to find out what it's going to be like to fight in a mine."

The next morning I found Caleb as he was forming up his posses. "We're going to need something sticky to apply to the spearheads. Do you know where we can find anything like that, or maybe some ingredients we can use to make some kind of glue?"

He pondered that for a second, then shook his head. "I don't. You'll need to talk to Harold. He has his fingers on the pulse of anything chemical that's used around here."

I grimaced, then nodded. "All right."

I found him in his lab. He was in his lab outfit again, the same as before. What had changed, however, was that now there were two other men in the lab with him. They were big, the same height as me, but wider, with unkempt beards and hair. They looked very similar to men I had run into in the Lawless Lands, men that believed they could take anything they had the strength to hold onto, and didn't care who they hurt in the process.

I ignored them and addressed Harold. "We're going to need something sticky, like a glue or maybe honey to apply to the spears, so the silver dust will stick to the spearheads. What do you think will work for that?"

He ignored me for a minute, putting me in my place, I guessed, then looked up with a cold smile. "You're not welcome here, witch. I suggest you leave or I'll have my men here escort you out. I promise you won't like it if they do."

I sighed. I could just leave and make Caleb deal with Harold, but time was a factor, and Harold needed to be taught a lesson. I motioned to the two thugs. "All right, gentlemen, let's get this over with."

They grinned, and when they started toward me, I moved, fast. Darting to one side, which put me out of line of the one on the left, I snapped a sidekick into the midsection of the right-hand guy, putting all the power of my body into it. It sank into his solar plexus, doubling him over, all of his air suddenly gone. As soon as my foot hit the ground, I shifted my weight and spun into a wheel kick that put my foot square into the other brute's jaw. He went down like a pole-axed ox. Normally I don't like to kick that high; it leaves you vulnerable to a counter from another trained fighter, but surprise was on my side here. They had no idea who they were facing.

I stepped over their bodies, and marched right up to Harold, grabbing his throat and squeezing. He choked and gurgled, his eyes opening wide in surprise at the strength of my grip.

"Listen to me carefully," I growled, leaning in close. "Just because someone is big, it doesn't mean they know how to fight. You might be the big swinging dick in this out-of-the-way little town, but that means nothing to me, and even less to those monsters in the dark. They'll rip your guts out and be feasting on your liver before you can blink twice." I gave him a little shake.

"Now, we don't want to be here any more than you want us here. The fastest way to get rid of us will be to give us everything we ask for, and to help us out as much as you possibly can. Cause trouble for us, and we'll get rid of you, one way or another. We won't even have to kill you ourselves; just take you out into the hills there and leave you. They'll take care of the rest. Understand?"

He nodded jerkily, his face purpling. I let go of his throat, shoving him away from me. He stumbled back, grasping at his throat, and gasping, chest heaving as he tried to get his air back. I turned my back on him and left.

That night the Sisters and I gathered in the saloon to discuss our findings. "There's only old spoor out in the hills," Winda began. "We did a complete circle around the town. There wasn't any trail fresher leaving the area. I think they're all holed up here, waiting for their opportunity, where there's a lot of easy prey. We did find the remains of some of the prospectors and their mules, however. I don't think any of them got away."

"That's something. Thanks Winda." I turned to Aadhya, who had been in charge of guarding the work parties. She had been a refugee in one of the villages that had been devastated by a Dragon raid eight months ago, had taken to the life of a Sister with joyful abandon, and had become a fierce, capable warrior.

"We caught scents in The Pancake and Silver Lady mines, but you knew that," she said. "We boarded them up first with heavy timbers. Nothing's breaking out of them easily, or quickly. We didn't see any signs in any of the other mines until we came to The Argent." She took a deep breath. "It's bad, Lyr. The whole place reeks to high heaven. Shiva knows how many of them are holed up there. And it's the biggest mine by far. I'm not sure we can clear it out."

"We have to, Aadhya. One way or another. If we have to lay siege to it and starve them out we will, but we'll leave that option for last. Maybe we can figure something else out after we clear out The Pancake and Silver Lady. In the meantime, we'll set guard details around the hotels and roving patrols in the streets. As soon as the blacksmiths make our weapons, and Harold refines our silver, we'll begin."

* * * * *

Two days later we were assembled at The Pancake, newly made spears in hand. In many ways, I wished we could have waited longer to give the blacksmiths more time to turn out more weapons. Even now they were hard at work, turning out more spears. The ringing of their hammers sang out in the distance, giving us our own musical accompaniment. Two thousand people armed with boar spears would be able to overwhelm any amount of abos hiding in these tunnels, but the more time we took, the more time it would give these creatures to figure out a way to find an escape route. We needed to finish this here and now.

"All right, listen up!" I bawled. "This is how we're going to do it..."

"Uh, excuse me, Lyr," Caleb said from my elbow. "This is my operation, remember?"

"Right. I'm sorry, Caleb," I replied, resisting the urge to roll my eyes. "You have the floor."

"Thank you. All right, listen up people!" he bawled. "This is how we're going to do it. I want teams of three, with at least one miner familiar with the layout of the tunnels with each team. Make sure the other teams stay far enough back to give the ones up front enough room to work. It will be the vanguard that will make the initial contact, but I want the rest of you packing the tunnel all the way to the entrance. Make sure they can't get by you. Do you have anything else to add, Lyr?"

I nodded. "Remember that these creatures will be much faster and stronger than even the strongest among you. Imagine you're going up against a rabid bear or man-eating lion. The trick to winning will be teamwork, and pinning them down. Don't forget to re-dip your spears in the silver powder after each stab. That's the key. I'll be in the front with Joseph and Samuel here," I motioned at The Pancake Mine foreman. "Caleb?"

Caleb continued. "There are a couple of branchings in this mine. When we get to one, another team will break off and work their way down that branch, clearing it out. Any questions?" There were none, and people started breaking up into teams.

"Winda?" I called. She hurried up. "Take a team and park yourself at the airshaft. We don't want anything escaping out that way." She nodded and scurried off.

"Yusi!"

"Yes, Lyr?" she said, appearing beside me.

"I want you to take another team and wait outside the main entrance here. I'm counting on you to be our final line of defense. Nothing gets past you, understand?"

She nodded. "Yes, Mother."

"Good! I have to go now, or they'll leave me behind." I started to trot off to join Samuel, when Yusi stopped me.

"Look after yourself, Mother," she said.

I nodded. "You too, Yusi," I replied softly.

The mine adit was dark, as these things tended to be, but dry. There wasn't a lot of moisture in the area, unusual for Kaler. It was also short, forcing me to crouch down to keep from banging my head on the ceiling. It was going to make things awkward.

"Couldn't make these things taller, huh?" I commented sarcastically, bending down.

Samuel shrugged his bony shoulders and spat a brown stream of tobacco juice on the tunnel floor. "Not my fault you're so tall. Works just fine for us normal-sized folk."

We walked along about 30 meters or so, the other teams falling in behind us, their boots scuffling in the dirt, until we came to a little side tunnel with a sturdy door set across it. An odd, acrid odor that I had never smelled before wafted from it. I looked at it then at Samuel, eyebrow raised in question.

He shrugged again. "Powder Room. One of Harold's new inventions. It's this black powder that explodes when you set fire to it. We use it in mining. Much faster than using just a hammer, or fire and water."

I tried sniffing for an abo, but the powder drowned everything out. I started for it, determined to check it out, but Samuel's hand on my arm brought me up short.

"What-" I started, anger blossoming due to his unexpected and unwanted touch on my arm, but he interrupted.

"You go waltzing in there with that lit torch you're holding, Missy and you'll blow us all sky high before we can fight those monsters. Let someone that works with that stuff check that room out."

I nodded, swallowing hard, and stepped back.

"Walter! Check out that powder room, will ya?"

Walter, back behind us with another team, nodded. They pushed forward to check out the room.

"Come on, Missy. Let's get going," Samuel said gently, and I nodded again.

We followed the tunnel's snaking way until we got to a slightly wider portion. Three tunnels lay before us, their openings gaping mouths of darkness.

"How many more branches are there, Samuel?" I asked, edging forward.

He shook his head. "This is it. This is a young mine. We haven't started stoping, yet, or creating new levels. So far the ore body is running level, and we're following along."

"Good," I mumbled. I crept forward, and gave all three tunnels a good sniff. The left tunnel smelled pretty clean; the rank feral scent of an abomination faded. There had been one there at one time, but probably not anymore. The center and right shafts stunk to high heaven. "Caleb," I called softly.

"What is it?" he replied, stepping to my side.

"Take that one, will you?" I said, pointing at the right-hand tunnel. "Chyanne, I want your and Aadhya's teams in there too. My team will take the center tunnel. Riya, take the left."

We all broke up and headed down our respective tunnels. I stalked down the middle one, torch held high. The mine track at my feet curved gently away from me, and slightly down, leading me further into the dark. The stench grew stronger, clogging my nostrils, leading me on, until it became like a wall.

"Stop," I ordered, holding the torch up. Everyone crashed to a halt behind me, murmurs building at the sudden halt. "Quiet!" I hissed, straining to hear. The sounds died down slightly. There, just beyond the torchlight, I could hear it, the low, raspy sound of a large animal breathing, combined with a building growl of anger at the audacity of us mere humans daring to invade its territory. Adrenaline spiked in me, running through my system like a flash flood, making my hands tremble. I took a deep, calming breath, hurled my torch toward the sound, then took my spear in both hands.

It tumbled, end over end and landed right next to my target, illuminating a gray furred nightmare with mismatched limbs and baleful eyes, crouching down on all fours. Just beyond the ring of light thrown by the torch, a second form could just be made out.

"There's two! Present!" I shouted, lowering my spear and jamming its butt into the ground. Then both forms leapt.

* * * * *

Chyanne

Chyanne had learned a lot about herself in this past year, what she was capable of, and what her limits were. And one of those limits she was just finding out about, was that she didn't like enclosed spaces. At all. Give her wide open spaces and a horse between her legs, and she was just fine. But this, this was hard. She could just feel the walls closing in around her, and the sense of uncountable tons of rock and dirt pressing down on her from overhead.

Her breath grew shaky, and her eyes began to dim as panic threatened to take over, so she concentrated on taking long, slow, deep breaths, and distracted herself by watching Caleb as he picked his way forward down the tunnel. At least the view was nice, she thought, admiring his slim, taut form ahead of her. She didn't know him well, yet, but she appreciated his witty, dry sense of humor. And the way he filled out those coarse cotton pants everyone in this town wore. What did they call that fabric? Denim.

A scent grew in her nostrils, clawing at her sinuses. Rank, musty, and wild, it screamed its warning to her. "Psst, Caleb! Hold up. We're close now." She moved ahead of him, spear held at the ready. He didn't like it, but she didn't give him time to protest.

Suddenly, a dim form barrelled around the corner of the tunnel and hit the end of her spear like a runaway bull, driving her back. The butt of the spear dug into the ground, then caught on one of the railway ties, stopping it cold. The thick spear shaft impossibly began to bend, then snapped like a dry twig. The form was suddenly on top of her, burying her beneath its revolting mass. She screamed as massive claws fastened on her shoulders, digging in deep, but her training took over and she ripped her dagger out of its sheath and plunged it into its side, between its ribs. It was its turn to shriek in pain as the silver on her blade burned it. It tried to bend its head down to bite her, but was hampered by her spearhead still embedded in its neck. A loop of a rope suddenly appeared in her peripheral vision, landing on the abo's head and drawing tight.

"Heave!" she heard Caleb shout, and the monster's weight suddenly disappeared from on top of her as it was dragged bodily away. Strong it might be, but it was no match for a dozen people hauling on the rope all at once. Rapidly it was dragged down the tunnel away from her, kicking and howling, people standing aside in the narrow passageway and stabbing it with their spears as it passed by them. She got shakily to her feet, and bent over, chest heaving as she tried to catch her breath, adrenaline still coursing through her.

A hand grasped her arm, and Caleb swam into her vision as he crouched down in front of her. "Are you all right?" he asked, concern painted plainly on his features.

She nodded weakly. "I'm fine." She straightened up and got her breathing under control. She rolled her shoulders around, feeling the unsettling, crawling sensation of her flesh knitting together as it grew rapidly, repairing the wounds the abo had inflicted on her. She thought it was creepy, but it was nothing compared to the feeling of her entire body transforming. "Come on. Let's make sure the rest of the tunnel is clear."

* * * * *

Lyr

Although they charged together at the same time, one was slightly faster, and therefore unluckier, as he was the one that ended up spitted on my spear. I dug the butt end into the ground to help me hold it, and luckily the butt caught on a cross tie, locking it down. I rushed forward, drawing my ax, and out of the corner of my eye, I saw the other one quickly overwhelm Samuel and bury him under its weight. The split second that took, however, opened it up to the spears from Dhitri's team. They didn't miss their opportunity, turning it into a pincushion.

My opponent was snarling, twisting and clawing at the spear buried in its chest, trying to free itself. I swung my ax at its side, aiming for the ribs. The ax crunched in heavily, burying itself deeply, and snapping at least three. I snarled, ripped it free, and struck again and again in a frenzy, chopping a hole in its side, to the symphony of its shrieks of pain. Its claws scrabbled uselessly in the tunnel dirt as it tried to get away from me, but the spear embedded in its chest and the tunnel wall blocked it.

I ripped my ax free from its side one more time, reversed, then buried my spike through its exposed eye and into its brain. Its struggles ceased, and it slumped in a heap, its system overwhelmed and dragging it down into unconsciousness. The damage it sustained would kill any normal animal or man, but its unnatural vitality meant it would heal the damage fairly quickly if given the chance. I tore my ax free from its skull and snapped my fingers.

"Silver!" I exclaimed, and stepped out of the way so the other teams could silver it, by means of repeated spear stabbings. The second abo was already dead, and I ignored it, kneeling down to check on Samuel. He was gone, his throat torn out in the split second that the creature had him down. I sighed. I had liked the crusty bugger. I straightened up, Dhitri appearing at my side as if summoned by magic.

"Come on," I said, "let's finish checking this tunnel."

Afterward, all of the teams convened outside of the mine to discuss what had happened. There had only been one in Caleb's shaft, and none at all in Riya's. Caleb was justifiably proud of his rope trick. All in all, despite the loss of Samuel, everyone who had participated was ecstatic that the mine had been cleared so easily. Backslaps and congratulations were passed around, and there was some talk among the crustier miners and townsfolk about taking some of the claws and teeth as trophies.

I felt the urge to caution them. "Remember. These creatures used to be men. Possibly men you knew once. This one," I toed the monster Caleb's team had dragged out, "could have been Pancake himself. We don't know, and never will. Do what's right." I walked away, leaving them to their celebration.

We met the next morning at the Bucket 'o' Blood with Caleb and Christopher, The Silver Lady's foreman, to plan clearing out that mine. He was about thirty-five, with tan, weathered skin, unusual in someone who spent most of their time underground, and a slim, wiry frame strengthened by a life spent shoveling rocks. His hazel eyes showed concern.

"The Silver Lady's not like The Pancake," he said. "We tunneled in underneath the main ore body, then stoped upward, following the veins, where we hit a big pocket. We've been following that ever since."

"So?" Dhitri said, shrugging. I gave her the side-eye. The last thing we needed was to get overconfident. That way lay disaster.

"So, it's going to be a lot more dangerous. The Silver Lady is twice the size of The Pancake, and riddled like a swiss cheese. There's a ton of places for these things to hide. And they'll be able to avoid us by moving between levels. I'm not sure if we mobilized the entire town we'd be able to cover everything, and I don't know how we'll know for certain if we've cleared it entirely."

Harold, who'd been silent so far, chimed in. "What's the draw like in The Silver Lady?"

Christopher shook his head. "Not great. Especially the upper level. It's been something we've been meaning to fix, but haven't gotten around to yet. Before we started using your explosive powder for mining, we'd set fire to the rocks, then douse them with cold water to get them to crack. Whenever we did it in the main adit, the smoke would linger in the upper tunnel for days."

Harold grinned, his eyes lighting up in delight. "Perfect!"

We settled on a plan. The whole town turned out, harvesting a noxious weed they called stinkweed from the surrounding hills, guarded at all times by teams of my girls, just in case. Then we piled the weed in all the mine carts we could find, along with other flammable brush. We were going to push the mine carts into the tunnel, then light the stinkweed on fire, hopefully smoking anything lurking in the upper tunnels out where we could deal with them. The more effective warriors were going to guard the people whose job it was to push the mine carts into the mine. It was a good plan. Something nagged at me, though, like we were missing something.

This time around, I had Chyanne and some of the more capable horsewomen patrolling around the mine, in case something broke free. I needed as many fighters as I could get to be guards, so couldn't spare the Sisters that I normally would outside.

"All right people!" Christopher bellowed. "The Silver Lady miners know where all the stopes and winzes are, so they'll be the ones pushing the carts! Lyr's ladies will be scouting ahead and clearing the way ahead of us. Each group will have a Silver Lady miner with them so they don't get lost. When we get the minecarts to the appropriate location, we'll light them on fire, and smoke those bastards out! All right, everyone, let's take them at a run!" He finished his speech to cheers from everyone, then we, as one, rushed into the mine.

It was a disaster. The plan was good, but we forgot to factor in what our enemy might do. That they wouldn't passively cower in their holes like they did at The Pancake. That *they* might be the aggressive ones, the ones that looked at *us* as prey. And there were too few Sisters; we were quickly spread too thin, and the townsfolk, brave as they were, were simply overmatched against creatures of the abos' strength and speed.

We started off fine, my team in the lead, Yusi, Winda, Aadhya, and Dhitri's following behind. Like The Pancake, The Silver Lady branched off, like the tributaries off a major river, shedding a team at each intersection. Pretty soon it was just me, Yumma, and our guide, Savage. Believe it or not, that probably wasn't his real name, which was probably something like Chester, or Chad. But that's the name he introduced himself as, so that was the name we used.

The tunnel branched again. I checked the smell of one, then the other. Both smelled dead. "How much further do these go?" I asked.

Savage pointed at the left one. "That one goes about a hundred more meters then stops." He pointed down the other one. "That's the main tunnel and goes for another thousand meters or so."

"Does the short tunnel have any stopes going up?" I asked.

He shook his head. "No. That was an exploratory tunnel where the vein petered out on us."

I nodded. "Good. I'm going to check it out. You guys wait here. I'll be right back." I ran down the tunnel to clear it, ignoring Savage's shout behind me. I should have paid attention, because I hadn't gone more than twenty-five paces, when I hit the roof of the tunnel with my forehead at a run. That knocked me back, stunning me, but that wasn't the worst of it. The force of my head hitting that random rock knocked it down causing part of the tunnel to collapse on me, partially burying me, and dragging me down into darkness.

I woke up on my stinking bed. Covered by that smelly blanket. Yusi sat in a chair by my bed. I groaned and hoisted myself up to a sitting position, noticing my clothes on the floor next to the bed. I let the blanket fall away from my torso, noticing that it was tightly covered in bandages. I looked over at Yusi.

She shrugged. "Your body got pretty crushed. We wrapped you up to give you some support until you could heal yourself."

I grunted. "How did it go?"

Yusi shook her head. "Not well. They were all up top. They waited for us to pass by, like they knew who was the real threat, then they dropped down onto the townspeople. The townsfolk did their best, but out of a dozen abos could only stop four. And mostly because they had packed the main tunnel so much, it slowed the abos down. They paid a heavy price for it, too. At least twenty, dead or wounded. We turned back as soon as we figured out what was happening, and helped them get a couple more. Nearest we can figure, six managed to escape from the mine. Chyanne's team ran down two more, but four got away. We don't know where they went. Could've left the country for all we know."

"Could have, but we should assume they haven't. If they have, we can hunt them down later. Did The Silver Lady get cleared at least?"

She nodded. "And we boarded it right back up. Nothing's getting back in, at least for a while."

"Good. Now I'm going to get dressed, and then let's figure out what to do with The Argent."

* * * * *

It was a somber group that gathered in the Bucket 'o' Blood that night. Our confidence after The Pancake had been shattered at The Silver Lady. The townsfolk had all lost friends or family in the attack.

Surprisingly, Harold took it the hardest. He sat at the table with his head buried in his hands, muttering to himself.

"What's wrong with Harold?" I muttered to Caleb. "Did he lose someone special at the Lady?"

Caleb shook his head. "He lost his mine foreman, but I think it's something else. He's never really lost at anything he's turned his hand to before. He might have inherited the mine from his father, but it's his work with his blasting powder that's made him more successful than even his parents could have dreamed up. Everybody here uses it. He's never failed at anything before, so today hit him kind of hard."

I nodded, then reached out and shook Harold's shoulder, startling him out of his reverie. He looked up at me, awareness filtering back into his eyes.

"You had a good idea. It should have worked, but it just didn't this time around. We forgot that the creatures we were hunting might have plans of their own, and we forgot how fast they are, me included. We'll have to learn from this and move on."

I gave his shoulder another shake, encouraging him. "Now, tell me all about the Argent."

Harold took a deep breath and took a long pull from his stein. He thunked it back down on the table, took another breath, then launched into lecture mode.

"The Argent is the largest mine in town. In fact, the town is named after the mine. The main ore body runs vertically from the top of Beauchamp Ridge down. We don't know how far. We've dug down six hundred feet so far, and still haven't hit the bottom of it.

In addition, there's rich veins radiating out from the central ore body that we've been following. If you look at a map, it looks like there's six levels, each level being about two miles in length, but in reality it's a crazy patchwork rabbit warren down there, with stopes connecting the different levels in random places. There's also drifts that end abruptly, twists, turns, odd branchings. For the life of me, I don't know how we'll be able to clear it, not without losing half the town at any rate."

He stopped talking, and stared glumly into space, lapsing into a brown study.

Chyanne piped up. "Could we just leave them there? Wait them out, until they starve?"

Harold spluttered. "Outrageous! That's a fabulously rich mine that employs half the town! We can't have it sitting idle for that long!"

"Would you rather lose the whole town, including yourself?" I shot back. "Corpses can't dig ore."

Harold fell silent, chastened.

Caleb shook his head as well. "It's a huge mine, with many air holes and exits. We don't have enough manpower to guard them all. Sorry, I just don't think that will work."

"Not to mention the chance that they'll be able to dig their way out somewhere. We can't take that risk," I said gently.

Chyanne fell silent, crestfallen.

I looked at one of the miners that was sitting at the table. "I noticed that the rock of The Silver Lady seemed to be different than The Pancake's. Less solid and more crumbly. What's The Argent's like?"

He shrugged. "It depends. There's areas where it's pretty solid, but there's levels where large sections needed cribbing to keep it from falling on our heads, and other spots where we had to put in stulls everywhere where we hit a big pocket."

Dhitri, always curious, raised her hand for attention. "I'm sorry, what is cribbing? And what are stulls? Some of us haven't lived here for years, you know."

"Cribbing is stacking timbers to support a mine ceiling, kinda like building a little log cabin, but underground. Stulls are jus' posts wedged here and there to keep the ceiling, or maybe the walls of a stope, from collapsing on our heads," Savage supplied helpfully.

"Hmm," I rested my chin on my hands, thinking. I wanted there to be some kind of flash of genius where a solution would pop into my head, but instead my thoughts just went round and round, like a mule team at a grist mill, going nowhere.

Harold, however, perked up. "You know, the main level of The Argent is the top level. It's not like The Silver Lady. We can fill bags or barrels full of blasting powder, send them down the ore chutes, then set them off. Maybe we can herd them into the less stable parts of the mine. A couple of strategic charges then could collapse whole sections, burying them alive with minimal risk to us."

"Do you have enough powder on hand, Harold?" Caleb asked.

Harold's eyes lost focus and he tilted his head up to the ceiling, calculating. After a bit, he shook his head. "Probably not. Not in my warehouse at any rate. Let me get together with the other mine owners. Between all of our mines, we might be able to gather up enough to do the job."

I nodded to myself. It seemed as good a plan as any, and I looked at Caleb, who was eyeing me as well. He shrugged at our unspoken communication, then said, "Sounds good, Harold. Let's go with it."

And so it began. Once his idea was given the go ahead, and determined not to fail again, Harold took the plan like a horse with the bit held in its teeth, and ran with it. The only problem was, what should have only taken a day at the most, stretched into two, going on three, while I gnashed my teeth down to bloody nubs, terrified that while we dicked around with the perfect delivery vehicle, the abos would find a hole we didn't know about, or dig themselves a new one and escape.

The thing was, while I danced in frustration on the sidelines, Harold was right, too. He determined pretty quickly that a burlap bag filled with powder did little other than make a big bang and create a lot of smoke. He quickly latched onto using metal shells that could be created easily. Stuffed full of powder, the resulting explosion created a satisfactory shockwave that could bring down unstable tunnel roofs, with the added bonus of spraying shrapnel everywhere. Any damage we could do before we actually faced those creatures was a benefit to us all.

Because of the amount we had on hand, our time constraints, and the relative ease of working with it because of its low melting temperature, it was decided we would use lead, even though iron or silver would have been more effective. But that still wasn't good enough. Harold had taken to enthusiastically experimenting with shell wall thicknesses, trying to determine what the optimal wall thickness was.

While he was doing his experimentation, I had deployed my girls on constant patrol of The Argent's known exits and entrances on a rotating basis. I had just come from hearing the current patrol's report and was now headed to the 'depot', an old gravel pit where Harold was setting off his explosions, hoping I could hurry things along a little. Surely he was almost done by now, I thought. I was so wrapped up in my thoughts that I wasn't aware of another presence until I heard the word "Catch!"

I looked up in surprise to see, in a split second, one of Harold's thugs throw a metal ball at me, smoke trailing from it. Instinctively I caught it, letting the heavy ball's momentum spin me completely around before I tossed it back at him. His shocked expression was the last thing I saw before it exploded between us. I felt the sting of dozens of metal shards hitting me, then everything went dark.

* * * * *

I woke up in my stinky bed again, Yusi sitting in a chair by my bed. Again. My head felt like it was twice its usual size, and my lips felt swollen. Something felt wrong with my mouth, and my tongue probed it, revealing that I was missing some teeth. I hoisted myself up to a sitting position with a groan.

"Yusi we have to stop meeting like this," I lisped, my swollen face and missing teeth making talking difficult, before I noticed that the rest of our little band had managed to cram itself into the small bedroom. How they managed it, I couldn't begin to guess. If somebody had asked me if it was possible, I would have said no.

"What's going on?" I asked.

She leaned over and covered one of my hands with hers. "When that bomb exploded, you got hit pretty hard with shrapnel, most of it centered on your face and chest. It took both of your eyes, and some of your teeth, as you've already found out. We spent forever digging pieces of lead out of you, including one that lodged in your neck, next to your jugular vein."

Zhong jumped in. "We had to use knives dipped in silver powder to slow down your healing long enough for us to get some of the deeper pieces out," she said, an odd, almost eager light in her eyes.

I studied her intently. "You sound like you might have enjoyed that a little too much," I said severely, but there wasn't a lot of force behind my words. Even after over a year of travelling in close company with Zhong, she still had walls up that no one had managed to breach yet. Truthfully, I was happy that she might finally have found something that interested her.

I looked back at Yusi. "What happened to the man who threw the bomb at me?" I asked

"Who, Elmer? He got peppered a little, but he's fine. We almost killed him ourselves, and most of the townsfolk wanted to hang him right then and there, but Caleb stopped us all. Said we needed every able-bodied person we had, and that he had a better idea."

"Which is?" I prompted when Yusi's pause grew a little too long for my taste.

"He said that since he's so into the new bombs that Harold is making, he can be one of the first ones into the mine. He'll be in the first assault wave."

A sudden suspicion flashed into my mind. "Was Harold behind this?"

She shook her head. "I don't believe so. Don't get me wrong, he wasn't broken up at all by what happened to you, but he was very annoyed at the interruption of his work by all the drama."

I grunted. Once I got out of bed, I was going to pay Harold a little visit to make sure. I didn't need someone of his intelligence coming after me. If he truly wanted to kill me, he just might manage it. I didn't need to be looking over my shoulder and ignoring the very real threat coming from the front. I looked over at Yusi again, then around the room at the rest of my Sisters. No one had moved. I sighed.

"What's wrong, Yusi? Obviously, I'm going to be fine, yet you all are hovering around me like mother hens. What's on your mind?"

She took a deep breath, her gaze darting around the room at everyone else, drawing strength from their presence. "Harold has declared he's found the optimal size and shape of the shells he wants to use. The blacksmiths are busy as ants from a kicked anthill making the shells. We're going in the day after tomorrow."

"So? That's good, right? What's the problem?"

Yusi took another deep breath, as if she was afraid something was going to blow up in her face. "We know how you are, Mother. And we don't think you should be part of the assault."

My skin heated up, and I thought my face was going to swell more than it already was in outrage. "What! That's silly! By the day after tomorrow, I'll be completely healed, except for my teeth, and those will come back in after my next transformation. There's no reason for me to not be in the fight. I'm the best warrior here, after all."

"We know, we know," Yusi soothed, patting my hand, trying to calm me down. "But the fact of the matter is, you were hurt at The Silver Lady, and you just sustained enough damage that would kill a normal person. You might be healed in time, but your body's reserves aren't going to be one hundred percent, and you know it. We had a talk, and we all agreed. If you're in the fight, then we'll be more worried about you than focusing completely on the fight itself. So please, we're asking you, help guard the town instead. You've trained all of us. We've got this."

I looked around at all of them, noticing for the first time their concerned faces, and it hit me forcefully, in a way I never let myself think about before, for multiple reasons. These weren't my Sisters. They were my daughters, every one of them, and I was their mother. My outrage drained away, replaced by an unfamiliar feeling that swelled up in me, one that I never let myself feel because it was so frightening. Love.

Love equated to vulnerability. Love could be used against you. But here we were. Run from it as I might, it finally caught up to me. And they were right. My reserves weren't going to be at one hundred percent. I'd be fine if I fought as I was, but if I was forced to Change for any reason, I would be running a real risk of not being able to Change back.

I slumped back down into that Makers-awful stinky bed. "All right, you win. I'll stay behind." Then I glared at all of them, seeing the relief etched on all of their faces.

"Don't get used to that feeling! It won't happen very often! Yusi, organize a homeguard. Winda, Aadhya, you're in charge of organizing the mine teams. Chyanne, you've got the cavalry detail. Now, bring me some meat. I've got to get back into fighting shape as fast as possible." I chuckled as they all sprang into action, bumping into and knocking each other over as they all tried to move at once.

And that was how the next couple of days went. Harold was in charge of the assembly line of bomb makers, the Sisters coordinated with Caleb on person-power, plans were made and discarded, then made and revised again. All while I sat on my ass, stuffing my face with as much food as I could hold, trying to build my reserves back up. It was probably all wasted effort, considering all the food that simply passed through my system. It took time for the necessary nutrients to accrete into the crystalline matrix that coated our bones, time that I didn't have. Still every little bit helped, although trying to chew around my missing teeth was annoying.

The day of our planned assault of The Argent Mine dawned. The original plan was to attack in the daytime. It wouldn't help anybody in the mine, but it would boost everyone's confidence outside of the mine itself, and give us the advantage. However, due to delays in bomb production and last minute organizational shifts, the sun had started sinking behind the mountains that surrounded us, giving the town a burnt orange overlay. There was talk about delaying another day, but we all agreed we had waited too long as it was, despite the elevated risk to us all as the advantage shifted to the monsters that were lying in wait for us.

Long torches were lit all around the town, bathing it in light, but delaying us another hour. The plan was to open up the top of the mine first and lower down a string of barrels filled with gunpowder and chained together with ropes and fuses. The resultant explosion would hopefully disorient anything hiding in there long enough for the teams to rush in, start rolling the shells down the ore chutes, and parking minecarts in strategic spots. Then they could set the charges off and hopefully cause controlled cave-ins that would trap most of the creatures, allowing for an easy mop-up of the ones that were left.

The teams assembled, then moved off toward The Argent mine, Harold in charge of the group that would set off the signal explosion. I stood in the middle of Main Street, and watched them go, leaning on my spear. I sighed, fear gripping my gut as I worried about everyone, about what they were going to face. Except Elmer, of course. I couldn't bring myself to give a fuck about *that* son of a whore. I sighed again, waiting for the big boom that would let me know when everything was going to kick off. Waiting was so much harder than being part of the action.

"Hello, Lyr," a voice murmured behind me, jolting me and spinning me around. I knew that voice. What met my eyes shocked me even more into a paralyzed disbelief. "Marie?"

* * * * *

Yusi

Yusi, true to form, had put herself in charge of the children, Zhong at her side. They had gathered all of the children in town and put them into the Bucket 'o' Blood, because it was one of the bigger buildings in town, as well as being more sturdily built than most of them. She didn't allow herself to dwell on the appropriateness of putting children in a house of ill repute. Survival first.

"How did I manage to get myself in this mess?" Zhong complained. "Stuck babysitting a bunch of kids that mean nothing to me."

"A series of events and decisions both in and out of your control led you to this time and place. Any other choice might have changed your destiny," Yusi replied absently. There was something wrong in the air tonight that portended doom. She could feel it, and it frightened her.

Zhong snorted. "Whatever."

Yusi snapped out of what was bothering her and focused on Zhong completely. "You've had a hard life. I get that. But so have we all. You're nothing special in that regard. But you're a survivor. *That* is what makes you special and why you've managed to handle everything that's been thrown at you so far. So here's a couple of hard truths. Even if you hadn't been attacked by The Ripper, there was a good chance you would be dead by now, whether it was from a client who decided to get a little too rough, a pimp trying to bring you under his control, or you finally Catching the Dragon in an opium den one night.

"So this is what you've been given, a completely fresh start, a do-over for your entire life. That is the Gift, not the Beast that you resent, and that you fight to control. And it can be a long life, a chance to live it to a depth that few people ever get. So you need to choose how you will live that life, whether you will be a beacon of light that stands against the forces of darkness forever, or be the darkness itself. But choose. The path is yours to take."

Something caught her attention. For the rest of her life Yusi couldn't tell what triggered her; whether it was an errant breeze that brought a scent to her nostrils or a premonition, but she was certain, down to her very bones, that Lyr needed her help.

"Stay here with the children," she ordered. "I'll be back."

* * * * *

Lyr

I saw her, but my mind refused to come to terms with it. Still, there she was, standing next to a large man whom I assumed was Fenrir. He was a large man, standing straight and tall with the muscled physique of a warrior. The planes of his face were sharply angled, and long lashes framed his chocolate brown eyes. Eyes that I assumed could be warm, but right now were frozen like a mud puddle in winter. A mane of straight black hair hung down to his shoulders, and clenched in his large fist was a slender leash that was attached to a collar around Marie's neck. The sight of that collar and leash nearly made me lose control, as red rage welled up from the depths of my soul and threatened to drown me.

I took a deep breath, then another, fighting for control. When I felt I had regained some modicum of it, I turned my attention to her, but watched Fenrir out of the corner of my eye at the same time. I had no idea where they had come from, but hopefully the bulk of their creatures were still trapped in that mine. If that was the case, then I had to keep them distracted until the townsfolk could set off the charges.

"You were dead. I came across your remains in that clearing so very long ago." I stared into her luminescent blue eyes, willing her to make me understand. I had always thought of her as a stunningly beautiful woman. She was very pale, with a slender, willowy figure, and thick brown, almost black hair. She smirked, a slight lifting of the corner of her mouth that managed to convey a sense of superiority. It struck a really incongruous tone with the collar and leash she was wearing.

"That's what we wanted you to think." She gazed up at Fenrir, adoration in her eyes. She sidled up to him and ran her hand down his chest. He glanced down at her expressionlessly for a second before returning his stare to me, trying to intimidate me. Unfortunately for him, he was a pale imitation compared to the force of personality that the one that Changed me wielded, nigh on to a century ago.

"I figured you out, you know. Why you insisted on being the only one to Turn us. It was a way for you to maintain control. I decided to figure out how to do it, and started to experiment on some of the lawless men that we captured. Most I had to destroy. Fenrir here was my first success. Then we fell in love." She stopped talking and resumed stroking his chest.

His expression didn't change as he continued to glare at me. I resisted the urge to roll my eyes. She might think she loved him, but I'd wager everything I had that her sycophantic worship wasn't returned in the slightest.

Her expression turned into a pout. "But then he escaped. I searched for him, didn't I? But I couldn't find him, not for a couple of months, anyway. While I was looking for him, he'd been very naughty, hadn't you, Fenrir? He had been making his own creations, and they ambushed us." Her expression changed, twisted by memories of pain and loss rising to the surface. "It was a hard battle, but we were losing, and then my love appeared. He saved me, but he required a sacrifice."

She turned to me. "I gifted him my hair and my arms, and he protected me from his servants. He left them behind to harass you, and took me with him. We've been travelling ever since, looking for a home. Someplace with a lot of raw material. For food. For soldiers."

"And he repaid you with a chain and collar," I sneered.

Her pale skin flushed red with rage. "I traded your chain and collar for his, is all! It might not have been physical, but you kept us all on a short leash!" she screamed.

"You knew the deal! And despite your high opinion of yourself, you're still just a pup, one who was still learning how to control her urges. A test you failed, as you can see for yourself!" I raged back at her, before gaining control of my temper, with difficulty.

I looked at Fenrir, who had stayed silent the entire time. "Can he talk for himself? Or did the Change make him mute?"

Fenrir threw his head back and laughed, a deep rich sound. He stopped abruptly, to fix me with his glare yet again. "I can talk. When it suits me," he rumbled.

"So how come you haven't created any more like you?" I asked. "Haven't figured it out yet?"

"I've only tried once. That mousy little bureaucrat in Li-Zhang. Then I figured out how to create my servants. Deliberately. They're easier to control. Why would I want to create future competition for myself? It didn't work so well for you, now, didn't it?" He smiled lazily, gently tugging on Marie's leash for emphasis. "Maybe one day, if I choose. I could always use sub-chiefs. But that's a long time in the future." He leaned toward me, focusing on me completely and smiling. "But a harem, now. I've always wanted one of those. And your Sisters would do admirably, once I break them."

Once again rage threatened to overwhelm me. My skin flushed and I trembled like a leaf, my Change threatening to overtake me. He was trying to get under my skin, forcing me to make a rash decision. Slowly I got myself under control. I just had to keep them distracted for a little while longer.

"Were you hiding in the mine with all your abominations? Or were you skulking out here? Couldn't abide their stink?"

His smile vanished like a blown out candle flame. "We were there. Shut in the dark for days. Argent will be paying for that insult to me in full measure, later. But I got my servants to start digging. We broke out today. In fact, they'll be joining us as soon as we've finished our little chat here. I'll be taking over the town, eating who I want and making soldiers of those worthy. Then it's off to the next town, until I've assembled a big enough army to carve out my own kingdom." He smiled at that, a feral baring of his teeth.

* * * * *

Harold

A hole just large enough to fit a barrel had been chopped into the wood planks covering the bottomless pit of the chimney. Harold stood over the hole, torch in hand.

"All right, everybody! Keep a hold on that rope! We only have one shot at this! Now, like we practiced... let's start letting the rope out!"

Carefully, hand over hand, a dozen townsfolk slowly lowered the heavy hawser into the blackness. Every fifty feet or so, a new barrel would be tied on, fuses braided together, and so on, until the first barrel hit the floor of the shaft. Quickly, the rope was tied off, and Harold touched his torch to the fuse. It was designed to burn all the way to the bottom, before touching off the lowest barrel, then burning back up, setting off the other barrels in a chain reaction.

"Go! Go! Go!" he screamed, waving his hands at the crowd. As one they turned and ran, some tumbling and rolling clumsily while others made it down the hill with all the grace of mountain goats. As one, everybody stopped and stared up at the top of the hill, waiting. Harold slid the last ten feet down on his butt, picked himself up, and kept running.

"Keep running, fools!" he screamed.

* * * * *

Caleb

Caleb sat his horse, waiting. For once he wasn't going to lead the assault in the mines. It was his crew's job to pick off stragglers if they managed to fight free of the mines, using the superior mobility granted to him by the horse. Chyanne sat next to him atop Prince, Astrid and Riya next to her. The fiery stallion fidgeted in impatience, but she quieted him with an expert hand.

"What do you think is going to happen?" she asked.

"Couldn't say," he replied absently, looking at the main portal entrance. "But I wager it's going to be epic."

* * * * *

Lyr

I was looking at Fenrir, trying to figure out how to answer his idiocy in a way that he would understand, when an explosion shook the ground under our feet. It wasn't a single explosion, either, but a series of explosions that rippled one after another, like the feeling of a knife edge riding on a fish's spine as you filleted it.

"You were saying?" I asked, baring my teeth in my own feral grin, before launching my spear at him.

* * * * *

Elmer

Elmer stood at his cart, gripping the steel edge with sweaty hands. His emotional state alternated between terror and rage. One second he was about to lose control of his bowels, and the next he was grinding his teeth in rage for being put in this position. This was all Caleb's fault, he thought to himself. Caleb, and all those strange bitches that rode into town on their high horses. When this was over he was going to make sure that everyone that slighted him paid him back in full measure. Just then, a series of explosions inside the mine almost knocked him off of his feet.

Jon Driver, the mine's foreman, shouted, "That's the signal!" and swung open the doors into the main tunnel. "Quick time, men! Hurry! Let's show them who's hunting who now! Go!" With a wild yell, everybody started pushing their carts in at a run. And Elmer was the very first one in line.

Panting, he pushed his cart deep into the adit. Everyone had their own jobs to do. His was to push his cart to where Tunnel Eleven changed from solid rock to a looser, much more dangerous rock that required timbering to support the tunnel where he was supposed to set off his explosive, hopefully causing a cave-in.

Other people stopped to light and then roll their bombs down the various ore chutes. Even more peeled off down different branchings, their own jobs to do. Elmer pushed grimly on. He had the furthest to go. He reached his objective, pushed his cart into place, and was about to light the charge with his torch, when other explosions began rumbling through the mine, jouncing the ground under his feet. He paused, his torch held shakily high, breath coming in great, panicked gasps, and waited until the ground stopped moving, at least for a couple of seconds.

It was the last mistake he would ever make. A low growl jerked his attention back to the tunnel in front of him. A pair of eyes lit up like lanterns in the dark beyond the torch light. He screamed and lunged to light the powder, but the eyes rushed at him and the body attached to them buried him under its weight, ripping and tearing.

* * * * *

The explosions rocked the mine, causing massive cave-ins as the explosives ripped apart the timbers and other supports that were keeping the mine from collapsing. But it was a huge mine, and a lot of Fenrir's creatures were crouched at the opening, waiting for him to call them. The loud noises and choking dust released caused them to boil out of the hole, like ants streaming out of a kicked anthill, squalling in fury. Suddenly, against all logic, the safest place to be in the entire town was *in* the mine. Carefully crafted plans were laid waste in an instant, and everything devolved into chaos as over a dozen abos flooded into the town.

"Shit!" Caleb cursed as howls of anger and screams of terror rang through the air. He leaned down in his saddle and grabbed a man who was fleeing by him. "Jonathon!" he snapped. "I want you to gather up anybody who can hit the broad side of a barn with their bow, get them up high, second story of the buildings that have them, roofs, whatever, I don't care. But get them up there double quick and have them start shooting those furry bastards! You got me?"

Jonathon nodded frantically and pelted off into the night.

"What's that going to do?" Chyanne asked him. "If they're not coated in silver, those arrows aren't going to do much."

"If my people stick enough arrows into them, it might slow them down enough for us to catch them and finish the job," he replied.

She nodded. "All right, I'll leave you to it. I've got some hunting to do myself."

He nodded. "Be safe, Chyanne," then spurred his horse forward, his men following him into the night.

"You too," she whispered, before reining Prince around. "Let's go, ladies. We've got abos to kill."

Winda and Aadhya were in the mine with their teams, guarding the miners who were setting off the charges. Smoke and dust billowed up from the different levels, filling the tunnels, clogging their eyes and nostrils, and quickly making the air in the mine unbreathable. The miners, their jobs done, were rushing by them, trying to get out of The Argent as quickly as possible. They were supposed to stay in the mine as long as possible, making sure the men got out and taking care of anything that showed up. The original plan was to leave the mine, reorganize, and head back in in the daylight to do any mopping up. That all changed when they heard the howling. Outside of the mine.

"Crap!" Aadhya cursed. "Winda, take your team and get out now. It sounds like you'll be needed outside. We'll be right behind you once everybody's cleared out here."

Winda nodded, clasped her forearm briefly in a gesture that communicated volumes, then took off, silently running toward the portal, her team following her.

Aadhya, sighed, then coughed, cursing some more. "Dhitri, Chaitri, on me. Let's make sure everyone's out and this level is clear."

* * * * *

Zhong

Zhong grumbled to herself, wondering when Yusi was going to get back. The kids were doing what any kid she had ever seen did. Being annoying. Getting into things they shouldn't, and hitting each other. Their screams and cries echoed through the building. She ignored them.

One of the older ones, a girl about ten years old, blond hair twisted into two braids, approached, carrying a baby about six months old. Zhong studied her. Ten she might be, but looking into her serious blue eyes, Zhong got the impression that this was an old soul.

"What?" she demanded.

"Do you think everything is going to turn out OK?" she asked, hitching the baby into a more comfortable position on her hip.

Zhong shrugged. "Who knows? Probably not, if my luck has anything to say about it." The baby screeched suddenly. Zhong looked down at it. It was a chubby baby, with plump brown cheeks, curly hair and chocolate eyes. She scowled at it, letting it know that she didn't appreciate the noise.

The baby found this hilarious, and laughed at her, its belly shaking as it giggled. Zhong scowled harder, which set the baby off on another long peal of laughter. Zhong couldn't help it, she smiled. There was such uninhibited joy in the child's laughter, it was impossible to not smile.

"I'm sorry, but Charlie here is such a happy baby. It's hard to keep her from laughing," the blond girl apologized.

"Charlie?" Zhong replied.

"Charlotte, but everyone calls her Charlie, for short."

"And you are?"

"Luna," she said. "My parents have a thing for the night sky, apparently."

Zhong grunted, then looked at Charlie again, who reacted by reaching out to her.

"She likes you," Luna said, holding Charlie out to her.

Hesitantly, Zhong picked Charlie out of Luna's grasp, and settled her uncertainly in her arms. Charlie studied her intently for a second, then her face split into a huge grin, toothless gums on full display. It was quite the most charming thing Zhong had ever seen.

Explosions rumbled in the distance, and Zhong looked up. "It's begun," she said. She handed Charlie back to Luna. "Gather the kids. Playtime's over."

With Luna's help, she corralled the kids back behind the bar, when the howls began.

"Shit!" she spat.

"You just said a swear!" one the girls declared, a dirty faced urchin.

"Shut up!" Zhong snapped. The howls sounded again, closer this time. Zhong looked around frantically. There was no way she could protect the kids by herself. Her gaze settled on the storeroom door. As she recalled, there was only one door, and no windows. "Luna, get the kids in there."

She shooed the kids into the room then shut the door. "No matter what you hear, keep this door closed until you're let out, you hear me?" she ordered, shutting the door. Quickly she stacked whatever she could find in front of the door. Hopefully it would slow them down a couple of seconds.

It was none too soon. There was a crash upstairs as something broke through one of the windows, followed by another crash as an abo burst through the swinging double doors. Zhong backed up to the storeroom door, spear held out in front of her, as the abo that burst through the front door slowly stalked towards her. Movement out of the corner of her eye caught her attention long enough to see another abo creep down the stairs from the second floor, joining the first. She shook like a leaf, adrenaline threatening to trigger her Change. There was no way she could beat two aberrations by herself. It was a death sentence. Briefly she considered fighting her way free and running away. She didn't owe anybody anything. But Charlie's happy face thrust itself into her mind's eye. Charlie deserved a chance at a happy life. Throwing her spear down, Zhong triggered her Change. She needed her Other's speed and ferocity now. Maybe she could damage them enough for her sisters to finish them off. Faced with the choice between her survival and the survival of innocents she had only just met, she made the right choice.

* * * * *

Aadhya

Aadhya led Dhitri and Chaitri deeper into the mine. When they hit a branch, one would stay at the intersection, acting as lookout, while the other two ran down the tunnel, looking for miners or abos. Aadhya and Chaitri were searching one such branch when something burst out of it. One of the abos had climbed up one of the ore chutes, and launched itself at them, hitting Chaitri, pushing her up against the wall, biting and tearing. It had obviously been caught in one of the explosions. Huge flaps of skin were hanging down from its face and torso, it was missing half of its face, and blood dripped down one of its haunches, refusing to clot. Chaitri did all she could to keep the thing from critically injuring her, but she was in a bad way, when Aadhya stabbed it in the ribs, putting all of her weight and strength behind the blow. She hit it like a runaway wagon, hurling it completely off of Chaitri, who sank down to her knees, her arms clutching at her middle, trying to hold in her guts.

Aadhya stabbed it again and again in a controlled frenzy, trying to damage it as much as possible so it would slow down enough for her to start applying silver, or Chaitri could heal enough to help her. Overwhelmed, the abo tried to break free, claws scrabbling against the dirt, but Aadhya wouldn't let up. Screaming in fury, she kept stabbing, until Chaitri appeared suddenly and buried her honor dagger, coated in silver powder, deep into one of its eye sockets. Leaving the spear buried, Aadhya drew her own dagger and stabbed it between the ribs, sliding it into its heart. That did it. Aadhya pulled out her dagger, wiped it off on the abo's fur, then sheathed it. She ripped her spear free from the corpse, and leaned on it, breathing heavily.

"How are you doing, Chaitri?" she asked between gulps of air.

Chaitri grimaced. "I'll live. It sure didn't feel good, though."

Aadhya snorted and was about to say something when a scream interrupted.

"Dhitri!" Aadhya gasped. She started to run off, then stopped to look at Chaitri.

"I'll be alright," she replied to Aadhya's unspoken question. "Go," she waved her off.

"I'll be right back," Aadhya said, and sprinted back the way they had come.

She reached the intersection where they had left Dhitri to find another abo worrying Dhitri's unmoving form. Unlike the one they had just fought, this one appeared unwounded, a bigger problem to be sure.

As she crashed to a halt, she distracted it from Dhitri and focused its attention entirely on her. Contemptuously, it dropped Dhitri's limp form and stepped over it, pausing long enough to scratch dirt over her with its hind legs, showing its complete and utter disdain for its prey. It tensed, eyeing her intently, capturing her gaze and holding it, trying to dominate her and make her freeze in terror.

Aadhya knew logically that she wasn't a match for it one-on-one. It was stronger and faster, and she knew she should be afraid. But all she felt was rage; all-consuming, red-tinged vision rage. That rage triggered a cascade of hormones that ripped through her body in a chain reaction that threatened a full on Change. She held it off, though, walking the knife edge, as her body swelled, building muscle in an instant. She lowered her spear at it.

"Well, come on, then. Come and get it, you scabrous goat fucker!" she roared.

It shrieked at her and leapt forward. The smarter move would have been to lodge the butt of her spear in the ground and wait for it, but Aadhya wasn't thinking all that clearly. She charged forward herself, but whether it was luck or instinctual timing, she got it right, catching it squarely in its chest when it was at the height of one of its leaps, arresting its charge.

It howled in pain as the spear pierced its body, but tried running down the shaft towards Aadhya anyway. It got stopped by the spear's crossbar. It strained to reach her, howling and swiping at her with her claws and snapping its maw at her while she struggled to hold it at bay. Aadhya wasn't sure how long this impasse lasted, but it seemed a little longer than eternity, when suddenly the abo's assault weakened. Its eyes opened wide in surprise, and it sank closer to the ground as one of its hind legs lost power. Aadhya blinked the sweat out of her eyes, and looked down to see Dhitri, half-changed, gnawing on its hind leg. Her eyes were glowing a furious yellow, like lanterns in the dark. Aadhya started chuckling, eventually giving way to roars of laughter.

"Meet Dhitri, you son of a whore," she laughed, then screamed with effort, lifting the abo up a little, then twisted hard, slamming it onto the ground and pinning it.

Dhitri, fully changed now, immediately let go of the leg and swarmed up its body, tearing into its soft underbelly in a frenzy.

It screamed and tried to push her away, but Dhitri's hind legs had its hindquarters pinned, and she just hunched her head and shoulders down, accepting the wounds it inflicted on her with its front paws while she dug ever deeper. It tried to curl in on itself and bring its teeth to bear, but Aadhya stomped her heavy boot down on its head, preventing that.

Chaitri staggered out of the passage a minute later, and fell on the creature, stabbing at it with her honor dagger. It was over in seconds.

* * * * *

Winda

Winda stumbled out of the mine to a scene of utter chaos. People were running in all directions, screaming, or trying to coalesce into organized knots of resistance. Abos flashed in and out of sight as they ran around, seeming as lost and confused as the humans they were supposedly hunting. Occasionally an arrow would bury itself in one of them as they paused a second too long.

"What do we do?" Amari asked, at a loss.

Winda shook her head wordlessly, not sure herself. Suddenly, from down the street, a scream of anguish tore through the air, so loud it managed to pierce even through the noise of general battle.

"That came from the Bucket o' Blood," Yumna said.

"That's where we put the children!" Yaa exclaimed.

Winda came to a decision. "Yumna, you and Yaa try to help whoever you can out here. Amari, come with me. We're going to the Bucket!"

They split up, Yumna and Yaa disappearing into the dark while Winda and Amari raced to the saloon. They burst through the swinging batwing doors to find two abos playing tug-of-war with Zhong's limp body. She was in her Other form, but it hadn't been enough. Amari saw this and screamed, triggering her own Change, while Winda launched her spear at one of the abos. It was a powerful cast, burying itself to the crossguard in the abo's side. The monster screamed as the silver-coated blade pierced it, burning like acid. It dropped Zhong and frantically clawed at its side, trying to pull the spear free.

Winda ripped her sword free of its sheath. She had to hold them off just long enough for Amari to complete her Change. It wasn't ideal, but life seldom was.

The second creature turned toward her and growled. Its eyes were empty sockets, blood oozing out of the holes in rivulets, and slowly dripping onto the floor in soft patters. Zhong had hurt it so badly its healing had slowed to practically nothing. It lifted its nose into the air, nostrils twitching as it sampled the air for new scents.

"So you're saying there's a chance," Winda muttered to herself. Now was the time to divide them, while the animal with the spear in its side was distracted. She sidled a few steps to the side, silently edging away from Amari, then stamped her boot on the floor.

"Hey! Over here!" she called.

The blind one focused on her position like a bat hunting insects at night, and charged at her, an arrow shot from a bow, growling angrily. Soft on her feet, she side-stepped like a matador in the ring, swinging her sword in a beautifully timed uppercut that sliced deeply into its throat as it rushed by her. She then reversed her momentum and pirouetted lightly on her feet, bringing her sword down on the back of its neck in a strong overhand chop, cutting through its spine, and almost beheading it completely. It collapsed, but its forward momentum carried it forward a couple more feet, sliding on the wooden floor.

Her total focus on the blind abo cost her, however, as the other one, having dug the spear out of itself, knocked her off of her feet, burying her under its bulk. Its maw gaped open, trying to engulf her entire head. Grimly she grabbed onto its lower jaw, trying to force it away from her face. It was like trying to lift a house. She wiggled further underneath it, trying to make it harder for it to reach her with its mouth, although she sacrificed leverage. She kept one hand on its chin, while her other groped for her dagger.

It shook its head sharply, breaking her hold on it, and hopped back enough to bring her in line with its head again. It dipped its head, aiming for her throat this time. She jammed her forearm in its mouth, screaming as its teeth tore into her flesh. She screamed again as it shook its head again, threatening to rip her arm from its socket, but her other hand found the hilt of her dagger. She was just starting to draw it from its sheath, when another weight landed squarely on top of the abo, and her as well, blasting the air from her lungs, and causing her to lose her grip on her dagger.

Amari's head appeared in her field of vision. Claws grabbed onto the abo's skull, piercing its eyes, and her mouth crunched down onto the abo's muzzle, biting deep. Amari threw the entire weight of her body back, trying to drag the abo's weight off of her lover.

The abo's mouth opened, and Winda jerked her shredded arm free, finally drawing her dagger. She slid it in between its ribs, right behind its shoulder.

It howled, blinded, and now stung by the acid burn of the silver. Amari continued to worry at it trying to find any vulnerable spot to attack and Winda stabbed it again and again, resheathing her dagger each time, like she'd been trained. Eventually its struggles stilled. With a mighty heave, Amari jerked its body off of Winda, who let her dagger hand flop onto the floor in exhaustion. She closed her eyes briefly, only to open them again for an up close and personal look at Amari's terrifying visage staring at her in concern.

"I'm fine, Amari. Although you didn't have to jump on me," she scolded.

Amari responded by running her tongue all the way up Winda's cheek.

"Ugh. Gross. Come on, let's see how Zhong's doing," Winda said, pushing Amari's nightmare form off of her. They hurried over to check on her.

During their battle, Zhong had reversed her Change, turning back into her human form. She lay there, naked and unmoving, bleeding on the floor. One arm and one leg had been completely shredded, most of the flesh ripped off. Bone gleamed whitely in several places, and Zhong's complexion had turned almost bone-white. Amari stood guard while Winda cradled Zhong's head in her lap.

"Hold on, Zhong. Hang in there and you can heal, eventually," she said, stroking Zhong's hair.

Zhong shook her head weakly. "Too much damage. They hurt me, over and over. I've got nothing left," she whispered.

"Please, Zhong. You're a fighter. You've been a fighter all of your life. Fight through this," Winda murmured. Tears gathered and started falling. Zhong and she had never been particularly close, but in the end, they were still Sisters.

"Life has been... pain. Where I'm going there will be no more pain. Tell me, are the kids alright?"

Winda nodded. "They're fine. You saved them," she sobbed.

Zhong smiled. "Good," and let go.

* * * * *

Lyr

The spear buried itself in Fenrir's stomach, and he gasped, grabbing at the shaft, then roared in pain as the burn of the silver registered. I started to charge him while he was distracted, when an arm of iron wrapped around my throat, yanking me up short.

"Where do you think you're going?" Marie whispered into my ear, before stabbing me in the liver with her blade. I screamed in agony, feeling blood gush down my side. For a normal human, this would prove quickly fatal, but we weren't normal. She withdrew the knife and tried to stab me again. "You taught me everything you know, remember? I'm your equal now!" she laughed.

I rocketed my head back into her face as hard as I could, crunching her nose flat, then grabbed the arm encircling my throat, I thrust my hips back and jackknifed forward, throwing her over my back and flat onto the ground.

"I taught you everything *you* know, Marie. You're still just a pup," I ground out, keeping hold of her arm. Flinging myself down on the ground, I wrapped her up in an arm bar and wrenched, breaking it. It was her turn to scream as her arm snapped like a chicken bone. I flipped myself back up to my feet and something flashed out of the corner of my eye, causing me to flinch. Fenrir had flung my own spear back at me, missing me by inches.

I turned and faced him, drawing my sword as Marie rolled onto her side, writhing at my feet, and holding her arm. He had started to rush me, but stopped when the sword came out. Staring at him, I thrust my sword straight down through her ribs. It wasn't much more than an inconvenience for her, but it would hurt her and slow her down. I didn't need to fight them both at the same time. She screamed again, bloody froth pouring out of her mouth.

"Well come on then," I told him, staring him right in the eye.

One corner of his mouth lifted in a smirk. "I am unarmed." He gestured at my weapons. "It's not exactly fair, don't you think?"

It was my turn to sneer. "Your lack of planning doesn't affect me. No mercy. No quarter."

His smirk turned into a savage scowl. He looked positively demonic at that moment. "I quite agree," he growled. Then he did something that truly shocked me. He turned and ran.

I muttered a curse and sprang after him, drawing my ax in my other hand. I'm a faster runner than average, but I wasn't a match for him, and he quickly left me behind. At the edge of town, an abomination rounded the corner of one of the houses and slid to a stop in front of me, blocking my way, its head lowered, glaring up at me. I didn't have time for this. My hands blurred as I shifted my ax to my right hand and my sword to my left. Drawing my arm back, I threw my ax at the abo as hard as I could. It flew straight and true, flipping end over end before burying itself to the haft in its skull.

Barely pausing in my stride, I followed the ax at a run. Snatching it out of the brute's head, I slammed it home again and again, until the monster's head was mush. Then I severed its spinal cord for good measure. It would heal from that eventually, but it would take a good long while, and by then somebody else might happen along and finish it for good. Then I raced off into the dark after Fenrir.

* * * * *

Marie

Marie rolled from her side to her knees, then struggled slowly to her feet, holding her ribs. Shakily, she knuckled the blood from her mouth, glaring out at the dark, feeling the hole in her ribs close and her lungs clear as her body quickly absorbed the bloody fluid that had filled them. A moment longer, and she would be able to trigger her Change, then she would be able to catch up to Lyr and Fenrir. Even Lyr wouldn't be able to triumph caught between the two...

Her thoughts slithered to a surprised halt and she shrieked in absolute agony as a silvered spear thrust itself through her chest, igniting a crescendo of blazing pain as the silver powder covering the spearhead diffused into her bloodstream, paralyzing her into immobility. A head reached around from behind her and wrenched her head back.

"Hello, Marie," Yusi crooned in her ear.

"You? I remember you. You're that pup that everyone thought was crazy." She tried to shake free from Yusi's grasp, but couldn't break free. The silver was working fast, weakening her. "Let me go, you crazy bitch! I'm your superior!"

Yusi ignored her, tightening her grip. "I always knew you were a traitorous bitch, Marie. Good-bye." So saying she slit Marie's throat, cutting all the way to the bone. She pushed Marie away, who slowly slumped to the ground, taking the spear with her. Yusi crouched down and stared at her face, watching the light slowly fade from her eyes. She knew she should probably go and help bring order to the chaos that was surging through the town, but it was important that Marie didn't cheat her fate this time.

* * * * *

Lyr

His trail led me into the badlands that surrounded the town of Argent. I followed him through sagebrush, following the tracks his feet left in the dry spongy ground. I followed him as he found a path up a canyon wall and climbed up onto the mesa. Barren sandstone stretched all around me, bands of varying shades of blue, purple, and black in my eyes. Tracking him just got a lot harder.

"No matter," I muttered. "This ends tonight, one way or another."

I followed my nose as it picked out his still fresh scent. It led me on until I found his clothes, abandoned in a heap by a pile of loose boulders. I squatted down on my haunches and considered this new development. He had all the advantages now, except two. His senses were now superior in every sense of the word; heightened sense of smell, hearing, and night vision. He was also even stronger and faster than he was before. The only things I had going for me were that I was still armed with silver, and I could still think. When one was in their Other form, it was a lot harder to suppress their base urges and think logically.

I had three choices in my mind. I could continue on as I had been doing. That would leave me wide open to being ambushed by something who could see, hear, and smell me long before I got into range. Chances were very good I wouldn't survive that. He could also simply outrun me, if he chose. I would never be able to catch up now.

I could turn around, and go back, organize my Sisters and the townsfolk, and hunt him down like the animal he was. But that would take a lot of time, and risk us losing his trail. Again. It would also give him time to clear out of the country and make more of his damn abominations. He could also circle back and ambush me.

The third option was for me to Change myself, and continue the hunt. I would still be at a disadvantage, but that would be less than me in my human form. It would also be harder to kill him without silver.

I straightened up, and began to take my clothes off. I wasn't confident I could win, but I didn't have to; I only had to damage him enough to slow him down. My Sisters would be coming after me soon. They would find him. I folded my clothes neatly, a nice change for once, then lay my weapons down on top of them. I looked at them wistfully. Hopefully the Sisters would find them before some enterprising individual with loose standards of ownership could, then triggered my Change. The familiar sensation of excruciating pain engulfed me as the Change invaded every cell of my being. With a monumental effort of will, I kept myself from crying out with the pain, choking it down and holding it to the occasional whimper.

When it was done, I rolled to my feet, shook myself, and scanned the night. Its entire vista opened up before me, like a newly opened blossom. Scents were sharper, more distinct, and sounds were amplified. What used to be a barren wasteland now teemed with insect and small mammal life. The night lost much of its shadow, although the colors were now muted. Fenrir's scent, which was faint, now blazed before me. I shook myself and growled softly, my rage, lust for The Hunt, and its bloody conclusion beginning to hammer at my awareness, making cool reasoning gutter like a candle flame in the wind. I set off at a trot, nose hovering off of the ground. Fenrir was mine. My prey.

His trail led off, and I followed it, all through the night, and the next day. His trail led on, straight and true, only changing as he went around the inevitable terrain obstacles. I paused only long enough to drink from whatever pool of water

I found, and to relieve myself. Urinating on the trail brought me some comfort. It would make it easier for my Sisters to track me.

As the sun began to set, painting the landscape in bloody hues of orange, I paused and rested. It was harder and harder to form coherent thoughts. My rational mind was under constant assault from my instincts, and the constant battering was taking its toll. I could only imagine what state Fenrir's mind was in right now. He would have to Change back soon or risk losing his mind. Idly I wondered if he even knew what kind of danger his mind was in. I almost hoped he had already lost it. He would still be incredibly dangerous, but his ability to create others of his kind would be reduced to almost pure chance. Creating one of us took *planning*. With an impatient huff I started off again. Enough woolgathering. There was prey to chase down.

Afternoon faded into night and I continued my course. I was indefatigable. I was invincible. Hunger gnawed at me, but I could go on forever. The only thing that mattered was my prey, his throat between my teeth, the taste of his blood as I drank it down. His scent trail ran along, straight and unchanging. I began to feel contempt for my prey. He was just running, like a coward. Like prey. And here I thought he might have been a worthy challenger for me.

My complete focus on the spoor, and my lapse of discipline, allowing the Other to have too much control, almost doomed me. The slightest sound of claws disturbing pebbles on the stone gave me an instant's warning, enough to jump over and to the side, spoiling his aim.

He had circled around and set up an ambush, climbing atop a boulder that overlooked his trail. His leap, if not for my jump, would have landed him on top of me, in perfect position to kill me with a single well placed bite.

I sprinted away, putting distance between us with great bounds. After a half-dozen strides, I whirled around to face him, crouching down, my full throated snarl both a warning and a challenge.

He pulled up short, and his own roar echoed back at me as his paws batted at me, claws out. My own claws flashed out, slapping his paws away. I snarled again. He startled, then appeared to change tactics. He took a step back, relaxing his posture, straightening up and then flexing, posturing for my benefit. Dominance pheromones began wafting out from him as he sought to subjugate me.

My lips curled back from my teeth, and I rumbled softly, continuing to warn him to keep his distance. I looked him over. He was the first male lycan I had seen in almost a century. He really was a handsome bastard, the thought whispered rebelliously in the darkest recesses of my mind.

Large, with dark chocolate, almost black fur, he carried the ruff of a fully mature male. Ropy muscle snaked underneath his glossy fur like ship hawsers. His eyes glowed at me, yellow and welcoming, like lanterns in the night, beckoning you home. His fangs gleamed whitely in the dark. Everything about him communicated youth and vigor, a beast in the absolute prime of his life. And his pheromones continued their insinuating assault, telling me to submit, to accept his place as my rightful lord and master.

A large part of my fuzzy mind wanted me to submit, to roll over, show my belly, and accept his place over me. But that growing instinct triggered something else in me, a growing righteous anger that came not from my Other, but *me*. An anger that bubbled up and brushed aside that compulsion like twigs before a spring flood. Magnificent he might be, but he didn't hold a candle to Constatine, Duke of Tansyl, and the one that Turned me so very long ago. I was a queen, a mother, a leader of monsters myself. I belonged to myself and no other. I rose up and spit a challenge at him, my own dominance pheromones flooding out of me in a massive wave and hitting him in the face like a bag of rocks.

He blinked in astonishment, and seemed to shrink down into himself for the briefest of moments before his own fury surged to the surface. He snarled and charged. I met him halfway, clawed fingers digging into his shoulders inside of his arms, and my teeth closing on his throat. He howled in pain as I bit deep and tossed me away as if I weighed nothing, tearing out a large chunk of his flesh in the process. I rolled back to my feet and spat out the bit of meat that was in my mouth.

He clutched at his throat, choking, as blood gushed from between his fingers, while he glared at me. I lunged at him, using the loose pebbles that covered the sandstone to my advantage, skidding across the slippery surface, underneath his clumsy swipe and hooking one of his haunches, which I used as an anchor to pivot myself behind him. I swarmed up his back, biting and clawing, ripping deep gashes in his flesh, reaching for anything vulnerable.

He howled again, reaching around with an unnaturally long arm, and ripped me from him. He tossed me away easily. I flew twenty feet, twisting in the air, and landing on my feet, clawing myself to a stop.

He straightened up and exhaled air in a sudden chuff. His whole manner broadcast satisfaction. I knew why. I was faster, but he was far stronger, and I couldn't hurt him fast enough. I would have to come up with a different strategy. I snarled at him, then whirled and sprinted away. He bellowed in victory, and gave chase.

It went against every instinct I had, but I couldn't match him one-on-one. Unless I got lucky, I wouldn't even be able to slow him down. My head start bought me a couple of jumps, but he started catching up to me in a couple of strides. I led him down a narrow wash where the walls closed in around us. I could feel him right behind me, imagined his breath blowing hot on my feet. Quick as thought, I launched myself up one of the walls, then flipped around, landing on his back. Surprised, he was slow to react, and I fastened onto one of his ears, before ripping it away at the root, reveling in his roar of agony. One of my claws found an eye, and I popped it like a grape. Then I was off, running in a completely different direction. Once again, he followed me, but slower, wary now of another ambush, and I used his hesitation to my advantage, building a sizable lead.

The marathon chase continued through the night, with both of us running as fast as we could, untiring as one of those mechanical men Jack used to tell me about. I continued to increase my lead, as he started to slow. Unnatural vitality he might have, but he also had greater mass to move, and over a long distance, that was starting to tell.

My path led us into a different landscape, one where boulders, huge rocks as big as one of our houses back home, lay piled haphazardly on top of each other. The land started to fracture, splitting into canyons that clawed themselves into the earth, heading out and down to a destination that I couldn't see. I stayed well away from those narrow gashes. They weren't going to help me.

The ground became more broken, and the footing got treacherous. I now risked rolling an ankle if I didn't pay attention to where I put my feet. The canyons grew shorter and petered out. Now cliffs hemmed me in on my left, stair-stepping down to a river that writhed through the tortured ground hundreds of feet below me. Then I saw it; my salvation. A huge boulder perched precariously among a nest of crumbling stones on top of the plateau. It looked like one good push would send it and thousands of tons of rock tumbling down. There was even a narrow shelf of rock directly below it. Perfect.

I slid carelessly down onto that shelf of rock, claws scrabbling for purchase amongst all of the loose scree. I urinated hurriedly, trying to expel liquid from a body dehydrated from the long chase, then scrambled up and out the other side to hide behind the pile of rocks. My lungs were heaving like a bellows after that long run, and I controlled my breathing with difficulty. The only way this would work is if he didn't know where I was.

I didn't have to wait long. He came out of the night like a nightmare given physical form, congealing from the darkness. I held my breath, hoping he would take the bait and follow my scent down onto the cliff shelf. However, he stopped at the cliff's edge and peered down, his own chest heaving in great gasps. I took satisfaction from the fact that I wasn't the only one suffering from the chase. Then he started casting about in a small circle.

I snarled to myself. He wasn't taking the bait. Cautiously, careful to stay upwind from him, I edged away from my hiding spot and wormed myself deeper into the tumbled rocks further away from the cliff's edge. Carefully, I crouched down, settling myself. I would only have one chance at this.

He carefully scented his way to where I had been hiding. There he paused, exhaling noisily in frustration when he didn't find me. In that instant, I charged, barreling into him with all the force I could muster. I was on him before I registered to his senses and I knocked him off the cliff. He fell twenty feet to the ledge, and rolled to his feet, staring at me in disbelief. I didn't give him a chance to recover, ramming my body against the boulder, pushing it with all the strength I could summon. For a frozen instant nothing happened, and I was terrified he would quickly climb his way up to me. I didn't have the energy to escape from him a second time. Terror gave me extra strength, and the boulder teetered in its nest, toppling slowly to where Fenrir was standing.

It hit the shelf with a tremendous impact, shaking the cliff. The shelf crumbled away, taking the boulder and Fenrir with it, tumbling down towards the river, picking up more stones and detritus with it, creating an avalanche of rocks and dirt.

As I was watching the spectacle, the ground I was standing on, weakened by the impact and the shelf below crumbling, suddenly gave way beneath me and I followed Fenrir down the cliff face. I tried riding the tumbling rocks down, like a child sledding in winter, but more of the cliff above me gave way, chasing me down. Then I tried making my way to the side of the avalanche, where I could find something to cling to, but my foot slipped and got pinched between two tumbling rocks. Instantly I was pulled down, rolling over and over again, getting hit repeatedly. I went airborne for a brief eternity, then cried out in pain when I landed again, my hips striking a rock with shattering force. The pain registered for an instant, then I was off again, rolling down. I was pushed off another cliff by the rolling stones and went airborne again, this time for what seemed like an eternity. I howled in alarm, then hit water with stunning force. It forced its way in my mouth and nose, choking me.

I panicked as I began sinking as fast as some of the rocks falling in the water around me. We in the Sisterhood can't swim. We're too dense, both in our musculature and our thickened bones. Terrified, I triggered my Change back to human as I began to claw my way back to the river's surface. This was probably a bad idea as it would deplete all of my body's resources, but drowning wasn't a good look either.

My limbs shrank as my body scavenged the now unneeded muscle and bone for energy. Shattered bones reformed as my body forced itself back to human, and I began to make headway in my panicky flight towards the surface and air. Dots began to swim in front of my eyes, my vision greying as I was running out of air. My legs still weren't working quite right, threatening to drag me back down when my face broke out of the water. Greedily I gasped in a huge lungful of sweet air, thrashing around clumsily, trying to keep my head above water.

A scrubby little pine tree floated by me, dislodged by the avalanche I caused, and I splashed towards it, grabbing onto it and using it to keep me afloat. I looked back behind me, studying the wreckage I had caused. Dust hung motionless in the night air, and errant rocks and gravel still slid to the water in decreasing amounts. I saw no sign of Fenrir. I would have to go back and look for his body. I was nearly certain of his death, but I needed undeniable proof.

A growing roar in my ears distracted me from surveying my handiwork, and I turned to look where I was going. Right in front of me, too close for me to do anything, the river plunged off the cliff in a massive waterfall. I opened my mouth and screamed as I went over the edge, tangled up in that damn pine tree. Then everything went black.

Epilogue

It was a subdued, somber group that gathered together in the Bucket o' Blood. The town and the Sisters had successfully beaten Fenrir's monsters, but at a great cost. Argent lost a quarter of its people, and the Sisters, in addition to Zhong, had lost Yumna and Yaa, who had sacrificed themselves saving some of the townsfolk. Chyanne and Caleb leaned on each other for support as they tried to come to grips with what happened. Yusi was kneeling on the ground, Zhong's head in her lap. Tears ran freely down her face as she stroked Zhong's face and hair. Killing Marie had been necessary, but Zhong's life was a high price to pay.

Astrid pushed through the crowd. "Where's Lyr?" she demanded. "I can't find her anywhere."

"She's gone," Yusi murmured. "She went after Fenrir."

Chyanne pushed herself wearily away from Caleb. "All right. I'm best on a horse. I'll go." A hard hand landed on her shoulder, halting her. She looked around into Winda's concerned face.

"No, you won't. You're dead on your feet. You stay here. Amari, Astrid, and I can find her. There's still some mopping up here to do. Don't worry, we'll find her."

Two days later, they reined their horses to a stop at the top of the cliff that had taken Lyr down into the river. Winda dismounted, and cast about in wider and wider circles, searching for any sign of her. They had found her clothes and weapons a day back, which were now stowed safely in their saddlebags or lashed securely to their horses' harnesses. When she was done, she looked up at the other two.

"Her trail ends here," she said.

Amari looked at the rubble strewn hillside. "This is fresh," she mused.

Winda looked down the hill speculatively. "So it is," she replied.

They ended up tying a rope to one of the horses. With Amari steadying the horse, Winda and Astrid carefully worked their way down the hill. They caught Fenrir's scent halfway down. Carefully rolling some boulders away, they found his body. Lyr's plan had worked. Of Lyr they found nothing. It was as if she had vanished.

Astrid looked at the river winding below her. "Do you think she died here?" she asked.

Winda shook her head. "Lyr is the toughest bitch I've ever met in my life. If anyone could have survived this, it would be her. Anyway, even if she managed to drown herself, she would have been swept that way," she motioned downstream, then looked at Astrid. "Go back to town and gather the Sisters that aren't involved with hunting down the last of the abos. Meet back here and start hunting for sign. I'll head downstream." She grasped Astrid's shoulder and shook it. "We'll find her. I promise."

* * * * *

Many miles downstream, after floating down many random tributaries and channels, a scrubby pine tree came to a stop on a small sandbar in the crook of a nameless stream. A tanned hand flopped down to rest limply on the damp yellow sand.

The End

About the Author

After stumbling across The Hobbit in the third grade, Jay has been an avid reader ever since. Having travelled through countless worlds of other people's imaginations, he is wanting to turn his hand to creating and sharing his own.

He lives in Oregon with his lovely and long-suffering wife, two youngest children that haven't left the nest yet, two dogs, and a cat gifted by the Cat Distribution Network. You can visit him at:

https://jayhobsonauthor.com